Rachel's house

Stephanie's house

School bus

School

B
F
F

TWO
NOVELS

ALSO BY JUDY BLUME

Judy Blume

BFF*

*BEST FRIENDS FOREVER

TWO NOVELS

DELACORTE PRESS

Published by Delacorte Press
an imprint of Random House Children's Books
a division of Random House, Inc.
New York

Delacorte Press and colophon are
registered trademarks of Random House, Inc.

www.randomhouse.com
www.judyblume.com

Educators and librarians, for a variety of teaching tools,
visit us at www.randomhouse.com/teachers

Library of Congress Cataloging-in-Publication Data
is available upon request.

ISBN 978-0-385-73407-3 (trade)
ISBN 978-0-385-90416-2 (glb)

Printed in the United States of America

10 9 8 7 6 5 4 3 2 1

First Delacorte Press Edition

judy blume

Hi, Friends and Readers!

I'm so happy that these two books, favorites of mine, are now available in one big volume. When I first got the idea for *Just as Long as We're Together*, I was remembering being part of a trio as I was growing up. Like Stephanie, I had two best friends all through elementary school. There were times when one or another of us felt left out by the other two. And there was a terrible time when one of us felt betrayed by the others. So I know that being part of a trio isn't always easy.

When the three of us started junior high, everything changed. We began to grow apart. It was hard and sometimes painful. I often felt that I was the one who no longer fit in. But maybe my two friends felt the same way. I don't know. We never talked about it. In time, each of us found new interests and new friends.

I had to find out for myself that you can't have a best friend without being one. Friendship depends on trust, caring, and loyalty. You have to work at it. You have to value your friend. In seventh grade, I met the girl who would become my best friend for life. There was a connection between us from the beginning. We were sometimes competitive, which wasn't good for our friendship, but somehow we got through that. Maybe we learned that boys and popularity come and go but neither is as important as a true friend. Together, we've learned what *BFF* really means.

Before I sat down to write these two books, I knew my characters well, or thought I did. But I like it best when my characters surprise me as I'm writing, and these three girls and their families certainly did. Nothing turned out the way I thought it would. By creating fictional families and situations that kids have no control over, I get to see how they cope. Sooner or later, most real-life kids find themselves in situations they can't control. You can't control your family. You can't control your friends, either—but at least you get to *choose* your friends.

Both Stephanie and Rachel have to deal with major family changes. Neither one wants to tell the other what's going on at home.

Sometimes friendships change. Rachel doesn't want to lose Stephanie, but she also wants to have other friends—friends from music camp, friends from math class. Steph is threatened by this. If Rachel finds new friends, what will happen to their friendship? At the same time, Steph wants to be friends with Alison. And she doesn't know how to do that without trying to make Alison and Rachel friends too. As the new girl in town, Alison comes up with a way to attract new friends. But she's careful not to give away much about her family. She wants to be liked for herself. It's not easy for her to come into a friendship that has a long history. It's not easy being caught between Stephanie and Rachel.

The thing is, it's good to have friends from different parts of your life—school, activities, the neighborhood, summer. They won't all become your BFF, but that's okay.

I hope you enjoy these two novels about Stephanie, Rachel and Alison. I'd always planned to write three books, one from each girl's point of view. But I never got around to writing Alison's story. Maybe someday.

I'd love to hear from you. You can visit me online at www.judyblume.com. Click on Book List, then on *Just as Long as We're Together* and *Here's to You, Rachel Robinson* to find out how I chose the titles for these two books, how I named the characters, and more.

Judy Blume

CONTENTS

Just as Long as We're Together

To my friend,

STEPHEN MURPHY

who touched my life with his courage, dignity
and never-ending sense of humor

Lola will always remember . . .

Hunks

"Stephanie is into hunks," my mother said to my aunt on Sunday afternoon. They were in the kitchen making potato salad and I was stretched out on the grass in our yard, reading. But the kitchen window was wide open so I could hear every word my mother and aunt were saying. I wasn't paying much attention though, until I heard my name.

At first I wasn't sure what my mother meant by *Stephanie is into hunks*, but I got the message when she added, "She's taped a poster of Richard Gere on the ceiling above her bed. She says she likes to look up at him while she's trying to fall asleep at night."

"Oh-oh," Aunt Denise said. "You'd better have a talk with her."

"She already knows about the birds and the bees," Mom said.

"Yes, but what does she know about boys?" Aunt Denise asked.

It so happens I know plenty about boys. As for hunks, I've never known one personally. Most boys my age—and I'm starting seventh grade in two weeks—are babies. As for my Richard Gere poster, I didn't even know he was famous when I bought it. I got it on sale. The picture must have been taken a long time ago because he looks young, around seventeen. He was really cute back then. I love the expression on his face, kind of a half-smile, as if he's sharing a secret with me.

Actually, I don't call him Richard Gere. I call him Benjamin but my mother doesn't know that. To her he's some famous actor. To me, he's Benjamin Moore, he's seventeen and he's my first boyfriend. I love that name—Benjamin Moore. I got it off a paint can. We moved over the summer and for weeks our new house reeked of paint. While my room was being done I slept in my brother's room. His name is Bruce and he's ten. I didn't get a good night's sleep all that week because Bruce has nightmares.

Anyway, as soon as the painters were out of

my room I moved back in and taped up my posters. I have nineteen of them, not counting Benjamin Moore. And he's the only one on the ceiling. It took me all day to arrange my posters in just the right way and that night, as soon as my mother got home from work, I called her up to see them.

"Oh, Stephanie!" she said. "You should have used tacks, not tape. Tape pulls the paint off the walls."

"No, it doesn't," I said.

"Yes, it does."

"Look . . . I'll prove it to you," I said, taking down a poster of a lion with her cubs. But my mother was right. The tape did pull chips of paint off the wall. "I guess I better not move my posters around," I said.

"I guess not," Mom said. "We'll have to ask the painters to touch up that wall."

I felt kind of bad then and I guess Mom could tell because she said, "Your posters do look nice though. You've arranged them very artistically. Especially the one over your bed."

Rachel

"I can't believe this room!" my best friend, Rachel Robinson, said. She came over the second she got home from music camp. We shrieked when we saw each other. Dad says he doesn't understand why girls have to shriek like that. There's no way I can explain it to him.

Rachel must have grown another two inches over the summer because when Mom hugged her, Rachel was taller. She'll probably be the tallest girl in seventh grade.

"I've never seen so many posters!" Rachel stood in the middle of my room, shaking her head. When she noticed Benjamin Moore she asked, "How come that one's on your ceiling?"

"Lie down," I said.

"Not now."

"Yes, now . . ." I pushed her toward the bed. "It's the only way you can really see him."

Rachel shoved an armload of stuffed animals out of the way and lay down.

I flopped beside her. "Isn't he cute?"

"Yeah . . . he is."

"My mother calls him a hunk."

Rachel laughed.

"You know what I call him?"

"What?"

"Benjamin Moore."

"Benjamin Moore . . ." Rachel said, propping herself up on one elbow. "Isn't that a brand of paint?"

"Yes, but I love the name."

Rachel tossed a stuffed monkey at me. "You are so bizarre, Steph!"

I knew she meant that as a compliment.

"Is that the bee-sting necklace?" Rachel asked, reaching over to touch the locket around my neck. As she did, her hair, which is curly and reddish-brown, brushed against my arm. "Can I see how it works?"

"Sure."

I stepped on a bee in July while I was at Girl Scout camp and had an allergic reaction to its sting. The camp nurse had to revive me because I went into shock. The doctor said from now on I've got to carry pills with me in case I get stung again. They're small and blue. I hope I never have to take them. I'm not the greatest at swallowing pills. When I got back from camp, Gran Lola, my grandmother, gave me this necklace. I'd written all about it to Rachel.

I opened the small gold heart. "See . . ." I said, showing it to her, "instead of a place for a picture inside there's room for three pills."

Rachel touched them. "What did it feel like to be in shock?"

"I don't remember. I think I felt dizzy . . . then everything went black."

"Promise you'll always wear the necklace," Rachel said, "just in case."

"I promise."

"Good." She closed the heart. "Now . . . what about those cartons?" she asked, pointing across the room. "When are you going to unpack them?"

"Soon."

"I'll help you do it now."

"That's okay," I told her.

"You've got to get organized before school starts, Steph." She crossed the room and kneeled in front of the biggest carton. "Books!" she said. "You want to arrange them by subject or author?"

"This isn't a library," I said, "it's a bedroom."

"I know . . . but as long as we're doing it we might as well do it right."

"I don't need to have my books arranged in any special order," I said.

"But how will you find them?"

"I recognize them by their color."

Rachel laughed. "You're hopeless!"

Later, I walked Rachel home. It's funny, because when I first heard we were going to move I cried my eyes out. Then, when my parents told me we were moving to Palfrey's Pond, I couldn't believe how lucky I was, since that's where Rachel lives. Now, besides being best friends we'll also be neighbors. And moving just a few blocks away really isn't like moving at all. I think the only reason we moved is that our house needed a new roof and Mom and Dad just about passed out when they learned what it would cost.

The houses at Palfrey's Pond are scattered all around, not lined up in a row like on a regular street. They're supposed to look old, like the houses in a colonial village. Rachel's is on the other side of the pond. When we got there she said, "Now I'll walk *you* home."

I looked at her and we both laughed.

When we got back to my house I said, "Now I'll walk *you*."

Then Rachel walked me home.
Then I walked her.
Then she walked me.
We managed to walk each other home nine times before Mom called me inside.

3

Alison

The day before school started was hot and still. I was hanging out by the pond, dipping my feet into the water. That's when I first saw the girl. She was crouching by the tree with the big hole in it. I figured she was trying to get a look at the raccoon family that lives inside. I've never seen them myself, but my brother has.

I shook the water off my feet, put on my sandals, and walked over to her. She looked about Bruce's age. Her red and white striped T-shirt came down to her knees. Probably it belonged to her father. Her hair was long. She hadn't brushed it that day. I could tell by her crooked part and the tangles at the ends. I guess she wasn't worried about stepping on a bee because she was barefoot.

She had a small dog with her, the kind that has fur hanging over its eyes. As soon as I came close the dog started to bark.

"Be quiet, Maizie," the girl said. Then she turned to me. "Hi . . . I'm Alison. We just moved in. You probably didn't notice because we didn't have a moving van. We're renting Number 25."

"I'm Stephanie," I said. "I live here, too. Number 9."

Alison stood up and brushed off her hands. She reached under her T-shirt, into the pocket of her shorts, and pulled out a card. I was really surprised because I got one just like it last week. On the front it said, *Looking forward . . .* And inside it said, *to meeting you next Thursday.* It was signed *Natalie Remo, seventh grade homeroom teacher, Room 203.*

"What do you know about Mrs. Remo?" Alison asked. "Because that's who I've got for homeroom."

I guess she could tell I was surprised. She said, "You probably thought I was younger. Everyone does since I'm so small. But I'm going to be thirteen in April."

I didn't tell her I'd thought she was Bruce's age. Instead I said, "I'll be thirteen in February." I didn't mention the date either—February 2—

Ground Hog Day. "I'm in Mrs. Remo's home-room, too. She sent me the same card."

"Oh," Alison said. "I thought she sent it to me because I'm new. I'm from Los Angeles."

"My father's there now, on business," I told her. He's been there since the beginning of August, ever since we moved. I don't know how long he's going to be away this time. Once he had to go to Japan for six weeks.

Maizie, the dog, barked. Alison kneeled next to her. "What'd you say, Maizie?" she asked, pressing her ear right up to Maizie's mouth.

Maizie made a couple of sounds and Alison nodded, then giggled. "Oh, come on, Maizie," she said, as if she were talking to her dog. Then Alison looked up at me. "Maizie is such a char-acter! She told me to tell you she's glad we're in the same homeroom because she was worried about me not knowing anyone in my new school."

"Your dog told you that?"

"Yes," Alison said. "But look . . . I'd really appreciate it if you didn't say anything about it. Once people find out your dog can talk, forget it. In L.A. there were always reporters and photographers following us around. We're trying to avoid the same kind of publicity here."

"You mean," I said, "that your dog actually talks . . . like Mr. Ed, that talking horse who used to be on TV?"

"That horse didn't really talk," Alison said, as if I didn't know.

"Well," I said, scratching the mosquito bite on my leg, "exactly how does Maizie talk? I mean, does she talk in human words or what?"

"Of course she talks in words," Alison said. "But she doesn't speak perfect English because English isn't her first language. It's hard for a dog to learn other languages."

"What's her first language?" I asked.

"French."

"Oh," I said, "French." Now this was getting really good. "I'm taking Introduction to French this year."

"I'm taking Introduction to Spanish," Alison said. "I already speak French. I lived outside of Paris until I was six."

"I thought you were Chinese or something," I said.

"I'm Vietnamese," Alison said. "I'm adopted. My mother's American but she was married to Pierre Monceau when they adopted me. He's French. Mom came to the States after they got divorced. That's when she met Leon. He's my stepfather."

I absolutely love to hear the details of other people's lives! So I sat down beside Alison, hoping she would tell me more. Bruce says I'm nosey.

But that's not true. I've discovered, though, that you can't ask too many questions when you first meet people or they'll get the wrong idea. They may not understand that you're just very curious and accuse you of butting into their private business instead.

Alison fiddled with a twig, running it across Maizie's back. I didn't ask her any of the questions that were already forming in my mind. Instead I said, "Would your dog talk to me?"

"Maybe . . . if she's in the mood."

I cleared my throat. "Hi, Maizie," I said, as if I were talking to a little kid. "I'm your new neighbor, Stephanie Hirsch."

Maizie cocked her head at me as if she were actually listening. Her tiny bottom teeth stuck out, the opposite of mine. My top teeth stuck out before I got my braces. The orthodontist says I have an overbite. That would mean Maizie has an underbite.

"What kind of dog are you," I asked, patting her back. Her fur felt sticky, as if she'd been rolling in syrup.

"She's a mixture," Alison said. "We don't know anything about her parents so we don't know if they could talk or not. Probably not. Only one in seventeen million dogs can talk."

"One in seventeen million?"

"Yes. That's what the vet told us. It's extremely rare. Maizie is probably the only talking dog in all of Connecticut."

"Well," I said. "I can't wait for Rachel to meet Maizie."

"Who's Rachel?" Alison asked.

"She's my best friend."

"Oh, you have a best friend."

"She lives here, too. Number 16. She's really smart. She's never had less than an A in school." I stood up. "I have to go home now. But I'll see you tomorrow. The junior high bus stops in front of the lodge. That's the building down by the road. It's supposed to come at ten to eight."

"I know," Alison said. "I got a notice in the mail." She stood up too. "Do you wear jeans or skirts to school here?"

"Either," I said.

"What about shoes?"

I looked at Alison's bare feet. "Yes," I said, "you have to wear them."

"I mean what *kind* of shoes . . . running shoes or sandals or what?"

"Most of the kids here wear Top-Siders."

"Top-Siders are so preppy," Alison said.

"You don't *have* to wear them," I told her. "You can wear whatever you want."

"Good," Alison said. "I will."

Rachel's Room

"Dogs can't talk," Rachel said that night, when I told her about Alison and Maizie.

I was sitting on Rachel's bed. Her cats, Burt and Harry, were nestled against my legs, purring. They're named after some beer commercial from Rachel's parents' youth.

Rachel was going through her closet, pulling out clothes that don't fit anymore. In her closet everything faces the same way and hangs on white plastic hangers.

In my closet nothing is in order. Last year Rachel tried to organize it for me. But a week later it was all a mess again and she was disappointed.

"Are you giving away your Yale sweatshirt?" I asked.

"No, that still fits."

"What about your red plaid shirt?"

"Yes . . . do you want it?"

"I'll try it on and see," I said.

Rachel took it off a hanger and handed it to me. "I've got to do some back-to-school shopping."

I did mine last week. I got a skirt, a couple of shirts, a sweater and a pair of designer jeans. Rachel's mother says designer jeans are an incredible rip-off and she won't let Rachel or her sixteen-year-old sister, Jessica, buy them. Rachel also has a brother, Charles. He's fifteen. He doesn't get along with the rest of the family so he goes away to school. I doubt that he cares about designer jeans.

My mother says she admires Mrs. Robinson. "Nell Robinson sticks to her guns," is how Mom puts it. "I wish I had such strong convictions." But she doesn't. That's how come I got a pair of *Guess* jeans. It's not that I care about labels. It's just that I like the way they fit.

I pulled my T-shirt over my head.

"Steph!" Rachel cried, lowering the window shades. "I wish you'd remember you're going into junior high. You can't run around like a baby anymore. Where's your bra?"

"At home. It was too hot to wear it."

I tried on Rachel's red plaid shirt. It's made of flannel that's been washed so many times it's almost as thin as regular cotton. It felt soft against my skin. I buttoned it and rolled up the sleeves. Then I jumped off the bed, waking Burt, who yawned and stretched. I looked at myself in Rachel's mirror. "I like it," I said.

"It's yours," Rachel told me.

"Thanks." I took the shirt off. Even though the shades were down the breeze from the window felt cool against my skin.

"Put your T-shirt on, Steph," Rachel said, tossing it to me, then turning away.

I slipped it on and flopped back onto Rachel's bed. Burt was chasing a rubber band around on the floor. Harry was still curled in a ball, fast asleep.

Rachel went to her desk. She held up her notebook. It was covered in wallpaper. I recognized the pattern—tiny dots and flowers in pink and green—from their bathroom. It looked great. "Do you have any extra?"

"I think we have some blue stripes left from the dining room. Want me to take a look?"

"Sure."

I followed Rachel into the hall. She opened the stepladder in the closet and climbed to the top. "Here it is," she said, handing me the roll.

Then we went downstairs. Mrs. Robinson was at the dining room table with stacks of papers and books spread out in front of her. She's a trial lawyer. "Stephanie . . ." she said, glancing up for a minute, "good to see you!"

"Mom's got a big case starting tomorrow," Rachel explained.

Mrs. Robinson is always either starting a big case or in the middle of one.

Mr. Robinson was at the kitchen table, also surrounded by books and papers. He teaches history at the high school. As we walked through the kitchen he popped two Pepto-Bismol tablets into his mouth. "I always get nervous before school starts," he said, chewing them. "You'd think by now I'd be used to it, but I'm not."

"I never knew teachers get nervous about starting school," I said.

Mr. Robinson nodded. "It starts in my stomach in August and doesn't let up until the end of September." The Pepto-Bismol made his teeth look pink.

"I'm going over to Steph's," Rachel said. "I'll be back in less than an hour."

"Okay," Mr. Robinson said.

Rachel carried the wallpaper. As we passed Number 25 I said, "That's Alison's house. She's in Mrs. Remo's homeroom, too."

Rachel froze. "That is so unfair!" She has someone named Ms. Levano for homeroom. "I don't know what I'm going to do if we're not in the same classes."

"Don't worry," I said, "we will be."

"I hope you're right."

The lights were on in Alison's house but the curtains were pulled closed so we couldn't see anything.

"What's she like?" Rachel asked.

"She's small and friendly," I said. "She seems okay."

"Except for that talking-dog business."

"It *is* possible," I said.

"Come on, Stephanie! There's no such thing as a talking dog. If there was we'd have heard about it."

"Maybe so," I said.

When we got to my house Mom was working at her computer. Since she got it she doesn't have to spend such long hours at the office. "Dad called, Steph. He's waiting for you to call him back."

"Okay . . ." I left Rachel in the den with Mom and called Dad from the kitchen phone. It's funny talking to him in L.A. because when it's eight o'clock here it's only five o'clock there. He was still at the office and I was about to get ready for bed.

"I miss you," Dad said.

"I miss you, too. When will you be home?"

"I'm not sure yet."

"I hope it won't be long."

"I'll definitely be home for Thanksgiving."

"Dad . . . that's more than two months away."

"There's no way I can get back before then, Steph. I have to make two trips to Hawaii and one to the Orient."

I didn't say anything for a minute. Neither did Dad. Then he said, "Well . . . have a good first day at school."

"Rachel and I aren't even in the same home-room," I said.

"Don't worry . . . you'll do fine without Rachel."

"I'm not worried. Who said I was worried? I'm just saying it's not fair since we're best friends."

"You and Rachel will still see each other after school."

"What do you mean *after* school?" I asked. "We'll be on the same bus and we'll probably be in all the same classes."

"So you'll be together all the time . . . just like before."

"That's right," I said.

"What's the weather like?" Dad asked. He loves to hear about the weather.

"Hot and humid with a chance of thunder-storms."

We talked for a few more minutes, then I went back to the den.

"Rachel's waiting upstairs," Mom told me.

"Surprise!" Rachel called, when I got to my room. She held up my notebook. She had covered it while I was talking to Dad. "What do you think?" she asked.

I wanted to cover my own notebook is what I thought. But I couldn't say that to Rachel. Her feelings would be hurt. So I said, "It looks good."

"It's really hard to get perfect corners with wallpaper," she said. "Want me to print your name and address inside?"

"I'll do it myself."

"Okay . . . but I'll draw the lines so the letters are even." She searched my desk. "Where's your ruler?" she asked.

"Don't worry about it," I said. "I'll do it later."

When Rachel left I took a bath and washed my hair. It feels funny washing short hair when you're used to having it longer. The other night, when Rachel first saw me, she'd asked, "What'd you do to your hair, Steph?"

"I got carried away," I'd told her. "It was so hot when I came home from camp I decided to cut it all off."

"Yourself?"

"No, I went to the Final Cut."

"It's kind of interesting," Rachel had said. "Especially from the back."

I liked my short hair for about a week. Now I wish I'd never done it. It'll probably take all year to grow back.

I wrapped myself in a towel and left the steamy bathroom. I still couldn't believe Dad wasn't coming home until Thanksgiving. He's never been away that long. But fall goes a lot faster than winter, I reminded myself. It's my favorite time of year, not counting spring. I also like summer a lot. And winter is fun because of the snow . . . I began to feel better.

Before I got into bed I found my ruler. It was under Wile E. Coyote, my number one stuffed animal. Dad won him for me last year at the Jaycees' Carnival. I drew four straight lines on the inside of my notebook, then printed my name and address. There, I thought, admiring my work.

I got into bed and looked up at Benjamin Moore. I hope I meet someone just like him at junior high.

Homeroom

I introduced Alison to Rachel at the bus stop the next morning. Alison was wearing baggy pants, a white shirt about ten sizes too big, and running shoes. She had sunglasses around her neck, on a leash, and a canvas bag slung over her shoulder. The tangles were brushed out of her hair but her part was still crooked. All in all she looked great.

Then Rachel introduced us to Dana Carpenter, a ninth grader who also lives at Palfrey's Pond. I was glad we'd have company riding the bus because I'd heard rumors that some people like to give seventh graders a hard time on their first day at junior high.

When the bus came Rachel and I found two

seats together. Alison sat two rows ahead of us with Dana Carpenter. Nobody seemed interested in giving us a hard time.

"You didn't tell me Alison's Chinese," Rachel whispered when the bus got going.

"She's Vietnamese," I told Rachel. "She's adopted."

"Oh," Rachel said. "She doesn't even seem scared."

"I don't think she's the type to get scared over school," I said.

"I wish I weren't," Rachel said. "I couldn't eat a thing this morning. I was shaking so bad I could hardly brush my teeth."

I tried to help Rachel calm down by offering her a chocolate chip cookie from my lunch bag. She nibbled at it, then handed it back to me. No point in wasting it, I thought, so I finished it myself.

At the next bus stop six kids got on the bus and one of them was the best looking boy I have ever seen in person in my whole life. He looked almost as good as Benjamin Moore.

"Hey, Jeremy!" a group of boys called. "Back here . . ."

The boy, Jeremy, walked right by me on his way to the back of the bus. As he did his arm brushed against my shoulder. I turned around to get a better look at him. So did Rachel. So did most of the girls on the bus. He had brown hair, brown eyes, a great smile and he wore a chartreuse colored jacket. I learned that color from my deluxe Crayola crayon box when I was in third grade. On the back of his jacket it said *Dragons* and under that, *1962*.

"He has a great body," Rachel whispered to me.

"Yeah," I said. "He's a real hunk." We started to laugh and I could feel Rachel relax, until the bus pulled up to school. Then she stiffened. But her homeroom, 7-202, turned out to be right next to mine, 7-203.

"Stay with me until the bell rings," she begged. "And promise that you'll meet me here, in the hall, before first class so we can compare schedules . . . okay?"

"Okay," I said. Alison was standing next to me. She kept putting her sunglasses on, then taking them off again.

"Look," I said to Rachel, "there go the Klaff twins. Kara's in your homeroom and Peter's in mine." The Klaff twins were in our sixth grade class. Their mother is our doctor. I figured Rachel would feel better knowing that Kara's in her homeroom.

"Well . . . I guess this is it," Rachel said. "I'm going to count to ten, then I'm going to go in."

"Okay."

She counted very slowly. When she got to ten she said, "If I live through this I'll see you later." She turned and marched into her homeroom. Sometimes Rachel is really dramatic.

Alison and I found desks next to each other. As soon as I sat down Eric Macaulay yelled, "Hey . . . it's Hershey Bar!" He *would* have to be in my homeroom! Last year he and some other boys got the brilliant idea of calling me Hershey Bar just because my last name is Hirsch. They're so stupid! Of course Eric had to go and take the desk right in front of mine.

Besides Eric Macaulay and Peter Klaff there were two other boys and two girls from sixth grade in my homeroom. One of them, Amber Ackbourne, I have never liked. She has such an attitude! The other one, Miri Levine, is okay. She took the desk on the other side of mine. I set my notebook, covered in Rachel's dining room wallpaper, on my desk. Miri Levine looked at it and said, "I like your notebook."

I said, "Thanks."

She had a plain spiral notebook on her desk.

"How'd you get the corners so perfect?" she asked.

"Rachel covered it for me."

"Oh, Rachel . . . everything she does is perfect."

"I know," I said.

Alison unpacked her canvas bag. She pulled

out a gray-blue stone, a roll of Scotch tape, a pad decorated with stickers, a Uniball pen, cherry flavored lip gloss and a small framed photo. Then she put everything back into her bag except the stone. She passed it to me. "It's my favorite," she said.

The stone was smooth and warm from Alison's hand.

When the bell rang a woman walked into our room. I was really surprised when she said, "Good morning, class. I'm Natalie Remo, your homeroom teacher."

I'd expected someone young, around twenty-four, with short brown hair . . . someone a little overweight, like me. But Mrs. Remo is about my mother's age, which is thirty-eight, and she's black. She was wearing a suit. I noticed when she took off her jacket that the lining matched her blouse. She also had on gold earrings which she pulled off and set on her desk.

"Still pretty warm out," she said, fanning herself with a yellow pad. "More like summer than fall." She walked around the room opening the windows. "There . . . that's better." She stood in front of the class again. "I hope you all received my cards."

No one said anything.

"Did you . . . receive my cards?"

Everyone mumbled, "Yes."

"Good," Mrs. Remo said. "Welcome to J. E. Fox Junior High."

I happen to know that our school is named for John Edward Fox. He was supposed to be the first principal here but he died right before the school opened.

"I teach math," Mrs. Remo said. "So eventually most of you will wind up in one of my classes."

Nobody said anything.

"Well . . ." Mrs. Remo continued, "either you're all still asleep or you're feeling pretty unsure about junior high. I think by the end of the day you're going to feel much better. Once you get used to changing classes you'll all relax."

Nobody said anything.

Mrs. Remo smiled at us. "All right . . . let's see who's here today." She called our names in alphabetical order. Amber Ackbourne was first. She always is.

When Mrs. Remo called my name I raised my hand and said, "Here . . ." As I did, Eric Macaulay turned around and whispered, "Hershey Bar." I tried to kick him but I missed and kicked the leg of the chair instead. I hurt my foot so bad I groaned.

"Yes, Stephanie? Did you have something to say?" Mrs. Remo asked.

"No," I said, and Eric Macaulay laughed.

When she got to Alison Mrs. Remo pronounced her last name Mon See U.

Alison corrected her. "It's spelled M-o-n-c-e-a-u," she said. "But it's pronounced Mon So. It's French."

"Of course," Mrs. Remo said. "I should have known."

Everyone turned and looked at Alison. Alison just sat there as if she didn't notice but I could see her clutching her favorite stone.

After that we got our locker assignments and our class schedules. Then Mrs. Remo told us when the bell rang we should proceed to our first class in an orderly way. We waited for the bell, then we all jumped up and raced for the door.

"Orderly . . ." Mrs. Remo reminded us.

Rachel was already in the hall, waiting. "Well," she said, "let's see your schedule."

I handed it to her. I knew from the expression on her face that the news wasn't good before she said, "I can't believe this. We don't have one class together. Not one!"

"Let me see," I said, reaching for her schedule and mine. I compared them. "Look at this," I said. "We both have first lunch period. And we're in the same gym class."

"Gym," Rachel sniffed. "Big deal."

I felt bad for Rachel because Alison, Miri
Levine and I are in the same English, math and
social studies classes. Rachel has math first period,
with Mrs. Remo. I said, "You're lucky. She's
nice."

"Out of my way, Hershey Bar!" Eric Macaulay
said, shoving me.

"Watch it," I told him.

"Watch it yourself," he said. "I've got to get to
my math class. If I can only find room 203."

"This *is* room 203," Alison told him.

He looked up at the number on the door.
"Hey, you're right. I've got math right here.
Right in my own homeroom."

"Oh no!" Rachel groaned. "I'm in *his* math
class. It couldn't be worse."

"Yes it could," I told her.

"You know your problem, Stephanie?" Rachel
said.

"No, what?"

"You're an eternal optimist!"

"What's an optimist?"

"Look it up!"

As soon as I got to English class I looked up
optimist in the dictionary. *Optimist: One who has a
disposition or tendency to look on the more favorable
side of happenings and to anticipate the most favorable
result.* Well, I thought, what's wrong with that?

30

Maizie's Story

That afternoon, on our way to the school bus, Rachel admitted school hadn't been that bad. She knew some kids in her classes from last year and one, Stacey Green, she knew from music camp.

"You see? I told you it would all work out. The Eternal Optimist strikes again."

Rachel raised her eyebrows at me.

" 'Optimist,' " I said, " *'one who has a tendency to look on the more favorable side of happenings.'* "

"I'm impressed," Rachel said.

The boy in the chartreuse dragon jacket sat behind us on the bus. I heard him say something about a left wing to the boy next to him. I wasn't sure if he was talking about a bird or a plane.

When we got off the bus Alison asked us both to come over to her house.

Rachel said, "I have a flute lesson at four-thirty."

"You play the flute?" Alison asked.

"Yes," Rachel said.

"Are you any good?" Alison asked.

I laughed. Alison didn't know yet that Rachel is good at everything. "She's practically a professional," I told Alison.

"I'm not *that* good," Rachel said.

Alison checked her watch. "Look, it's only three-thirty . . . so why don't you come over for a little while? My dog can talk."

Rachel glanced at me. I wasn't supposed to have told anyone about Maizie so I hoped she wouldn't give me away.

"Your dog can talk?" Rachel asked.

"Uh huh," Alison said.

"Well . . ." Rachel said, "I guess I could come over for a little while."

Maizie met us at Alison's kitchen door, shaking her little rear end from side to side, then leaping into the air. Alison put her books on the kitchen table and scooped Maizie up into her arms. She put her face right up close to Maizie's. It looked like they were talking—in French, I think. It was hard to tell because Alison spoke very softly. But

Maizie nodded, made small sounds and sometimes let out a bark.

Rachel looked skeptical as she watched the two of them. I learned that word—skeptical—from her. It means to question or doubt.

"What's new with Maizie?" I asked Alison.

Alison put Maizie down and giggled. "She told me the silliest story."

"What story?" Rachel asked.

"I'm not sure it's true," Alison said as she poured three glasses of grape juice and set a box of pretzels on the table.

"Tell it to us anyway," Rachel said, taking a handful of pretzels.

"Well . . ." Alison began. She told us this story about her stepfather, Leon, who took Maizie for a walk in the woods. While they were walking Leon tripped over a branch and fell into the brook. He got soaked, which Maizie thought was a big joke.

"That's the whole story?" Rachel asked.

"Yes." Alison looked at me. "Of course, Maizie might have made it up. Sometimes when she's bored she sits around making up stories."

Rachel still wasn't convinced and Alison could tell. "I suppose we could ask Leon if it's true," she said.

Alison pressed the button on the intercom.

Every house in Palfrey's Pond has an intercom. Ours doesn't work but probably when Dad comes home he'll fix it.

"Hi, Leon . . ." Alison said. "I'm home."

"Be right down," a man's voice answered.

In a minute Leon came down the stairs and into the kitchen. He was tall and mostly bald.

"Hello, Pumpkin," Leon said to Alison, ruffling her hair.

Pumpkin? I thought.

"This is my stepfather, Leon Wishnik," Alison said, introducing us.

Leon smiled. He had very nice teeth. I notice everybody's teeth. Mom says it's because I wear braces. She says once they come off I won't be so interested in teeth. But Dad says my interest in teeth could mean that I want to be a dentist.

"Glad to meet you, Rachel," Leon said to me.

"I'm Stephanie," I told him.

He laughed. "Well, glad to meet *you*, Stephanie. And glad to meet you, too, Rachel." Leon lifted the lid off the pot on the stove and stirred. It smelled great.

"Maizie told me about your walk," Alison said to Leon. "Is it true . . . did you really trip and fall into the brook?"

Leon turned away from the stove and wagged his finger at Maizie. "I asked you not to tell anyone about that," he said to her.

34

Maizie ran under the kitchen table to hide.

"Then it's true?" Alison asked.

"Yes," Leon said. "My shoes will never be the same."

"Are you saying that your dog *really* talks?" Rachel asked Leon. I stared at her. She'd lowered her voice by an octave and sounded exactly like her mother. I could tell Leon was impressed. Tonight, while they were eating dinner, he would probably say to Alison, *That Rachel . . . she's certainly mature for her age.* He wouldn't know that this morning she was shaking with fear over the idea of junior high.

"Yes," Leon said, sighing, "Maizie talks . . . usually too much." He rested the wooden spoon on a saucer. "I've got to get back to work now. Nice to meet you, Stephanie and Rachel."

"Nice to meet you, too," we said.

Rachel still had a handful of pretzels and was licking the salt off them one at a time. She always licks pretzels until they're soggy.

Alison asked if we wanted to see her room. "But I'm warning you . . . it's incredibly ugly."

"So what'd you think?" I asked Rachel, as I walked her home from Alison's house.

"Obviously she's very insecure," Rachel said. "That's why she uses that talking dog story."

"But Maizie *can* talk," I said. "You heard what Leon said."

"You're so gullible, Steph!" Rachel said. "But I suppose that's part of your charm."

I had no idea what gullible meant and I wasn't about to ask so I just nodded and said, "It runs in my family."

Rachel gave me one of her skeptical looks, then said, "Well . . . I think we should try to help her get adjusted here. I think we should try to be her friends."

"I think so, too," I said.

Bruce

Bruce's fifth grade teacher is Mrs. Stein. I also had her. But she taught fourth grade then. "She remembers you, Steph . . ." Bruce said at breakfast the following Friday. "She said you came in second in the reading contest." He reached across the table for the box of Cheerios.

"Rachel came in first," I told him, as I buttered my toast. I like my toast very dark. I try to catch it just before it burns and is ruined.

"Mrs. Stein says she remembers Rachel, too," Bruce said.

"Rachel's teachers always remember her," I said. In fourth grade Rachel started reading the kinds of books her sister, Jessica, was reading for eighth grade English. When we gave book talks in class Rachel never reported on those books, though. She'd choose a book she thought a normal fourth grader would like instead.

By sixth grade everybody knew Rachel was smart but she didn't like it if the teacher made a big thing out of it. During math she'd go around helping kids who didn't understand. Our sixth grade teacher called Rachel his teaching assistant.

I was still sitting at the kitchen table, finishing my toast and thinking about Rachel, when Mom opened a kitchen drawer and said, "Oh, no!"

"Did you get a mouse?" I asked.

Mom slammed the drawer. "I give up!" she said. "They ate the peanut butter right off the traps. I'm going to have to call Mr. Kravitz."

"Who's he?" Bruce asked.

"The exterminator," Mom said. "He's the one who bought the yellow house from us."

"I never knew we sold our house to an exterminator," I said. "I thought Mr. and Mrs. Kravitz owned a shoe store."

Mom laughed. "Where did you get that idea?"

"I don't know."

"Well, Mr. Kravitz is an exterminator," Mom said.

That night Aunt Denise asked Mom to go to the movies with her. Besides being sisters, Mom and Aunt Denise are also best friends. I wish I had a sister, even though Rachel says she and Jessica don't get along that well. Mom has two sisters, Robin and Denise. Mom is the middle one. Her name is Rowena.

"Maybe I should call Mrs. Greco," Mom said at dinner.

"I'm too old for a sitter," I told her. Mrs. Greco sat for us when we lived in the yellow house. "I could be a sitter myself."

"You're not too old for companionship," Mom said.

"I have Bruce."

Bruce smiled. "She has me," he said, as if it were his idea. "And the mice."

"Very funny." Mom poured her tea. She took a few sips, then said, "Tell you what . . . if I'm going to be home by midnight you two can stay by yourselves . . . that is, if it works out tonight. But if I'm staying out later than that, you'll have a companion."

"You mean someone like Rachel?" I asked. "That kind of companion?"

"We'll see," Mom said.

We'll see is what Mom says when she wants to change the subject.

As soon as Mom left I took the phone into the pantry and called Rachel. The pantry is small, like a closet, but it's the only place in this house where I can talk on the phone in private. There's a light inside and enough room to sit on the floor, as long as I don't try to stretch out my legs. There's a nice spicy smell, too, which makes me hungry, even if I've just finished dinner.

While I was talking to Rachel I munched on the macadamia peanut brittle one of Mom's clients brought her from Hawaii. I tried Alison's number after I'd talked to Rachel, but her line was busy so I went into the den to watch TV with Bruce.

Next year, when we get cable, we'll have MTV. Aunt Denise's neighborhood already has cable, and my cousin, Howard, watches MTV all the time, even while he's doing his homework. Mom says I'll never be allowed to do my homework in front of the tube. I say, *We'll see.*

Bruce went to bed at ten. One thing about Bruce, he falls asleep really fast, as soon as his head hits the pillow. Same as me.

I went to the bathroom and used the Water Pik. Then I scrubbed my face. Some nights I don't bother washing my face at all. I keep forgetting to ask Mom if scrubbing your face will keep you from getting acne. I scrubbed mine until it turned very pink, to make up for all the nights I'm too lazy to do anything.

Next, I decided to call Dad. I went down the hall to Mom's room and looked up Dad's number in the little phone book she keeps in her night table. There was also a flashlight in her drawer, and some lip goo.

I dialed the number of Dad's apartment. The phone rang three times before Dad's answering machine clicked on with Dad's voice saying, "This is Steve Hirsch. I'm not home right now but if you leave a message . . ."

"Hi Dad," I said at the sound of the beep. "It's Stephanie. I just wanted to say hello."

I went back to my room. The house was so quiet. There was a half moon outside my window and it lit up Benjamin Moore's poster. Well, Benjamin, I thought, as I got into bed. It's just you and me tonight. I wish you were real. I wish you could come down off the ceiling and kiss me goodnight. You look like you'd be a great kisser.

I rolled over and fell asleep. I slept until a frightening sound woke me. I sat up in bed, my heart pounding. Then I raced down the hall to Mom's room. But Mom wasn't home yet. I grabbed the baseball bat from under her bed. She keeps it there when Dad is away, just in case. I glanced at the clock—11:20—not even an hour since I'd gone to bed. I listened for other sounds, trying to decide if I should call the police or a neighbor, but all I heard was Bruce, crying and calling for Mom. I ran to his room, clutching the baseball bat, and that's when I realized nothing was wrong in the house. It was just Bruce, having one of his nightmares.

I sat down at the edge of his bed. He threw his arms around me, sobbing. I held him tight. I would never put my arms around him during the day. Not that he'd let me. His face felt hot and wet with tears. He smelled like a puppy.

"The usual?" I asked.

"Yes . . . I saw it," he said, gulping for air. "I saw the bomb . . . it was silver . . . shaped like a football . . . rolling around in the sky. When it got to our house it started to fall . . . straight down . . . and then there was a flash of light . . . and I heard the explosion . . ."

"It's all right," I told him. "It was just a bad dream."

"It's coming," Bruce said, "the bomb is coming. . . ."

"But it's not coming tonight," I told him, stroking his hair. His hair was soft and damp around the edges.

"How do you know?"

"I just know. So there's no point in worrying about it now."

"It could be the end of the world," Bruce said, shuddering.

"Look," I told him, "if it happens, it happens." I don't like to think about the end of the world or the bomb so I don't. I'm good at putting bad things out of my mind. That's why I'm an optimist.

I lay down on Bruce's bed and held him until he fell back asleep. The good thing about his nightmares is that he never has more than one a night. It's as if he just needs to be reassured that the end of the world isn't coming yet.

I guess I fell asleep holding Bruce because soon my mother was gently shaking me and whispering, "Come on, Steph . . . let's go back to bed."

She walked me down the hall to my room. "He had a nightmare," I said, groggily.

Mom tucked me into bed and kissed both my cheeks.

The next morning, when I came into the kitchen, Bruce was sitting at the table, writing a letter.

I poured myself a glass of orange juice. "Who are you writing to today?" I asked.

"The President," Bruce said.

"Oh, the President." I set out a bowl for my cereal.

"You should write, too," Bruce said. "If everybody writes to the President he'll have to listen. Here . . ." Bruce shoved a piece of notebook paper at me.

"Not while I'm eating," I said. I finished my cereal, rinsed the bowl, then brought the box of doughnuts to the table. Mom is a doughnut addict but since we moved she's buying only the plain or the whole wheat kind. No artificial flavors or colors, no preservatives. Mom will eat only one a day now, at the most two, because she's trying to lose weight. I miss glazed doughnuts. I miss chocolate and jelly filled too.

"Mom is going to kill you," Bruce said.

"For what?"

"Polishing off three doughnuts."

Three? I counted the ones left in the box. He was right. Sometimes when I'm eating I forget to keep track.

I washed my doughnuts down with another glass of juice and then I started my letter.

Dear Mr. President,

I really think you should do more to make sure we never have a nuclear war. War is stupid, as you know. My brother, who is ten, has

44

nightmares about it. Probably other kids do, too. I have mainly good dreams. My friend, Rachel, says I am an optimist. Even so, I don't want to die and neither do any of my friends. Why can't you arrange more meetings with other countries and try harder to get along. Make some treaties. Make them for one hundred years so we don't have to worry for a long time. You could also get rid of all the nuclear weapons in the world and then maybe Bruce, my brother, could get a decent night's sleep.

Yours truly,
Stephanie B. Hirsch

I like using my middle initial for formal occasions. The *B* stands for Behrens. That's my mother's maiden name.

I shoved my letter across the table, at Bruce. He read it. "This is about dreams," he said.

"No, it's not," I told him. "It's about nuclear war."

"But there's a lot in it about dreams."

"So . . . what's wrong with that? If *you* didn't have bad dreams about nuclear war we wouldn't be writing to the President, would we?"

"I don't know," Bruce said. "And you didn't make paragraphs, either."

"I didn't make paragraphs on purpose," I said. That wasn't true but I wasn't going to admit it to Bruce. "I think it's an outstanding letter," I said. "I think the part about the hundred year treaties is really brilliant."

"In a hundred years we'll be dead," Bruce said, sounding gloomy.

"So will everybody."

"No . . . people who aren't born yet won't be."

"That doesn't count," I said. "Everybody we know will be dead in a hundred years."

"I don't like to think about being dead," Bruce said.

"Who does?" I passed him the doughnut box. "Here," I said, "have one . . . it'll make you feel better."

"I don't like these doughnuts," he said, "especially in the morning."

Saturdays

Ever since Dad went to L.A. Mom takes Bruce and me to the office with her on Saturdays. She's got a travel agency in town. Going Places is the name of it. Aunt Denise says Mom is a real go-getter. She says she hopes I take after her. I don't know if I do or not. Mom had puppy fat like me when she was a girl. And we both have brown hair and blue eyes if that means anything.

I reminded Mom this was the Saturday Rachel and I were going to shop with Alison, to help her fix up her room. "Rachel says it's very depressing the way it is. It's all gray."

"Gray is a sophisticated color," Mom said.

"But it's so blah . . . it doesn't suit Alison," I told her. "Alison is a very cheerful person."

"She sounds like a good match for you," Mom said.

"I think she is. I think we're really going to get along."

"What about Rachel?" Mom asked.

"She wants to be Alison's friend, too. She wants to help her get adjusted here. We're meeting in front of the bank at one o'clock. Is that okay?"

"I think we can arrange to give you the afternoon off," Mom said. "But try and get as much as you can done this morning."

"You know I'm a hard worker," I said.

My job is filing. Craig taught me how to do it. He's one of Mom's part-time assistants. He wears a gold earring in one ear and has a scraggly moustache that he's always touching to make sure it's still there. He wants to write travel guides to places like Africa and India when he's out of college. So far he's only been as far away as Maine.

There's no big deal to filing as long as you know the alphabet. The only thing I have to remember is that we file front to back here, which means I have to put the latest papers at the end of the folder, not at the beginning.

While I was filing, who should come into Going Places but Jeremy Dragon, that good-looking boy from the bus. Only Rachel and Alison know my secret name for him. I named him that because of his chartreuse jacket with the dragon on the back. He wears it every day. He was with two of his friends. I recognized them from the bus, too.

"Can I help you?" Craig asked them.

"We need some brochures," Jeremy Dragon said, "for a school project."

"Help yourself," Craig said.

"How many can we take?" one of Jeremy's friends asked.

I came running up front then. "How about five apiece?" I said.

Jeremy and his two friends looked at me. So did Craig.

"Aren't you supposed to be filing?" Craig asked.

"In a minute," I told him and hoped that he would go do something else. When he still didn't get the hint I said, "*I'll* take care of this, Craig." I've heard Mom say that to him lots of times.

Finally Craig got the message and said, "Oh . . ." and he excused himself to go back to the desk where he'd been working.

"You should try the Ivory Coast," I said to Jeremy, handing him a brochure. "And Thailand . . . that's a good one." I handed him that brochure, too. "I also recommend Alaska . . . and then there's Brazil." Each time I handed Jeremy Dragon a brochure our fingers touched and I got a tingly feeling up my arm.

"We're doing a project on marketing and advertising," Jeremy said, "not on travel."

"Oh," I said, as his friends helped themselves to more than five brochures apiece. Then I quickly added, "If you ever do want to plan a trip this is the best travel agency in town. My mother owns it so I should know."

"We'll keep that in mind," Jeremy said. He kind of waved as he went out the door.

"My name is Stephanie," I called after him. But he didn't hear me.

I couldn't wait to tell Rachel and Alison about my morning.

Gena Farrell

Here's what we bought for Alison's room: two lamp shades, one comforter, a set of flowered sheets, four throw pillows, three posters and one box of push pins.

We shopped all over town, walking from store to store, until my feet ached. Rachel said it was important to see everything available before making a decision. She took notes on what we saw, and where. I hoped we'd run into Jeremy Dragon again but we didn't. Eventually we wound up where we started, at Bed and Bath. I couldn't believe how Alison just bought whatever she wanted. Even though the sheets and the throw pillows were on sale, they were still very expensive. Alison charged everything on her mother's American Express card.

"You mean she just gave you her credit card . . ." I asked, "just like that?"

"She trusts me," Alison said.

"I know, but still . . ." I said. "Did she tell you how much you could spend?"

"We talked about what I needed," Alison said.

"At least you got some of it on sale," Rachel said. "My mother buys everything on sale. And you got very good things. It pays to buy the best because it lasts longer."

I don't necessarily agree with that. Take my flowered sweatshirt. If I had bought the expensive kind I'd be stuck with it as long as it fit. But I bought the rip-off sweatshirt which only cost half as much so when it fell apart in the wash after a couple of months I didn't mind.

"Let's meet tomorrow morning at my house," Alison said, "around eleven. And you guys can help me fix up my room . . . okay?"

"Sure," I said.

"I'm going to visit my grandmother in the morning," Rachel said, "but I should be back around noon."

Rachel's grandmother had a stroke last spring. Once, I went with her family to the nursing home, but I got really upset because Rachel's grandmother couldn't walk or talk. Rachel says her grandmother understands everything they say and someday she may even be able to speak again. I don't know. I hope that never happens to Gran Lola or Papa Jack. It would be too sad.

On Sunday morning I got to Alison's house right on the dot of eleven. I rang the bell and a woman opened the door. She was wearing jeans and that red and white T-shirt Alison had been wearing on the day that we met. She looked very familiar.

"Hello," she said, "I'm Alison's mother. Are you Stephanie?"

"Yes."

"Alison's in her room. You can go on up . . ."

I started up the stairs. Then Alison's mother called, "Thanks for helping Alison find such beautiful things yesterday."

I stopped and turned at the landing, looking down at her. I know who she looks like, I thought. She looks like Gena Farrell, the TV star.

I went to Alison's room. She was unrolling her posters and laying them out on the floor. "Hi," I said. Maizie was on the bed. She barked at me. "Hello, Maizie." As soon as I spoke she turned her back. I guess she wasn't interested in having a conversation.

"Your mother looks a lot like Gena Farrell," I told Alison.

"I know," Alison said.

"I guess everybody tells her that."

"Yes. Especially since she is Gena Farrell."

"Your mother *is* Gena Farrell, the TV star?"

"She's an actress," Alison said, "not a TV star." She held a poster of Bruce Springsteen against the wall. "What do you think?"

"I can't believe this!" I said. "Your mother is Gena Farrell and you never said anything?"

"What should I have said?" Alison asked, holding up a second poster. This one showed a gorilla lying on a sofa. "Do you like it here or do you think I should hang it over my desk?"

"Over your desk," I said. "I just can't believe that you didn't tell us!"

"Would it have made a difference?" Alison put the posters on her bed.

"No," I said, "but . . ."

"But what?" Now she looked directly at me, waiting for me to say something.

"Nothing . . ."

"Get down, Maizie!" Alison shooed her off the bed.

Maizie growled.

"She can't stand it when people gush over my mother," Alison said. "She'll try to bite anyone who does. You wouldn't believe how many times she's tried to bite reporters."

"Really?"

"Yes," Alison said, taking the comforter out of its plastic bag. "Give me a hand getting this on the bed."

The comforter had tiny rosebuds all over it. And the lamp shades, which had been my idea, were made of the same fabric. Rachel said the lamp shades were unnecessary and too expensive, but Alison bought them anyway. At the time I thought it was to please me, since everything else had been Rachel's idea. But now that I knew Alison's mother was Gena Farrell I wasn't so sure. I mean, Gena Farrell is famous! She must be very rich.

I helped Alison hang her posters. I wished I had thought of push pins when I was hanging mine. They don't take the paint off the wall and they make such tiny holes that no one would ever notice them.

When we'd finished Alison said, "Do you know how to play Spit?"

"Spit as in saliva?" I asked.

Alison laughed. "Spit as in the card game."

"There's a card game called Spit?"

"Yes." Alison opened her desk drawer and took out a deck of cards. She shuffled, divided them into two piles, then explained the rules of the game.

By the time Rachel got there Alison and I were in the middle of a really fast hand and couldn't stop laughing. "We're playing Spit," I told Rachel.

"What?" Rachel said.

"It's a card game."

"You want me to teach you?" Alison asked Rachel.

"No . . ." Rachel said. "I came over to help with your room but I see it's all done."

Alison collected the cards and wrapped a rubber band around them.

"Doesn't it look great?" I asked Rachel.

"Actually, it does," Rachel said. "It looks just like a flower garden. Maybe I should be an interior designer."

"Did you recognize Alison's mother?" I asked Rachel.

"No, should I have?" Rachel asked.

"She's Gena Farrell," I said.

Maizie began to bark.

"Who's Gena Farrell?"

"Alison's mother!"

"I got that part," Rachel said. "The part I didn't get is *who* is Gena Farrell?"

"The TV star," I said.

"Actress," Alison said, correcting me.

"The actress," I repeated. "You know . . . she's on *Canyon Crossing*."

Maizie jumped off the bed and began nipping at my feet.

"Quit that," I told her.

"I warned you," Alison said.

"I've never seen *Canyon Crossing*," Rachel said.

"Yes, you have . . ." I told her. "Last year we watched it at my house . . . more than once."

"I don't remember," Rachel said.

"It's been cancelled," Alison said. "Mom's doing a new series. It's called *Franny on Her Own*. It won't be on until February. They're shooting in New York now. That's why we moved east. Leon's the head writer. He gets to decide what happens to all the characters."

"That's so exciting!" I said. "What's it like having Gena Farrell for a mother?"

"She's the only mother I've ever known." Alison stacked the books on her desk.

"But she's so famous!" I said.

Maizie growled. I wondered if it was true that she tried to bite reporters who asked too many questions.

"It doesn't matter that she's famous," Alison said. "When she's home she's Mom. The other stuff is just her work. It has nothing to do with me."

"You sound so well adjusted," Rachel said. "Kids of stars aren't supposed to be well adjusted. They're supposed to be neurotic."

"I can't help it if I'm not. Now could we please change the subject?"

I looked at Rachel. All three of us were quiet

for a minute. Then I said, "When you were little and you lived in France did you eat frogs' legs?"

Alison laughed. "Even when we change the subject you're still asking questions!"

"Stephanie likes to know everything about her friends," Rachel said, linking her arm through mine. "It's a sign that she cares."

Left Wing

The window in the second floor girls' room at school looks down on the playing field. I discovered this on Monday at the end of lunch period when I happened to look out that window. The soccer team was at practice. And who should be playing but Jeremy Dragon! I ran down to the cafeteria to tell Rachel and Alison. Then the three of us raced back up to the girls' room.

"He plays left wing!" Alison said.

"What does that mean?" I asked.

"That's his position," Alison said. "Look . . . he's trying for a goal!"

We held our breath. But he missed.

Since then we don't waste a lot of time in the cafeteria. As soon as we finish eating we come up to the girls' room and spend the rest of lunch period looking out the window. Jeremy Dragon has hairy legs. Rachel says that means he's experienced.

"Experienced how?" I asked.

"Experienced sexually," Rachel said.

"Really?" I asked. "How do you know that?"

"I read it," Rachel said.

"How far do you think he's gone?" Alison asked.

"Far," Rachel said.

"All the way?" Alison asked.

"Possibly," Rachel said.

"Just because he has hair on his legs?" I asked.

"That and other things," Rachel said.

"Like what?"

"I think what Rachel means," Alison said to me, "is that his body is very mature."

"Well, so is Rachel's," I said. "She has breasts and she gets her period."

"Really?" Alison said to Rachel. "You get your period?"

"Yes," Rachel said. "I've had it since fifth grade."

"I haven't had mine yet," Alison said.

"Neither has Steph," Rachel said.

"And that's the whole point," I told her. "*Your* body is developed and you don't have any experience. You haven't even kissed a boy."

"Jeremy Dragon is in ninth grade," Rachel said. "I certainly expect to have kissed a boy by the time I'm in ninth grade."

"I've already kissed two boys," Alison said.

Rachel and I looked at her. "Real kisses?" I asked.

"Yes."

"When did this happen?" Rachel asked.

"Last year. I kissed one at the beach and the other in the courtyard at school."

"How old were these boys?" Rachel asked.

"My age. Sixth grade."

"Kissing a sixth grade boy isn't the same as kissing someone like Jeremy Dragon," Rachel said. "Kissing Jeremy Dragon would be a whole different story."

Alison looked out the window. After a minute she said, "I see what you mean."

Mr. Kravitz

Mr. Kravitz, the exterminator, came to our house in a white truck that had KRAVITZ—SINCE 1967 printed in small letters on the door. He wore a dark blue jumpsuit with *Ed* stitched on the pocket. He had a brown and white dog with him. A beagle, I think. He brought the dog into our house. "This is Henry," Mr. Kravitz said. "He's trained to find termites."

"We don't have termites," Mom told him. "We have mice."

Mr. Kravitz looked at his notebook. "Oh, that's right." He laughed and shook his head. "Well, Henry's not a bad mouser, for a dog."

Mr. Kravitz and Henry followed Mom into the kitchen. Then, as if she'd just remembered I was there, she said, "This is my daughter, Stephanie."

"How do, Stephanie," Mr. Kravitz said.

"Mr. Kravitz bought the yellow house," Mom reminded me.

"I know," I told her.

"And we're certainly enjoying it," Mr. Kravitz said.

"I'm glad," Mom said. "Well . . . I'll let you get down to business, Mr. Kravitz. I hope you can clear up our problem."

"I'll do my best," Mr. Kravitz said.

Mom went upstairs to work at her computer, which she's moved from the den to her bedroom. I went to the refrigerator to get a glass of juice. "Do you use traps?" I asked Mr. Kravitz.

"No."

"What do you use?"

"Something else."

"What?"

"Does it make a difference?"

"Yes."

"Why?"

"Because my brother and I don't believe in violence."

"I don't use anything violent."

"What do you use?"

Mr. Kravitz let out a deep breath. "I use something to discourage them from coming back."

"Poison?" I asked.

"We don't think of it that way."

"Oh," I said, drinking my apple juice. Then I remembered my manners. "Would you like a glass of juice?"

"No thank you," Mr. Kravitz said. His dog, Henry, was sniffing inside the cabinet under the sink.

"So, who sleeps in my old room?" I asked.

Mr. Kravitz was inside the cabinet now, poking around with a flashlight. "Which room would that be?" he said. His voice was muffled.

"Top of the stairs . . . first room to the left," I told him.

"Hmm . . . that would be my youngest son's room. He's in ninth grade at Fox Junior High."

"Really," I said, talking louder. "I go to Fox. I'm in seventh grade."

"Maybe you know Jeremy," Mr. Kravitz said.

"Jeremy?"

"Yes. Jeremy Kravitz. He's my son."

"I only know one Jeremy," I said. "And he's not your son. He wears a chartreuse jacket with a dragon on the back."

Mr. Kravitz backed out of the cabinet. "That's *my* jacket," he said, laughing.

"Your jacket?"

"Nineteen-sixty-two," Mr. Kravitz said, standing up. "I was a senior in high school then."

"Are you saying that the boy who wears that dragon jacket is your son?"

"That's right."

"And his name is Jeremy and he sleeps in my old room?"

"That's right."

"Excuse me," I said to Mr. Kravitz. "I've got to do my homework now." I had to call Alison and Rachel right away! I ran into the den to use the phone.

I called Rachel first. "You won't believe this," I began, "but . . ." I told her the whole story. "You've got to come right over."

"I'm practicing my flute now," Rachel said.

"Rachel . . ." I said, "we are talking about Jeremy Dragon whose father happens to be standing in my kitchen. . . ."

"All right. . . ." Rachel said. "I'll be over in a few minutes."

I didn't have to convince Alison. She ran all the way around the pond and arrived at my house breathless. When Rachel got here the three of us went into the kitchen and I introduced them to Mr. Kravitz.

"Are you really Jeremy's father?" Rachel asked in her most mature voice.

Mr. Kravitz was spreading a white powder inside our cabinets. "Has Jeremy been giving you trouble?" he asked, looking up at us. "Has Jeremy been rude to you?"

I love how parents always assume the worst about their kids. "No," I said. "We're just curious because he rides our bus."

"And we're interested in that jacket he wears," Rachel said. "It's a very unusual jacket."

I tried to catch her attention but I couldn't.

"Actually it could be a valuable antique," Rachel continued. "I know because my aunt, who lives in New Hampshire, is in the antique business."

"The jacket was his," I said to Rachel, nodding in Mr. Kravitz' direction.

"Oh," Rachel said. "I didn't mean to insult you, Mr. Kravitz. I only meant that some day that jacket could be considered an antique. I didn't mean it was that old right now."

"I'm not insulted," Mr. Kravitz said.

Henry continued to sniff around our kitchen.

"Does your dog talk?" I asked Mr. Kravitz.

"Henry communicates," Mr. Kravitz said, as if my question was perfectly normal, "but he doesn't speak."

"Only one in seventeen million dogs can talk in words," I told him.

"Is that right?" Mr. Kravitz asked.

I didn't tell him about Maizie. It wasn't my business. If Alison wanted him to know she could tell him.

"Now, girls . . ." Mr. Kravitz finally said, "I'd really like to spend more time chatting with you but I've got work to do here."

"Well . . . it's been very nice meeting you, Mr. Kravitz," Rachel said.

"Same here," Alison said.

"Likewise," Mr. Kravitz said, from inside another cabinet.

The three of us went outside and ran down to the pond. "Can you believe Jeremy Dragon sleeps in my old room?"

"Too bad you didn't sell your house with the furniture," Rachel said. "Then he'd be sleeping in your bed!"

The idea of Jeremy Dragon sleeping in my bed made me feel funny all over.

"You're blushing, Steph!" Alison said.

"Your face is purple!" Rachel sang.

"Excuse me," I said, walking between them. "I think I need to cool off." I went down to the edge of the pond and waded into the water, scaring the ducks, who paddled out of my way.

Rachel yelled, "Steph . . . what are you doing?"

And Alison called, "Steph . . . come out!"

"It feels great!" I sang, splashing around. "Come on in . . ."

"Stephanie!" Rachel shouted, "it's not a swimming pond!"

"So . . . who's swimming?"

They couldn't believe I'd gone into the pond with all my clothes on. Neither could my mother, who happened to be in the kitchen when I came home. "Stephanie . . . what on earth?"

"I didn't mean to get wet," I told her. "It just happened."

Dad's Laugh

Dad called from Hawaii. "Are the waves huge?"
I asked.

"I haven't had a chance to get to the beach."

"Dad . . . how can you be in Hawaii and not
get to the beach?"

"I'm here to work, Steph."

"I know . . . but still . . ."

"I'll try to get to the beach tomorrow . . .
okay?"

"Okay. And send us some of that peanut brittle
. . . the kind with macadamia nuts."

"I don't think peanut brittle is good for your
braces."

"Well, then . . . send shells from the beach
. . . or sand."

"I'll try," Dad said. "So what's new at home?"

I told him about our first dead mouse. "Mom found him in the cabinet under the sink . . . she practically fainted . . . so I lifted him out by his tail . . . dropped him into a Baggie . . . and tossed him in the trash can."

Dad laughed. I love to make him laugh. When he does he opens his mouth wide and you can see his gold fillings. "Wait . . . I'm not finished," I said, "because after I tossed him in the trash I forgot to put the bunjie cords back on the can . . . so that night the raccoons got into it and made a mess! So guess who had to clean up . . . and guess who almost missed the school bus?"

Dad kept on laughing. I'm definitely best in my family at making him laugh. But we don't get to laugh that much over the phone.

"So how's the weather?" Dad finally asked.

"Nice," I told him. "It's getting to be fall."

Remarkable Eyes

Mrs. Remo wears contact lenses. She's always telling us about them. She got them before school started so she's worn them for two months now. This morning she was rubbing her eye. Then she said, "Oh no . . ." and motioned for us to be quiet. "I think I've lost a contact lens. I need someone to help me find it."

Hands shot up around the room.

Eric Macaulay called out, "I've got perfect vision, Mrs. Remo. I'll find it for you."

"All right, Eric," Mrs. Remo said.

Eric shoved his chair back so hard it crashed into my desk, knocking over my books, which I had stacked like a pyramid. He raced up to the front of the room.

"Be careful where you step, Eric," Mrs. Remo said. "The lens is very fragile. I hope it's fallen onto my desk, not the floor."

But Eric didn't even bother to look on Mrs. Remo's desk. He stood right up close to her and seemed to be examining her dress, which was a dark green knit, with short sleeves. He didn't touch her, but the way he stared must have made her uncomfortable because she laughed nervously and said, "What *are* you doing, Eric?"

"Trying to find your lens," Eric said, "so please don't move."

I would have been very embarrassed to have Eric Macaulay examine me that closely, especially across my chest.

But then, halfway between Mrs. Remo's left shoulder and her waist, Eric plucked something off her dress. "Aha!" he said. "Got it!" He held it up for Mrs. Remo to see.

"Why, Eric . . ." Mrs. Remo said, taking the lens off his finger, "you must have remarkable eyes! How did you know it would be on my dress?"

"My mother wears contacts," Eric said. "Whenever she thinks she's lost one it's always stuck to her clothes."

"Thank you, Eric," Mrs. Remo said.

The class applauded and Eric took a bow.

Alison leaned across the aisle and whispered, "He's so cute!"

I made a face. Eric is too impossible to be cute.

On his way back to his desk Eric stopped next to Alison's. "Do you wear contacts, Thumbelina?"

He's been calling her Thumbelina since the second week of school but she doesn't seem to mind.

"No," Alison told him. "My eyes are as perfect as yours."

"Too bad . . ." Eric said, "because I wouldn't mind finding your lost lenses."

Alison started to giggle and once she gets started she can't stop.

As soon as Mrs. Remo had her lens back in place she held up a flyer and said, "I've got an announcement, class. The seventh grade bake sale will be held a week from Monday. The first . . ." She stopped and shook her head. "All right, Alison . . . either calm down or share the joke with the rest of us."

Alison covered her mouth with both hands to keep from laughing out loud but I could tell she still had the giggles.

Mrs. Remo continued with her announcement. "The first $150 will be used to donate food baskets to the needy. Anything over that will go to the seventh grade activity fund. Last year's seventh grade class earned enough to hold a winter dance."

A winter dance, I thought. Now that sounds interesting.

"So . . ." Mrs. Remo went on, "we need to appoint a bake sale chairperson . . . someone to keep track of who's baking what."

"Mrs. Remo . . ." Eric called, waving his arm.

"Yes, Eric?"

"I nominate Peter Klaff as chairperson. He's very organized. When I run for President he's going to be my campaign manager."

Was Eric planning to run for President of Fox Junior High, I wondered, or President of the United States?

"Peter . . ." Mrs. Remo said, "would you like to be chairperson of the bake sale?"

Everyone looked at Peter Klaff. He's shorter than me and much thinner. He has pale blond hair and eyebrows and lashes to match. Also, his ears stick out. I think it must run in the family because his mother and sister have the same kind of ears. You could see the red creeping up Peter's neck to his face. And you could see him gulping hard, as if he couldn't get enough air to breathe. He's so shy! But he managed to answer Mrs. Remo's question. He said, "Yes."

"Fine," Mrs. Remo said, "then it's all settled."

As Alison and I walked through the hall on

our way to first period class she began to sing a song she'd made up about a boy with remarkable eyes. "Well?" she said, when she'd finished.

I pretended to stick my finger down my throat. "That bad?"

"No . . ." I said. "Worse!"

She bumped hips with me and we both laughed. But the next time she sang her song I found myself humming along.

Debate

Rachel says she has more important things on her mind than baking. She's trying out for the school debating team. Only two seventh graders will make it. She has to prepare a five-minute speech and present it at assembly on the afternoon of the bake sale.

"What's the subject of your speech?" I asked.

"Should wearing a seat belt be law or should it be up to the individual to decide?"

"That's easy," I said. "It should be law."

"I have to be able to argue both sides of the issue," Rachel explained, "even if I disagree with it."

"That's stupid."

"No . . . that's what debating is all about."

A few days later I went to Rachel's house after school. I couldn't stay long because I had an appointment at the orthodontist at four-thirty. Alison couldn't come over at all because she's got a rash on her foot and Leon took her to see Dr. Klaff.

Rachel was a wreck over her speech. "Look at my notes," she said, holding up a stack of 3x5 cards. "I've been working every night till ten."

"Don't worry so much," I told her. "After all, it's just five minutes."

"Do you have any idea how long five minutes really is?"

"Five minutes is five minutes," I said.

"I mean," she said, "do you know how it feels?"

"How it feels?" I asked.

"Yes," she said. "Look, I'll show you. Stand right there . . . right where you are . . ."

I was standing in the middle of her bedroom.

"Don't move," Rachel said.

"Okay."

"Now . . . tell me when you think five minutes is up. And don't look at your watch," she said. "Ready, set, go . . ."

I stood very still. I didn't move, except to scratch my leg. Burt and Harry were asleep on Rachel's bed. Rachel sat at her desk, shuffling

77

her note cards. I wondered how Alison was doing at Dr. Klaff's. Alison says Peter Klaff likes me. She says he's always looking at me and that's how you can tell. But I'm not sure she's right. When Peter asked what I was bringing to the bake sale I told him I was partners with Alison and that we were baking brownies from an old family recipe. He didn't seem impressed.

I looked over at Rachel again. She was still at her desk, making more note cards. "Okay," I said. "Five minutes is up."

Rachel checked her watch. "Ha! It's only been one minute, twenty-four seconds."

"I can't believe it!"

"I told you five minutes feels like a long time!"

Mom made me puree of carrot and a baked potato for dinner that night, because after my braces are tightened I can't eat anything but soft, mushy foods. "Rachel's trying out for the debating team," I said, as I mashed my potato with butter. "She's got to make a five-minute speech about seat belts."

"I'm sure she'll do fine," Mom said.

"I'm sure, too, but Rachel's worried. She wants to be the best."

"She's such a perfectionist," Mom said.

"I wouldn't mind being perfect," Bruce said.

"You mean you're not?" I asked.

"Very funny," he said.

"Be glad you're not," Mom said. "It's a hard way to go through life."

I tasted the carrot puree. Even though it looked like baby food it was delicious. Bruce watched me eat it. "I hope I never need braces," he said.

"It's temporary," I told him. "Some day I'll have a beautiful smile."

"Yeah . . . but what about the rest of your face?"

"Bruce!" Mom said.

"It's just a joke, Mom," he told her.

"He really wishes he looked like me," I said.

Bruce chuckled to himself.

We had vanilla pudding for dessert. "I'm thinking of trying out for symphonic band," I announced, as the pudding slid around in my mouth.

"Since when do you play an instrument?" Bruce asked.

"I'm trying out for percussion."

"Since when do you play drums?" Bruce asked.

"Ms. Lopez says I can learn . . . as long as I have a good sense of rhythm." I finished my pudding. "Do you think I have a good sense of rhythm?" I asked Mom.

"When you were little I'd give you a pot and a wooden spoon and you were happy for hours. If that's an indication I'd say yes."

"A pot and a wooden spoon," Bruce repeated, shaking his head and chuckling again.

The next time Dad called I asked him if he thought I had a good sense of rhythm.

He said, "You used to have a great time with a pot and a wooden spoon."

"That's exactly what Mom said."

"I guess we remember the same things."

I told him about the seventh grade bake sale and that Alison and I are going to bake Sadie Wishnik's brownies.

"Who's Sadie Wishnik?" Dad asked.

"Leon's mother."

"Who's Leon?"

"Alison's stepfather. And you know who Alison is," I told him, "she's my new friend."

"So Sadie Wishnik is her stepgrandmother?" Dad asked.

"I guess so," I said. "Anyway, we're going to Sadie's house to bake, on Sunday. She lives in New Jersey, near the ocean. And speaking of oceans . . . thanks for the box of shells from Hawaii. I've never seen such pretty ones. Did you find them yourself?"

Dad hesitated. "The truth?"

"Yes."

"I never did get to the beach. I bought them at a gift shop."

I knew it! I could tell by the way they were wrapped. But I didn't want Dad to feel bad so I said, "Maybe next time you'll get to the beach."

"Maybe so."

"Anyway . . . I love the shells!"

"I'm glad," Dad said. "So . . . what else is new at school?"

Dad is always asking what's new at school. I tell him what I think he wants to hear. What I don't tell him about is boys. I don't think he'd understand. If I told him that Peter Klaff stares at me he'd probably say, *Doesn't he know it's bad manners to stare?* And I certainly don't tell him about watching Jeremy Dragon at soccer. Dad would never understand that.

"What about your grades?" Dad asked.

"We haven't gotten any yet."

If Mom and Dad were in a debate and the subject was grades, Mom would say that what you actually learn is more important than the grades you get. Dad would argue that grades are an indication of what you've learned and how you handle responsibility. If I had to choose sides I'd choose Mom's.

Sadie Wishnik's Brownies

The rash on Alison's foot is called contact dermatitis. That means Alison's foot came into contact with something that caused the rash. What I don't get is, how can one foot come into contact with something the other foot doesn't? Dr. Klaff gave her a cream and told her to wear white cotton socks until the rash was gone.

Sunday morning, when I got to Alison's, she was waiting on her front steps. She had invited Rachel to come to Sadie Wishnik's, too. But Rachel said she had to stay home to work on her speech. I think the real reason Rachel wouldn't come is she gets carsick.

Gena Farrell came out of the house carrying

Maizie and a straw bag. She was wearing mirrored sunglasses. Her hair was tied back and she didn't have on any makeup. You couldn't tell she was famous. Leon followed, locking the door behind him. He carried the Sunday newspaper tucked under his arm.

As soon as we got going Gena pulled a needle-point canvas out of her bag and began to stitch it.

"That's pretty," I said, trying to get a better look from the back seat. "What's it going to be?"

Gena took off her mirrored glasses, turned around, and faced me. She has big eyes—deep blue, like the color of the sky on a beautiful spring day. She held the needlepoint out, studied it for a minute and said, "A pillow, I think."

"Mom gave away twenty pillows last Christmas," Alison said.

Gena laughed. "I spend a lot of time sitting around and waiting on the set," she said. "So I do a lot of needlepointing. It relaxes me."

I couldn't believe Gena Farrell was talking to me as if we were both just regular people.

It took two and a half hours to get to Sadie's. Alison and I played Spit the whole time. Sadie lives in a place called Deal, in a big, old white house with a wraparound porch. She belongs to a group that brings food to people who are too old or sick to cook for themselves. It's called Meals on Wheels. When Leon told me about her, he sounded very proud.

Hearing about Sadie made me think of my grandparents. Gran Lola, who gave me my bee-sting locket, isn't the cooking kind of grandmother. She's a stockbroker in New York. She wears suits and carries handbags that match her shoes. I once counted the handbags in her closet. She had twenty-seven of them. Mom says that's because Gran Lola never throws anything away. Papa Jack is a stockbroker, too. He has an ulcer.

My father's parents are both dead. They died a week apart. I hate to think of Mom and Dad getting old and dying. It scares me. So I put it out of my mind.

Sadie was waiting for us on her porch. When she saw the car pull into the driveway she came down the stairs to greet us. She was very small, with white hair and dark eyes, like Leon's. She was wearing a pink sweat suit. She hugged Alison first. "My favorite granddaughter," she said, kissing both her cheeks.

"Your only granddaughter," Alison said. Then she introduced me. "This is Stephanie, my best friend in Connecticut."

I smiled, surprised by Alison's introduction.

Sadie shook my hand. "Any friend of Alison's is a friend of mine."

You could smell the ocean from Sadie's front porch. I took a few deep breaths. Sadie must have noticed because she said, "It's just three blocks away. You'll see for yourself this afternoon."

Inside, the table was set for lunch. As soon as Leon walked Maizie we sat down to eat. Everything tasted great. There's something about salt air that makes me really hungry.

After lunch Alison and I helped Sadie do the dishes. Then Sadie pushed up her sleeves and said, "Okay . . . now it's time to get down to business."

I love to bake. I especially love to separate eggs. Aunt Denise taught me how to do it without breaking the yolks, but for brownies you don't need to separate eggs.

"Grandma," Alison said, after we'd measured, mixed and divided the batter into six large baking pans, "don't you think we should write down the recipe for next time?"

"It's better to keep it up here," Sadie said, tapping her head. "That way, if you find yourself in Tahiti and you want to bake brownies, you won't have to worry."

We slid the pans into the ovens. "So . . ." Sadie said, "you'll have one hundred twenty full sized brownies or, if you cut them in half . . ."

"Two hundred forty," I said.

"I don't think we should cut them in half," Alison said, "because we want to sell each one for fifty cents. And that way we'll make . . . uh . . ."

"Sixty dollars," I said.

Sadie looked at me. "A mathematician!" she said. "A regular Einstein!"

"Not really," I told her, feeling my face flush. "Rachel's the mathematician. She couldn't come today because she gets car—" I caught myself just in time. "She couldn't come because she had to work on her speech."

"If we earn enough at this bake sale," Alison told Sadie, "the seventh grade will be able to have a winter dance."

"A dance!" Sadie said. "I used to love to go dancing. Nobody could hold a candle to my rumba. I could wiggle with the best of them. And you should see my mambo and samba and cha cha . . ." She began to sing and dance around the kitchen. "Come on . . ." she said, holding her hands out to us. "I'll teach you."

"I don't think we'll be doing the rumba at the seventh grade dance," Alison said.

"You never know," Sadie told her. "This way you'll be prepared."

First, Sadie taught us the basic box step. *Forward, to the side, together . . . backward, to the side, together.* Once we had that she taught us the rumba. She was about to teach us the samba when the timer on the oven went off. Sadie stuck a toothpick into the center of each pan to make sure the brownies were done. Then we set them on racks on the counter to cool.

"Now . . ." Sadie said, "if you'll excuse me, it's time for my siesta."

"Your siesta?" I said.

"Grandma never says nap," Alison explained. "Naps are for babies . . . right, Grandma?"

"Right."

While Sadie was taking her siesta Alison and I went to the beach with Leon and Gena. Leon held Maizie on a leash until we got there. Then he turned her loose and she took off, running first in one direction, then the other.

Leon and Gena sat on a jetty to watch the waves. Alison and I took off our shoes and socks. "What about your rash?" I asked. "I thought you have to wear a sock on that foot."

"I'm sure the salt water is good for it," Alison said.

It was windy on the beach, but sunny and warm for October. We rolled up our jeans and ran along the water's edge, laughing. Alison's long, black hair whipped across her face, making me wish mine would hurry and grow. Maizie ran alongside us, looking up, as if to say, *How much longer are we going to play this game?*

I was having the best time. I like being with Alison. I like being her friend.

Maizie barked.

"Are you having fun, too?" I asked her.

She barked again.

"What's she saying?" I called to Alison, who was ahead of me.

"Nothing," Alison called back. "She's a dog."

"What do you mean?" I asked, catching up with her.

Alison flopped down. Maizie rolled over and over in the sand. "Do you really believe that dogs can talk?" Alison asked.

"Only one in seventeen million," I said, sitting beside her.

Alison laughed and lay back. Maizie jumped on her.

"You mean she *can't* talk?"

Alison shielded her eyes from the sun and looked at me. "You didn't really believe me, did you?"

"Of course not," I said, drawing a face in the sand with my finger. "I was just playing along with you."

Alison sat up. Sand fell from her hair. "You *did* believe me!"

"I suppose now you think I'm *gullible*," I said.

"I don't know what that means," Alison said.

"It means when a person is easily tricked . . . when a person believes anything. I know because I looked it up one time."

"I don't think you're like that," Alison said. "I think you're a lot like me." She wrestled with Maizie for a minute. When Maizie escaped she said, "I only told you she could talk because I wanted you to like me. I wanted us to be friends."

"We are friends," I said.

"Best friends?"

I picked up a handful of sand. "Rachel and I have been best friends since second grade," I said, letting the sand trickle through my fingers.

"You mean you've never had more than one best friend at a time?" Alison asked.

"No . . . have you?"

"Sure . . . almost every year."

I looked at her. "So you're saying the three of us can be best friends?"

"Sure," Alison said.

"Great!"

"But don't tell Rachel about Maizie, okay? I'll tell her myself . . . when the time is right."

"Okay." I looked down the beach at the jetty. Leon and Gena were kissing.

La Crème
De La Crème

Sadie's brownies were a big hit. Kids kept asking, "Who baked these? They're great!" We saved one for Rachel. She was too worried about her speech to get to the bake sale.

Jeremy Dragon came back for a second brownie, then a third. Alison handed him the brownies and I took his money. That way we each got to touch him three times. It's good the brownies were individually wrapped because his hands were dirty.

Even Mrs. Remo bought one and when she tasted it she said, "These are incredible . . . they're so moist. Do you have the recipe?"

"It's in my grandmother's head," Alison told her.

"See if you can get her to write it down," Mrs. Remo said, licking her lips. "These are definitely *la crème de la crème*."

Alison smiled. Ever since Mrs. Remo mispronounced her name on the first day of school she's been trying French phrases on her.

"What's *la crème de la crème* mean?" I asked Alison when Mrs. Remo was gone.

"It means *the best of the best*."

At the end of the day we had the debate assembly. Five kids from seventh grade were trying out. The only one I knew, besides Rachel, was this boy, Toad. His name is really Todd but everyone calls him Toad, including his family. He went to my elementary school but he wasn't in my sixth grade class.

Toad spoke first, then two girls I didn't know, then a boy who's in my social studies class, then Rachel. She had brushed her hair away from her face, making her look younger than usual, and prettier. I know her so well I never think about her looks. I forget about the way her lower lip twitches when she's scared.

That morning, when I'd called for Rachel, her mother had been giving her a last minute lecture about the debate. "Wear your height as if you're proud of it . . . shoulders back, head high."

"Yeah . . . yeah . . ." Rachel had said. She'd heard it all before.

Mrs. Robinson had planted a kiss on Rachel's cheek. "I know you'll be the best. You always are."

Now, as Rachel walked across the stage, my heart started to beat very fast. I could tell she was trying to take her mother's advice but somehow she wound up walking as if she were in pain.

When she got to the lectern she tapped the microphone to make sure it was still working, then cleared her throat twice. Her voice trembled as she began to speak but once she got going her body relaxed and her voice changed into that grown-up one she uses when she wants to get attention. A hush fell over the audience. You could tell everyone was listening to what she had to say. She was definitely *la crème de la crème* of debaters.

When she finished the audience applauded the same way they had for the others. Then Mr. Diamond, my English teacher, stepped up to the microphone to make some announcements. The first was that we had made $316 at the bake sale that morning. Everyone cheered, especially Alison and me because Sadie's brownies had brought in close to a fifth of the total! Next, Mr. Diamond told us we'd be able to donate food baskets to the needy on both Thanksgiving *and* Christmas. Everybody cheered again. And then he said we'd earned enough to have a winter dance on Ground Hog Day, February 2. The cheering grew louder.

"That's my birthday," I whispered to Alison, who was sitting next to me.

"You're so lucky!" she said.

Another teacher handed Mr. Diamond a slip of paper. "Okay . . ." he said, "here are the results of this afternoon's competition. The two newest members of the debating team are . . ." He hesitated for a minute, making my stomach turn over, "Todd Scrudato and Rachel Robinson."

Toad and Rachel came forward to shake Mr. Diamond's hand. Rachel was smiling and she walked more like herself. I felt myself choke up. I reached over and squeezed Alison's hand. She squeezed mine back.

The Alison Monceau Story

I have never understood what makes some kids so popular. I've been trying to figure it out for years. Almost from the first week of school you could tell Alison was going to be the most popular girl in our homeroom and it's not because her mother is Gena Farrell. Nobody knows about that but Rachel and me and we are sworn to secrecy. The funny thing is, Alison doesn't even try to be popular. It's just that everyone wants to be her friend. I've made a list with reasons why.

1. She is very friendly.
2. She never has anything bad to say about anyone.

3. She doesn't have bad moods.
4. She laughs a lot.
5. She is funny.
6. She has nice hair.
7. She looks different than the rest of us because she is Vietnamese. Looking different can either work for you or against you. In Alison's case it works for her.

Alison knows how to be popular without being snobby, which is more than I can say for Amber Ackbourne. She's the leader of the snobbiest group of girls in seventh grade. And now she wants to be Alison's friend. She's always coming up to her in homeroom. But Alison can see right through her.

The boys like Alison, too. They just have different ways of showing it. They like to tease her, the way Eric Macaulay does, calling her Thumbelina and shooting rubber bands in her direction. Rachel says it's demeaning to be called Thumbelina. She says Alison should put a stop to it right now, before it gets out of hand.

"He only calls me that because I'm small," Alison said the other day at my house. "You know that fairy tale about the girl who's smaller than a thumb . . . there's even a song about her." Alison began to sing and dance around my room. She's a very good dancer. She must take after

Sadie Wishnik. When she finished she fell back on my bed, laughing. I laughed too. Finally, so did Rachel. Alison has a way of making people feel good.

Soon all three of us were singing the Thumbelina song and by the time Rachel went home she said, "Well . . . maybe it's not so demeaning."

Alison also knows how to flirt. I've been watching to see how she does it. She kind of teases the boys and giggles. You can learn a lot by watching a popular person in action. You can learn how to act and how not to act. Mom is always telling me to be myself but there are times when I don't know what being myself means. Sometimes I feel grown up and other times I feel like a little kid. I seem to be more than one person.

That's exactly how I felt last Wednesday. It was raining really hard. Alison came to my house after school. Rachel couldn't come because she had a music lesson. We were sitting in the kitchen, eating doughnuts and playing Spit, when we got to talking about the games we used to play when we were little. It turned out we'd both collected Barbies. So I got the idea to go down to the basement and dig out my old Barbie dolls, which I haven't seen since fourth grade. I found them in a carton marked *Steph's Old Toys*. I carried the Barbie case up to my room, closed the door and Alison and I played all afternoon, dressing and undressing my three Barbies, while we made up silly stories for them to act out.

One of the stories was *Barbie Is Adopted*. After we'd finished, I asked Alison how it feels to be adopted for real.

"How would I know?" she asked. "I was adopted when I was four months old. I don't know what it feels like not to be adopted."

"But do you ever think about your biological mother?" I asked. I had seen this movie on TV about an adopted girl and when she was eighteen she decided to search for her biological mother.

"Sometimes I think about her," Alison said, "about how young and poor she was. She was just fifteen when she had me. But I'm happy with Gena and Leon. If I had to choose parents I'd choose them."

"I'd choose mine, too," I said, "except I'd make sure my father got a job where he didn't have to travel."

"What does he do anyway?"

"He's in public relations."

"When's he coming home?" Alison asked.

"Not until Thanksgiving."

"You must really miss him."

"Yeah . . . I do."

Later, when we packed up my Barbies and put them away, we vowed never to tell anyone we had played with them that afternoon.

The next day I was sitting in French class day-dreaming about Alison. About how her life sounds just like a fairy tale. It would make a good movie, I thought. It would be called *The Alison Monceau Story*. It would star Gena Farrell as Alison's mother and Alison as herself and I would play her best friend. *Stephanie Behrens Hirsch* it would say on the screen. Maybe Rachel could play Alison's biological mother. With makeup and a wig she could probably look Vietnamese and she could certainly look fifteen. Jeremy Dragon could play . . .

"Stephanie!" Mrs. Hillerman shouted. "Will you please wake up!"

"What . . . me?"

The class laughed.

"I've lost my place," I said.

"I don't think you ever had it," Mrs. Hillerman said. And then she said something to me in French, something I didn't understand, and the whole class laughed again.

Macbeth

Double, double, toil and trouble;
Fire burn and cauldron bubble.

Rachel taught us this poem from *Macbeth,* by William Shakespeare. We're going to dress up as the three witches from the play and recite the poem instead of saying "Trick or Treat" on Halloween. We're not interested in "Trick or treating." We're interested in using it as an excuse to get into a certain person's yellow house.

On Halloween night we put on the weirdest clothes we could find, plus junk jewelry and witches' hats. We also used gobs of makeup from Gena Farrell's makeup collection. Alison showed us how to do our eyes. When Gena saw us she said, "The three of you are really something!"

It took us twenty minutes to walk to my old house. Once you're on Pine Tree Road you still have to go down a quiet lane to the end, then up a long, steep driveway, through the woods.

"How long did you live here?" Alison asked.

"Almost all my life until last summer."

The outside lights were on and a carved pumpkin sat on each side of the front door. "It's a big house," Alison said, looking around.

"Yeah. . . ." I nodded and rang the bell. It was hard to think of another family living in my house.

Jeremy answered the door. He wasn't wearing his chartreuse jacket. "Witches," he said, looking us over.

We stepped into the foyer. "Not just any witches," Alison told him. "We're the three from *Macbeth*."

"*Macbeth* . . ." Jeremy said. "Wasn't that on TV?"

"*Macbeth* is a play by William Shakespeare," I told him, as if I knew all about it.

"Oh, *that Macbeth*," Jeremy said.

Rachel, who hadn't spoken yet, gave us the sign to recite our poem.

"Double, double, toil and trouble;
Fire burn and cauldron bubble."

"Yeah, I know what you mean," Jeremy said, when we'd finished. Henry, the termite dog, came down the stairs and sniffed us. Then he wandered off through the dining room.

"I used to live here," I told Jeremy, as he dropped a Heath bar into each of our bags.

"Oh, yeah . . ." he said, "my father mentioned something about a girl who used to live here."

"Stephanie," I said. "Stephanie Hirsch. We met at my mother's travel agency . . . remember?"

He gave me a blank look.

"You and your friends needed brochures for a school project," I reminded him.

"Oh, right . . ." he said. "You look different."

"I wasn't wearing a witch's hat that day."

"And you bought brownies from us at the bake sale," Alison said.

"Those brownies were the best," Jeremy said. "I could've put away a dozen." Then he looked right at Rachel and he said, "You're Rachel, right?"

Rachel didn't say anything. She just gave us the sign to recite our poem again.

"Double, double, toil and trouble;
Fire burn and cauldron bubble."

101

When we were outside I grabbed Rachel's arm and said, "He knew your name."

Rachel ignored me. So I asked, "How does he know your name?"

"How should I know?" Rachel said, sounding angry, as if it were my fault Jeremy knew her name. She ran the rest of the way down the driveway and when we were back on the road she said, "We're too old for this! I don't know what got into me! I don't know why I agreed to it!" She sounded on the verge of tears. "I'm going home!"

"Don't go now," Alison said, running to catch up with her. "We haven't been anywhere yet. We haven't been to Eric Macaulay's or Peter Klaff's or . . ."

"You're going to spoil all our fun!" I called, chasing Rachel, who was walking very fast. "How can we be the three witches from *Macbeth* without you?"

Rachel sniffled. "Okay . . . but I'm never doing this again."

"Fine," I told her. "You don't have to."

But we didn't have much fun after that. So we headed for home.

The next day, at the end of math class, Mr. Burns gave me a note to take to another math teacher, Mrs. Godfrey. I got to Mrs. Godfrey's room just as the bell rang and the door opened. Jeremy Dragon was the first one out. "Hey, Macbeth . . ." he said when he saw me.

At least he recognized me this time.

Then Dana Carpenter came out. "Hi, Steph . . . what are you doing here?"

"I've got a note for Mrs. Godfrey," I said. "What class is this?"

"Enriched math."

"Oh," I said.

"I've got to run," Dana said. "See you later."

"Okay."

I waited while the ninth graders trudged out of Mrs. Godfrey's room. Then, just as I was about to go in with the note, who should come out but Rachel!

We stared at each other.

"What are you doing here?" Rachel asked, sharply.

"I've got a note for Mrs. Godfrey," I said. "What are *you* doing here?"

Rachel brushed past me and began to walk down the hall. I followed her. "I *said* what are *you* doing here?"

"They switched me to this class."

"They switched you to this class . . . to *enriched* math?"

"Yes."

"And you never told me?" I said. "You never said anything about it?"

"What should I have said?" Rachel stopped and we faced each other.

"You should have said that you were switched to *enriched* ninth grade math!" I told her. "That's what you *should* have said."

"Will you stop saying it like that!" Rachel's lower lip quivered.

"Like what?"

"Like it's something bad I've done."

"I didn't say it was bad," I told her. "I just said it's a big surprise!"

Rachel didn't say anything.

"So how long have you been in this enriched ninth grade class?" I asked.

"Since the second week of school," Rachel said, quietly, looking at the floor.

"The second week of school!" I said, my voice growing louder. "Well, isn't that interesting! Were you ever going to tell me?"

"I wanted to," Rachel said, "but I was afraid you'd be mad."

"Mad!" I said. "Why should I be mad? Just because Jeremy Dragon knows your name and you tell me you don't know how? *I* should be mad over a little thing like that? Just because I'm supposed to be your best friend and you keep a secret like this from me?"

"I wasn't sure I would like the class," Rachel said. "I didn't think there was any point in telling you until I'd made up my mind. And I didn't know, until last night, that he knew my name."

I felt this huge bubble of anger rising from my stomach. When it got to my throat I shouted, "Oh . . . who cares!" and I marched away from Rachel, holding my books tight against my chest.

"Look," Rachel said, keeping up with me, "I didn't ask to be born this way."

"What way?" I snapped.

"The way I am."

"What way is that?"

"Smart." Rachel practically spit out the word.

"You're not just smart," I told her.

"Okay . . . so I'm not just smart. It still isn't my fault. It just happened. It's not something I work at, you know. It's not something I especially like about myself. Most of the time I wish I could be like everyone else . . . like you!"

"Thanks a lot!"

"I meant that in a friendly way, Steph."

I didn't respond. I didn't know what to say. I didn't even know what I was feeling. All I knew was this was the first time Rachel had ever kept a secret from me.

"Does this mean you don't want to be my friend anymore?" Rachel's voice broke, as if she might cry any second.

"No," I said. "It doesn't mean anything except you should have told me about that math class yourself."

"You're right," Rachel said, "I know that now."

The second bell rang. I ran to my next class and didn't realize, until I got there, that I still hadn't given Mrs. Godfrey the note from Mr. Burns. So I ran all the way back to Mrs. Godfrey's class and was late getting to my own.

Confessions

I know, deep down, it's not Rachel's fault she's so smart or that she was switched to enriched math. But that doesn't mean I have to like it. How can you be best friends with someone who keeps secrets from you? Important secrets, like being in enriched math.

I didn't say anything to Alison about Rachel that afternoon. I didn't say anything because I didn't have the chance. Leon picked us up after school and drove us to town. It was raining. The three of us had to go to the library to look up information for our first social studies report. All the seventh graders have the same assignment: to do a report on someone who has made a major difference to the world.

Leon dropped us off at TCBY, the frozen yogurt place. The letters stand for The Country's Best Yogurt. Alison is really into frozen yogurt. She says everybody in California loves it. Rachel likes it, too. I used to think it was gross but now I'm getting used to it. I ordered a hot fudge sundae which the menu describes as swirls of french vanilla yogurt with hot fudge and whipped topping sprinkled with pecans. Alison and Rachel ordered Smoothies. A Smoothie is a yogurt and fruit juice drink.

When our order was ready we carried it to a table. As soon as we sat down Rachel said to Alison, "I have something to tell you." She took a long sip of her Smoothie. "Remember those math tests we took the first week of school?"

"Uh huh," Alison said. "That's how Mr. Burns found out I'd lost my skills."

Mr. Burns is always telling Alison she's lost her skills. Alison keeps trying to explain she never had those skills in the first place.

"Well . . ." Rachel said, glancing at me, then turning her attention back to Alison. "After those tests I got transferred to another math class." She paused and took another sip of her Smoothie. "I got transferred to a more advanced math class."

"I'm not surprised," Alison said.

"It's enriched ninth grade math," Rachel said.

"No kidding," Alison said. She licked some Smoothie off her upper lip.

"I'm in Dana Carpenter's class," Rachel said.

"I like Dana," Alison said.

"And Jeremy Dragon is in my class, too."

Alison put down her glass and did look really surprised. Now she's going to let Rachel have it, I thought. Now she's going to tell her that friends don't keep secrets like that.

But all Alison said was, "I never knew Jeremy was smart. I mean, he thought *Macbeth* was a TV show!"

"I guess he's smarter at some things than others," Rachel said.

"So is that what you wanted to tell me?" Alison asked, slurping up the rest of her Smoothie.

"Yes," Rachel said.

"Well, congratulations," Alison said. "Maybe you could help me with my decimals and per-centages. I can't do pre-algebra until I've got them down."

"Sure," Rachel said, "any time."

I could see the relief on Rachel's face, and to tell the truth I couldn't understand why Alison reacted to Rachel's news as if it was just ordinary school stuff. But I didn't say anything. I just sat there spooning up my yogurt sundae, wishing it were ice cream instead.

"I have something to tell you, too," Alison said to Rachel. "Maizie doesn't talk. I made that up to get you and Steph to like me."

"I've always known that." Rachel looked at me. "It's Steph who believes everything she hears."

"She already knows about Maizie," Alison said.

"Really?" Rachel said. "Since when?"

"Since the day we went to Sadie Wishnik's house to bake brownies," Alison told her.

"That was weeks ago," Rachel said, glaring at me. I spooned up the sauce from the bottom of my dish and licked it off the spoon.

"I asked Steph to let me tell you myself," Alison explained.

"I see," Rachel said, quietly.

"Just like you got to tell Alison about your enriched math class yourself," I said to Rachel.

"You knew about her math class?" Alison asked me.

"I wouldn't exactly say I knew . . . I just found out today . . . by accident."

We just sat there. No one said anything. Finally Rachel stood up and gathered her books. "We should get going. We've got a lot to do at the library."

Alison and I got our things together, too. Outside, it had stopped raining.

"Who are you doing your report on?" Rachel asked Alison as we headed for the library.

"Martha Graham," Alison said. "She practically invented modern dance. What about you?" she asked Rachel.

"Margaret Mead. She was a famous anthropologist. How about you, Steph . . . who are you doing?"

"Jane Fonda."

"Jane Fonda!" Rachel said. "What major difference has she made to the world?"

"She got a lot of people to exercise," I said.

Rachel snorted. "I don't think that's the kind of difference our teachers have in mind."

"I'm not so sure," Alison said. "Jane Fonda is a very important person. Everybody in L.A. . . . ."

"We're talking about the world," Rachel said, "not L.A."

"I know," Alison said, "but besides exercise she's a very good actress. My mother's always saying she'd love to be offered half the roles Jane Fonda gets."

Rachel shook her head. "I don't know about the two of you."

That night I went to Mom's room. She was stretched out on her chaise lounge, reading.

That's her favorite place to relax. "Rachel's been transferred to enriched math and she never even told me."

Mom looked at me over the top of her glasses. They're half glasses. She wears them for reading. She tucks in her chin when she looks over them, giving her face a funny expression.

"She's so smart!" I said, sitting on the edge of the chaise lounge.

"You're smart, too, honey," Mom said.

"Not smart like Rachel." I picked up a small, white pillow and held it to me.

"Rachel is gifted," Mom said.

"Gifted," I repeated, trying out the word.

"Does it bother you that she's been placed in enriched math?"

"It's not just any enriched math," I said. "It's ninth grade enriched math."

"You know, Steph . . . life isn't easy for Rachel."

"Are you kidding? She can get straight A's without even trying."

"I'm not talking about grades," Mom said.

I didn't say anything.

"You're not going to let this math class come between you, are you?"

I played with the lace ruffle on the pillow. "I guess not . . . unless Rachel does." I didn't want to think about Rachel anymore. So I looked across the room at the group of family photos on the wall. There's one I especially like of Mom and Dad. He's carrying her piggy-back and she's laughing so hard her eyes are closed. "I can't wait until Thanksgiving," I said. "I can't wait to see Dad!"

I told Dad I was counting the days when he called the next night.

"So am I," Dad said. "What's new in school?"

"I made symphonic band . . . percussion."

"Congratulations!"

"And in math we're following the stock market."

"That sounds interesting."

"It is. We each get to pick three stocks and pretend they're ours. I picked Reebok, Revlon and Jiffy Lube."

"That's quite an assortment."

"I know."

"How's the weather?"

"It's been raining," I said. "But today the sun came out again." I paused, trying to come up with something else that would interest Dad. "Have you heard about Bruce?" I asked.

"What about him?"

"Well . . ." I began, but Bruce grabbed the phone out of my hand and said, "I'll tell him myself."

Bruce has entered a national contest. *Kids for Peace* it's called. He's made a poster and sent it to Boston, where it will be judged. The three winners will get a free trip to Washington where they'll meet the President. In some ways I hope Bruce does win the contest. In other ways I hope he doesn't. I don't know how I'd feel having a famous brother. Probably everyone would compare me to him and ask, *What contests have you won, Stephanie?* And I'd have to think of some clever answer like, *I don't believe in contests. Contests don't prove anything.*

I wonder if Jessica and Charles feel that way, having a younger sister like Rachel. I wonder if they're always trying to prove that they're as good as she is. Lucky for me Bruce isn't gifted. He's just a regular kid who happens to have made a great poster.

Things

Mom and Aunt Denise are trying to decide whether to make a vegetable stuffing or a chestnut stuffing for the Thanksgiving turkey. They don't actually put the stuffing inside the turkey. They make it as a side dish. Mom says it's healthier to roast the turkey without stuffing it. I don't see why they call it stuffing when it isn't.

We're going to have fourteen to dinner. Everyone is family except for Carla, Mom's best friend from college, and her little girl, Katie, who is eight. Carla is a widow. Her husband was killed while he was crossing the street. Some guy in a van plowed into him. The guy didn't even have a driver's license. Katie was only a baby at the time. She never got to know her father. Mom says some people have more than their fair share of trouble. But Carla has a very good job. She produces a news show for NBC.

I asked Mom if I could make place cards this year because everyone always stands around at Thanksgiving waiting to be told where to sit. And while they're waiting the food gets cold. Mom said place cards sounded like a good idea. I made them out of purple colored paper. I drew a flower on each one and tried to keep my letters from going uphill when I printed the names.

Then I made a seating chart, like the one Mrs. Remo used the first week of school, before she'd memorized our names. I put myself between Dad and Katie. I put Bruce next to Cousin Howard. I would never sit next to Howard. He's seventeen and disgusting. He burps after every mouthful. Then he tells us that in some countries burping is considered a great compliment to the cook. If you don't burp, Howard says, you're a very rude guest. Howard also lets it out the other end. I asked him at our Passover seder, last spring, if that's also considered a compliment in some countries. He just laughed. I'm so glad I don't have a brother like him.

Mom says he's just going through a phase and that in a few years he'll be just like his brother, Stanley, who goes to college. I don't know if that's good or bad. Stanley is such a bore!

On Wednesday, the day before Thanksgiving, I couldn't concentrate in school. I kept thinking that in a few hours I would see Dad again. I pictured him in my mind. He's tall and thin, with a bony face. His eyes are grayish-blue and he wears aviator glasses. He's got a dimple in his chin, like Bruce. When he's very tired his shoulders slump. He'll probably be very tan from all that California sunshine, I thought. And he'll have presents for all of us—sweatshirts for Bruce and me, saying something about California, and for Mom, perfume and a lacy nightgown.

I was glad we had only half a day of school. During the last hour we had an all-school Thanksgiving assembly, which made the time go even faster. The chorus sang, the dancers danced and the symphonic band played. This was my debut as a percussionist. I got to play cymbals twice and chimes once. I made a mistake on chimes. But Ms. Lopez, the music teacher, gave me a reassuring look, as if my mistake hadn't mattered at all.

Aunt Denise picked me up after school. I always help her bake the pies for Thanksgiving dinner. She says she wishes she had a daughter like me. I don't blame her. Imagine someone as nice as Aunt Denise being stuck with sons like Howard and Stanley!

While the pies were baking Aunt Denise and I cleaned up the kitchen. "Has your mom been talking to you?" she asked, as she handed me the green mixing bowl to dry.

"About what?" I asked.

"You know," Aunt Denise said, "things . . ."

"Oh, *things*," I said. "Yeah . . . Mom bought me a book."

"A book?"

"Yeah . . . *Love and Sex in Plain Language*."

"Sex?"

"Yes, isn't that what you meant?"

Aunt Denise hesitated. "Sort of . . ."

"I'm home!" I called, when Aunt Denise dropped me off at five. I wanted to change before Dad got here. He's renting a car at Kennedy Airport and driving up to Connecticut.

"I'm upstairs . . ." Mom called back. I went to her room. She had just stepped out of the shower and was wrapped in a big striped towel.

"What a day," she said, holding her head, "I have a headache *this* big . . ." She took a bottle of aspirin from her cabinet and gulped down two of them with water. "I've made reservations at Onion Alley for you and Bruce and Dad . . . at seven."

"What about you?" I asked.

"I'm going over to Denise's to help with the stuffing and the sweet potato pudding."

"But, Mom . . . this is Dad's first night home."

"I know, honey . . . but we've talked it over and he understands."

"But, Mom . . ." I began again. Then I remembered that they would be alone later. "Oh, I get it," I said, giving Mom a sly look.

"Really, Steph . . ." Mom said.

Dad

It was a nippy night and I shivered in my sweater as I waited outside for Dad. To keep warm I jumped in the leaves on our front lawn. I was glad it was already dark. I wouldn't want anyone to see me fooling around that way.

A car drove slowly down our street. I brushed myself off and watched, wondering if it could be Dad. It passed our house, stopped, then backed up, parking right in front. The door opened and Dad got out. I ran toward him. "Dad!" He hugged me and held me close. It felt so good to smell his special smell again, a combination of after-shave, butterscotch Life Savers and something else...something that's just him. He was wearing his same old brown suede jacket. It felt soft and familiar against my cheek.

When we were inside the house I noticed the bald spot on the back of his head had grown, or maybe it was just the way the wind had blown his hair. Also, he had no tan. I asked him about that right away.

He said, "I'm working long hours. I don't have time to sit in the sun."

He did look worn out. It's not good for him to be away from us, I thought. He probably has no one to cheer him up after a hard day at work.

"Didn't anybody ever tell you it's impolite to stare?" Dad said, laughing.

"What?"

"You were staring," he said again.

"I was?"

"Yes . . . so now it's my turn." He looked me over carefully. I don't know why but I suddenly felt shy. I guess it's because I'm a different person now, different than when Dad left. I hadn't even started seventh grade then. Now, I'm almost a teenager. Dad ruffled my hair.

"It's growing," I said, self-consciously, as I touched it. "It should be long again by spring."

"It looks fine the way it is," Dad said.

Bruce came racing down the stairs. Dad picked him up and swung him around. Then they kind of nuzzled and swatted each other's arms the way they do to show affection. "You look so big," Dad told Bruce.

"I haven't grown at all," Bruce said. "Not an inch."

"Well, you could have fooled me."

Mom came downstairs right behind Bruce. She and Dad hugged, but just for a minute. "How are you, Row?" Dad asked.

"I'm okay," Mom said.

You could tell they didn't want to get started in front of us.

I was right about the sweatshirts. Dad brought one for me that said *Los Angeles, City of Angels* and one for Bruce that said *Los Angeles Dodgers*. I don't know what he brought for Mom.

Dad had never even seen my new room so I grabbed him by the hand and led him up-stairs.

"Look at all these posters," Dad said. "How come that one is on the ceiling?" He strained his neck to get a better view of Benjamin Moore.

"That one is special," I said. "You have to lie on the bed to really see him."

"Maybe later," Dad said.

He didn't seem surprised that just the three of us were going out to dinner. I guess he and Mom had worked out the details over the phone. We got to sit in a booth at Onion Alley. I ordered a calzone but I didn't eat much because Bruce and I talked non-stop through dinner. I told Dad all about Alison and how she used to live in Malibu, which she says isn't that far from Marina Del Rey, where Dad has his apartment. I told him about how she's lost her skills in math but that Rachel is going to help her get them back. I told him how well Alison and I get along and how much fun she is.

"It sounds as if you and Alison are best friends," Dad said, picking at his veal.

"I'm best friends with Rachel *and* Alison," I told him.

"Two best friends?" Dad asked.

"Two are better than one," I told him.

"Two best friends means she's never off the phone," Bruce said. "She just about lives in the pantry."

"The pantry?" Dad looked confused.

"That's where she hides with the phone," Bruce explained.

"If I had my *own* phone in my *own* room I wouldn't have to lock myself up in the pantry for privacy. At Crazy Eddie's you can get one for just $19.95. That's what I'd really like for my birthday."

"I don't think it's a question of how much a phone costs," Dad said. "I think it's more the idea of it."

"But you'll think about it, won't you?" I asked. "For my *thirteenth* birthday?"

"I'll discuss it with Mom."

I'll discuss it with Mom is Dad's version of *We'll see.*

When Bruce started telling Dad about his computer teacher my mind drifted. It would be great to have my own phone. I'd get a pink one with a really long cord so I could carry it from my desk to my night table. And I'd get a name number so my friends could just dial 662-STPH, the way you can dial 662-PIES when you want to order a pizza.

"So what do you think, Steph?" Dad asked.

"What?"

"She wasn't listening," Bruce said. "Her mind was someplace else."

"I was talking about our weekend plans," Dad said, "about staying at a hotel in the city. I thought we'd get out early to see the windows on Fifth Avenue. You know how crowded it gets over Thanksgiving. Then we could head up to the Museum of Natural History . . . and maybe to the Metropolitan . . . see a play on Saturday night . . ."

"That sounds great!" I said. "I didn't know we were going to the city for the weekend."

"That's because you were busy daydreaming," Bruce said.

"I wasn't daydreaming," I told him. "I was thinking."

"That's enough!" Dad said. "All that matters is that we have a good time together. And that means no fighting."

"We hardly ever fight anymore," Bruce told Dad.

"Well, that's good news," Dad said.

I wished I could call Rachel and Alison that minute and tell them about our plans, but Alison had already left for Sadie Wishnik's and Rachel had gone to her aunt's house, in New Hampshire.

As soon as we got home Bruce ran for the bathroom. Dr. Klaff says he has a small bladder. So if he drinks a lot he has to pee a lot. And he had two glasses of water plus a Coke at dinner. Dad says when he was a kid he had the same problem.

"See you tomorrow," Dad said, kissing my cheek.

"What do you mean, tomorrow?" I asked.

"I'm driving down to the city now. I've got a meeting first thing in the morning."

"You've got a meeting on Thanksgiving morning?"

"Yes," Dad said, "a breakfast meeting. It's the only time we could get together. But I'll be back in plenty of time for dinner."

"What about Mom?" I asked.

"What about her?"

"She's going to be so disappointed. You two haven't seen each other since summer."

"Did she tell you that?"

"Not exactly," I said.

"She knows about my meeting," Dad said. "And she's going to be busy with Thanksgiving dinner."

"Not that busy!"

"Don't worry about it . . . okay?" Dad kissed me again, this time on top of my head. "I'll be here tomorrow by two, at the latest."

Bruce had a nightmare that night. I heard him calling for Mom. I heard Mom padding down the hall to his room. I heard her talking softly to him. I guess I must have fallen right back asleep because when I opened my eyes again it was morning and I could smell the turkey roasting.

T-Day

Dad drove Carla and Katie up from the city. They got here before two, just as Dad had promised. Carla is tall and thin with wispy blonde hair. She wears suede and leather clothes, even in summer, and silver jewelry.

"Stephanie . . . look at you!" she said. Her voice was breathy, making her sound as if she'd just run around the block. "Aren't you something!" When she hugged me I could smell her perfume. Then she reached into her bag for a Kleenex and blew her nose. Mom says Carla developed allergies right after her husband died. She sneezes all year round.

"Can I help in the kitchen?" Carla asked Mom.

"Everything's ready," Mom said, wiping her hands on her jeans, "except me."

"I'll keep you company while you get dressed," Carla said.

"Will you watch the turkey, Steve?" Mom asked. "It needs basting every fifteen minutes."

"No problem," Dad said.

"Come on," Bruce said, grabbing Dad's hand and dragging him toward the den. "The game's on . . ."

Katie stood watching as everyone went off in different directions. She's small for eight, with chubby pink cheeks. She reminds me of a Cabbage Patch Kid. "You want to see my room?" I asked her.

"Sure."

We went upstairs. "This is nice," Katie said, looking around. "I like your posters. How come that one's on the ceiling?"

"That's my boyfriend," I told her.

"What's his name?"

"Benjamin."

"That's a nice name. How old is he?"

"Seventeen."

"That's really old. Are you going steady?"

"Yes, but my family doesn't know so don't say anything, okay?"

"Okay."

I took a deck of cards out of my desk drawer. "I'll teach you to play Spit."

"I already know how."

"You do?" That surprised me because I had never heard of the game until Alison taught me. "You want to play?" I asked her.

"Sure," she said.

Katie was really fast. She beat me twice before the rest of our guests arrived. They all came at once.

Aunt Robin and her live-in, Scott, brought their poodle, Enchilada. Gran Lola calls Enchilada her granddog. Aunt Robin and Scott are investment bankers. Their hobby is money. That's all they ever talk about. So they were extremely interested when I told Gran Lola and Papa Jack about my three stocks and how I came to choose them. "I picked Jiffy Lube because I liked the name, Revlon because Mom uses their makeup and Reebok because everybody wants to wear their shoes. So far I'm doing all right."

Uncle Richard, who is married to Aunt Denise, said that from his experience with the stock market, my reasons for choosing Revlon, Jiffy Lube and Reebok seemed as good as any.

At four we sat down to dinner. Everyone oohed and aahed as Mom carried in the turkey and set it in front of Dad. Then she took her seat at the opposite end of the table.

"Breast or leg?" Dad asked each of us as he carved the turkey.

"Breast!" Bruce called out and he and Katie started laughing.

"Oh, to be ten again," Cousin Stanley said, sighing, as if he were ninety years old instead of nineteen.

Papa Jack took his ulcer medicine before he ate anything.

After the main course Howard burped three times. "An excellent meal," he said, patting his middle.

During dessert a piece of pumpkin pie fell to the floor. Enchilada gobbled it up. I don't know if anyone besides me noticed. But a few minutes later Enchilada threw up on Bruce's shoe. Bruce took it personally. "These are my only shoes," he said. "What am I supposed to wear to school on Monday? If I wear these all the kids will hold their noses and say, *Yuck . . . barf!*"

"Take them off and put them in the laundry room," Mom said. When Bruce didn't move she added, "Hurry up!"

Aunt Robin took Enchilada outside, just in case, while Scott cleaned up under the table. "You'd be better off with a baby," Gran Lola said, when Aunt Robin came back. "A baby isn't any more trouble than that dog."

"Babies grow up," Aunt Robin said, looking at Howard.

Howard burped.

Papa Jack took some more ulcer medicine.

By eight, our company had left, including Carla and Katie, who drove back to the city with Aunt Robin and Scott. Suddenly the house seemed very quiet. The four of us cleared the table. Then Mom loaded the dishwasher and Dad scrubbed the pots and pans, while I wrapped the leftovers. I guess Mom and Dad were too tired to talk.

When I finished I went upstairs to change because I'd dropped a blob of cranberry sauce on my shirt. While I was in my room Dad poked his head in and said, "If you hurry and pack we can still get down to the city tonight."

"I didn't know we were going tonight."

"Yes."

"But Mom has to work in the morning, doesn't she?"

"Stephanie," Dad said, "sit down."

There are times when you know you're going to hear something that you don't want to hear. Something that you've kept yourself from thinking. I sat on the edge of my bed, chewing on the insides of my cheeks.

Dad paced the room. Finally he sat beside me. "I know you've guessed by now . . ."

"Guessed what?"

"About Mom and me . . . about our separation."

"What separation?"

"This separation," Dad said, sounding impatient. "About how we're living apart for a while."

"No!"

"I thought you knew," Dad said, shaking his head.

"What am I supposed to be . . . some kind of mind-reader?"

"But all those questions last night . . ." Dad said.

"What about them?"

Dad stood up. "Wait here . . ."

He went into the hall and called, "Row . . . would you come upstairs for a minute?"

I looked at Benjamin Moore. I forced myself to concentrate on him. If he were really my boyfriend I'd be getting ready to go out with him now. Probably we'd go to a movie first, then to Arcudi's for a pizza. While we were eating, Jeremy Dragon would come in with some of his friends and say, *Hey, Macbeth . . . how's it going?* Then I'd introduce him to Benjamin and he'd be really impressed, not just because Benjamin is so cute but because he's seventeen. Later, Jeremy would take me aside and ask for my phone number. I'd say, *Just dial 662-STPH.*

I heard Mom and Dad walk down the hall. I heard the rise and fall of their voices but I couldn't make out what they were saying. What exactly had Dad meant by a separation? And why had he acted as if it were my fault that I hadn't known all about it? I tiptoed down the hall. The door to Mom's room was closed. I stood outside and listened.

Dad said, "I thought we agreed not to hide it."

Mom said, "I wasn't hiding anything. They never asked. *I* thought we agreed that if they didn't seem concerned we wouldn't bring up the subject."

Then Dad said, "Well, the cat's out of the bag . . . and Stephanie's upset."

"Who's fault is that?" Mom asked.

And Dad said, "How was I supposed to know she really didn't have a clue . . ."

That did it! I threw open the door and shouted, "I suppose now you think I'm gullible!" I could see the look of surprise on their faces. "Well, I'm not. I can't be easily tricked by you or by anyone else!" I turned, slammed the door and ran back to my room where I threw myself face down on my bed.

"What's going on?" Bruce asked, standing in my doorway.

"Plenty," I told him. "And none of it's good!"

Weekend

I refused to go to New York with Dad. Bruce went without me.

"Don't you think you're being hard on him, Steph?" Mom said on Friday morning.

"Is that supposed to be a joke?" I asked, wolfing down my second bowl of cereal. "In case you're wondering," I added between mouthfuls, "I'm just as mad at you as I am at Dad."

"I can see that," Mom said, "and I'm sorry. I should have talked to you about the separation before but you seemed so happy . . . enjoying school and your friends . . ."

"So you let me go right on thinking that everything is the same as always."

"Well, in a way it is," Mom said. "Your life isn't going to change."

"How can you say that?"

"It's no different from when Dad's on a business trip, is it?"

"Until last night it wasn't any different." I cut myself a slice of apple pie and heated it in the microwave. "I suppose that's why we sold the yellow house and moved here," I said, "because of the separation."

"That's one reason."

"And I suppose everyone in the family knows."

"My sisters do," Mom said, "and Gran Lola and Papa Jack."

"And Carla?"

"Yes, Carla knows."

I finished my pie and stomped out of the room, leaving my dirty dishes on the table.

"Where are you going?" Mom called after me.

"Back to bed," I told her.

"I wish you'd get dressed and come to the office with me."

"No, thank you." I went upstairs and got into bed, pulling the quilt over my head.

When I woke up, two hours later, I heard Mom talking on the phone. Now that was really unusual because she never takes off from work. When one of us is sick and has to stay home from school, she gets Mrs. Greco to come in for the day.

I went to the kitchen and ate the leftover sweet potato pudding. All of it. I might have spaced out in front of the TV then, but Mom was still on the phone in the den. I couldn't tell if it was a business call or if she was blabbing to Aunt Denise, because when she saw me standing there, she covered the mouthpiece with her hand and waved me away. So I went back to bed. I slept on and off, all afternoon.

Mom looked in on me twice. The second time she felt my forehead, but I didn't let on that I knew.

By dinnertime I still hadn't gotten dressed. I went downstairs. Mom was on the phone again. "I'm going to eat now," I told her. This time she held up her hand, motioning for me to wait, but I didn't. I made myself a gigantic turkey sandwich on bread sliced so thick I could hardly fit it into my mouth. I ate half the left-over stuffing and the last piece of apple pie. Then I went back to bed.

On Saturday morning Mom came to my room. "As soon as you're dressed I'll drive you down to the station. Dad's waiting for you . . . he doesn't want you to miss the windows on Fifth Avenue."

"I'm not going anywhere," I said.

"He's got three tickets for a musical tonight."

"Let him take someone else," I said. Then I burped. I didn't mean to. It just slipped out.

"I know how much you like musicals, Steph . . ."

"I am *not* going to New York!"

Mom stayed home again and worked on the computer. That afternoon she found me in the kitchen, gnawing on a turkey leg. "Stuffing yourself isn't the answer," she said. "You're going to get sick if you keep this up."

"It's all your fault," I said.

"What do you mean?" Mom asked.

"I mean, if you weren't such a go-getter this wouldn't be happening. If we had all gone to California you and Dad wouldn't be separated now."

"That's not true," Mom said. "I don't know where you got such an idea."

"Then explain it to me," I said, searching the refrigerator for the jar of dill pickles.

Mom closed the refrigerator door and stood blocking it. "Dad and I have some problems. We're trying to work them out."

"What problems?"

Mom sighed. "He's bored with his life. He wants to make changes. I like my life the way it is . . ."

"But he *had* to go to California," I said. "He had no choice."

"He *asked* to go to California," Mom said.

"I don't believe you!" I said. "I don't think you even care about this separation. If you did you'd be crying!"

"When I feel like crying I do it in private," Mom said, raising her voice. "I don't tell you everything."

For a minute neither one of us spoke. Then Mom softened. "Look," she began, trying to put her arm around me. I jumped out of the way. I wasn't about to let her touch me. "We're not going to make any hasty decisions . . . I can promise you that. This is just a trial separation."

"How long does a trial separation last?" I asked.

"As long as necessary," Mom said.

I ate a piece of pumpkin pie without even tasting it.

That night, when I went to bed *again,* I thought over what Mom had said about Dad being bored with his life. I don't understand how he could be bored. He's got a wonderful family. He's got a good job. He makes enough money. Maybe what he needs is a hobby, I thought. Maybe he needs to get interested in something like scuba diving or refinishing furniture. Or maybe he's having his mid-life crisis. Yes, that's probably it! When Rachel's father had his mid-life crisis, a few years ago, he changed his job. He used to be a lawyer and now he's a teacher. Maybe Dad should become a teacher, too. Then he could get a job at the high school, like Mr. Robinson. He could even coach football since that's his favorite sport. And that way he wouldn't have to commute to the city or fly away on business trips. I fell asleep wondering what subject Dad should teach.

I slept until noon on Sunday. When I got up I threw on a pair of jeans and a sweatshirt. Then I hit the kitchen. I polished off the rest of the pumpkin pie, the stuffing and most of the turkey. I was beginning to feel like I might explode. I needed to get out of the house. I put on my new winter jacket, the one I got two weeks ago. Mom wanted me to buy it in either red or blue but I held out for purple. I zipped it up and went out the back door. It was cold out, and gray. Winter was definitely coming. I burped twice. Too bad Howard wasn't there. He'd have been proud of me.

The wind whipped around my head, hurting my ears. I covered them with my hands and kicked stones as I walked down to the pond. When I got there I sat on a log, facing the water. I sat until my feet were numb from the cold. Then I jumped up and down trying to get the feeling back in my toes. But that made the food slosh around in my stomach and I started to feel sick. I grabbed a handful of stones and tossed them one by one, into the pond, hoping to get them to skim the water. But none of them did. Then I sat on the log again.

I don't know how long I'd been sitting there when I saw Dad's rental car. It slowed down, stopped briefly, and Bruce jumped out. "Hey, Steph . . ." he called, running toward me. "What are you doing?"

"What does it look like I'm doing?" I asked.

"Sitting by the pond and freezing your butt."

"Very good."

"We had a great time in New York. We saw the best show."

"What show?"

"Little Shop of Horrors."

"I saw the movie."

"Yeah . . . but the show was better. It was so funny." He imitated Audrey II, the talking plant. "Feed me, Seymour . . . feed me!"

I almost laughed.

"Dad gave your ticket to Carla."

"Carla took *my* ticket?"

"Yes . . . and she liked the show a lot."

"That's disgusting!" I said.

"What is?"

"That Dad would give my ticket to Carla and that she would take it!"

Bruce shrugged. "What'd you do all weekend?"

"I did nothing . . . that's what!"

"Oh." He picked up a stone and tossed it. It

skimmed along the water. "Let's go home now, okay? Dad wants to talk to you before he leaves."

"I'm staying here until he's gone."

"But . . ."

"Why don't you go tell him that for me?" I shivered and hugged myself, trying to keep warm.

Bruce reached into his pocket and pulled out a ski hat. "Here," he said, dropping it in my lap. Then he ran up the hill to our house.

My eyes filled with tears. I sniffled and checked my pockets for a tissue to blow my nose. But the pockets were empty. I pulled on Bruce's hat.

A few minutes later Dad parked his car by the side of the road. "Steph . . ." he called, waving for me to join him.

I acted like I didn't even notice.

So Dad came down to the pond. "We missed you this weekend," he said, sitting beside me on the log.

I didn't say anything.

He picked up a stick and began scratching the ground with it. "I'm sorry you found out the way you did. Mom and I should have told you sooner."

I still didn't respond.

"Look . . ." he said, "I just want you to know that no matter what happens I'll always be your father."

"Did you read that in some book?" I asked.

"Some book that tells you how to talk to your kids when you're separating because you're bored with your life?"

"I didn't read it anywhere," Dad said. "It's how I feel. And who told you I was bored with my life?"

"Mom . . . who do you think?" A squirrel ran in front of us. I watched him for a minute, then I looked over at Dad. "Is it true?"

"I suppose it is in some ways . . ." Dad said. "But it has nothing to do with you or Bruce."

"Does it have to do with Mom?"

"Not with Mom exactly . . . but with the direction of our marriage."

"And all this time I thought you *had* to go to California." I practically spit out those words.

"We needed time apart . . . to think things through . . ."

"So how come you couldn't think in Connecticut or New York? How come you had to go across the country to think?"

"It seemed easier at the time." He glanced at his watch. "I've got a plane to catch."

"Planes are more important than families, right?"

He sucked in his breath but he didn't deny it. "I want you and Bruce to come out to L.A. over Christmas," he said. "We'll have more time to talk then." He leaned over to kiss me but I pulled away from him. "You're making this very hard, Steph."

"Good," I told him.

Rachel called that night. "Our weekend was a disaster!" she said. "My brother was so obnoxious . . . he had Mom and Jessica in tears . . . Dad lost his temper . . . and finally, Charles stormed out of my aunt's house and went to stay with friends. I don't know why he has to be so impossible. I don't know why he can't get along with us. Anyway, I can't think of a worse Thanksgiving!" She paused to catch her breath. "So how was yours?"

"Great."

"How was your father?"

"Great."

"What'd you do?"

"We ate a lot."

Rachel laughed. "Did you go to the city?"

"No."

"I thought you would."

"No time."

"When will your father be back?"

"He's not sure."

"For Christmas?"

"Probably."

"Well . . . the time between Thanksgiving and Christmas always goes fast."

"Yeah . . . right."

"Oh, I almost forget," Rachel said, "I made All-State Orchestra."

"You did?"

"Yes. The letter was waiting for me when I got home. Stacey Green made it, too. We're going to be really busy with rehearsals. In April there's a concert. You'll come, won't you?"

"Sure."

"Well . . . I'm glad you had a good weekend."

"Yeah. See you tomorrow."

An hour later Alison called. "Hi . . . I'm home."

"How was your Thanksgiving?" I asked.

"Leon and Sadie had a fight."

"How could anybody fight with Sadie?"

"She says Leon's the only one who ever does."

"I thought he's so proud of her."

"Yeah, but see . . . Sadie's friends are always dropping off manuscripts for Leon to read. They all know somebody who's trying to write. But Leon can't stand to look at other people's work. So he tells Sadie, *If I wanted to do that I'd be a teacher instead of a writer.* So then Sadie says, *What will I tell my friends?* So then Leon says, *Tell them your son is a selfish man who guards his free time.* So then Sadie says, *My friends will be very disappointed.*

So then Leon blows up and tells Sadie she has no understanding of his work. Then he slams out of the house, Sadie winds up in tears and Mom locks herself in the bedroom and won't come out. It was all very depressing."

"Was this before Thanksgiving dinner or after?"

"After. Sadie didn't show him the manuscripts until Friday night."

"That was smart. So did they finally make up or what?"

"Yes, but not until Saturday morning." She paused. "So how was your weekend?"

"Great!"

"Well, I'm glad somebody had a great time."

Later, as I came out of the bathroom on my way to bed, Bruce called to me from his room. "What?" I asked, standing in his doorway.

He was sitting up in bed with the atlas in his lap. "Dad says I should pretend he's on a business trip. He says it's just a trial separation."

I walked over and sat on the edge of his bed. The atlas was opened to a map of California. "Did he tell you what that means?"

"It means they live apart and think things over."

"Did he tell you anything else?"

"No . . . except we're going to L.A. over Christmas. Would you rather go to Marineland, Disneyland or Universal Pictures?"

"I may not go at all," I said.

"Then I'm not going either." He closed the atlas, looking very sad.

"We don't have to decide yet," I said, in my most cheerful voice. "And I think pretending he's on a business trip is a good idea. I think we should both do that . . . because before you know it, they'll probably be back together. I'll bet they're back together by my birthday." I could see that made Bruce feel better so I kept going. "You know Miri Levine . . . this girl in my class? Well, her parents got divorced when we were in fourth grade and when we were in sixth . . . they got married again . . . to each other."

"Really?" Bruce asked.

"Yes. So let's not say anything to our friends about this separation or we'll just have to explain all over again when they get back together."

"You don't think they'll get divorced?" Bruce asked.

"No! Who's talking about divorce?"

"I think I'll go to sleep now," Bruce said. "Tell Mom I'm ready for my kiss, okay?" He snuggled down under his quilt.

"Good night," I said.

As I was leaving he called, "Steph . . ."

"Yeah?"

"It wasn't that much fun in New York without you."

"I'm not surprised." I danced out of his room singing, "Feed me, Seymour . . . feed me."

I got into bed feeling a lot better. It's funny how when you try to help somebody else feel better you wind up feeling better yourself.

Peter Klaff

At school everything was the same, except that Jeremy Dragon was wearing a winter jacket. On Monday morning we had a fire drill before first period. On the way back to homeroom Peter Klaff told me he'd had two warts removed from his middle finger over the holiday weekend.

"Did your mother do it?" I asked.

"Yeah . . . with dry ice," Peter said. "It burned." He held his finger up to my face. "You see that . . . right there . . . that's where they were."

Peter Klaff had never stood so close to me. I pretended to be really interested in the black marks on the back of his finger. I even touched them, just to show how interested I was. Peter is growing. He comes up past my eyes now. "It

148

must be weird having your mother for your doctor."

As soon as I said that I got a mental picture of the Klaff family sitting around their dinner table. I could hear Dr. Klaff saying, *Stephanie Hirsch was in for her yearly check-up today. Her breasts are beginning to develop.*

It's about time, Peter would say, between mouthfuls.

She's probably going to get her period soon, Dr. Klaff would say, helping herself to more linguini.

I'm glad you mentioned that, Mom, Peter would say. *From now on I'll keep a look-out for anything red on the back of her pants.*

That's very thoughtful of you, Peter, Dr. Klaff would say. *So many boys your age act foolish about menstruation. Here, have some more bread.*

I must have had a strange expression on my face because Peter said, "What?"

"Nothing . . ." I said. "I was just wondering if your mother talks about her patients at home . . . like when you're sitting around the dinner table?"

"Nah . . . she talks about the Mets. She's a baseball fanatic."

"What about when baseball season's over . . . like now?"

"Movies," Peter said. "She's a movie fanatic, too."

"Oh . . ." I felt relieved. "I thought maybe she talks about diseases and stuff like that."

"Hardly ever," Peter said.

This was definitely the longest conversation we'd ever had. And I didn't want it to end yet. So I said, "Do you use apple shampoo?"

"Yeah . . . how did you know?"

"I can smell it," I said. "It smells nice."

He came even closer to me, stood on tiptoe, and sniffed my hair. "Yours smells nice, too. Like uh . . ."

"Almonds," I told him.

"Yeah . . . like almonds."

The next morning, when I got to homeroom, I found a small plastic bottle on my desk. On the side there was a picture of an apple. I opened it and sniffed what was inside. Apple shampoo! I looked over at Peter Klaff. We smiled at each other and I put the bottle in my bag. This was the first gift I'd ever had from a boy. I was glad Alison was busy talking to Miri Levine and that neither one of them had noticed the private look Peter and I shared.

The following morning Mrs. Remo was late getting to homeroom. While we were waiting to see if we'd have a substitute, Eric Macaulay told us a gross joke. Alison threw her shoe at him and said, "That is the sleaziest joke I've ever heard!"

Just as her shoe hit Eric's head Mrs. Remo came into the room.

"Really!" Mrs. Remo said. "This is not the kind of behavior I expect from my homeroom when I'm late. Alison and Stephanie . . . you can both report to me after school this afternoon."

I was shocked. First of all, I hadn't been doing anything wrong. Second of all, I'd never seen Mrs. Remo in such a bad mood.

We told Rachel about it at lunch. She couldn't believe it either. "Just because you threw your shoe at him?" she asked Alison.

"Yes," Alison said.

Then I said, "And when Alison tried to explain that I didn't have anything to do with it, Mrs. Remo said, *Maybe next time you'll think before you act.* Now what does that have to do with anything?" I asked Rachel. "I mean, does that make any sense to you?"

"No," Rachel said.

"She's been acting that way since we came back from Thanksgiving," Alison said.

"Maybe she didn't have a good holiday," Rachel suggested.

"Probably plenty of people didn't have a good holiday," Alison said.

I didn't say anything. I just unwrapped my lunch and started to eat.

On Thursday night I was in the pantry with the phone, talking to Alison and finishing off a bag of oatmeal cookies. As soon as I hung up, the phone rang again. I picked it up, expecting Rachel or maybe Alison, who sometimes forgets to tell me something and has to call back. But it was Peter Klaff. He asked for our math assignment. I gave it to him. Then he said, "Thank you very much," and he hung up.

I couldn't believe it. Peter Klaff calling me! How come he didn't ask his sister, Kara, for the assignment? She's also in our math class. There must have been more to his call than math.

Later, Dad called, but I refused to speak to him. "Tell him I'm in the shower," I said to Bruce.

Before I went to sleep I *did* take a shower. And I washed my hair with Peter Klaff's apple shampoo. When I got into bed I looked up at Benjamin Moore. Peter's not a hunk, like Benjamin. And he's not as sexy as Jeremy Dragon. But for a seventh grade boy, he's okay. I think I might decide to like him.

The Sharing
Season

The symphonic band is playing for the Christmas-Hanukkah show. It's an original musical called *The Sharing Season*, about a modern couple named Mary and Joe who come from different religious backgrounds. They want their kids to understand and respect both holidays so they take turns telling them about Christmas and Hanukkah.

Dana Carpenter is playing Mary and Jeremy Dragon is playing Joe so I'm very glad I'm in symphonic band. On the first day of rehearsals I couldn't take my eyes off Jeremy. That's why I missed my cue and Ms. Lopez had to stop the symphonic band. "We should have had a drum roll there," she said. "Let's try to stay awake on the snare drum, please." I was so embarrassed!

After a week of rehearsals Dana and Jeremy started acting as if they really *were* Mary and Joe. Instead of hanging out in the back of the school bus with his friends, Jeremy sat up front with Dana now. And in the halls at school they held hands and looked at each other like sick dogs. I wondered if she knew he had hairy legs.

I was so busy at school I didn't have time to think about my parents. But sometimes, when I least expected it, I'd get a gnawing pain in my stomach or my leg would start twitching. That's what happened in the locker room today, while we were getting changed for gym. I sat down on the bench and rubbed my leg.

"What's wrong?" Rachel asked.

"Nothing."

Rachel stepped into her gym shorts and tucked her shirt inside. "Maybe you're getting your period."

"What does my leg have to do with getting my period?"

Alison didn't wait for Rachel to answer. "How come you never tell me I'm getting *my* period?" she asked Rachel.

"Steph is more developed than you," Rachel said.

"I've been eating a lot of bananas," Alison said.

"Bananas?" Rachel repeated.

"I heard bananas put weight on you fast," Alison said. "And if I gain weight maybe I'll grow on top . . . and if I grow on top . . ."

"How old was your mother when she got it?" Rachel asked.

"Gena was twelve," Alison said.

"Because these things are basically inherited," Rachel continued.

"Oh . . ." Alison said. "I have no idea how old my biological mother was."

"But she must have had it by the time she was fifteen," I told Alison, "because that's when she had you . . . right?"

Alison nodded.

I stood up. My leg had stopped twitching.

"I still think you're getting your period," Rachel said.

"I promise when I do you'll be the first to know."

"What about me?" Alison asked.

"You'll be the first *two* to know . . . okay?"

"Okay," they both said.

On Saturday afternoon the three of us were at Rachel's, discussing Dana and Jeremy.

"It's obvious they're in love," Alison said.

"If he has to be in love with a ninth grade girl I'm glad it's Dana," I said.

"Me too," Rachel added. "At least she's smart."

"Yes, but I wish she'd stop humming under her breath at the bus stop." I stretched out on the floor with a bag of potato chips.

"No crumbs, please," Rachel said.

"You're so fusty!" I learned that word from her.

"I think you mean fussy," Rachel said, "because *fusty* means either *musty* or *old-fashioned*."

"Then you're fussy," I said, shoveling the chips into my mouth.

"Better to be fussy than slovenly," Rachel said.

"I'm not exactly slovenly," I said. "I'm just not as perfect as you."

"I'm not perfect," Rachel said. "I'm just organized."

"I wouldn't mind being half as organized," Alison said. She circled the room, running her hand over the row of framed pictures on Rachel's dresser, the tray of miniature perfume bottles, the collection of painted jars and boxes.

Sometimes, when Alison is at Rachel's she'll stare at the clothes in her closet, admiring the way everything faces the same direction. "I'll bet you never have trouble finding anything," she'll say.

"Never," Rachel will answer.

Alison ran her hand across the books on Rachel's shelves, arranged in alphabetical order by the author's last name. "Oh . . . I read this one," she said, taking down a copy of *Life With Father*. "It was funny."

"Yeah," I said, "but if it were written today it would probably be called *Life Without Father*." I forced a laugh at my own joke. Rachel and Alison looked at me. "I mean," I said, trying to explain, "so many fathers have to travel for their jobs."

Alison nodded. "I'm so glad Leon doesn't have to travel." She put the book back on the shelf. "Speaking of travels . . . we're going back to our house in California for Christmas."

"Really?" I said. "My father wants us to come out over Christmas, too."

"Maybe you can visit me in Malibu," Alison said.

"You're both going to be gone over Christmas?" Rachel asked. "You're both deserting me?"

"Stacey Green will be around, won't she?" I asked.

"I don't know," Rachel said. "She's not the same kind of friend as you. She's a music friend, that's all."

"But she slept over last weekend, didn't she?" I asked.

"Yes, because we had rehearsals for All-State."

"It's just for two weeks," Alison told her.

"Two weeks!" Rachel cried. "Did you know that Christmas vacation is the time when more people get seriously depressed than any other time of the year? And it's because they have no one special to share their holidays!" Her voice broke.

No one spoke for a minute, then Alison said, "I'm going to ask my mom if you can come to Malibu with us."

"I couldn't possibly leave my family at holiday time," Rachel told her. "They need me." Then she made a small noise, almost like a yelp, and ran out of the room, hands over her face. We heard the door to the bathroom close and lock. Then we heard Rachel crying.

Alison and I looked at each other. "She's very sensitive, isn't she?"

"Yes . . . and it was really nice of you to invite her," I said.

"Even so . . . I feel bad. I shouldn't have said anything about you visiting me in Malibu."

"She'll be okay."

"I hope so."

Mom isn't coming to L.A. with Bruce and me. She's going to Venice, Italy. She says it will be hard to be away from us but she's always wanted to see Venice and this is the perfect opportunity because a group of travel agents are going together. She seems excited about her trip, a lot more excited than I am about mine.

I haven't talked to Dad on the phone since Thanksgiving. I get tense when he calls. I always ask Bruce to make excuses for me. But when the phone rang on Sunday night I answered without thinking and it was him.

"You've certainly been busy lately," he said.

"Yes." My palms were sweaty. I reminded myself that this was my father. There was no reason to panic just because he was on the other end of the phone.

"How's the weather?" he asked.

"Sunny but very cold."

"What are you doing in school?"

"Rehearsing for the holiday show. Too bad you won't be here to see it."

"I wish I could be."

"I'll bet."

"Stephanie . . ."

"I really have to go now," I told him. "I'll get Bruce."

Mom came to my room later. I was lying on my bed, staring up at Benjamin Moore. "I overheard part of your conversation with Dad," she said, "and I think I should set the record straight.

You're blaming him for something that's not entirely his fault."

"I thought you said it was all his idea."

"Going to California . . . yes. But I wanted this separation, too. I just wasn't willing to initiate it. Dad forced it out into the open. Probably, in the long run, that's good."

"I'm glad you both like the idea so much!"

The next night, when Mom came home from work, she dropped a bag on my bed. "I was passing the sports store and they were having a special on Speedo bathing suits. I thought you might need one for L.A."

I think Mom's noticed that I've gained weight. I've been using a safety pin to hold my jeans together and wearing big shirts over them to hide the evidence. My gym shorts are getting tight but they have an elastic waistband so I can still squeeze into them.

I tried on the bathing suit. It was blue, with a diagonal white stripe. I looked terrible in it. I looked fat.

The Sharing Season was a big success. Mom and Bruce came to the evening performance and after it, Rachel and Alison came back to our house. It was our last chance to exchange holiday presents before vacation began. Our gifts to each other all turned out to be purple. We hadn't planned it that way. It just happened. I guess it's because purple is our favorite color.

I gave Alison and Rachel sets of barrettes, hand-painted with little purple flowers. Rachel gave us each purple T-shirts that said *FRIENDS* and Alison gave us purple leather picture frames. Inside was a photo of the three of us, plus Maizie, Burt and Harry. Leon had taken the picture right before Thanksgiving. We'd had to carry Burt and Harry to Alison's in their cage, the one the Robinsons use to take them to the vet. In the picture we're sitting on Alison's bed, laughing our heads off. Alison is holding Maizie, Rachel is holding Burt and I'm holding Harry, who is trying to escape. It's a great picture.

But when Rachel looked at it she started to cry. "I'm going to die of loneliness without the two of you!" That got Alison started and a minute later, I was in tears, too.

Finally Mom came to my room and asked if everything was all right. We explained that it was and Mom asked if we'd like a pizza. Of course we said "Yes."

While we were waiting I taught Rachel and Alison a song I'd learned at camp. It's called *Side by Side*. The part I like best goes:

Through all kinds of weather
What if the sky should fall
Just as long as we're together
It doesn't matter at all

We sang it about twenty times, until we were laughing so hard we had to stop.

Iris

Dear Rachel,

Well, here I am in sunny California! It's so weird here! It smells like summer but there are Christmas decorations everywhere. You can sit on the deck of Dad's apartment and watch the volleyball games on the beach. And there's a marina with hundreds of boats just a block away. Bruce likes to hang out there with his new friend, Shirley. Shirley is visiting her father, who's divorced. She's ten, same as Bruce. I'm glad Bruce has found a friend here because now I am free to do whatever I want and there's just so much to do . . .

I went on for three pages in my letter to Rachel but I didn't tell her the real truth except for the description of Dad's place. I didn't tell her how unhappy I was feeling or how homesick, or how Bruce has been having nightmares. We were sleeping next to each other on rollaway beds in the living room. So every night I'd get up with him and comfort him until he fell back to sleep.

I didn't tell Rachel that it wasn't always sunny here, that sometimes it was damp and foggy and the ocean was freezing and nobody in his right mind would get wet. I didn't tell her that Mom wasn't with us. And I certainly didn't tell her about Iris.

Iris is Dad's friend. That's how he'd introduced her to us on our first night in California. "Kids . . . this is my friend, Iris. She lives down the hall. We met in the laundry room."

"I've heard a lot about you," Iris said.

"I haven't heard a word about you," I answered.

Before we went out to dinner that night Dad looked me over and said, "Wow, Steph . . . you've really been putting it on."

I was hoping he would add something else. Something like, *But you still look great to me!* When he didn't, I said, "I haven't gained an ounce. You've just forgotten what I look like."

Then Iris said, "Maybe you could come to exercise class with me. I go every day at four."

"That's a fine idea," Dad said.

"I have other plans," I told them both. Right away I could tell it was going to be a long two weeks.

I suppose it could be worse. Iris could look like one of those girls on the beach who are always playing volleyball. They're tall and tan and skinny with long blonde hair and they say *Hi* as if it's a six syllable word. But Iris is small with short dark hair and pale, creamy skin. She isn't even young. She's thirty-six. She's divorced but she doesn't have any kids. I knew from the start that Dad and Iris weren't just friends. I knew from the way they looked at each other— the same way Dana and Jeremy do—like sick dogs.

Iris works for an entertainment agency. Her job is finding books that would make good movies. It sounds like a really easy job to me. All she has to do is read. But over the holidays she was reading at home instead of at the office. Except *home* seemed to mean Dad's place. After a couple of days I'd asked Dad, "Doesn't Iris have any other friends?"

"Sure," Dad said. He was also taking time off from the office.

"Then how come she's always hanging around here?"

"I think her other friends are away for the holidays."

"What about family?" I asked. "Doesn't she have any family?"

"No," Dad said, "she doesn't."

I thought about what Rachel had told us. About how people can get very depressed during the holidays if they don't have friends or family. So I didn't say anything else about Iris hanging around. Not then, anyway.

I decided the only way to get through the two weeks was by telling Dad I had a lot of school work to do. "Tons of reading," is how I put it. Dad and Iris were impressed, which meant they left me alone.

I still hadn't worn the bathing suit Mom bought for me. Nobody thought that was strange because Iris doesn't wear a bathing suit either. She says she's allergic to the sun. I told her that's a real coincidence, because so am I. When Iris does sit outside she wears a wide-brimmed straw hat. The only makeup she uses is lip gloss, which she carries around in her pocket and smears on her lips at least a hundred times a day. I wonder if Dad gets it on his face when they kiss. I hate to think of them kissing! But I'm sure they do. Iris is always touching Dad. She touches him a lot more than he touches her but I haven't heard him complaining. I wonder if Mom knows about her.

We were eating out every night at medium

fancy restaurants where I ordered huge dinners and finished every mouthful. "You certainly have a healthy appetite," Iris said one night.

"Yes," I said, "isn't Dad lucky . . . suppose he had a daughter with anorexia instead?"

"Mmm . . ." Iris said. She says that a lot.

Everyone around here is thin. Everyone except me. Well, who cares! Since I've been here I eat as much as I feel like eating, whenever I feel like eating.

After dinner, we'd usually play a game of Scrabble and I'd eat either ice cream or cookies, depending on what I'd had for dessert at the restaurant. I'm getting good at Scrabble. Once I scored thirty-two points on the word *fusty*. Iris asked if I knew what it meant. "Yes," I told her. It has two meanings—one is *musty* and the other is *old-fashioned*. She couldn't believe I knew so much.

Yesterday, Dad took Bruce on a fishing trip. The boat left at five AM. Dad wanted me to come, too, but I said, "No, thanks." I don't like the idea of fishing. It's bloody and disgusting. I was really shocked that Bruce wanted to go. After all, fishing is a violent act. But I didn't discuss that with him. I was afraid if I did he'd have more nightmares, about fish getting nuked.

"If you won't come with us I'll ask Iris to keep you company," Dad said.

"I don't need a babysitter," I told him.

"Iris won't mind. And the two of you can spend the day reading."

There was no point in arguing.

I slept until ten that morning. And when I got up Iris was already there, reading on the deck. I heard her radio. She plays classical music all the time. In some ways she reminds me of Rachel, like the way she reads a book a day and the kind of music she enjoys. I wonder if Rachel will be like Iris when she grows up. I wonder if Iris and Rachel would get along if Iris were Mr. Robinson's friend.

I threw on my shorts and shirt and carried the container of orange juice out onto the deck.

"Good morning," Iris said.

"Morning," I answered, taking a swig of juice directly from the carton.

"Why don't you get a glass, Stephanie?" Iris said. "It's more sanitary that way."

"I don't mind," I said, taking another drink.

"I was thinking about the rest of us," Iris said.

I ignored that and wiped the juice off my mouth with the back of my hand. "So . . ." I said, "how long have you and Dad known each other?"

"About six weeks," she said. "We met in the

laundry room right before Thanksgiving." She smiled when she said that. She and Dad must think that meeting in the laundry room is really cute.

"We had a fabulous Thanksgiving," I told her. "Mom and Dad were so glad to see each other!" I drank from the carton again. "Dad was hoping Mom would come out here for the holidays but she had to go to Italy . . . on business."

I didn't wait for Iris's reaction. I went back inside and pulled my wallet out of my duffel bag. Then I went out to the deck again. "You want to see a picture of my mother?" I asked, flipping through the photos in my wallet. When I came to Mom's I flashed it in front of Iris's face. "Isn't she pretty?"

Iris studied the picture.

"She's got a very successful travel agency," I said. "She's a real go-getter . . . she makes a lot more money than Dad." I had no idea if that was true but it sounded good. "They've been married fifteen years," I added. "May twenty-fourth is their anniversary."

Iris marked her place in the book she'd been reading with a piece of Kleenex. Then she closed the book and rested it in her lap. "I know how you feel about me, Stephanie," she said, looking directly at me.

"No, you don't," I told her.

"Okay . . . maybe I don't know, exactly, but . . ."

"That's right. You don't know exactly."

"Well, you're making it pretty clear," Iris said.

I leaned over the railing of the deck and looked down. "My parents are trying to work out their problems," I told her, "and I don't think Dad can work his out with you hanging around night and day."

"Will you please watch what you're doing!" Iris said as I leaned over even farther.

I could taste the orange juice coming up. If I do fall, I thought, I probably won't die. I'll probably just break an arm or leg. We're only three stories up. "You're wasting your time if you think Dad's going to marry you," I said, "because this is just a trial separation which means you're just a trial girlfriend." I straightened up and sat in the canvas chair, opposite Iris, with my arms folded across my chest. "So why don't you go and find somebody else?"

Tears sprang to Iris's eyes. "You know, at first I wanted you to like me," she said, "but now I really don't care if you do or you don't." She jumped up. "Excuse me . . . I just remembered there's something I have to do at home."

"Take your time . . ." I called after her.

I spent the rest of the morning sitting in the

deck chair, looking out at the ocean, and wondering why I didn't feel better now that I'd told Iris my true feelings.

While I was eating lunch Alison called and asked me to come to Malibu either tomorrow or the next day. I told her I couldn't.

Alison was disappointed. "Mom says she'll send a car for you so your folks won't have to make the trip."

"I wish I could," I said, "but . . ."

"Are you trying to tell me something?" Alison asked.

"What would I be trying to tell you?"

"That you're embarrassed to ride in a car with a driver?"

"No," I said.

"Are you embarrassed because you think we'll have a house full of movie stars?"

"No . . . I never even thought of that." Actually, a house full of movie stars sounded pretty good to me. And I'd love to see Alison's house. Most of all, I'd love to see Alison. But I just can't do it. I can't explain what's going on here. And I can't pretend that I'm having a great time when I'm not. Alison would know in a second that something is wrong.

"It's very quiet around here," Alison said. "Mom hasn't been feeling well so she's resting a lot."

"What's wrong with her?"

"Leon says she's exhausted from filming the series."

"That's too bad."

"I suppose I could come to your father's place."

"No," I said, quickly. "It's very crowded here and . . ."

"I guess you want to spend as much time as possible with him," Alison said.

"Yes."

"I understand," Alison said. "I'd feel the same way."

Just as I hung up the phone Iris came back. She didn't say a word. She just went out to the deck and settled in again, with her books and her radio.

I ran out of the apartment and down the outside stairs leading to the beach. Oh, I hated Iris! And I hated Dad for having her around when this was supposed to be our vacation! I walked along the ocean's edge for more than an hour. I came back full of sand, my eyes stinging from the salt air. I knew Iris would tell Dad what had happened between us so I spent the rest of the afternoon in the bathtub, planning my defense.

That night, instead of going out to dinner, Dad decided to cook the fish he and Bruce had caught.

"We don't like fish," I said.

"You've never had fish this fresh," Dad said.

"Does it have bones?"

"If you get one you just spit it out."

"I think I'll have tuna," I said.

"Tuna *is* fish," Dad said.

"But it's in a can," I told him. "And it doesn't have any bones."

"I'll have tuna, too," Bruce said.

Dad sighed. "You two don't know what you're missing. Maybe Iris will come over and help me eat this fish."

But Iris told Dad she thought she'd stay at home for a change. So Dad took some fish down the hall to her apartment. He was gone for an hour.

After dinner, instead of playing Scrabble, Dad called me into his room. He shut the door and said, "You were very rude to Iris today."

"I told her the truth," I said. "I told her that you and Mom are trying to work out your problems, which is what *you* told me."

"I expect you to treat my friends with respect, Stephanie."

"Respect has to be earned," I said.

"Where did you hear that?" he asked.

"I read it in one of Mom's books about raising kids."

"I see," Dad said.

"It wouldn't hurt you to read some of those books."

Dad raised his voice. "I don't need you telling me what to read!"

"I think I'll go home tomorrow," I said, my voice breaking. "I think I'll stay with Gran Lola until Mom gets back."

"You're not going home until January second," Dad said.

"We'll see!" I told him, turning on my heels.

He came up behind me and grabbed my arm. "You are *not* going home until the second!" he repeated.

I shook free of him. "What am I . . . a prisoner here?"

"Prisoners don't get to go to Disneyland," Dad said. "And that's where we're going tomorrow."

"Is Iris coming with us?"

"No . . . Iris has other plans."

"Too bad," I said as I left Dad's room. I went directly to the refrigerator and took out the jar of peanut butter. I've told Iris that we don't keep our peanut butter in the refrigerator but she doesn't listen. I opened the jar, stuck in my finger and dug out a cold blob. I put it in my mouth all at once. Then I got ready for bed.

On the plane going home, I said to Bruce, "Mom and Dad probably won't be back together by my birthday."

"I know," Bruce said. He was working one of those puzzles where you have to move small plastic tiles around until you get the numbers in the right order. Shirley's father gave it to him. "They're probably going to get divorced."

"They are not," I said.

"Then what about Iris?"

"Iris is just a fling."

"What's a fling?" he asked.

"A romance that doesn't last."

"How do you know?"

"Because I've read a lot of romances."

"Oh," Bruce said. "I hope you're right." He moved around a few more tiles, then he held the puzzle up for me to see. "Look at this . . . I got it!"

Reunion

I was so glad to get home! I called Alison, then Rachel. We made plans to get together that night, right after dinner. Rachel said she'd come to my house first, then we'd walk over to Alison's.

When Rachel rang the bell I answered the door. "Hi . . ." she said, "welcome home." She didn't shriek or jump up and down so neither did I.

As soon as Mom heard Rachel's voice she came into the hall and gave her a hug. "Happy New Year!"

"Happy New Year to you, too," Rachel said. "How was Venice?"

Mom glanced at me. "It was wonderful," she

said, slowly. "Of course it was hard to be away from the family . . ."

"I know what you mean," Rachel said. "I could never be away from my family over the holidays."

"Did Charles get home?" Mom asked.

"No, he went to visit a friend from school . . . in Florida."

"That's a good place to have a friend this time of year."

"I know."

"We're going over to Alison's now," I told Mom.

"Be back by eight-thirty," Mom said. "Tomorrow's a school day. And take your flashlight."

As soon as we were outside Rachel said, "Your father must have been really disappointed."

"About what?"

"That your mother went to Venice."

"Oh, yeah . . . but he understood. She had to go. It was a business trip."

"At least she had a nice time, though," Rachel said.

"Yeah." I shined the flashlight on my wrist. "Look what she brought me." I was wearing a bracelet made of something called Murano beads. Each one is a different color and decorated in a different way.

"It's pretty," Rachel said.

"Thanks."

"Did you and Alison see a lot of each other in California?" Rachel asked.

"No."

"How come?"

"No time," I explained.

"But you at least got to her house in Malibu . . . right?"

"No . . . we never got together at all."

"What?" Rachel said. "I can't believe it!"

"I know."

"But why?"

"I told you . . . no time. My father had so many plans. Fishing trips, Disneyland . . . every day it was something else."

"How was Disneyland?"

"Bruce thought it was great but I think we're getting kind of old for it." I didn't add that Dad had accused me of acting sullen and unpleasant that day or that I had told him it was all his fault. Actually, Dad and I never really talked again after the night we argued over Iris. I kept hoping he'd call me into his room and say, *I've been doing a lot of thinking, Steph . . . and I realize that you and Bruce and Mom are the most important people in my life.* But he didn't. He didn't even say he loves me, that no matter what he'll always love me.

When we got to Alison's the three of us hugged.

178

"I can't *believe* you and Steph didn't see each other even once!" Rachel said to Alison.

"I know," Alison said. "I was so disappointed but . . . c'est la vie!"

C'est la vie is French for *that's life.*

Gena and Leon came out to greet us and wish us a Happy New Year.

Then we went upstairs to Alison's room. Rachel stretched out on the bed and began to brush Maizie. I sat on the floor with Alison. She pulled a gauzy blue shirt and skirt out of a Christmas box and held it up. "Mom and Leon gave it to me. I'm thinking of wearing it to the dance."

"What dance?" I asked.

"The Ground Hog Day dance," Alison said. "Remember?"

"Oh, that." I had forgotten all about it. "I'll bet none of the seventh grade boys even know how to dance."

"So, we'll teach them!" Alison said.

I thought about teaching Peter Klaff to dance. Would I say, *Forward, to the side, together . . . backward, to the side, together . . .* the way Sadie Wishnik had the day she'd taught Alison and me to rumba in her kitchen?

Maizie turned and grabbed the brush out of Rachel's hand. She jumped off the bed with it between her teeth, carried it across the room and hid it, like a bone, behind Alison's desk.

"You are the silliest dog!" Alison said, scooping her up and kissing her. Maizie wriggled out of Alison's arms and attacked the tissue paper on the floor.

Rachel kind of rolled off the bed, sat behind Alison on the floor and said, "Can I braid your hair?"

"Sure," Alison said.

Last year, when I had long hair, Rachel liked to braid mine.

I made a ball out of tissue paper and tossed it across the room. Maizie chased it.

"Show Alison the bracelet your mother brought you from Venice," Rachel said, as she divided Alison's hair into sections.

"I love Venice!" Alison said. "Muscle Beach . . . the crazies on roller skates . . ."

"Not Venice, California," Rachel said. "Venice, Italy."

"Oh, she went to *that* Venice," Alison said. "Mom and Pierre took me there when I was little. We rode in a gondola."

"This is what she brought me," I said, holding my wrist in front of Alison's face.

"It's beautiful," Alison said.

"Thanks." I made another tissue paper ball and called, "Go get it, Maizie . . ." Then I said, "It was a business trip. Mom had to check out the hotels and restaurants for her clients." I glanced over at Rachel, who was fastening Alison's braids with the barrettes I'd given to her for Christmas.

Alison held her braids out to the sides like Pippi Longstocking, making us laugh. "Want to play Spit?" she asked.

"Sure," I said. Alison has figured out a way for the three of us to play at the same time, by using two decks of cards.

She grabbed them off her desk and handed them to me. I shuffled them and handed them back to her, to cut. Then she handed them to Rachel, to deal.

"When are the two of you going to grow up and quit playing this ridiculous game?" Rachel asked. I couldn't tell if she was serious or joking around.

"Probably never!" Alison said, taking it as a joke.

Rachel began to deal our hands but before we got going Alison said, "If you could dance with only one boy at the Ground Hog Day dance who would it be?"

"I can't think of any boy in seventh grade," Rachel said.

"Suppose it could be any boy at school?" Alison asked.

"Ummm . . ." Rachel said, sticking her tongue into her cheek, "I guess it would be Jeremy Dragon."

"He's in love with Dana," I reminded her.

Rachel put down the cards. "We're not talking about reality," she said. "We're talking about fantasy."

"Even so," I said, "that's a dumb fantasy because you know it can't happen."

"There's no such thing as a dumb fantasy," Rachel said. "Besides, every girl needs a fantasy boyfriend. Isn't that why you have that stupid poster over your bed?"

"But if I had to choose one boy to dance with at the Ground Hog Day dance I wouldn't choose Benjamin Moore. I would know that Benjamin Moore isn't going to be there!"

Rachel shook her head at me. Her eyes had turned very dark. "I have never . . . ever . . . seen anyone act so pre-menstrual in my life! Even Jessica doesn't get as tense as you."

"You know," Alison said, looking me up and down, "I think Rachel might be right this time. You look really puffy and my mother says that's a sure sign."

I didn't tell Alison that the reason I look puffy is that I've gained weight. And I didn't tell Rachel that if I'm acting tense it's for reasons that have nothing to do with getting my period.

"You better start carrying your equipment around with you . . ." Rachel said, "just in case."

"Imagine getting it at school!" Alison said. "What would you do? Where would you go?"

"I'd go to the nurse," I said. "And she'd give me a pad."

"Stephanie doesn't worry about things like that," Rachel said.

"Why should I?" I asked. "Worrying is just a waste of time!"

When I got home I found Mom at the kitchen table folding laundry. Bruce and I had come back from L.A. with our suitcases full of dirty clothes. We hadn't washed anything while we were with Dad. I sat down at the table and Mom pushed the basket of clean clothes toward me. "Rachel says I'm acting pre-menstrual," I told her, as I folded a T-shirt.

Mom hooted. "Sometimes Rachel is just too much!"

"You can say that again!"

"Did you tell her I went to Venice?"

"No."

"Have you told her about Dad and me?"

"No . . . there's nothing to tell."

Max Wilson

"Want to see what Jeremy gave me for Christmas?" Dana asked at the bus stop on Monday morning. It was freezing, with snow expected, and we were stomping our feet, trying to keep warm.

I'd never seen Dana look prettier. She was wearing a fuzzy white hat and her cheeks were rosy from the cold. She held out her arm and shook her wrist. "It's his I.D. bracelet. See . . . there's his name."

The bracelet was too big for Dana so she had threaded a small chain through the links. I ran my finger over the letters spelling out *Jeremy Kravitz*. "It's really nice," I said.

"What'd you give him?" Alison asked.

"I gave him my favorite pin. It's a small gold dove. He wears it on his . . ." Dana blushed, then paused as she looked around, but there was no one else listening. "He wears it on his underpants," she whispered, "but nobody knows so don't say anything, okay?"

"Don't worry," I told her. "The three of us know how to keep a secret."

The bus came along then and as soon as we were seated Rachel said, "How does she know?"

"Know what?" I asked.

"Know that he actually wears that pin on his underpants?"

"I see what you mean," I said.

Alison, who was sitting in the row in front of us, started to giggle.

"And does he wear it pinned to his waist or his butt?" I asked.

"Or someplace else?" Rachel said.

"Oh, no . . ." Alison said, "that's too disgusting!"

"Besides," I said, "wouldn't that hurt?"

By the time Jeremy Dragon got on the bus we were laughing so hard we just about fell off our seats as he passed us. "What's so funny, Macbeth?" he asked. Sometimes he calls the three of us Macbeth as if we are just one person. He didn't wait for us to answer, not that we would have been able to, anyway. He walked to the middle of the bus where Dana was saving a seat for him.

When Alison and I got to homeroom we found a substitute teacher at Mrs. Remo's desk. She was cleaning her glasses, a routine she repeated about twenty times before the last bell rang. Then she stood and introduced herself. "Good morning, class," she said, in a high-pitched voice. "I'm Mrs. Zeller. This is my first day as a substitute teacher."

Admitting that was a real mistake! Notes started flying across the room.

"I used to teach," Mrs. Zeller continued, "before my children were born, but I taught in high school, not junior high."

That did it. Everyone began to laugh out loud.

Mrs. Zeller looked around, trying to figure out the joke. She didn't know she was it. "I taught in Ohio," she said, "not Connecticut."

Now we were roaring, as if that was the funniest line in the history of the world.

Mrs. Zeller fiddled with the blue beads around her neck, tucked a loose strand of hair back into place, then tugged at her skirt and looked down. She probably thought she was losing her underwear.

"Well . . ." she said, "I guess I have to tell you

the bad news. Mrs. Remo's father passed away over the holidays so she's going to be out all week."

A hush fell over the room. I never even knew Mrs. Remo had a father. I hardly ever think of my teachers as regular people with families and lives outside of school. I wonder if they ever think of us that way. I wonder if they know that sometimes kids can't concentrate in class because of what's going on at home. I'm lucky that I can put my family problems out of my mind while I'm at school. I looked over at Alison. She was clutching her favorite stone. I thought back to that day right after Thanksgiving when Mrs. Remo had shouted at Alison and me, then kept us after school. Rachel had said, *Maybe she didn't have a good holiday.* Rachel could have been right.

Amber Ackbourne, who had been laughing harder than anyone before Mrs. Zeller told us the bad news, was crying now. Her shoulders shook and she sounded like a sick cat. I thought how weird it is that one minute you can be having the greatest time and the next . . . *wham* . . . just like that everything changes.

The door to our homeroom opened and a tall boy walked over to Mrs. Zeller. He handed her a yellow card and said, "I'm Max Wilson. I'm new."

Amber Ackbourne blew her nose and pulled herself together.

"Oh, dear," Mrs. Zeller said, her hands fluttering around her blue beads. "A new boy. What do we do about new people, class?"

Eric Macaulay called, "Give him a desk."

"Yes," Mrs. Zeller said, "of course. A desk. That would be a good place to start. Why don't you find a desk, Max, and make yourself at home. I'm a substitute and this is my first day, so I don't know the ropes yet." She sounded less nervous than before.

Max walked around the room looking for a desk. When he didn't find one he said, "Excuse me, but there's no desk."

"No desk," Mrs. Zeller said. "What now?"

"Give him a chair," Eric Macaulay said. "Then you can ask the janitor to bring up another desk. A big desk because this guy is tall."

"Thank you," Mrs. Zeller said. "That's very good advice. What did you say your name was?"

"Eric Macaulay."

"Well, thank you, Eric, for being so helpful," Mrs. Zeller said.

Max found a chair and sat down.

"Now, Max . . ." Mrs. Zeller said, "why don't you tell us something about yourself . . . something to help us get acquainted with you."

"There's nothing to tell," Max said.

"There must be something," Mrs. Zeller said. "Tell us where you came from and about your family."

Max sat low in his chair, his legs stretched straight out in front of him. He was wearing black hi-tops. "I'm from Kansas City," he said, looking into his lap. "That's in Missouri. There is a Kansas City in Kansas but that's not the big one. My father got transferred up here so that's how come we moved. I've got two sisters and a brother. My brother's older than me and my sisters are younger. That's about it." His voice cracked on every other word. "Oh yeah . . ." he added and this time he looked up. "I was thirteen on New Year's day and I like basketball." He smiled. He looked good when he smiled.

He had short brown hair, hazel eyes and a nose that was too big for his face. Mom says people have to grow into their noses. She says sometimes it takes until you're thirty. That's a long time to wait for your face to catch up with your nose.

"That was very interesting, Max," Mrs. Zeller said.

Eric Macaulay waved his hand and called, "Mrs. Zeller . . . how about if I introduce the rest of the class to Max?"

"What a good idea, Eric," Mrs. Zeller said.

I loved the way Eric was doing his Remarkable

Eyes number on Mrs. Zeller. He walked up and down the rows of desks saying our names, then giving each of us a title. Peter Klaff was Mr. Shy, Amber Ackbourne was the National Enquirer and Alison was Miss Popularity. When he came to me he rested his hand on my head. I squirmed, trying to move away from him. "And this is Stephanie Hirsch," he said, "also known as Hershey Bar, also known as El Chunko."

El Chunko! I didn't wait for another word. I shoved my chair back and stood up so fast it toppled over. "And this . . . in case you're wondering . . ." I said, pointing at Eric, "this is the Class Asshole!"

Everyone laughed like crazy for a minute, then the room fell silent again. Mrs. Zeller looked right at me and said, "I'm going to forget I heard you use that word in class . . . but I never want to hear it again. Do you understand?"

I wiped my sweaty palms off on my jeans. "Yes," I said.

Then the bell rang and everybody rushed off to their first period classes.

At lunchtime the first one of us to reach the cafeteria gets on line and buys three cartons of milk. Today it was me. But Alison met me at the cash register. "Eric didn't mean anything, you know," she said. "It was just his idea of a joke."

"Some joke!" I walked across the cafeteria in a huff.

Alison followed. "Please don't be mad at me."

"I'm not mad at you. I just don't see how you can like him."

"Mom says there's no accounting for taste," Alison said.

"I guess this proves she's right!"

The three of us share a lunch table with Miri Levine, Kara Klaff and two other girls. Eric Macaulay, Peter Klaff and their friends sit two tables away from us. Today they also had Max Wilson with them. I set the milk cartons down and took a seat with my back to the boys. Rachel sat opposite me. "Who is that guy?" she asked.

"What guy?" I said.

"That comely guy with Eric and Peter."

"What's comely?" Alison asked.

"Attractive . . . good looking . . . cute . . ."

"You think he's cute?" I said.

"Yes," Rachel said, "very."

"Then why didn't you just say so in the first place?" I asked.

"Because I like the way comely sounds," Rachel said. "I think it suits him."

"His name is Max Wilson," Alison told her. "He's new . . . he's in our homeroom . . . he's from Kansas City."

"The one in Missouri," I added, as I opened my lunch bag and spread out a tunafish sandwich with lettuce, tomato and mayonnaise, a bag of Fritos, two doughnuts and an apple.

"He's in my Spanish class," Alison continued, "and he couldn't answer one question. He's a complete airhead."

"I'll bet he's at least 5'8"," Rachel said, staring.

"Did you hear what Alison said?" I asked. "She *said* he's a complete airhead."

"You can't judge a person's intelligence by how he behaves in one class on his first day at a new school," Rachel said.

"Especially if he's a *comely* new person," Alison said.

"Oh, right," I added, "especially if he's *really* comely." Alison and I laughed and laughed.

Rachel pushed up her sleeves. "Sometimes the two of *you* act like complete airheads!"

El Chunko

Aunt Denise gave Mom an exercise tape for Christmas. When Mom got home from work on Monday night, she put on shorts and a T-shirt, shoved the tape into the VCR and jumped around doing something called Jazzercise.

I made myself a snack of rye bread slathered with cream cheese, then curled up in my favorite chair in the den and watched as Mom huffed and puffed her way through the tape. Mom is shaped like a pear, small on top and wider on the bottom. She says there's nothing you can do about the way you're built. It's all in the genes.

I draped my legs over the arm of the chair and devoured the rye bread as Mom lay on her mat doing some kind of fancy sit-ups to an old Michael Jackson song. Mom copied everything the Jazzercise leader did. When the leader asked, *Are you smiling?* Mom smiled. When she asked, *Are you still breathing?* Mom shouted, "Yes!"

"You know what Eric Macaulay called me today?" I asked Mom.

"What?" she said, without missing a beat.

"He called me El Chunko . . . so then I called him an asshole."

I expected Mom to give me a lecture about using unacceptable language at school. But instead she said, "You have gained weight, Steph. Why don't you join me . . . Jazzercise is fun!" She was on her hands and knees raising one leg to the side, then the other. Each time she did, she groaned.

"It doesn't look like fun," I said.

"It's not as bad as it looks." She was panting so hard she could barely talk.

When that number was over the Jazzercise leader applauded and said, *Give your glutes a hand!*

Mom sat up and applauded, too.

"Where are your glutes?" I asked.

"Back here," Mom said, grabbing the lower part of her backside.

"Oh," I said.

194

The next day Mom brought home a digital scale. When she stepped on it her weight flashed across the screen in red numbers. "You're next, Steph."

"No thanks."

"Come on . . ."

"I *said* no thanks!"

"Look," Mom said, "I know you don't want to talk about this but I'm concerned about your health. I need to know exactly how much weight you've gained since the school year began."

"A few pounds," I said. Actually, I had no idea how much weight I'd gained. The school nurse weighs us the first week of school but other than that I haven't been near a scale.

"Stephanie," Mom said, sounding very serious, "get on the scale."

"Not with my clothes on."

"Okay . . . then get undressed."

"Not in front of you."

"I'm your mother."

"I know! That's the point."

"Then get undressed in the bathroom . . . but hurry up."

I could tell Mom was losing patience with me. So I went to the bathroom, took off all my clothes, wrapped myself in a towel, then ran back to Mom's room and stepped on the scale.

"Stephanie!" Mom said, as the numbers flashed.

"This scale is at least ten pounds overweight," I told her.

"No, it's not. It's exactly right. I'm calling Dr. Klaff in the morning. We've got to do something about this."

"Don't call Dr. Klaff!" I said. I could just see the Klaff family at the dinner table talking about me. *Stephanie Hirsch has gained quite a bit of weight,* Dr. Klaff would say.

And Kara would say, *I'm not surprised. I'm at her lunch table and she's been pigging out since Thanksgiving.*

Then Peter would say, *I used to like her, but that was before she turned into El Chunko. Now I'm not so sure. I don't even know if I'm going to dance with her at the Ground Hog Day dance.*

Then Kara would say, *But Peter . . . if you don't, who will?*

"I want Dr. Klaff to recommend a sensible diet," Mom was saying, "not one of those fad diets that ruins your health."

"Who said anything about a diet?" I asked.

"How do you expect to lose weight without a diet and exercise?"

"I don't know."

That night after dinner Mom cleaned out the pantry. She got rid of every cookie, pretzel and potato chip. Then she attacked the freezer, pulling out the frozen cakes and doughnuts. "From

196

now on," she said, "it's carrot and celery sticks for snacks."

I watched as Mom packed all the goodies into a shopping bag. "What are you going to do with them?"

"I'm taking them to Aunt Denise's house. Howard and his friends can have it all."

"Don't you care about his weight and health?"

"Howard is as thin as a flagpole," Mom said.

"I'm going to starve," I said. "I won't have enough energy left to exercise."

"You'll have more energy than you do now," Mom told me. "Wait and see."

That night I stood naked in front of the full length mirror on the back of the bathroom door. It was steamy from my bath, but I could see enough. My breasts were growing or else they were just fat. It was hard to tell. Maybe if I lost weight, I'd lose them, too. My glutes were pretty disgusting. When I jumped up and down they shook. The hair down there, my pubic hair, was growing thicker. It was much darker than the hair on my head. My legs weren't bad but my feet were funny-looking. My second toes were longer than my big toes.

"Stephanie!" Bruce called, banging on the bathroom door. "I've got to go."

I put on my robe and opened the door. "It's all yours."

"I can't breathe in here," he said, fanning the air. "Why do you have to steam it up every night?"

"Steam is good for you," I told him. "It opens your pores."

"Where are your pores?"

"You'll find out when you're my age."

Flings

The phone rang just as we were finishing dinner the next night. It was Dad.

"How's school?" he asked me.

"Fine."

"How are Rachel and Alison?"

"Fine."

"How's the weather?"

"Cold with a chance of snow."

"What's new?"

"Nothing."

After that there was a minute of silence. Probably Dad was trying to think of some other question for me. When he couldn't he said, "Well . . . why don't you put Bruce on?"

I was at my desk later, doing math homework

and humming along with the Top Forty songs on my radio, when Mom came to my room. She stood behind me with her hands resting lightly on my shoulders. "Did something happen between you and Dad over the holidays?" When I didn't answer Mom continued, "I couldn't help noticing how distant you were to him on the phone."

"It has to do with Iris," I said. This was the first time I'd said Iris's name at home.

"Is she the woman Dad's seeing?"

"Yes. I wasn't sure if you knew."

"I don't know the details," Mom said, "but I know he's met someone."

"Doesn't it bother you?" I asked.

"I guess I don't like the idea of being replaced so easily."

I turned around and faced Mom. "You're not being replaced! Iris is just a fling."

Mom laughed.

"It's not funny!"

"I know . . . and you're probably right . . . it's just a fling."

I was glad Mom agreed with me. I felt a lot better until she said, "I imagine I'll have my own fling one of these days."

"You!" I said. "When?"

"I don't know."

"Will it be before or after my birthday?"

Mom laughed again.

"I'm serious," I told her. "I want to know."

"Forget it, Steph."

"No, I'm not going to forget it. Is having a fling part of a trial separation? Is it something everyone does?"

"I was just kidding," Mom said.

But I knew she wasn't.

Thoughts

Jeremy Dragon is available again! But the three of us can't be happy about it because Dana is so miserable. She came to the bus stop the following Monday morning with red and swollen eyes. "It's all over," she said, holding up her naked wrist.

"What happened?" Rachel asked.

"We went to a party and he made out with Marcella, that eighth-grade slut." Tears spilled down her cheeks.

Alison put her arm around Dana's waist. "I'm really sorry."

I gave Dana a tissue to blow her nose.

"I trusted him," Dana said. "I trusted him with my innermost feelings and he betrayed me."

I felt a lump in my throat. If this was love you could have it!

"I don't know how I'm going to face him on the bus this morning," Dana said. "Do you think I could sit with the three of you . . . because my closest friends don't ride this bus and . . ."

"We'd be honored," Rachel said.

"And we'll never speak to Jeremy again!" I promised.

When the bus stopped we got on and found seats together. At the next stop, when Jeremy got on and greeted us in his usual way, "Hey, Macbeth!" we turned away from him.

I was very glad to see Mrs. Remo back at her desk in homeroom. Mrs. Zeller had never forgiven me for saying the A-word in class, and I'd felt uncomfortable around her all week long. After Mrs. Remo took attendance she stood and said, "I want to thank all of you for your kind thoughts and generous contribution to the Cancer Society in memory of my father. He was a fine man and I'm going to miss him very much." She choked up. "But he had a long, productive life and that's what counts."

I felt another lump in my throat. This one was even bigger than the one at the bus stop. This one made me think about my father. Sometimes I feel guilty because I don't miss him that much, especially since the holidays. I think if he would just stay in L.A. everything would be okay. Maybe it would be different if Mom cried all the time or seemed depressed, but she doesn't. I think it would be a lot harder for us if Dad lived nearby and we had to go visit him and Iris.

Still, as Mrs. Remo told us about her father, I imagined all the terrible things that could happen to Dad. I imagined him crashing into a van on the Freeway, drowning in the ocean, having a heart attack at work. I couldn't stand the idea of anything happening to him, especially if he didn't know I still love him.

As soon as I got to math class I opened my notebook and started a letter.

Dear Dad,

I was thinking of you this morning. And I was wondering if you think I don't love you anymore? In case you don't know, I still do. But sometimes I get really mad and I don't know how to tell you. I got really mad about you and Iris because Bruce and I thought we were coming to L.A. to spend the holidays just with you. So naturally we were surprised and disappointed to find Iris there. Also, I hate it when you ask me so many questions over the phone. I especially hate it when you ask me about the weather. You never ask Bruce about the weather. If you want to know about the weather that much why don't you listen to the national weather report? Another thing is, I was wondering how you feel about me . . .

Alison tugged at my arm. "Steph . . . he just called you to the board."

I looked up and Mr. Burns was staring at me. "I won't even ask where your mind is this morning, Stephanie. It's clear that it's somewhere else. But if you wouldn't mind taking your turn at the board . . ."

I walked up to the blackboard and stood between Peter Klaff and Emily Giordano. Somehow I was able to solve the problem quickly and get it right. I would have to finish my letter to Dad during English.

But once a week, when we come into Mr. Diamond's class, we have a special writing assignment. And today was the day. Mr. Diamond had printed the topic on the board: *I Used To Be . . . But I'm Not Anymore*. Mr. Diamond never grades these papers. He just writes comments. Also, spelling and grammar don't count. What counts is our ideas and how we present them. The following week he'll choose two or three papers to read out loud but he never tells us who wrote them. Sometimes you can figure it out, though.

He always picks the best papers to read, papers that make you think.

I sat for a long time before I started to write. I looked up at the ceiling for inspiration, then out the window, but all I saw were the tops of bare trees. I nibbled on my pencil. *I Used To Be . . . But I'm Not Anymore.* I looked around the classroom. Almost everyone else was hard at work.

I thought about the letter I'd started to Dad during math class. I thought about how my life has changed. And then an idea came to me and I began to write. I wrote and wrote, filling up one sheet of paper after another. When the bell rang I looked up at the clock and couldn't believe the time had gone so quickly. I clipped my five pages together and wrote across the bottom: *Please do not read this aloud in class.*

At lunchtime Rachel begged me to introduce her to Max. "Please, Steph . . . I have to meet him!"

"Okay . . . okay . . ." I said. The two of us got on line right behind him. "Hey, Max!" I said, tapping him on the back. "How're you doing?"

He looked at me.

"Stephanie," I said. "From your home-room . . ."

"Oh, yeah . . ." he said. "You're El Chunko, right?"

I gritted my teeth. "You can call me either Stephanie or Steph, but that's it!"

"Sure," Max said. "It's nothing to me . . . you know? I'll call you whatever you want."

Rachel gave me a little kick, reminding me to introduce her to him.

"Oh, Max," I said, "I'd like you to meet my friend, Rachel Robinson. She's in 7-202 . . . that's the homeroom right next to ours."

"You're in seventh grade?" Max asked Rachel.

"Yes," Rachel said.

"You're tall for seventh grade," Max said.

"So are you," Rachel told him.

Max laughed. He sounded like a horse.

"So . . ." Rachel said, "everything's up to date in Kansas City . . . right?"

"Huh?" Max said.

"Never mind," Rachel said. "It's just a song."

"You know a song about Kansas City?" Max asked.

"Yes . . . it's from a musical called *Oklahoma!*"

"Whoa . . ." Max said, "this is going too fast for me."

We reached the food counter and Max took fish cakes, mashed potatoes and peas. Nothing makes the cafeteria smell as bad as fish cakes.

Max put mustard on his. "Aren't you getting anything?" he asked us.

"We bring our lunch," I told him. "But we buy our milk."

Max followed us to our table. "Mind if I join you?"

"Uh . . . all the seats at this table are taken," Rachel said. "Why don't you sit with Eric and Peter?"

"They're not as pretty as you," Max said to Rachel.

Rachel turned purple and took a deep breath.

Max leaned over and spoke softly. "Some day I'd like to hear that song about Kansas City."

As soon as he was gone Rachel said, "I've got to get something new to wear to the Ground Hog Day dance."

"He seems to like you fine just the way you are," I told her.

"He did seem to like me, didn't he?"

"Yes."

"You think he really does or was it just an act?"

"I don't think it was an act."

"Suppose he really *does* like me?"

"So . . . you want him to, don't you?"

"I think I do but . . ." Rachel watched me as I unpacked my lunch. "A hardboiled egg and carrot sticks?" she asked.

"Mom and I are watching our weight."

"Is it because the boys are calling you El Chunko?"

"It has nothing to do with them!"

The Celebrity

Bruce won second place in the *Kids for Peace* poster contest. The reporters who came to our house to interview him had questions for me, too. "Tell us, Stephanie . . . how does it feel to have a brother who's so involved in the peace movement?"

"I'm very proud of my little brother," I told them. I kept stressing *little* and *younger* when I talked about Bruce. And I didn't say one word about his nightmares.

"Your brother seems to have a very supportive family. Would you say that's true?"

"Oh, yes . . . definitely."

"Have your parents encouraged him in his quest for peace?"

"Let's put it this way," I told them. "They haven't discouraged him."

"Then they're not activists themselves?"

"Pardon?" That's the word Rachel uses when she's talking to grown-ups and she doesn't get what they mean.

Mom had been standing across the living room with Bruce, who was being interviewed by another reporter. Now she walked over to me and put her arm around my shoulder.

"Mrs. Hirsch . . ." the reporter said, "I was just asking Stephanie if you or Mr. Hirsch are activists in the peace movement?"

"Well, no . . ." Mom said, "not exactly . . . although we certainly believe in it. My business takes up most of my time."

"And your husband?"

"He's in California . . . also on business."

"So what you're saying is that your ten-year-old son did this on his own?"

"Yes, that's right."

War Is Stupid! Says Ten-Year-Old Poster Winner, the headline read in the Sunday paper. Under that was a picture of Bruce and a story about him.

Bruce called Dad to tell him the good news. And Dad called Bruce two more times over the weekend. The first time I answered the phone. He said, "Isn't it great about your brother!"

And I said, "Yes."

"I'll bet the phone hasn't stopped ringing."

"Mom's thinking of taking it off the hook."

"Wish I were there to celebrate with you."

I didn't respond.

"Well, let me talk to Bruce."

After he called *again* I asked Bruce, "What'd he want this time?"

Bruce said, "You know . . . more about being proud of me. And he wanted to remind me to wear a tie and jacket to the White House."

On Monday, at the bus stop, Dana said, "I saw Bruce's picture in the paper yesterday. He's so famous!"

"Yeah . . . he is," I said.

"Did he leave for Washington yet?" Rachel asked.

"He's leaving at nine," I told her. Mom is going with him. Bruce and the other poster winners are meeting the President this afternoon. Then they're flying to New York and staying overnight at a hotel because tomorrow morning they're going to be on the *Today* show. I'm going to spend the night at Aunt Denise's.

"Have you heard about me and Jeremy?" Dana asked.

"No . . . what?" I asked.

She shook her wrist. She was wearing Jeremy's I.D. bracelet again.

"What happened?" Rachel asked.

"He realized he'd made a terrible mistake and he begged me to forgive him."

"That's so romantic," Alison said.

"I wouldn't have forgiven him that easily," Rachel said.

"Just wait until you're in love!" Dana said.

Rachel didn't tell her that she's halfway there.

At school everybody was talking about Bruce, including my teachers. Mrs. Remo said, "What a special brother you must have, Stephanie."

By the end of the day I was sick of hearing about Bruce and how great he is. So when Mr. Diamond called me up to his desk after class I figured it was going to be more of the same. "Stephanie . . . that paper was amazing!"

"It wasn't that great," I told him, thinking he meant the story in the newspaper.

"Believe me," he said, "it was very special."

It wasn't until he tapped the paper he was holding that I realized he wasn't talking about the newspaper. He was talking about the paper I'd written in class last week. Across the top in green ink he had printed, *Interesting, revealing and straight from the heart!*

"I've asked Mrs. Balaban to see you this afternoon," Mr. Diamond said.

"Who's Mrs. Balaban?"

"The school counselor. She might be able to help you sort out your problems."

"I don't have any problems."

"I know these things are hard to face, Stephanie . . ."

"What things?"

"The kinds of problems you wrote about."

"No," I said, "you've got it all wrong!"

"Stephanie . . ." Mr. Diamond said, "go and see Mrs. Balaban."

"Sit down, Stephanie," Mrs. Balaban said.

I sat in the chair at the side of her desk. She was wearing a white sweater with a design knitted into it. On one hand her fingernails were long and polished pink. But on the other, three of her nails were very short and not polished at all. There was a picture of a baby on her desk.

When she caught me looking at it she turned it toward me and said, "This is Hilary . . . she's a year old now but she was only eight months when this was taken."

"She's cute."

214

Mrs. Balaban smiled and flicked her long, dark hair out of her way. "Do you have brothers or sisters?"

"I have one brother. He's ten. You probably read about him in yesterday's paper. He won second place in the *Kids for Peace* poster contest. He's going to meet the President and be on the *Today* show."

"Really . . ." Mrs. Balaban said. "And how do you feel about that?"

"Me? Well . . . I'm glad for Bruce but I wouldn't mind being famous myself." I laughed. It didn't sound like my regular laugh.

Mrs. Balaban lowered her voice as if she were telling me a secret. "Everything said in this office is strictly confidential, Stephanie."

"Good," I said.

Then we just looked at each other for the longest time. It reminded me of the staring contests we'd had at Girl Scout camp, where whoever blinks first, loses. Mrs. Balaban blinked first. "In February I'm starting an after school group for kids whose parents have split up."

"My parents haven't split up."

"Oh?" Mrs. Balaban studied the hand with the long fingernails. "Well, Stephanie . . . we can talk about anything that's on your mind . . . anything that's bothering you."

"Nothing's bothering me."

"I see." She sharpened two yellow pencils. Then she said, "If you ever do want to talk I'll be here. I'm on your side. I hope you'll remember that."

"Okay."

"Thanks for stopping by." She reached across her desk and shook my hand. "I'm trying to meet as many new students as I can."

"There's a new boy in my homeroom," I said. "Max Wilson. He's very tall. Maybe you should meet him."

"Max Wilson . . ." Mrs. Balaban repeated, writing it down.

On Tuesday morning Aunt Denise and I watched the *Today* show together. Bruce came on right after the eight o'clock news. Aunt Denise grabbed my arm and held on during the entire interview, which lasted five minutes. Bruce looked like he was having a good time. The other two poster winners seemed scared. I was glad when the interview was over because Aunt Denise stopped crying and finally let go of my arm.

I decided I'd send Dad the paper I wrote in Mr. Diamond's class.

I Used To Be An Optimist But I'm Not Anymore

It's not as easy to be an optimist now that I'm almost thirteen because I know a lot more than I used to . . .

Dad is always asking how I'm doing in school. This would prove that some of my work is *interesting, revealing and straight from the heart.*

Making Plans

Mom bought new earrings. They're shaped like bolts of lightning and they sparkle. "What do you think?" she asked. The earrings dangled from her ear lobes to her chin.

"They're different," I said.

"I hope that's a compliment."

I didn't want to hurt Mom's feelings so I didn't tell her the earrings were much too flashy. "Are you going to wear them to the office?"

"No," Mom said, "I'm going to wear them to Carla's party on Saturday night."

"I didn't know Carla's having a party."

"Yes," Mom said, "and I told her I'd come in for the weekend to give her a hand."

"Who's coming to this party?" I asked.

"Carla's friends."

"Women *and* men?"

"Yes," Mom said, "of course."

"Married *and* divorced?"

"I really don't know. I imagine there will be some of each."

"And you're going to wear *those* earrings?"

"Yes," Mom said, "but I'm also going to wear a dress and shoes and . . ."

"This is it, isn't it?" I asked.

"This is what?"

"You're going to New York to have your fling."

Mom threw back her head and laughed. The earrings danced around her face.

"It's not funny!" I said. I hate it when I'm being serious and Mom thinks it's a big joke.

But Mom couldn't stop laughing. Finally, she managed to say, "Sorry . . . it just struck me as funny that you should be worried about me having a fling." She gulped, holding back another laugh.

"I'm not worried!" I told her. "I never worry! I just don't like the idea of you with some guy. I'll probably hate him as much as I hate Iris."

"I didn't know you hate Iris," Mom said, quietly.

"Well, now you know. It may be fun for you and Dad to have your flings but it's not fun for Bruce and me."

"I'm sorry, Steph . . . I keep forgetting this is hard on you."

"People who are separated are supposed to be miserable," I told her.

"On some days I am," Mom said, "but I try to keep busy and not give in to it."

I thought about how I do the same thing.

"Look . . ." Mom said, "I need to get out and be with people. That's all there is to it." She took off her new earrings and dropped them into her jewelry box. "So would you rather spend the weekend at Aunt Denise's or with a friend?"

"With a friend," I said.

As I was getting ready for bed I decided I'd ask Alison if I could spend the weekend at her house.

"It's all set," Mom said, when she came to my room to say goodnight. "Nell Robinson would love to have you for the weekend."

"But Mom . . . I was going to ask Alison."

Mom shook her head. "I assumed when you said you wanted to stay with a friend you meant Rachel."

"You should have asked me first," I told her.

"I can see that now," Mom said, rescuing Wile E. Coyote from the floor. She set him on my chair. "You don't mind going to Rachel's, do you?"

"It's not that I mind . . ."

"Good . . ." Mom said, before I'd finished. "Because it would be awkward to try to explain to Nell now. Besides, I'll feel more comfortable knowing you're at the Robinsons'."

"I keep telling you that Gena Farrell is just a regular person," I said. "You don't have to be afraid of her."

"I'm not the least bit afraid of her," Mom said. "It's just that I've known Nell longer."

I happen to know that Mom thinks of Gena Farrell as a famous TV star, not as Alison's mother. One time, when Gena came by our house to pick up Alison, Mom talked too fast and offered Gena a cup of tea at least ten times, until finally Gena said, "Thanks . . . I'd love a cup." Alison says that just because Gena is famous and beautiful people don't treat her the same as they would somebody else. And that makes *her* feel uncomfortable.

Bruce understands. He told me he's sick of being famous. The other night he said, "It was fun for a few days but I never want to see another reporter. I hate their dumb questions. And I'm never entering another contest. From now on I just want to be a regular kid and play with David after school."

"But if you had it to do over again, would you still enter this contest?" I asked.

"Maybe," Bruce said. "Because it wasn't that bad meeting the President and having cocoa at the White House."

At the bus stop the next morning Rachel said, "I hear you're coming for the weekend."

"Yes," I told her. "Mom is going to New York to help her friend give a party."

"So what do you want to do?" Rachel asked.

"I don't know . . . whatever you want to do."

"I was planning on rehearsing a new piece with Stacey Green but I can cancel," Rachel said.

"You don't have to cancel," I told her. "I can do something else while you're rehearsing."

"Really . . . you wouldn't mind?" Rachel asked.

"No . . . when are you going to rehearse?"

"Friday night."

"We can go to the movies," Alison said to me. "And you can sleep over at my house."

"No," Rachel said. "My mother's looking forward to having Steph stay at our house."

Her *mother* is looking forward to having me stay? I thought. I guess that proved Mrs. Robinson hadn't discussed Rachel's weekend plans with her, either.

"And don't forget . . ." Alison said, "on Saturday we're going shopping for the Ground Hog Day dance."

"I won't forget," Rachel said. "I'm going to get something really wild!"

"What do you mean by wild?" I asked.

"You know," Rachel said. "Wild!"

Like Mom's earrings, I thought.

Getting Even

Dad called. "I got your letter and essay, Steph."

"Just forget about it," I told him.

"I don't want to forget about it," Dad said. "It took me a while to digest everything you said but now I think I understand."

"There's nothing to understand. I was in a weird mood that day . . . that's all."

"No . . . it was foolish of me to expect you and Bruce to accept Iris on such short notice," Dad said.

"You mean on *no* notice."

I could hear Dad sigh. "I should have told you about her before you came."

"It doesn't matter," I said. "I understand now that you and Mom have to have your flings."

"What do you mean?"

"Nothing . . . just that after this weekend you and Mom will be even."

"What are you talking about?" Dad said. "What's this about Rowena having a fling?"

I could tell from the change in his voice that he didn't like the idea at all. So I added, "You should see the earrings she got for Carla's party. They're really wild!"

"Put Mom on the phone," Dad said.

"She's not here."

"Where is she?"

"She drove Bruce over to Aunt Denise's. Uncle Richard's taking him and Howard to a hockey game."

"Ask her to call as soon as she gets back," Dad said.

"She might be too busy packing for the weekend," I told him.

"Well . . . tell her I called."

"Okay."

"And Steph . . ." Dad said, "about your birthday . . ."

I was glad to hear he remembered.

"I'm thinking of flying in for the weekend."

No! I thought. I don't want him flying in for the weekend. Look how excited I had been about Thanksgiving and then he came home and spoiled everything with his news about the separation. I

don't want any bad news over my birthday weekend! So I said, "I'm going to be really busy.
We're having a dance at school on Friday night
and on Saturday Gran Lola and Papa Jack are
taking Rachel, Alison and me to a play. And on
Sunday Mom's having the family over for cake.
She's already ordered it . . . it's going to have
purple roses . . ."

"Maybe I should wait until spring break," Dad
said.

"That would be better."

"But I'm sending your birthday surprise now."

"What is it?"

"If I tell you it won't be a surprise."

Probably another sweatshirt, I thought.

Sleep-over

On Friday morning at the bus stop Dana held out her arm and the bracelet was gone. "This time it's for good!" she told us.

"What happened?" Alison asked.

"He says he wants to be free to go out with other girls . . . like Marcella."

"Don't worry," Rachel said, "it's probably just sexual attraction."

"Please don't say that!" Dana started to cry.

"All she means is that Jeremy's had a lot of experience," I said, trying to make Dana feel better.

"How do you know that?" Dana stared at me.

"Because he's got . . ." I was going to say "hairy legs" but Rachel kicked me.

"What Stephanie means," Rachel said, "is that some boys are so interested in sex they forget about everything else. He'll come to his senses one of these days."

"I don't know," Dana said, blowing her nose. "I'm very confused. My friends tell me he's trying to make me jealous. They say he's trying to pressure me into going further than I want to go."

"You should never allow yourself to be pressured into having sex," Rachel said, sounding like an expert.

"That's right," I added, as if I knew all about it, too.

"Absolutely," Alison agreed.

"Your generation is just amazing!" Dana told us. "When I was your age I didn't know anything."

That night at the movie theater I bought a small container of popcorn. So did Alison but she got hers with butter and I didn't. As soon as we sat down I found out that popcorn without butter is very dry. It sticks in your throat. I started choking on the first piece I ate. So I excused myself to go back to the lobby for a drink of water. The people in our row had to stand to let me out. After I got a drink I stood on the refreshment line again, this time to have my popcorn buttered. It's probably not real butter anyway, I told myself, remembering my promise to Mom—that I'd watch what I ate over the weekend. It's probably just something to wet down the popcorn so you can eat it without choking to death.

While I was waiting Jeremy Dragon came into the theater with Marcella. She was wearing the tightest jeans I'd ever seen, tucked into white cowboy boots. And she was chewing bubble gum. I hoped she'd blow a bubble big enough to get stuck in her eye makeup.

By the time my popcorn was buttered the lights had gone down inside the theater and I had trouble spotting Alison. But I didn't have any trouble spotting Jeremy and Marcella. They were sitting in the last row, over on the side, and they were already making out. I wondered what Marcella had done with her bubble gum. Or did she kiss with it still in her mouth? No, she was the type who'd stick it under her seat.

By the time I found Alison the movie had begun. Everyone in our row had to stand so I could pass. As soon as I was seated I told Alison about Jeremy and Marcella. The woman behind us tapped me on the shoulder and said, "Shush . . ."

Right after the opening scene Alison whispered, "I'm going out for a drink."

I nodded. Everyone had to stand again, as Alison made her way to the end of our row.

She was gone for at least ten minutes and when she came back the man on her other side said, "Will you girls either quit running around or find yourselves some other seats!" So the two of us got up and went to look for other seats.

We stood at the back of the theater for a while, watching Jeremy and Marcella, until the usher told us that we either had to find seats or leave the theater. The only seats we could find were in the first row. We were so close to the screen we had to strain our necks to see. The movie wasn't worth it.

After, we went to the frozen yogurt place, where Leon was going to pick us up at ten. I ordered a cup of pineapple yogurt. That's about as simple as you get. Alison had her favorite—a PeachBerry Smoothie. As we were waiting for our orders Jeremy and Marcella came in. "Hey, Macbeth . . ." Jeremy called, "enjoy the show?"

I was really surprised. First of all I didn't know he'd seen us in the theater. Second of all I didn't know which show he meant—the movie or the show he and Marcella had put on. So I just looked at him and said, "I've seen better."

He laughed. "I'll bet."

Marcella ordered a waffle cone with pecan praline yogurt. She didn't speak to either one of us.

When Leon pulled up, twenty minutes later, he asked Alison to run back inside to buy a quart of pistachio to go. "Gena's got a craving for pistachio," he told me, as I got into the back seat of the car.

Rachel was sitting up in bed, reading, when I got to her house. Her face was covered with some kind of white goo.

"What is that?" I asked.

"It's a mask," Rachel said. "It dries up your skin so you won't break out."

"You sleep with it?"

"No, you wash it off after fifteen minutes. So how was the movie?"

"I've seen better," I told her. "But Jeremy and Marcella were there . . . making out."

"Making out in public is *so* disgusting!" Rachel said.

"I know. It was very embarrassing to have to watch them kiss."

"You actually saw them kiss?"

"Yes, more than once," I told her. "So how was rehearsal with Stacey?"

"Frustrating. We tried a really hard piece," Rachel said. "So how did they kiss?"

"The usual way."

"French?"

"I wasn't *that* close," I said.

"I'll never make out at the movies for the whole town to see," Rachel said.

"Me neither."

"If you feel like reading there's a really good book on my desk."

I walked over to Rachel's desk. "Which one?" I asked. There was a whole stack.

"It's called *Gone With the Wind*," Rachel said. "You'll like it. It's very romantic."

"I'm not into romances the way I was last year," I told her.

"This isn't like some teenage romance," she said. "This is the real thing."

I thumbed through the book. "It's very long."

"But it goes fast once you get into it."

"I think I'll wait a while to try this one."

"Okay," Rachel said, yawning. "I'll wash off my mask . . . then we can go to sleep."

I got undressed while Rachel was in the bathroom. If only we were as close as we used to be, I thought, I would tell her about my parents. I wish I could . . . I wish I could tell her *and* Alison. I hate having to keep secrets from my best friends. I've never kept a secret from Rachel

232

before and until this year she's never kept one from me. But everything is different between us now. I can't explain it but I can feel it.

I pulled my nightgown over my head, then settled into my sleeping bag, which was spread out on a foam pad on the rug. It would be easy to tell Alison about my parents, I thought. She'd understand, especially since she's been through it herself. But I could never tell her without telling Rachel, too.

Rachel came back and got into bed. " 'Night," she said, turning out the light.

"Rachel . . ."

"Yeah?"

"Remember when we used to play dress-up with your parents' terry robes . . . pretending they were strapless gowns . . . and we'd stuff the tops with socks and tie the belts underneath . . ."

"Uh huh."

"And remember when we decided to cook dinner for my parents and we burned the bottoms of the pots?"

"Uh huh."

"And that day your new mattress came . . ." I began, trying to laugh. "Remember how we jumped up and down on it pretending it was a trampoline?"

"All of that was a long time ago, Steph . . ."

"I know . . . but don't you ever think about all the fun we used to have?"

"Not that much." She rolled over in bed.

I bit my lip, scared I might cry. I thought, Rachel doesn't want to be my best friend anymore. She probably wants to be best friends with Stacey Green.

Burt snuggled next to my legs. His purring put me to sleep. In the middle of the night he and Harry must have changed places because when I woke up on Saturday morning Harry was next to me and Burt was gone.

Rachel was already dressed and sitting at her desk.

"What are you doing up so early?" I asked. "It's Saturday."

"I like to get my homework out of the way on Saturday morning," Rachel said. "Then I have the rest of the weekend free to enjoy myself."

I rolled over thinking that I'm just the opposite. I always let my homework go until Sunday night. Rachel and I are opposites in so many ways.

By the time we went down to breakfast Mr. and Mrs. Robinson were getting ready to leave. Every Saturday morning they go for a hike in Devil's Den. If there's snow they take their cross-country skis. I wished my parents would find something to do together.

Mrs. Robinson was tying up her boots. "It's

good to have you here, Steph . . . you've been such a stranger lately."

What did she mean by that? "It's just that junior high keeps us so busy," I said.

Mr. Robinson kind of patted my head. "Don't let yourself get so busy you forget your friends."

I looked at Rachel but she was slicing a banana into her cereal.

"So I'll pick you up at the bank around five," Mr. Robinson said to us, as he wrapped a plaid scarf around his neck.

"We'll be there," Rachel said.

After breakfast Rachel changed the litter in Burt and Harry's box, then she cleaned her room. She dusted everything and vacuumed everywhere, including under her bed. She sprayed Windex on her mirror and the insides of her windows. She rearranged all her dresser drawers and made sure her closet was perfect.

"This must be the cleanest, neatest room in Palfrey's Pond," I said, "maybe even in all of Fairfield County."

"I like my room to be clean," Rachel said.

"Is Stacey Green like you?"

"What do you mean?"

"You know . . . does she clean her room and keep her drawers and closet the way you do?"

"Stacey is basically neat and organized, but not like me."

Rachel was lining up the photos on her dresser. One of them was the picture in the purple leather frame, the one Alison had given to us for Christmas. She held it for a minute before setting it back in its place. We look so happy in that picture, I thought. If only it could be that way again. "Rachel . . ." I began.

"What?"

I wanted to ask if she liked me anymore but I couldn't. So I just shook my head and said, "It's almost twelve-thirty. We should get going. Alison will be waiting for us."

Something Wild

All the stores in town were having mid-winter sales. I suggested that we go to Enchantment first because they don't have three-way mirrors. I hate three-way mirrors. At Enchantment there are no mirrors in the dressing rooms. If you want to see how you look you have to come out onto the floor. In some ways that's just as embarrassing because the sales people stand around saying how great you look even when you don't.

I liked the first outfit I tried—a dark green skirt and top, made of something that felt like sweatshirt material. The skirt swirled around and the top had a lacy collar and little animals marching up and down the sleeves.

"This is it!" I announced, taking a quick look

at myself in the full-length mirror. "I'm all set for the dance."

"But, Steph . . ." Rachel said, "it's the first thing you've tried. Who knows what you might see someplace else?"

"I like it," I told her, "and it's a good price. I'll have enough left to buy shoes."

"You're just trying to avoid having to make a decision later," Rachel said.

"I am not!" Actually, I've always been the type of shopper who buys the first thing that looks good and Rachel knows it. I save a lot of time and trouble that way, plus I don't have to keep changing my clothes in stuffy dressing rooms.

"She's not going to find anything more becoming," the dark-haired saleswoman said to Rachel, as if Rachel were my mother.

"And that color was made for her," the blonde saleswoman added, trying to convince her.

I loved the way they were discussing me as if I wasn't there. On my way back to the dressing room I said, "I'm the one who's going to wear it and *I'm* completely satisfied!"

When I came out of the dressing room Rachel was trying on some gold knitted thing and the saleswomen were raving about it. Alison and I smiled at each other. "I'm glad you're taking that outfit," she said to me. "It looked great on you."

Rachel tried on everything in the store but

couldn't find anything wild enough so we headed down the street. We went to three more stores and at each of them Rachel asked a salesperson to hold aside a skirt or a top for her. She kept a list of who was holding what, the way she had the day we'd shopped for Alison's room.

Alison already had her outfit for the Ground Hog Day dance. All she needed was a camisole and tights to go under the gauzy blue skirt and shirt. She found them at Underpinnings. She was so sure of her size she didn't even bother to try them on.

After that we had to pee. The stores in town won't let you use their bathrooms. They claim they're for employees only. And the restaurants also give you a hard time unless you're eating there. Lucky for us there's a very nice, clean bathroom at Going Places, Mom's travel agency. It's even got lemon scented soap and pretty paper towels to dry your hands. I felt a little funny because Mom wasn't there, but I knew no one in the office would mind.

The chimes rang as I opened the door. Business looked good. Three clients were talking to agents and two more were waiting. Mom says that during January and February people start dreaming about spending a week in a warm and sunny place.

"Well . . . well . . ." Craig said, coming forward

to greet us. "Look what the wind blew in. I missed you this morning, Stephanie. I had to do all the filing myself."

"I'm glad to know you appreciate my hard work."

"I do . . . I do . . . I can hardly wait until you come back next Saturday."

"I won't be here next Saturday. Next weekend is my birthday."

"I don't know . . ." he said. "You take a lot of time off. I guess when your mother owns the business you can get away with anything."

Alison nudged me. She really had to go. I said, "Actually, we came to use the . . ." I don't know why I had trouble saying *bathroom*. I say it all the time.

Rachel finished the sentence for me. "The facilities," she said to Craig.

As soon as Rachel said that Alison got a fit of the giggles and once she gets started, forget it! In a minute she had me laughing, too. Even Craig couldn't keep a straight face. But Rachel was annoyed and in the bathroom she said, "Are you two ever going to act your age?"

When we left Mom's office we hit four stores in a row. At the last one, Class Act, we ran into Amber Ackbourne and two of her friends. "We're shopping for the dance," Amber told us.

"So are we," Alison said.

240

Amber had on the same gold knitted thing Rachel had tried at Enchantment and her friends were oohing and aahing over how great she looked. Personally, I thought she looked as silly as Rachel had. "I wonder if Max will like me in this?" she said, posing in front of the mirror.

"Max?" Rachel said.

"Yes . . . he's the new boy in our homeroom and he's *sooo* cute. I may dance with him all night."

Rachel just stood there, with her mouth half opened.

"Haven't you heard?" I said, setting the record straight. "Max likes Rachel."

Amber turned away from the mirror and faced Rachel. "Is that true?"

"Of course it's true!" I said.

"I'm asking Rachel, not you," Amber said.

Rachel mumbled something.

"What?" Amber asked.

"I *said* it could be true," Rachel told her.

"*Could be* isn't the same as *definitely,*" one of Amber's friends said.

And the other one said, "Just wait until he sees you in that gold sweater, Amber."

"I don't steal other people's boyfriends," Amber said.

"He's not exactly my boyfriend," Rachel said.

That was a really stupid thing for Rachel to

admit. So I had to set the record straight again. "He may not be her boyfriend but you should see them in the cafeteria."

Alison nodded but she didn't speak.

"You have the same lunch period as Max?" Amber asked Rachel.

"Yes," Rachel said, "but Max is a free person. He can dance with anyone he wants." She grabbed my sleeve. "We've got to go now."

"But we haven't see anything here," I said.

"We've seen enough!" Rachel spoke through clenched teeth.

" 'Bye . . ." Amber called. "See you in school on Monday."

Outside, Rachel walked very fast. Alison and I had to hurry to keep up with her.

"How could you tell her that?" Rachel finally asked me.

"Tell her what?"

"That Max likes me."

"It's true, isn't it?"

"Even if it is, you had no business blabbing it to her."

"I wasn't about to let her think she can have any boy she wants," I said.

"Max is *my* business, not yours!"

"Come on, Rachel," Alison said, "Steph didn't mean anything . . . she was just trying to help."

Rachel marched down the street to Ollie's, a

store that's much too expensive for us. We never go there, even to browse. But Rachel went inside and announced to the saleswoman, "I want something really wild!"

The saleswoman was tall and thin. She was wearing a suede skirt, a denim shirt and boots. She had about twenty strands of beads around her neck. Her hair was bright red and frizzed around her face. She looked exactly the way I imagine Rachel wants to look at the Ground Hog Day dance. The name pin on her pocket said *Glory*.

"I guess I'm not quite sure what you mean by wild," Glory said to Rachel. "Because what's wild to you might not be wild to me and vice versa . . . if you get my point."

I thought about Mom's earrings and wondered if she was having a wild time in New York.

"So are we talking formally wild or informally wild?" Glory asked.

"Informally wild," Rachel said. "It's for a school dance."

"Hmmm . . ." Glory studied Rachel. "What size jeans . . . 28 long?"

"How did you know that?" Rachel asked.

"It's my job," Glory said, walking across the store to a rack of pants. She flipped through, pulled off a pair of white pants and handed them to Rachel. "While you're trying these I'll see what we have in wild tops. Do you want a covered or a bare look?"

"Not too bare," Rachel said, "but a little bare would be okay."

We followed Rachel into the dressing room. Alison sat on the floor, cross-legged, and I stood in the corner, trying not to block Rachel's view of herself in the three-way mirror. She pulled on the white pants, then turned round and round, examining herself from every angle.

That's when I noticed the label. "Oh-oh," I said, "they're designer jeans."

"So?" Rachel asked.

"So . . . your mother doesn't let you buy designer jeans."

"What are you . . . my conscience?"

"I'm just reminding you."

"I don't need you to remind me!"

"But your mother will see the label."

"If I decide to buy them," Rachel said, "which I haven't . . . I'll cut off the label."

"You'd lie to your own mother?"

"You're a good one to talk about lying!"

"What's that supposed to mean?"

"Forget it."

"No, I don't want to forget it."

Rachel spun around. "Okay, fine . . ." She pointed her finger at me. "You told us your mother went to Venice on business!"

"That's true."

"No, that's not true."

"What does she mean?" Alison asked me.

But Rachel didn't give me a chance to answer. "I mean that Stephanie has been lying to us since the beginning of the school year and I'm getting sick of it!"

"Lying?" Alison said.

"I haven't been lying!" Why was Rachel doing this to me?

"Her parents are separated," she told Alison. "They've been separated since the summer. They're probably going to get a divorce."

"No!" I said. "They're not getting divorced. It's a trial separation . . . that's why I didn't tell you!"

"Oh, please!" Rachel's yellow sweater had crept halfway up her middle. "You say you want to know everything about your friends' lives but when it comes to your own you don't see anything you don't want to see. You don't face reality. You live in some kind of sick fantasy world!"

"If anybody's sick around here it's you!" I cried. "You and your perfect room and your perfect grades and your perfect flute and . . ."

Rachel sucked in her breath. "When are you going to grow up?" she hissed.

"When I feel like it!"

"Stop it!" Alison covered her ears with her hands.

"This has nothing to do with you," Rachel yelled at her. "So just stay out of it."

"Don't tell her what to do!" I shouted. "You don't rule the world!"

Alison began to cry.

"Oh . . . you're both such babies!" Rachel yelled. "It's impossible to be friends with such insensitive, immature babies!"

"And it's just as impossible to be friends with somebody who thinks she knows everything . . . even when she doesn't!"

Rachel lunged and for a second I thought she was going to punch me. So I grabbed her first, by the arm, and I yelled, "Why don't you take your big brain and just shove it!"

She shook free of me and shouted, "And why don't you stay home and play Spit for the rest of your life like the big baby you are!"

"Girls!" Glory opened the curtain to the dressing room. "This is very unbecoming behavior. I'll have to ask you to leave if . . ."

"You don't have to ask me," I told her, "because I'm on my way!" I stormed out of the dressing room.

"I'm never speaking to you again!" Rachel yelled after me.

"That's the best news I've heard all day!" I yelled back.

Several customers stared at me as I ran through the store and out the glass door. Let them stare, I thought. Who cares? I had had enough of Rachel Robinson. This proved that not only wasn't she my best friend, she wasn't even my *friend*.

I didn't realize I'd left my jacket on the floor of the dressing room until Alison came through the door carrying it. I didn't even know I was crying until she handed me a tissue. Then I felt the hot tears on my face and the drip from my nose freezing on my upper lip and chin.

"I'm sorry about your parents," Alison said, softly. "I had no idea."

"It's not your problem," I told her.

"Yes, it is," she said, draping my jacket over my shoulders.

At five, Alison and I went to the bank where we had arranged to meet Mr. Robinson. If I had had enough money I'd have called a cab. But I'd spent my last few dollars buying shoes for the dance.

Rachel was already there, waiting for her father. She was carrying two packages. I wondered what she'd bought. As soon as she saw us she turned away. When her father pulled up she got into the front seat of the car and Alison and I got into the back.

"Well," Mr. Robinson said, eyeing our packages. "I see you've had a successful afternoon."

When we didn't respond he said, "I guess you're tired out. Shopping will do it to you every time."

When we still didn't answer he laughed and said, "Better you than me. I'd rather do anything than shop." After that I think he got the message and he didn't say anything more.

When we got to Rachel's I whispered to Alison, "Can I stay at your house tonight?"

"Sure," Alison said.

"I'll get my things and be right over."

Rachel ran into the house, tore upstairs and locked herself in the bathroom.

I tossed my things into my canvas bag, found a sheet of paper in Rachel's desk drawer and wrote a note:

Dear Mrs. Robinson:

Thank you for inviting me to spend the weekend. I can't stay over tonight for very personal reasons. I hope you understand. If you don't, you can ask Rachel. I will be at Alison's, if my mother calls.

Sincerely,
Stephanie

Personal Stuff

I would never forgive Rachel for the horrible things she said about me. My parents' separation was none of her business. Besides, what did she know about how I was feeling inside? Which proved that Rachel Robinson was the one who was immature and insensitive, not me!

Mom came back from New York on Sunday afternoon but I didn't tell her about Rachel and me until we sat down to supper. Then, while she dished out tomato-rice soup, I said, "Rachel and I had a fight. We're never speaking to each other again!"

Mom said, "I'm sure you can patch it up if you try."

"I don't want to try."

Mom covered the pot of soup and bit into a cracker. "That's not like you, Steph. After all, you and Rachel have been best friends since second grade."

"Well, we're not anymore!"

"But you've got so much in common."

"No," I said, "we don't have anything in common. That's the problem."

"You shared your childhoods," Mom said. "You'll always have that in common."

"That's not enough!"

"It's stupid to fight with your friends," Bruce said, slurping his soup.

"Rachel is *not* my friend."

"But she was . . . before you had the fight . . . right?"

"Before we had the fight doesn't count," I told Bruce.

"That's how wars get started," he said.

"Nobody is talking about war!" I shouted.

"Calm down, Steph . . ." Mom said, "and eat your soup before it gets cold."

When I got into bed that night I went over the fight in my mind again, trying to figure out how it had started. But all I could remember was the part about the designer jeans, and the shouting, and the tears. I had trouble falling asleep. When I finally did, I dreamed I was at the Ground Hog Day dance, naked. *Baby . . . baby*

. . . *baby,* Rachel sang, taunting me. Everyone else laughed and pointed. Finally, Mrs. Remo covered me with her coat.

When Dad called the next night I told him that Rachel and I were never speaking again.

He said, "You two will make up in no time."

"We will not."

"Want to bet?" Dad asked.

"No."

"Well, I do. I'll bet five dollars that before your birthday you and Rachel are best friends again."

"My birthday's this Friday, so you're definitely going to lose."

"I'll take that chance."

Parents always think they know so much about their kids when really, they hardly know a thing.

"So," Dad said, "how was Mom's weekend in New York?"

"Why don't you ask her yourself?" I thrust the phone at Mom, who was relaxing at the kitchen table, sipping tea and reading the newspaper.

"Yes, Steve . . ." Mom said, taking the phone, "everyone's fine."

I began to peel the label off the jar of mayonnaise that was still sitting on the counter. If I'm really careful I can sometimes peel labels off in one piece, which feels almost as good as peeling sunburned skin.

"A fling?" Mom said into the phone. "No, I

did not have a fling in New York . . . not that it would be any of your business if I had."

I put the mayonnaise jar in the refrigerator and tried to sneak out of the kitchen but I didn't make it. "Stephanie!" Mom called, as she hung up the phone. "Did you tell Dad I was going to New York to have a fling?"

"I might have mentioned something about that," I said. "And by the way . . . how was Carla's party?"

"Don't try to change the subject," Mom said and I could tell by the tone of her voice she was serious. "You had no business discussing my social life behind my back."

"Dad was jealous, wasn't he?"

"This is a marriage, not some junior high romance," Mom said. "We've got to work it out ourselves."

"I don't see why I can't help."

"Because you don't have the power to make it turn out the way you want . . . you'll only wind up disappointed. Do you understand?"

"No!" I shouted, as I ran out of the kitchen and up the stairs. If you asked me, Mom and Dad were behaving just like Jeremy and Dana. I slammed my bedroom door and threw myself on my bed, on top of my stuffed animals. I hated the way Rachel, and now Mom, accused me of butting into their social lives when all I was trying to do was help. I lay there for a long time, crying. I was sure Mom would come to my room to apologize, but she didn't.

Word gets around fast at school. By lunchtime on Tuesday everyone knew that Rachel and I weren't speaking. On the bus Rachel sat with Dana, as far from Alison and me as possible. And in the cafeteria she sat at Stacey Green's table. I saw her fooling around with Max, too.

Kara Klaff asked, "What'd you two fight about anyway?"

"Personal stuff," I answered.

Miri Levine said, "Do you think you'll make up soon, or what?"

"Never," I told her.

Amber Ackbourne came up to me in homeroom. "I can't believe that you and Rachel aren't speaking. I mean, you and Rachel have been friends forever. I hope it didn't have anything to do with Max or that gold sweater I bought for the dance."

"Don't flatter yourself," I said. "It didn't."

After school Alison said, "Everybody's asking if I'm on your side or Rachel's. They don't know she called me an insensitive, immature baby, too. I hate fights!"

"It wasn't my idea to have this fight," I told her.

"I know," Alison said. "I was there . . . remember?"

We squeezed hands and I thought how lucky I am to have Alison for my best friend. Because if Rachel had been my only best friend imagine how lonely I'd feel now. As lonely as Rachel would feel if she didn't have Stacey Green.

That night it began to snow and by the time I went to bed it was coming down hard. I had another bad dream. This time Rachel and I were walking along a highway but there was no traffic. Then, suddenly, a speeding car came out of nowhere and headed straight for us. We tried to run but our feet wouldn't move. The car smashed into Rachel. Her body flew up in the air, sailed across the highway and landed with a thud. I raced to her side but it was too late. When the police came they arrested me even though I hadn't done a thing. The policeman who handcuffed me looked exactly like Benjamin Moore. He said, *You planned the whole thing, didn't you?* I screamed, *No! No!* and woke up shaking and covered with sweat.

Bruce raced into my room. "What was that?"

"I had a bad dream," I said.

"Scary?"

"Sort of . . ."

"About the bomb?"

"No."

"You want me to stay with you?"

"I'm okay now."

He went to my window and looked out. "It's still snowing. I hope school is closed tomorrow."

"Yeah . . . we could use a snow day."

"I guess I'll go back to bed now."

When he got to my door I said, "Bruce . . ."

"Yeah?"

"Thanks for coming to my room."

"That's okay," he said. "I know what it's like to have bad dreams."

What's weird is, Bruce hasn't had a nightmare since he won second place in the poster contest. Mom says he feels better now that he knows he's not the only one who cares. He's even been invited to become an honorary member of two national organizations that work for peace.

It was still snowing when we woke up on Wednesday morning. School was closed. Bruce and I whooped for joy, then went back to sleep.

The snow stopped and the sun came out around eleven. Bruce and his friend, David, built a snowman in our yard. I tied a scarf around his neck and set Dad's brown felt hat on his head.

Seeing the hat on the snowman reminded me of the old days, when Dad would play with us in the snow. I wonder if we'll ever do that again.

After lunch Alison and I went down to the pond to skate. Rachel was there, too, with Dana, but she just gave me a haughty look. So I gave her one back. I learned that word from Rachel. It means arrogant, which means hoity-toity, which means thinking you are great, which definitely fits Rachel. While I was showing off, skating backwards, I tripped and fell. Alison had to help me to my feet. She sat on a log with me for a while, until the pain in my backside went away. After that I stuck to ordinary skating and when Rachel did a series of figure eights, I didn't act impressed like everyone else at the pond.

Mom had gone to the office for a few hours that afternoon and when she got home, around five, I was sitting in the den nibbling a bowl of carrot sticks and reading. I'd decided to try *Gone With the Wind* after all, proving that Rachel isn't the only person in seventh grade who can read grown-up books. Mom changed into her exercise clothes and shoved her Jazzercise tape into the VCR. When the leader came on the screen Mom began her warmup stretches.

I put down my book. "I think I'll try that today," I said, standing behind Mom and copying her movements.

When we got to the number where the leader says, "Okay . . . now I want you to make believe you're punching someone you really can't stand! Remember . . . it's a lot better to punch the air than someone you know," I punched as hard as I could. First to the right, then to the left. *Take that* . . . I thought, *and that!* Punch . . . punch . . . punch . . . until Mom touched my arm and said, "The number's over, Steph. You can stop punching now."

Slow Dancing

A package arrived from Dad on Friday. I took it to my room. The card showed an older elephant talking to a younger one. It said *Happy Birthday to someone young enough to enjoy it but old enough to know better.* Under that, Dad had written, *Wish I could be with you to celebrate your thirteenth! Love, Dad.* I turned it over to see if it was made of recycled paper. It was. I unwrapped the box and opened it slowly. Inside was an amethyst heart on a gold chain. Amethyst is my birthstone.

I ran downstairs. Mom was fixing an early dinner because the Ground Hog Day dance was starting at seven-thirty. "Look what Dad sent for my birthday," I said, dangling the necklace under her nose.

Mom glanced up from the chicken and vegetables she was stir-frying. "Very pretty."

"You think he picked it out himself?" I asked.

"I hope so," Mom said.

"Me too . . . because if Iris picked it out I'll never wear it. I'll flush it down the toilet first!"

"Really, Steph . . ." Mom laughed. But I think she was glad I said that.

"How would it look with my green outfit?"

"When you get dressed for the dance you can try it and see," Mom said.

"But how can I wear this *plus* my bee-sting necklace?"

"There are no bees at night," Mom said, "especially in the winter."

"Then I guess I'll wear Dad's necklace tonight and tomorrow, when I go to New York, I'll wear Gran Lola's." I paused for a second. "And I'll wear my new boots tomorrow, too." I added that because Mom had given me a pair of cowboy boots for my birthday. They're something like the ones Marcella wore to the movies the night I saw her with Jeremy Dragon, except mine are a soft grayish color and Marcella's are white. I didn't get my own phone. Oh, well . . . there's always next year.

"Steph . . ." Mom began.

"I really love the boots you gave me!" I said. I

didn't want to hurt Mom's feelings, making her think I liked Dad's present better.

But Mom had something else on her mind. "Don't you think we should ask Rachel if she needs a ride to the dance tonight?" she asked.

"No!"

Rachel had written a note to my mother:

Dear Mrs. Hirsch,

Due to a change in plans I won't be able to go to New York on Saturday to help celebrate Stephanie's birthday.

Sincerely,
Rachel Robinson

"I talked to Nell today," Mom said.

"You called Mrs. Robinson?"

"She called me. Rachel is suffering."

"Good," I said. "Rachel deserves to suffer!"

"Stephanie . . . I'm surprised at you. Where's your compassion?"

"It's my birthday," I said. "Where's her compassion? Besides, you don't know the terrible things she said about me."

"Maybe she's sorry," Mom said

"Then let her tell me herself."

The gym looked great. Besides crepe-paper streamers and balloons in different colors, huge letters spelling out *Ground Hog Day* were strung across one wall. The other walls were covered with murals of ground hogs looking for their shadows. My two favorite teachers, Mrs. Remo and Mr. Diamond, were chaperones, along with the other seventh grade homeroom teachers.

When Alison and I got there Eric Macaulay, Peter Klaff and Max Wilson were already gathered around the refreshment table, stuffing their faces with cookies and fruit punch. Nobody was dancing yet.

We were there for at least ten minutes before Rachel came in with Stacey Green. She was dressed all in white. I couldn't tell if her white pants were the designer jeans she'd tried at Ollie's on the day of the fight, or not. But I know we hadn't seen her top, which was pleated and shaped like a lamp shade. She had a white flower in her hair, too. A gardenia, I think. I was too far away to smell it. She didn't look like a person who was suffering at all.

We stood around for a while, girls talking to girls and boys talking to boys, until Amber Ackbourne dragged Max Wilson out to the middle of the floor, to dance. Then Toad asked Alison to dance and soon all the boys were cutting in on each other to get their turns with Alison. All but Eric Macaulay. He just watched. So I was really shocked when he suddenly grabbed my hand and said, "Come on, El Chunko . . . let's dance!"

"My name is Stephanie!" I reminded him.

"Yeah . . . yeah."

Eric surprised me. He actually knew how to dance. And even though we didn't touch because it wasn't a slow number, he managed to dance me over to where Peter Klaff was standing. When we were right in front of Peter, Eric shoved me at him. "Catch . . ." Eric called to Peter, laughing. I almost fell over but Peter caught me. He didn't let go of me right away either.

Next, Eric grabbed Rachel around the waist. He only came up to her chest but he danced her over to Max and Amber. When he was right up close he shoved Rachel at Max, the way he had shoved me at Peter. Rachel went flying, nearly knocking over Amber. Eric rescued Amber and before she knew what was happening he danced her away, leaving Max and Rachel together. Then Eric danced Amber over to Alison and shoved her at Alison's partner. Finally, Eric had Alison to himself.

"I can't believe this!" I said to Peter, who was standing with his hands in his pockets.

"He planned the whole thing," Peter said, "and it worked." He looked at me. "So . . . you want to dance?"

"Sure."

"Okay . . . there's just one problem."

"What's that?" I asked.

"I don't know how," he said.

"I'll teach you." A slow song was playing. "Put your arm around my waist," I told him.

"I know that part," Peter said. "The part I don't know is what to do with my feet."

"Try this," I said. "Forward, to the side, together . . . backward, to the side, together." I kind of dragged Peter around with me.

Peter kept repeating, "Forward, to the side, together . . . backward, to the side, together." And soon he said, "Hey, we're dancing." Sometimes we stepped on each other's feet, but so what? We danced for six numbers, fast and slow, before Peter said, "I drank a lot of punch. I've got to go . . ."

"Me too."

"Meet you back here in five minutes or less," he said, pushing the timer on his stop watch.

I headed for the girls' room mainly because my pantyhose were falling down. Probably I'd bought the wrong size. I'd had trouble figuring out the height and weight chart printed on the back of the package. Two other girls were in there. One of them, Emily Giordano, I know from my math class. She was putting on lip gloss. We greeted each other, then I went into a booth.

When I pulled down my pants I saw a reddish-brown stain inside. What's this? I thought. Could it be? No . . . probably not. But if it's not, then what is it? By the time I flushed the toilet I knew for sure because there were a few drops of menstrual blood in there. Imagine that . . . my period on my thirteenth birthday! I had to think fast. "Emily . . ." I called. "Are you still out there?"

"Yes."

"Could you pass me some paper towels?"

"What for?" Emily asked.

"I've got my period," I said, trying it out. It sounded so grown-up!

"Don't you want a pad?"

"I don't have any money with me . . . do you?"

"No, but I could go ask somebody."

"That's okay," I said. "Just pass me the paper towels."

"Here . . ." she said, shoving a whole stack under the door.

"Thanks." I stuck half a dozen of them inside my pants but they felt hard and rough against me. Still, they were better than nothing. I couldn't wait to tell Alison what had happened! But when I got back to the gym she was dancing with Eric

Macaulay and Peter was waiting for me at the refreshment table. "I thought you fell in," he said, checking his watch. "You were gone nine minutes, seventeen seconds."

We started dancing again but I couldn't help thinking: Suppose the paper towels aren't enough? Suppose it gets on my skirt and Peter says, *What's that . . . your period?*

"You're not doing *forward, to the side, together* the way you were before," Peter said.

"Oh, sorry . . ." How could I concentrate on dancing at a time like this? I tried to get Alison's attention. I beckoned to her but she thought I was waving and she waved back. She and Eric never stopped dancing. Finally I broke away from Peter and said, "I just remembered . . . I've got to tell Mrs. Remo something."

"Now?"

"Yes."

"Are you trying to get rid of me?" Peter asked.

"No . . . this has nothing to do with you."

"Okay." He pushed the button on his watch again. "You've got five minutes . . . starting now!"

I went over to Mrs. Remo and asked if I could talk to her in private. She put her arm around me. "Are the boys giving you a hard time?" she asked.

"No." I wondered why she thought that. "It's my . . ." Then for some reason I started to laugh.

"What?" Mrs. Remo asked.

"I just got my period and I don't have any . . ." I couldn't stop laughing.

"Is this your first time?"

I nodded because I was laughing too hard to speak.

"Let's see what we can do." Mrs. Remo went to the girls' room with me, deposited the right coins in the machine on the wall and handed me a pad. "Just peel off the bottom and stick it to your panties," she whispered. "I'll wait here . . . just in case."

I tried to stop laughing. I'm not the type to get giggling fits, like Alison. I attached the pad to my pants, pulled everything up again and came out of the booth just as Alison burst into the girls' room. "Are you okay?" she asked. "Peter said something's going on."

"I'm fine," I told her. "I just got my period."

"Oh, Steph . . ." Alison hugged me. "That's so exciting! And on your birthday, too."

"It's your birthday?" Mrs. Remo asked.

"Yes. I'm thirteen today."

Mrs. Remo also gave me a hug, which was kind of embarrassing. "Happy Birthday, Stephanie!"

Peter and Eric were waiting for Alison and me. "That was twelve minutes, four seconds," Peter said. I wished he hadn't gotten a stop watch for Christmas.

Mrs. Remo went to the microphone and tapped it. "Attention everyone . . ." she said, "I want to make an announcement. I just found out something special about Stephanie Hirsch."

Oh, no! I thought. She's going to announce my period to the entire seventh grade. This was worse than the dream I'd had about the dance, where I was naked and Mrs. Remo had to cover me with her coat. I felt my face turn hot. I felt dizzy. I'm going to pass out, I thought. I reached for Peter's arm to steady myself, which he took to mean I wanted to hold hands.

Mrs. Remo began to speak. "Today . . ."

"No!" I called in a weak voice, hoping to stop Mrs. Remo. But Peter thought *no* meant I didn't want to hold hands and he quickly moved a step away from me.

"Today is Stephanie's thirteenth birthday," Mrs. Remo said. "Let's all wish her a very happy one." The whole class began to sing and my dizzy spell passed. I glanced over at Rachel, who was standing close to Max Wilson. She wasn't singing. Our eyes met for a minute before she turned away. I remembered my promise, that she and Alison would be the first to know when I got my period. But promises to someone who isn't your friend anymore don't count.

During the last half hour of the dance Rachel and Max were wrapped together, barely moving in time to the music. Her head was buried in his neck and his eyes were half-closed. They were definitely the most intense couple at the dance.

When the music ended there was a dash for the coat room. As soon as we found our coats Peter and I went outside. It was a cold, clear night and Peter pointed toward the sky. "Look . . . there's Orion."

When I looked up he kissed me. "Happy Birthday, Steph."

I was so surprised I couldn't think of a thing to say.

"I never did that before," he confessed.

"Neither did I."

"Let's do it again," he said.

"Okay." This time I was careful to keep my lips closed. I wasn't taking any chances that our braces would get stuck together. I didn't get the same kind of tingles from kissing Peter as I do from standing close to Jeremy Dragon or pretending that Benjamin Moore is my boyfriend, but kissing him felt warm and friendly.

Peter left as soon as he spotted his mother's car. I stood alone for a minute, thinking about everything that had happened to me tonight.

"Oh, there you are," Alison said. "I had the best time! Eric kissed me goodnight."

"Peter kissed me, too."

"Eric kissed me twice."

"Same here."

"Do you think they planned it?" Alison asked.

"Did he tell you to look up at Orion?"

"Yes," she said.

"Then they planned it."

"So . . . who cares?" we said at the same time. And then we laughed.

Mom couldn't believe I got my period. She was more excited than I was. "Come on, Mom . . ." I said, "it happens to every girl sooner or later."

"I know," she said, sitting on my bed after the dance, "but it's very special when it happens to your own daughter. I'm so proud of you, Steph!"

"Just because I got my period?"

"No . . . just because." She was getting kind of teary and had to stop to blow her nose. "I just wish you and Rachel would make up. Nell stopped by tonight while you were at the dance. She left a package for you. I'll go get it."

Mom came back to my room with a box wrapped in silver paper, tied with a purple ribbon. I opened the card. *With love to the birthday girl, from all the Robinsons*, it said in Mrs. Robinson's handwriting. Inside the box was a long, white Victorian nightgown, the kind the girl in *The Nutcracker* wears. I've always wanted one. I held it up for Mom to see.

"It's beautiful," she said. "Why don't you phone and thank them."

"I'll write a note instead," I said.

I called Dad the next morning to thank him for my birthday necklace. But I forgot about the time difference and I woke him. "Should I call back later?" I asked.

"No . . . that's okay." He sounded groggy. I hoped Iris wasn't there. "What time is it, anyway?"

"It's almost ten here so I guess it's almost seven there."

He yawned. "I wanted to get up early today."

"I called to thank you for the necklace. It's beautiful. I love amethyst."

"I'm glad. How was the dance?"

"It was great!" I thought about telling him I got my period but decided against it. I didn't want him blabbing it to Iris. It was none of her business. "By the way . . . you owe me five dollars."

"I do?"

"Yes . . . you lost your bet."

"What bet?"

"That Rachel and I would be best friends again by my birthday."

At eleven, Alison, Bruce and I took the train to New York. I asked Bruce to take Rachel's place because it was too late to invite another friend from school. And, in a way, I was glad to take him. Bruce can be very good company. Also, he made a beautiful decoupage box for my birthday. Mom said he'd been working on it secretly for a month.

Mrs. Robinson

The following week there was another snowstorm and school was closed again. I spent the afternoon at Alison's and as I walked home the sun began to set, turning the sky pink and purple. I breathed in the clean, fresh smell of the new snow. It had been a perfect afternoon. I began to hum a song I'd heard on Alison's stereo. As I passed Rachel's house I noticed Mrs. Robinson, trying to shovel her car out of a snowdrift. I should have walked the other way around the pond, I thought. I bent my head and walked faster but Mrs. Robinson saw me anyway.

"Steph . . ." she called.

I looked up as if I was really surprised. "Oh—hi, Mrs. Robinson. I didn't see you."

She came toward me, carrying her snow shovel.

"You need a hand with your car?" I asked.

"No, it's hopeless," she said. "I'll have to wait for the plow." She kind of leaned on her shovel. "Thanks for your note. It was very sweet."

"I really like the nightgown," I told her.

"Rachel said you would."

I wish she hadn't said Rachel's name. Every time I hear it I get a pain in my stomach.

"Stephanie . . ." Mrs. Robinson began, and I knew from the serious tone of her voice I didn't want to hear what was coming. "What happened between you and Rachel?"

"You'll have to ask her," I said.

"I have . . . but she won't tell me."

I didn't know what to say so I just stood there, wishing Mrs. Robinson hadn't seen me.

"Surely you two can talk it over and make peace," Mrs. Robinson said. "I know Rachel wants to be your friend. I know how important you are to her."

I looked away, to the Robinsons' house. I thought I saw Rachel, watching us from her bedroom window.

"She's terribly hurt, Steph. You know how sensitive she is. You know how much she needs you."

"She needs me?" I said. Imagine Rachel needing anyone!

"Yes," Mrs. Robinson said, "she needs you very much. She depends on you."

"Did she tell you that?" I asked.

"She doesn't have to tell me. I can see it. Isn't there anything I can do to help the two of you get back together?"

I shook my head.

"Your parents' separation must be very hard on you and I don't mean to make it worse," Mrs. Robinson said.

I wanted to tell her to shut up, that she had no business discussing my parents' separation but she went right on talking. "Taking your anger out on Rachel isn't fair, Steph."

"That's what you think I'm doing?"

"Am I wrong?" Mrs. Robinson asked.

"Yes, you're wrong!" I said, choking up.

"Then I'm sorry." She tried to put her arm around me but I pulled away and began to run. As I got closer to my house I tripped and landed in a snowdrift, soaking my jeans.

"Can you believe Mrs. Robinson said that to me?" I asked Mom that night. "Can you believe she thinks I'm taking out my anger on Rachel? Have you ever heard such a stupid thing?"

"Maybe she's right," Mom said. "Maybe that is what's happening."

"Mom!"

"Hasn't this nonsense with Rachel gone on long enough? Why don't you apologize, Steph?"

"Me, apologize! For what? I wish you'd stop trying to get us back together!" I shouted. "This is *our* problem, not yours!" I ran upstairs and slammed my bedroom door. My perfect afternoon had been ruined!

Dad called a few days later. "I thought you'd want to know," he said, "as of May first I'm coming back to the New York office."

"What?" I asked, switching the phone from one ear to the other. "What did you say?"

"I'll be working out of the New York office beginning the first of May," Dad said, slowly, as if we didn't speak the same language.

"Is Iris coming with you?"

"Iris and I aren't seeing each other anymore."

This was news to me! "Since before or after my birthday?"

"Before," Dad said. "But look, Steph . . . I don't want you to blame yourself."

Blame myself? I thought.

"I know that kids always blame themselves for these things," Dad said.

They do?

"It wasn't your fault," Dad continued. "Iris

and I finally sat down and talked it over and we realized we have different priorities."

"So you broke up?"

"Please try not to feel guilty."

Feel guilty?

"There was a lot more to our decision than what happened at Christmas."

Oh . . . Christmas. So that's why he thought I'd feel guilty. My head was filled with questions. "Where will you live?" I asked. What I really meant was, *Will you and Mom get back together? Will you come home?* But it was too hard to come right out and say what was on my mind.

"I'll probably take an apartment in the city," Dad said, "at least in the beginning."

What did that mean? "So you'll be living in New York starting May first?"

"Yes," he said. "Life out here isn't what I expected. And I miss you and Bruce very much. Once I'm in New York we'll be able to see each other every week."

Every week? Did that mean he would come up here or Bruce and I would go to the city? My stomach started growling but I didn't feel hungry.

When I hung up I went to see Mom. "Did you know Dad's coming back to the New York office?"

Mom was at her computer. "Yes," she said, quietly.

"And his fling with Iris is over, too."

"Yes," she said again.

"So what does it mean?" I asked.

"We don't know yet, Steph. We've still got a lot of thinking to do."

"But you might get back together . . . right?"

"Don't get your hopes up."

"But it's a possibility, isn't it?"

"I suppose it's a possibility . . . but it's not likely."

"I hate not knowing what's going to happen!" I shouted. "I'd almost rather know you're getting a divorce. I want it to be settled one way or the other so I can get used to the idea, so I can stop thinking about it."

"I'm not going to lie to you, Steph," Mom said. "We just don't know . . ."

"You're supposed to be grown-ups," I shouted at her, "so why can't you make up your minds?" I ran to my room and slammed the door.

This time Mom followed me. "I'm getting tired of your moody outbursts!" she shouted. "Other people live here too, you know. And it's time you showed some concern for their feelings."

"I show a lot of concern for Bruce's feelings!" I shouted back at her.

Killer Flu

In March everyone got the flu. Everyone but Alison and me. Rachel had it. Dana had it. Miri Levine and Peter Klaff have it and I think Eric Macaulay is coming down with it because he coughed all day today and fell asleep in homeroom, with his head on his desk. Mrs. Remo says if we develop symptoms we should definitely not come to school. I heard her tell Mr. Diamond, "They're dropping like flies in my homeroom."

I called Peter to see how he was feeling.

"This flu is a killer," he said. "I cough half the night."

"Can't your mother give you something?"

"She's working on it."

"When are you coming back to school?"

"Not until I'm better, which at this rate means next fall."

"Well, cheer up," I told him. "You're not missing that much. Half the class is absent."

"Yeah . . . Mom says it's an epidemic."

"Probably I'll be next," I said.

"Then I'll call you."

"Deal," I said. The thing I like best about Peter is he's not just a boy, he's a friend.

When Alison called a few nights later, in tears, I figured it was to tell me that she had the flu, too. But instead she said, "This is an emergency." Her voice quivered. "I've got to see you right away."

"You want me to come over?" I asked. Never mind that it was close to nine on a school night and outside it was windy and raining. If Alison needed me I would go. That's what friends are for.

"I'll come to your house," Alison said.

"Did somebody die?" I asked, thinking of Sadie Wishnik.

"No . . ." Alison said, "nobody died."

"That's a relief."

Alison came to the kitchen door carrying her overnight bag in one hand and Maizie tucked under her other arm. This was the first time Alison had brought Maizie to our house. I wondered why she'd picked a rainy night for Maizie's first visit. And how come she was carrying an overnight bag.

Maizie shook herself off, then sniffed around the kitchen.

Alison took off her wet slicker and hung it over the back of a kitchen chair. Her eyes were red and puffy.

"What's wrong?" I said.

"Where's your mother?"

"In her room. Why?"

"Where's Bruce?"

"He's upstairs too. What's going on?"

"What I have to say I have to say in private."

"Okay . . . fine."

"Can we get to your room without anyone seeing us?"

"We can try," I said.

Alison grabbed Maizie and held her jaws together so she couldn't bark. We crept up the stairs slowly and ducked into my room. Then Maizie leaped out of Alison's arms and hid under the dresser. Alison sat on the edge of my bed, her hands clasped tightly in front of her. "My mother is pregnant," she announced.

"No!"

"And they don't know how it happened."

"You mean it didn't happen in the usual way?"

"I mean, she's forty years old and she's never been able to get pregnant and now, all of a sudden, she is."

"That's amazing!" I said.

"It's more than amazing."

"What's she going to do?"

"She's going to have it. She and Leon think it's the greatest news they've ever heard. It doesn't bother them that when the kid is my age Mom will be fifty-three and Leon will be sixty-five."

I tried to picture Gena Farrell pregnant, but I couldn't. I couldn't picture her old either.

"What about the series?" I asked.

"How can you think of a TV series at a time like this?"

"I don't know. It just popped into my head." I like Gena's new TV series. It's funny but not silly. I watch it every Tuesday night. Maybe Leon could give Franny—that's the name of the character Gena plays—a baby on the show. That would be very interesting.

Alison was crying again. "Mom says she didn't tell me until tonight because they just got the results of the amniocentesis . . ."

"What's amniocentesis?" I asked.

"Some test they do on older women to make sure the baby is okay. They even know what sex it is."

"What?"

"It's a . . ." She shook her head. I sat beside her and put my arm around her shoulder. "It's a boy," she finally managed to say.

"So you'll have a younger brother, same as me."

"You don't get it, do you?" she cried. "This isn't anything like you and Bruce."

"Because you'll be thirteen years older?"

"No . . . because it will be *their* baby. Their *own* baby. Not some baby Gena adopted because she couldn't get pregnant. This baby will look like them."

"I hope it looks like Gena," I said. "Not that there's anything wrong with the way Leon looks . . . but Gena's a lot . . ." I stopped when I realized that wasn't what Alison meant. She meant this baby won't be Vietnamese.

"They won't need me anymore."

"Come on, Alison! I never saw a kid as loved as you."

"Until now! But who knows what's going to happen in July?"

I wanted to tell her about Dad and how he was coming back to the New York office on May first. I wanted to tell her that I don't know what's going to happen either. But it didn't feel like the right time to bring up my family problems.

"I'm going to France tomorrow," Alison said. "I'm going to find my biological mother."

"How?"

"There are ways."

"I think you're making a big mistake," I said.

We both heard the doorbell ring. Alison rushed to the window and looked out. "It's them," she whispered. "I'll hide in the closet."

"Alison, I wish you'd . . ."

"Shush . . ."

She was in the closet, with Maizie, when Mom opened my door. "Is Alison here?"

You could tell Alison was trying to keep Maizie from barking by the muffled sounds coming from the closet.

"Your parents are downstairs waiting, Alison," Mom said, as if nothing unusual was going on.

As soon as Mom was gone Alison opened the closet door and came out with Maizie in her arms. "I guess I'll go home now," she said. Her voice sounded hoarse. "I guess I'll wait until tomorrow to decide what to do."

"You look kind of funny," I told her.

"I feel kind of funny," she said. And then she just keeled over.

"Mom!" I called, "Come quick . . ."

Mom, Gena and Leon raced up the stairs. "Pumpkin!" Leon said. He lifted Alison onto my bed.

Gena felt her forehead. "She's burning up!"

"It's probably the flu," I told them. "The kids at school are dropping like flies."

"What's going on?" Bruce asked, standing in my doorway.

Alison opened her eyes. "My dog can talk," she said.

"What was that all about?" Mom asked, after Leon and Gena took Alison home.

"Family problems," I said.

"I hope it's nothing serious." Mom turned out the lamps in the living room.

"Gena's pregnant but no one's supposed to know. And Alison thinks once they have their own baby they won't love her anymore."

"Of course they will," Mom said, as we went upstairs.

"That's what I told her," I said. "I never saw a kid as loved as Alison."

"What about you and Bruce?" Mom followed me into my room.

I shrugged.

"You don't think we love you as much as they love Alison?"

"I don't know."

"Stephanie . . . of course we do!"

"Maybe."

"Just because we have disagreements from time to time doesn't mean we don't love each other," Mom said.

"I guess."

"I was tough on you that night, wasn't I?" Mom asked.

"What night?"

"That night I told you to think of other people's feelings."

"Oh . . . *that* night."

"From now on," Mom said, "if we have something to say we should say it. It's not good to hold in feelings . . . anger and resentment build up that way."

"Did you know I went to see the counselor at school?" I asked.

"No."

"Only one time . . . she wanted to help me with my problems but I told her I didn't have any. Rachel says I don't face reality."

"Is that what your fight was about?"

"That's part of it. Do you think I face reality?"

"I think you handle it in your own way. I don't see you hiding from the facts. I don't see you withdrawing."

"Sometimes I pretend everything's okay when it's not."

"So do I," Mom said. "That's how I make it through the day."

"We're a lot alike, aren't we?" I asked. "We're both optimists."

Mom hugged me. "We sure are."

Spring

It's been seven weeks since Rachel and I stopped speaking. At the bus stop in the morning she doesn't even look at me. She and Dana stand together, talking and laughing. Sometimes they talk so softly I can't hear what they're saying. I wish Alison would hurry and get better. I hate standing at the bus stop by myself. I've never felt so left out in my life. It's as if I'm invisible, as if I don't exist. Well, fine. Because as far as I'm concerned, Rachel Robinson doesn't exist either. Besides, I have more important things on my mind, such as what happens on May first when Dad starts working in New York?

I took Alison's homework assignments to her but the first three days she was too sick to do anything. Leon let me peek into her room. Seeing her like that, so small and pale with her eyes closed, frightened me. I guess Leon could tell because he said, "It looks worse than it is. She's going to be fine."

Later that week when I got to her house, Alison was sitting up in bed, sipping grape juice. "I feel a little better," she said, coughing.

"I can tell."

She held up a book—*What to Name the Baby*. "I'm trying to find a good name for him. You'd be amazed at how many names there are. So far Mom likes Alexander, Leon likes Edward and Sadie Wishnik likes Nelson . . ."

"Nelson?" I said.

"I know," Alison said, "it's terrible." She laughed a little but that made her start coughing again. "You better not come too close."

"I'm not afraid of catching it," I said. Actually, the idea of a week in bed, with Mrs. Greco making me cinnamon toast and camomile tea, didn't sound all that bad.

"It's good I didn't go to Paris after all," Alison said. "I'd have been stuck there with the flu."

"Yeah . . . and without Leon to take care of you."

"I've decided to wait and see what happens. Maybe it won't be that bad. And if it is, I can always leave after the baby is born."

"Right," I said. Maizie came in and jumped up on Alison's chair. "Guess what?" I asked, running my fingers along Maizie's back. "My father's coming back to work in New York."

"When?" Alison asked.

"May first."

"What's going to happen?"

"I wish I knew!"

"Well, at least you'll be able to see him whenever you want."

I nodded.

"Leon says you can feel spring in the air today," Alison said, lying back against her pillows. "I wish I could go outside. I hate staying in bed."

"You'll be better soon," I told her. "Did you hear that Dana and Jeremy are going to the ninth grade prom together?"

"No. . . ."

"I heard Dana telling Rachel at the bus stop this morning."

"Is she wearing his bracelet again?"

"No, they decided it was the bracelet that was the problem."

"That doesn't make sense. Are you sure you heard right?"

"Yes. I listen to everything they have to say. Besides, she's humming under her breath again."

"The way she did when they first started going out?"

"Yes . . . the same way, only louder."

Alison yawned. "I think I'll take a nap now."

"Okay . . . see you tomorrow."

Jeremy Dragon is back to wearing his chartreuse jacket. He bumped into me in the hallway at school. I saw him coming but he didn't see me and we collided. I suppose I could have stepped aside but I didn't. He knocked my books out of my arms.

"Hey, Macbeth!" he said. "Long time, no see."

"I'm still on your bus."

"Well . . . long time, no notice."

I could smell his breath and his hair and a woodsy scent coming from his shirt as he crouched next to me, helping to gather my books. I got tingles everywhere. Dana is so lucky!

I had trouble concentrating for the rest of the day. I was still thinking about him that afternoon when I got off the bus. Rachel and I were the only ones to get off at Palfrey's Pond. I walked behind her, humming to myself. The crocuses were beginning to bloom. I love the way they work themselves out of the ground. One day there's nothing there and the next, little blue, yellow and white flowers.

Rachel walked with her books under one arm. Her hair bounced up and down, instead of side to side, like Alison's. I thought about catching up with her and saying, *What's new?* But I didn't know how she'd react.

I followed Rachel all the way to her house without thinking. When we got there she turned around and faced me. For a minute I thought she was going to tell me to get lost and I started thinking of what I'd say if she did. But instead her face softened. "I'll walk you home . . ." she said, as if she were asking my permission.

I nodded.

This time we walked next to each other but we didn't speak. When we got to my house I said, "I'll walk *you* home."

Then she nodded. Halfway there I said, "You want to talk about it?"

"Do you?" she asked.

"I don't even remember how it started."

"You told Amber that Max liked me."

"Oh, right . . . I never did get what was so bad about that."

"It was just the last straw," Rachel said. "I was *so* mad at you by then."

"For what?"

"Because you didn't like me anymore."

"No," I said, "you were the one who didn't like me!"

"I didn't like *you* because you didn't like *me*!"

Rachel said. "You were best friends with Alison and everyone knew it."

"But you had Stacey Green," I told her. "You didn't want to be my best friend anymore."

"That's because *you* didn't want to be *mine*!" Rachel shifted her books from one arm to the other. "I felt it was some kind of competition . . . me against Alison . . . and I was always losing."

"You acted like you were too grown-up to hang around with us."

"I was trying to get back at you for leaving me out."

"We never left you out. It was always the three of us."

"I *felt* left out. I *felt* you weren't my best friend anymore."

"You can have more than one best friend at a time," I said.

"No, you can't."

"Why not?"

"Because best means *best*."

I thought about that. "What about close?" I asked. "You can have more than one *close* friend at a time, can't you?"

Rachel thought that over. "I guess so."

"And close is as good as best!"

"I don't necessarily agree," Rachel said.

"But it's better to be friends than not to be friends . . . you agree with that . . . right?"

"Well, yes," Rachel said, "if you're talking about true friends."

"Yes, I'm talking about true friends."

"Then it's definitely better to be than not to be." Rachel stuck her tongue into her cheek. "I think that's a line from Shakespeare," she said.

"I wouldn't know," I told her.

"I hear you got your period," Rachel said.

"Yeah, I did. But only one time, so far."

"And you've lost weight, too."

"I'm not as hungry as I used to be. Mom says my hormones are adjusting."

"Do you still have that stupid poster over your bed?"

"You mean Benjamin Moore?"

Rachel laughed. "I always liked that poster."

"Are you still throwing around big words?"

"You mean literally or figuratively?"

"Ha ha," I said. I had no idea what those words meant.

When we got to Rachel's house we stopped. "I hear you broke up with Max."

"He was a complete airhead," Rachel said. "I hear you're going with Peter Klaff."

"We're not exactly going together. We're friends, is more like it."

Rachel put her books down on the front steps and fished her key out of her bag.

"My father's coming back to work in New York," I said.

"I know. My mother ran into your Aunt Denise."

"Is that how you found out about my parents in the first place?"

"Yes." Rachel unlocked her front door but didn't go inside. "Look . . . I shouldn't have said those things about your parents. I'm sorry. I guess I was trying to hurt you the way you hurt me."

"I never tried to hurt you."

"But you did."

"Then I'm sorry, too," I told her.

"So . . . you want to come to my concert on the fifteenth? I've got a solo."

"Sure."

"You don't *have* to come," Rachel said. "I just want you to know you're invited. And you can bring Alison."

"I don't *have* to bring her."

"No, I want you to. I like Alison."

"Okay, I'll ask her. She's got the flu. I'm on my way to her house now."

"Tell her I hope she feels better."

"I will."

"See you tomorrow," Rachel said.

"Yeah . . . see you tomorrow."

I saw a bee buzzing around the forsythia bush in front of Alison's house. I'll have to start wearing my bee-sting necklace, I thought. I wonder what Alison will say when I tell her Rachel and I are speaking again, that maybe we are even friends. Probably she'll be glad. I broke off a sprig of forsythia and rang Alison's bell.

Here's to You, Rachel Robinson

To Amanda

1

Trouble in our family is spelled with a capital *C* and has been as long as I can remember. The *C* stands for Charles. He's my older brother, two years and four months older to be exact. Ever since the phone call about him last night, I've felt incredibly tense. And now, at this very minute, my parents are driving up to Vermont, to Charles's boarding school, to find out if he's actually been kicked out or if he's just been suspended again.

I tried to take a deep breath. I read an article about relieving tensions in *Psychology Today*. You take a deep breath, then count to ten as you slowly release it. But as I inhaled, I caught the scent of the fresh lilacs on Ms. Lefferts's desk and I started to cough. Ms. Lefferts, my seventh-grade English teacher, looked over at me. She was discussing the three most important elements in making a biography come alive for the reader. When I coughed again, she crossed the room and opened two windows from the bottom, letting in the spring breeze.

The class was restless, shifting around in their seats, counting the hours till school let out so they could enjoy the first really warm day of the year. But the clock on the wall read 10:17. The day was just beginning. And the date on the chalkboard said FRIDAY, MAY 8. Still seven weeks of school to go.

I forced my mind back to class.

"So now that we've come to the end of our unit on biographies," Ms. Lefferts was saying, "I have an assignment for you." She walked back to her desk and stood there, looking at us, a half smile on her face. She knows exactly how to get our attention. She makes good use of pregnant pauses. I once used that expression in class and have been paying for it ever since. Now I would know better. Now I would say *dramatic* pauses.

"I want you to write a biography of your own lives," Ms. Lefferts continued. "Not an *autobiography*, but a biography. Who can explain the difference?" She took a hair clip out of her desk drawer and held it between her teeth while she gathered her streaked blond hair into a ponytail. She looked around the room as she fastened it, waiting for someone to respond to her question.

Max Wilson raised his hand.

"Yes, Max?" Ms. Lefferts said.

"An autobiography is about the life of a car," Max said.

The class cracked up. Ms. Lefferts didn't.

"Get it?" Max asked. "Auto . . . biography."

"Yes, Max . . . I get it," Ms. Lefferts said. Then she sighed deeply.

I cannot believe that just a few months ago I liked Max Wilson. I actually spent the entire seventh-grade dance with my head nestled on his shoulder. We even kissed in the parking lot while we were waiting for our rides home. What a revolting thought! Now I understand that I never really liked Max, the person. It's just that he is the only boy in seventh grade who's taller than me.

"Rachel . . ." Ms. Lefferts said.

I snapped to attention. Ms. Lefferts was calling on me even though I hadn't raised my hand. I hate when teachers do that. But I said, "The difference between a biography and an autobiography is that in an autobiography the writer is writing about his or her own life. In a biography the writer is writing about the life of someone else."

"Exactly," Ms. Lefferts said. "Thank you, Rachel." Then she went on to explain that she wants us to write a short biography of our own lives, as if we don't know anything about ourselves until we go to the library to do research. "And try to hold it to five pages, please."

Ms. Lefferts never says a paper *has* to be at least five pages. She uses reverse psychology on us. And it always works.

I began to think about my biography right away. Luckily my French teacher was absent, and the substitute told us since she doesn't know one word of French, we could use the period as a study hour. I opened my notebook and started writing, ignoring the kids who were using the period to torture the substitute.

RACHEL LOWILLA ROBINSON
A Biography
Part One — The Unexpected Visitor

Rachel Lowilla Robinson was born tall. The average infant measures nineteen inches at birth but Rachel measured twenty-three. She was the third child born to Nell and Victor Robinson, following Jessica, who was four, and Charles, who was twenty-eight months. The Robinsons had planned on only two children, so Rachel was, as they sometimes put it, the unexpected visitor.

From her mother, Rachel inherited her height and her curly auburn hair. From her father, dark eyes and a love of music. Although her mother was from Boston and her father from Brooklyn, the Robinsons settled in Connecticut to raise their family, in an area of cluster housing called Palfrey's Pond, located just one hour from New York City by train.

Nell Robinson liked to say Rachel was mature from the day she was born. "She was born thirty-five," Mrs. Robinson joked with her friends. But obviously that wasn't true. Rachel was born a baby, like everyone else. She just did things a little earlier. For example, at eight months Rachel was walking. At eighteen months she was speaking in three-word sentences. She could read at three and at four she could pick out tunes on the piano. Her favorite was the theme from "Sesame Street," which Jessica and Charles watched on TV every day. Rachel's first memory was of Charles biting her on the leg, right above her knee. She was barely two at the time.

By first grade it occurred to Rachel that she was different. As her classmates were learning to read, she was finishing the Beverly Cleary books and starting the *Little House* set. As they were learning to add and subtract simple numbers, she enjoyed adding up long columns of figures, especially the register tape from the supermarket. This difference did not make her happy.

I was careful, in Part One, not to tell too much. I told just enough to show Ms. Lefferts I've given serious thought to this assignment. And even though I tried to use interesting details, little-known facts and humorous anecdotes—the three most important elements in making a biography come alive for the reader—I was not about to share the private details of my family life. I was not about to discuss Charles.

The bell rang before I had the chance to start Part Two. I didn't notice until then that I hadn't had any trouble breathing while I was writing. I guess *Psychology Today* is right when they tell you to get your mind off whatever is making you feel tense and onto something else. I picked up my books and went to the cafeteria to meet Stephanie and Alison for lunch.

"What's wrong?" Steph asked, the second I sat down. She was already halfway through a bologna sandwich.

"What do you mean?" I said.

"You're doing that *thing* with your mouth."

"I am?" Last year the dentist made me a kind of retainer to wear at night, to keep me from clenching my jaw, but I left it at Steph's in January and haven't seen it since. My parents still don't know I lost it.

"You get an A *minus* or something?"

"No," I told her.

"Then what?"

"Charles."

"Again?"

I nodded and began to peel a hard-boiled egg. All three of us bring our lunch. We're convinced we'll live longer that way.

"Why doesn't Charles ever come home?" Alison asked, chewing on a carrot stick. She's small and delicate and eats so slowly she hardly ever has time to finish her lunch. But that doesn't bother her. Hardly anything does. She's probably never had trouble breathing in her entire life. She's probably never even felt tense. We are total opposites, so it's amazing that we're friends. "I mean, doesn't he *want* to?" she continued.

"I guess not." I salted my egg, then bit into it.

"I don't get it," Alison said. She's never met Charles, since he left for Vermont last August and she didn't move here from L.A. until Labor Day. Actually Steph met Alison first and they hit it off right away. She didn't even tell me Alison's adopted or that her birth mother's Vietnamese until school started. I used to worry that Steph, who's been my best friend since second grade, would forget about me. Actually, I still do. But at the moment it seems to be working out okay, even though I know she and Alison prefer each other's company to mine.

"There's nothing to get," I told her. "Except that he's impossible! Now, could we please change the subject?"

"Impossible how?" Alison asked, ignoring my request.

"Rude and obnoxious."

Alison looked over at Stephanie to see if she agreed. Stephanie nodded. "He's definitely rude." Steph took a mirror out of her backpack and set it on the table. She opened her mouth wide to make sure food wasn't caught in her braces. Stephanie is the least self-conscious person I know.

"How'd he get that way?" Alison asked.

I was really getting annoyed and Alison could tell. She offered me her bag of potato chips. "How does anybody get that way?" I said, reaching in and grabbing a handful.

When I got home from school, my cousin Tarren was at the house. She's twenty-two and has a ten-month-old baby, Roddy. She could tell I was surprised to see her. "Nell and Victor had to go to Vermont," she said, using my parents' first names. "It has something to do with Charles," she added, as if I didn't know.

"Jess and I could have managed on our own," I told her, irritated that Mom had asked her to come over without discussing it with me.

Tarren bent down to tie her running shoes. She's tall, like all the women in our family, but her hair is black and her eyes blue. Jessica and I were brides-maids at her wedding two years ago. Now she's divorced. She and Bill, the guy she married, didn't get along even though they went together all through high school and two years of college. Tarren says Bill couldn't accept adult responsibilities, like being a father. He moved out west after the divorce and spends all his time hang gliding. His picture was on the cover of *Hang Glider* magazine a few months ago. He looked like some sort of strange prehistoric bird.

"Nell asked me to spend the night," Tarren said, "since tonight is Jessica's junior prom and all. . . ."

I had totally forgotten about Jessica's prom. I'd be devastated if it were my junior prom and Mom and Dad were away because of Charles.

"I promised we'd take lots of pictures," Tarren said. "I brought my new camera." She grabbed it off the kitchen counter. "It's a PHD. The guy at the store claims you can't take a bad picture with it." She pointed it at me. "You know what PHD stands for?" she asked. *"Press Here, Dummy!"* She laughed as she pressed but I jumped out of the way.

"Rachel! That was my last shot."

"Sorry."

"I guess it doesn't matter. Nell said you've got two rolls of film in the fridge."

I couldn't believe that in the midst of a family crisis Mom would remember we had film in the refrigerator. I guess Tarren could tell what I was thinking because she said, "Nell is the most amazing woman!"

I've heard that expression more times than I can count. It's true Mom is a successful trial lawyer, but

I don't see what's so amazing about that. I expect to do just as much with my life.

"Between you and me," Tarren continued, "I think it's grossly unfair that Nell has to spend so much of her time worrying about your brother. A lot of kids would jump at the chance to change places with him. He doesn't appreciate what he has. That's his problem!"

I didn't feel like talking about Charles, so I told Tarren I had homework and went up to my room.

Later the two of us had supper in the kitchen while Jessica soaked in a bubble bath upstairs. Tarren likes to hear about school since she's studying to be a teacher. So I told her about the biography and what Max Wilson had said in class. She laughed and laughed. She'll probably be a good teacher. She wants to teach fourth grade, which should be just right for her. We ate standing at the counter—tuna right from the can, lettuce leaves pulled off the head and, for dessert, frozen Milky Ways left over from Halloween. We're lucky we didn't break our teeth on them.

"Is this how you eat every night?" I asked, thinking of the way we sit down to dinner, the table set with place mats and pretty dishes.

"Rachel," Tarren said, "when you have a ten-month-old to worry about, *plus* papers and exams, you just don't have time to think about meals. If my mom doesn't fix supper, I'm happy grazing. When Roddy's older, it'll be different. I'll have a teaching job and my own place and . . ." Her voice drifted off for a minute. "But not everyone can be a wonder woman like your mother."

"Dad helps. He does all the grocery shopping."

"Well, I'm a single parent. There won't be anyone around to help me."

"Maybe you'll get married again," I suggested, causing Tarren to choke on her Natural Lime Spritzer, which she was swigging straight out of the bottle.

"Pul-eeese . . ." she said, wiping her mouth with the back of her hand. She sounded exactly like one of my friends.

We could hear Jessica rustling in her magenta taffeta prom dress before we actually saw her. She let me try it on last week. It fit perfectly. Jess and I could be doubles except she has a major case of acne. She uses a heavy medicated makeup that hides some of it on good days. On bad days nothing can hide it.

As Jess came down the stairs, Tarren snapped away. I was surprised when Jess posed for the camera. Usually she refuses to have her picture taken. But tonight she put her arms around me, as if I were her date, and twirled me across the room until we were both laughing our heads off and so dizzy we fell back onto the sofa.

"You two are so great!" Tarren said. "You remind me

of me and my friends when we were your age." She turned serious. "Enjoy it now," she told us, "because life isn't always all you thought it'd be." She paused for a minute, then added, "I speak from experience."

Neither of us knew how to respond. Finally Jessica cleared her throat and said, "Tarren . . . didn't you say you have to run over to the library?"

"Well . . . yes," Tarren answered, "but only for a little while."

"Why don't you go now?" Jess suggested. "The library closes at nine."

I found it strange that Jessica was suddenly so anxious for Tarren to go to the library.

"I've just got to pick up some books," Tarren explained to me. "We're studying the gifted and talented child this month."

I felt my face turn hot.

"I won't be long," she said.

As soon as she was gone, Jessica let out a sigh and raced upstairs. Ten minutes later she returned transformed in Mom's slinky black dress, satin heels and dangling earrings. She'd put on dark, wine-colored lipstick and had pinned her hair back on one side, letting the rest fall over her face.

I almost passed out. "Jessica . . ."

She held up her hand. "Don't say it, Rachel. We'll have pictures of me in pink."

"But Mom will—" I began again.

"Mom's not here, is she? And if someone at school tells Dad, it will be too late. The prom will be over."

Dad teaches history at the high school and coaches the track team. Someone will definitely tell him about this. Someone will say, "That was some outfit your daughter wore to the prom, Victor!"

A car horn tooted. Jess took a quick look out the window. "My chariot," she said.

I followed as she ran down the front walk. "And not a word about this to anyone," she called over her shoulder, tripping on Mom's heels. "Understand?"

Her friends Richie, Ed, Marcy and Kristen whooped and whistled when they saw her. Jess says she has the best friends ever. She says she can tell them anything. But I think they were surprised tonight.

"Get the camera, Rachel," Jess called. I ran inside for Tarren's PHD and snapped one group photo before they all piled back into the car.

I tried to imagine the three of us—Stephanie, Alison and me—going to our junior prom four years from now. Will we go in a group like Jess and her friends, or with individual dates? Jess says it's better to go in a group. There are fewer disappointments that way. I don't know. I think it would be more romantic to go with someone you really like. But if it came down to Max Wilson or my friends, I would definitely choose my friends.

As they pulled out, I called, "Drive carefully!"

"We always do," Jess called back, laughing.

I watched them drive away. Then I went back into the house, wondering what Mom will say if she finds out Jess wore her black dress. *She'll probably blame herself,* I thought. *She'll probably say Jess is* acting out.

3

cting out is exactly the expression Dr. Sparks used to describe Charles's behavior. He's the psychologist who evaluated him last year, the one who suggested he go away to school.

I admit it was a great relief when Charles left for Vermont last August—even though boarding school is a luxury we can't really afford, not with three kids who will soon be ready for college. I know my parents sometimes feel guilty about the decision to send him away to school. But I don't. Now I can invite my friends over without worrying.

I never told anyone I'd read Dr. Sparks's report. I'd found it by chance on the dining room table, mixed in with Mom's legal pads and reference books, while I was searching for a letter from music camp. It said Charles was *acting out* as a way of getting the attention he craved. Well, I could have told my parents that for free!

Thinking about Charles made me feel weak, so I took the last piece of watermelon out of the refrigerator and sat at the kitchen table slurping it up while I waited for Tarren to return from the library. When I finished, I collected the seeds and stood halfway across the kitchen. Then, one by one, I tried spitting them into the sink. Stephanie had a party on the last day of school last year and spitting watermelon seeds from a distance was one of the games we played. I was hopeless, missing the target every time. Even though I think it's incredibly stupid, I've been practicing in secret ever since. Tonight I hit my target eight out of eleven times.

The watermelon reminded me of dinner last night. We'd sat down to eat early, as soon as Mom had walked in, because Jess was in a hurry to get back to school. She and Ed were on the decorating committee for the prom. They were transforming the gym into some kind of futuristic fantasy with a hundred silver balloons and yards and yards of tinsel.

We'd been talking about the prom all through dinner, but just as we were finishing the watermelon Mom said, "Guess who's on the governor's short list for Superior Court?"

I had no idea what she was talking about, but Dad pushed back his chair, practically leaped across the table and lifted Mom out of her seat. "I've always wanted to make it with a judge," he said.

They kissed, then Mom told him, "You'll have to wait till the end of the month to find out."

"Find out what?" I asked.

"I've been nominated for a judgeship," Mom said.

"A judge?" Jessica asked. "You're going to be a judge?"

"Maybe," Mom said.

"What would that mean?" I asked. "Would you have to quit your job at the firm?"

"Yes," Mom said. "Being a judge is a full-time job."

"I can't imagine you as a judge," Jess said.

"I can," I told her. "Mom would make an excellent judge."

"I didn't say she wouldn't," Jess said.

"Would you get murder cases?" I asked Mom.

"That would depend on which court I'm assigned to," she said. "If it's criminal court, I could get murder cases. If it's domestic court, I'd get divorces and child custody cases, and if it's civil court . . ." She paused. "But it's too soon to think about the details. First we have to see if I'm actually appointed."

My mind was racing. What if Mom gets criminal court and sends a murderer to jail and he escapes and finds out where we live and comes after her. . . . I'd read about a case like that in the paper. Maybe we'll have bodyguards to protect us like the President. Not that I want to live with bodyguards. And I certainly don't want to be escorted to school every day. I don't think that would go over very well with my friends. Probably they won't want to come to my house if that happens. Probably their parents won't even let them!

Jessica brought me back from my *what ifs* when she jumped up from the table. "I'm going to be late! Be home around ten," she called as the screen door slammed.

Mom flinched. She hates it when the door slams.

It was my night to help clean up the kitchen. Mom makes out lists every Sunday night—household jobs, groceries, errands, appointments. Steph is envious of the chalkboard in our kitchen with the dinner menu printed on it every day. She never knows what's for dinner until her mother gets home from work with some kind of takeout. If it were up to Dad and Jess, our household would be chaotic. But Mom says if you're organized, everything in life is easier. I agree. Except maybe dealing with Charles.

I started clearing the plates off the table. When the phone rang, I ran for it, sure it was Stephanie or Alison. I wouldn't tell them anything about Mom being a judge yet. I'd wait until it was definite.

But it wasn't Alison or Steph. It was Timothy Norton, the director of the Dorrance School. I put my hand over the receiver and whispered to Mom and Dad, "It's about Charles."

Dad turned off the water at the sink and dried his hands on his jeans. I held the phone out to him as Mom raced upstairs to pick up the extension in their room. I felt my dinner sloshing around in my stomach. Yet from the tone of Dad's voice, I didn't think it was as serious as last time, when Mr. Norton called to tell us about Charles's accident.

That was last January, right after the holidays. Charles had gone for a joyride on his teacher's Yamaha. It was a wet night and he'd lost control, skidding across the road and crashing into a tree. He'd wound up with cuts and bruises plus a gash in his leg requiring twelve stitches.

Still, they said he was lucky because he hadn't been wearing a helmet and he could have been killed. I am somewhat ashamed to admit this, but at the time I'd let that thought run through my mind. *He could have been killed.* Then I'd pushed it away. I don't want Charles to die. Dying is too final. My parents would blame themselves and never get over it. Besides, he's my brother. I'm supposed to care about him. Even though the teacher didn't press charges, Charles was suspended for a week. But he didn't come home. He went to Aunt Joan's house in New Hampshire, instead.

A minute after Dad hung up the phone, Mom came back into the kitchen. She'd aged ten years in ten minutes. She thinks she's good at hiding her feelings because she doesn't talk about them. But she can't fool me. I can read her thoughts by the changes in her face. The crease in her forehead was deeper, her mouth was stiff and her shoulders hunched.

Dad put an arm around her. She gave him a pained look.

"What?" I asked.

Mom didn't answer.

"What?" I said again, this time to Dad.

"He hasn't handed in his papers and he refuses to take any exams," Dad explained. Then he went back to the sink, turned the water on full blast and began to scour the lasagna pan as if his life depended on it.

"What does that mean?" I asked Mom. "Will he have to do ninth grade a third time?"

"Absolutely not!" Mom said, pulling herself together. She stood tall and erect and looked me straight in the eye. "And he *didn't* repeat ninth grade. The system at Dorrance is different from public school. You know that. It was in Charles's best interest to start over as a freshman."

Mom marched across the kitchen and started loading the dishwasher, with all the dishes facing the same direction. She can't stand how Dad does it, shoving things in any which way.

"He's always been too young for his class, emotionally," Mom continued, building her case as if she were in court. She's full of excuses when it comes to Charles.

321

"And I don't want you to discuss this with anyone, Rachel."

"Mom!" I was annoyed that she thought I needed reminding.

"We should have held him back a year before first grade," Mom said, drumming the counter with her fingertips, "but who knew then?"

"Nell . . ." Dad said. "Rachel doesn't need to worry about this."

They looked at each other for a minute. Then Mom said, "You're right." But she kept drumming the counter. It was amazing how one phone call about Charles could change everything.

"This doesn't mean he's coming home, does it?" I asked. My mouth felt dry, as if I couldn't swallow.

"We won't know until we meet with Mr. Norton at Dorrance," Dad said.

"You'd better call for a substitute," Mom told Dad. "And I'll have to cancel my deposition." She opened a kitchen drawer, pulled out a pad and pencil and began to make a list. Without even looking up, she said, "Let the cats in, would you, Rachel. They're scratching at the screen."

I held the screen door for Burt and Harry, then bolted from the room with them at my heels. I raced up the stairs and locked myself into my room, throwing open all the windows. The night air smelled like summer. I wished it really *were* summer. I wished I could go to music camp tomorrow. Then I wouldn't have to think about Charles or what might happen if he came home.

I took my flute out of its case, sat at my music stand and began to play a Handel sonata. Music takes me someplace else. To a world where I feel safe and happy. Sometimes I make mistakes but I can fix them. Sometimes I don't get exactly the sound I want, but I can find it if I keep trying. With music it's up to me. With music I'm in control.

"Tell me more about Charles," Alison said.

It was Saturday morning and the three of us—Stephanie, Alison and me—were walking along the water's edge at the town beach. It's not an ocean beach. It's on the Sound. In fourth grade we had to memorize the difference between a sound and a bay. It's funny how you remember things like that.

The weather was still balmy but more humid than yesterday, and we wore shorts and T-shirts for the first time since last September. A few people on the beach were in bathing suits, working on an early tan. I hate baking in the sun. My skin gets freckled, my eyes sting and sometimes I get sneezing fits.

I've decided Alison's fascination with my brother has to do with the fact that until now she's been the only child in her family. Actually she's still the only child. Her mother is pregnant but the baby isn't due until July.

"Well, for one thing, Charles has a great sense of humor," Steph told Alison. "That is, when he wants to." She paused for a minute. "And he's extremely cute."

"Really?" Alison asked me. "I didn't know he was cute."

"I refuse to participate in this conversation!" I told them both.

Maizie, Alison's small, furry-faced dog, was digging up a bone buried in the sand. When we first met Alison, she told us her dog could talk and Stephanie believed her. Steph is incredibly gullible. She believes anything you tell her. She even believed her father was away on a business trip when it was painfully obvious to the rest of us her parents had separated.

Alison turned to Steph. "If Charles comes home from boarding school, will he finish ninth grade at Fox?" She acted as if Steph had all the answers. I never should have told them my parents went to Vermont. I never should have told them anything. My mother was right. This is family business. You can't expect anyone else to understand.

"Maybe he'll be in Jeremy Dragon's class," Alison said to Steph. I loved the way they were carrying on this conversation as if I weren't there.

"Oh, that'd be perfect!" Stephanie said, jabbing me in the side. "Right, Rachel?"

"I find that a totally revolting idea!" I said. Jeremy Dragon is our name for the best-looking boy in ninth grade. He wears a chartreuse satin team jacket with a black dragon on the back. I'm the only seventh grader in his math class.

"But it *is* possible," Alison said.

"Anything's possible!" I admitted. My mind was filling with *what ifs.* What if Charles comes home today? What if he *does* have to do ninth grade again, and at *my* junior high? What if he makes friends with Jeremy Dragon and Jeremy Dragon starts hanging out at our house and Charles humiliates me in front of him and my parents won't listen and . . .

"Rachel . . ." Stephanie sang, waving a hand in front of my face. "Where are you?"

I don't know why but as soon as Stephanie said that, I took off. I ran as fast as I could, with Maizie at my heels, barking.

I could hear Alison and Stephanie laughing and shouting, "Rachel . . . what are you doing? Rachel . . . wait! Ra . . . chel!"

There was no way they could catch me. My legs are twice as long as Alison's. And Steph isn't fast enough. Only Maizie could keep up with me. I kept running, from one end of the beach to the other. Finally I collapsed on the sand, totally out of breath, with a stitch in my side.

We went to Alison's house for lunch. Leon, her stepfather, made us grilled cheese and tomato sandwiches.

Alison's mother, Gena Farrell, was at the counter squeezing lemons. Suddenly she put her hands on her belly and said, "Ooh . . . Matthew's playing soccer this morning." Gena is a famous TV actress with her own series. But at home she acts like a regular parent. Alison says her pregnancy is a surprise to everyone since she's forty years old and the doctors told her long ago she'd never be able to have biological children. That's why she adopted Alison.

"Let me feel," Leon said. He put his hands on Gena's belly. "Good going, Matthew. That's a goal!"

They talk about the baby as if he were already born. Gena's had tests to make sure he's okay. That's how they know it's a boy. His full name will be Matthew Farrell Wishnik.

Before we finished lunch there was a rumble of thunder. Maizie whimpered and hid under the table. After lunch, while the rain poured down, the three of us watched a movie. Alison's family has a great collection of tapes. By the time it was over, it was close to four and the rain had stopped. I looked out the window and saw Dad's Explorer parked outside our house.

"I have to go," I said.

"Promise to call right away and tell us what's happening," Alison said.

But I wasn't making any promises.

5

The front door to our house was open. I called hello but no one answered. I ran upstairs, looking for Mom or Dad. Instead I found my worst fears coming true. Charles was in my room, at my desk!

I stood in my doorway, frozen. For just a minute I saw Charles the way Steph does—as a boy with dark hair, dreamy hazel eyes and a scar on his forehead. The scar makes him look interesting, not just handsome. Suddenly Grandpa Robinson's voice popped into my head. "Too bad the boy got all the looks in your family, Victor," he once told Dad. I was incredibly hurt when he said that, even though I was only eight.

Charles began to read aloud from my biography. "Rachel is credited with having discovered the vaccine, now widely used, to prevent hair balls in lions."

"Put that down!" My heart was pounding but I spoke slowly and quietly.

"Hair balls in lions?" Charles asked, acknowledging my presence. He didn't seem concerned that I'd caught him red-handed. "Hair balls in lions?" he repeated, laughing.

"I *said* put that down!" I sounded just like my mother when she turns on her lawyer voice. But that wasn't enough to stop Charles. He kept right on reading from Part Two of my biography, the part I call "Rachel, The Later Years." I'd handwritten it on one of Mom's legal pads early this morning. I'd enjoyed inventing my three brilliant careers—first as a veterinarian doing research on large cats in Africa, then as a musician with the New York Philharmonic, and finally as a great stage actress specializing in Shakespeare. I'd also given myself a husband and two children, all wildly successful.

"Her son, Toledo . . ." Charles paused, looking at me. "You named your son for a town in Ohio?"

"Spain, you idiot!" I tore across the room and reached for my biography. "Toledo, Spain!" I'm taller than Charles, but he's fast and he held the pages high above his head. Every time I grabbed for them, he'd transfer them to his other hand and dance around the room.

I felt so desperate I kicked, catching him on the shin. Then I dug my nails into his arm. I've never had a physical fight in my entire life. But I would have kept it up if he hadn't yelled, "Cut it out, Rachel . . .

or kiss your biography good-bye." He had both hands on my paper now, ready to rip it in half.

I didn't doubt that he'd do it. And there was no other copy. Even though I'd meant to enter it in my computer, I'd been rushing to meet Stephanie and Alison and figured I'd do it later. Tears stung my eyes but I would never cry in front of him. I would never give him that satisfaction!

I backed away and stood at the foot of my bed, my hands grasping the white iron rail. "You mess that up and you're dead!" I told him.

"Then you'll have to rewrite your biography," he said. "At thirteen Rachel Lowilla Robinson murdered her brother, Charles. She spent the rest of her life in jail. All eighty-four years of it."

"No," I said. "It would go more like, Since the judge and jury agreed that her brother provoked her, Rachel was acquitted and lived happily ever after."

"You won't get off that easy," he said. "They'll get you for manslaughter, at the very least."

"I'm a juvenile," I told him. "At the most I'll get probation."

"I wouldn't count on that."

"Really," I said. "Well, let's go and ask Mom, since she's just been nominated as a judge."

I could tell by the expression on his face I'd caught him by surprise. *Good!* He laid my biography on the desk. "Isn't that something!" he said. "Another milestone for our extraordinary family." He flopped in my favorite chair and draped his legs over the arm. "So . . . are you surprised to see me, little sister?"

"I'm never surprised by you," I said, which was a big lie. His moods can switch so fast you never know what to expect, which is the single worst thing about him. "When are you going back to school?" I asked, trying to sound as if I didn't care. "Or were you actually kicked out this time?"

"Expelled, Rachel. The expression is *expelled*."

"Were you *expelled* on purpose?" I asked, wondering what exactly this would mean.

"Yeah. I missed you so much I couldn't wait to come home." He inspected his arm where I'd dug in my nails. He could have smashed me. But that's not Charles's style. Instead he gave me his best, dimpled smile. "You've done a real job on your room. What color do you call this?"

"Peach," I answered.

"Peach," he repeated, looking around. "Maybe I'll switch rooms with you. This one is bigger than mine. And since I'm older, I should have the bigger room, don't you think?"

Was he serious? I couldn't tell. This *used* to be his room. When we were younger, Jess and I shared her room. But then Charles campaigned for the small room on the first floor, and when Mom and Dad finally agreed, I got this one.

Aunt Joan sent my bed and the wicker furniture from her antique shop in New Hampshire. And Tarren gave me the rag rug for my birthday. I'm not about to give up my room! But Mom and Dad wouldn't ask me to, would they?

Now I felt totally confused, the way I always do around him. I wanted to scream, *Go back to school! Go anywhere! But leave us alone!* Except in our family we don't scream. We swallow hard, instead.

Charles stood up and stretched. "I think I'll go down and unpack. My room has several advantages over yours. . . ." He walked in front of the bed, where I was sitting. He put his face close to mine and I could smell onions on his breath.

"Besides," he said, "if I had to sleep in a room with peach walls, I'd puke." He made a disgusting retching sound, and as I jumped back, he laughed.

When he was gone, I closed the bedroom door, lay down on my bed and cried.

Mom and Dad tried to make Charles's first supper at home a festive occasion, even though being expelled from school isn't normally an event to celebrate. Charles came to the table wearing a T-shirt that said I Don't Need Your Attitude . . . I Have My Own. None of us commented. Dad grilled chicken with mustard sauce and Mom made Charles's favorite coleslaw, so full of vinegar it choked me. But Charles loved it. The sour taste agreed with him.

In the middle of dinner he said, "So I think I'll drop out for a while . . . maybe get a job or something."

"That's not an option," Dad said.

"You have to be sixteen to drop out, don't you?" I asked. "And your birthday's not until November."

"Aha . . ." Charles said. "The child prodigy speaks."

I hate it when he calls me that. It makes me feel as if I've done something wrong, something to be ashamed of.

"It's just a matter of finding the right school," Mom said to Charles softly.

Charles exploded. "There is no right school for me! Don't you get it by now? I'm allergic to school!"

"Excuse me," Jessica said. "I've got to pick up my prom pictures before Fotomat closes."

"Excuse me, too," I said, shoving back my chair. "I have a ton of homework."

Charles shook his head. "Those daughters of yours need to be taught some manners," he told Mom and Dad. "They shouldn't be allowed to leave the table when the rest of us are still eating. If I didn't know better, I'd think it has something to do with me. I'd think they're not really as glad to see me as they pretend."

"They might be if it wasn't for your attitude," Mom said.

"Attitude?" Charles said, looking down at his T-shirt. "If we're talking attitude here—"

But Mom didn't wait for him to finish. "Just stop it, Charles!"

"Nell . . ." Dad said, quietly. "Let it go."

"Right," Charles said snidely. "Let it go, Mom. We don't want to upset Dad, do we?"

Later, I think we all regretted how badly dinner had gone and we gathered in the living room. "What's this?" Mom asked, examining the red marks on Charles's arm where I'd dug my nails into his skin. They were sitting next to each other on the small sofa.

"Harry," Charles said, using the cat as an excuse.

"I don't like the way it looks," Mom told him. "Put some peroxide on it."

"Yeah . . . yeah . . ."

"I'm serious, Charles. It could get infected."

Charles smiled at me.

Dad perched on the sofa arm, next to Mom, and Jess passed around her prom pictures. As she did, she gave me a private look, letting me know she'd already removed the group shot showing her in Mom's slinky black dress.

"Oh, Jess . . ." Mom said, studying the pictures. "That shade of pink is perfect on you."

"Magenta," I said.

Everyone looked at me.

"Well, it's more magenta than pink, isn't it?" I asked.

"*Magenta*," Charles said, making me wish I'd never heard the word. "Glad to know you're keeping up with your Crayola colors, Rachel."

Before I could think of something to say back, Dad held out one of Jessica's pictures and said, "Brings back memories, doesn't it, Nell?"

Mom said, "In my day you had to be *asked*."

Dad put his arm around Mom's shoulder and nuzzled her. "If they could see you now, those guys would be eating their hearts out."

"Good," Mom said, smiling at him.

Mom isn't beautiful like Alison's mother but she is very *put together*. She wears classic clothes and her hair is always perfect, whether it's loose or tied back. She says grooming is more important than looks. I hope that's true because when Mom was young she was awkward—too tall like me—and had a serious case of acne, like Jess.

"So, Jessica . . ." Charles said, studying one prom picture after the other. "Do they still call you *Pizza Face*, or is it mostly *Jess the Mess*?"

Jessica grabbed the pictures out of his hand. "Asshole," she hissed. "I wish you'd never been born!" She started from the room in tears, then turned back to face him. "And I hope you get the worst zits ever. I hope they swell and ooze and hurt so bad you go to bed crying every night!"

"Thanks, Jess . . ." Charles called, as if Jess had given him a compliment. "I appreciate that."

Mom ran after Jessica, and Dad said, "Dammit, Charles . . . we're a family. Could we please try to act like one?"

"I am trying," Charles said. "It's just that my sisters are so sensitive they can't even take a joke."

I lay in bed for a long time that night, stroking Burt and Harry, as I listened to Jess crying in her room. I don't understand Charles. I don't understand how he can be so cruel and hateful.

Unfortunately cystic acne runs in our family. Mom and Dad actually met at a drugstore, buying the same medicated skin cream, when they were first-year law students at Columbia. They started going together right away and were married the week they graduated. Mom says Dad is the first person who ever talked to her about acne. Everyone else shied away from the subject. It made them too uncomfortable.

Until then, Mom never even went out with a guy. Looking back, she says her acne was a blessing in disguise. It freed her to concentrate on schoolwork. She won a scholarship to college and another to law school, and she always graduated with honors. But she never kissed a guy until she met Dad and she was twenty-two at the time! I'm glad I've already had my first kiss. Not that I'm proud of having kissed Max Wilson, but at the time it seemed like the right thing to do.

There are a lot of things in life I consider unfair and cystic acne is one of them. I'm not talking about your basic teenage acne. I'm talking about painful lumps and bumps that swell and distort your face. I don't know what I'll do if I get it. Jess has tried antibiotics but they haven't helped much. Mom is always saying, "It cleared up before my thirtieth birthday," as if that will help Jess feel better. Imagine waking up every day with your problem right there on your face for the whole world to see! And having to deal with stupid guys calling you *Pizza Face* and *Jess the Mess*.

I consider Jess one of the bravest people I know. She gets up and goes to school five days a week. She has friends. She even manages to have a sense of humor.

When I finally did fall asleep, I tossed and turned and had bizarre dreams. I woke at dawn, sweaty and anxious, so I crept down to the kitchen and made myself a bowl of Cream of Wheat, with just a drop of brown sugar and milk. Whenever I feel my stomach tying up in knots, I eat comfort food—bananas, mashed potatoes, cooked cereal.

I was thumbing through the Sunday paper and feeling better when Charles waltzed in, humming to himself. "Good morning, little sister," he sang, as if we were old friends. "Did you get your beauty sleep?" He looked at me, then answered his own question. "I guess not."

I mumbled a few choice words under my breath.

"What was that?" he said.

"Never mind."

He began pulling out baking pans, mixing bowls and ingredients from the refrigerator.

"What are you doing?" I asked.

"It's Mother's Day, Rachel."

"I *know* it's Mother's Day."

"So . . . I'm going to bake something special for our dear old mom."

"Since when do you know how to bake?"

He shook his head. "There's so much you don't know about me."

That was certainly true. I never would have guessed Charles would remember Mother's Day. I thought about the gift Jess and I had bought for her—a subscription to *Metropolitan Home*. Mom's always saying she needs to redo the living room, if only she could find the time. We hope this will encourage her.

I read the rest of the paper while Charles baked. I have to admit, when he pulled a scrumptious-looking coffee cake out of the oven forty-five minutes later, I was pretty amazed. He tested it with a toothpick, then set it on a cooling rack. The smell made my mouth water.

I watched as he prepared a steaming pot of coffee, poured a pitcher of orange juice, and arranged it all on a tray. At the last minute he plucked a flower from the bunch on the table and set it on top of his cake. Then he took the Sunday paper, including the section I was reading, folded it up and tucked it under his arm. Before he started out of the room, he looked at me. "Impressed?" he asked.

He knew I was, even though I didn't say a word.

A minute later Jessica came into the kitchen, still in her nightshirt, her hair disheveled, her face covered with dark green goo that smelled faintly of seaweed. She yawned.

"What are you doing up so early?" I asked.

"Couldn't sleep." She opened the refrigerator and stuck her head inside. "I just met our *nightmare* on the stairs."

"He was bringing Mom breakfast in bed . . ." I told her, "in honor of Mother's Day!"

"Oh, God . . ." Jess said from inside the refrigerator. "He's such a hypocrite!"

"Suppose they don't find another school for him?" I asked. "What do you think will happen? I mean, he won't finish ninth grade at Fox, will he?"

"Mom and Dad are smart. They'll figure out something."

"But I've got to know now!"

"There's no way you can know, Rachel. And worrying about it isn't going to help." She backed out of the refrigerator and touched her face to see if the mask had hardened yet. It hadn't.

"Does that mean you think he's going to stay here?" I asked.

"It's his home, isn't it?" she said. "Mom and Dad are his parents, aren't they? They can't just *give* him away."

"Maybe they could send him to live with someone else," I suggested.

"Like who?"

"I don't know . . . Aunt Joan? She took him when he was suspended."

"That was for a week," Jess said. "Don't get your hopes up." She stuck her face back inside the refrigerator.

Mom came downstairs, beaming. "Charles baked a fabulous coffee cake," she said to me. "You've got to try it. It's light and fluffy and the topping's perfect." Then she noticed Jess. "Jessica, please close the refrigerator. Everything will spoil."

Jess touched her cheek. This time she was satisfied. The seaweed mask had set, leaving her with a hardened green face and white circles around her eyes. She looked like a green raccoon.

"Maybe I'll get a job as a baker," Charles said, following Mom into the kitchen.

"That could be a wonderful summer experience for you," Mom said, "if you don't have to go to summer school."

"I wasn't talking about a *summer* job."

"We've already been through that," Mom reminded him. "Let's not spoil our day."

"Oh, right!" He thumped his head with the back of his hand. "Today is Mother's Day . . . a family holiday. I hope my sisters remember that."

"Excuse me," I said. "I'll be in my room, practicing."

"Practicing?" Charles sneered.

"The flute!" I shouted.

"Oh, the flute," he said. "I thought you had something more exciting in mind."

"Grow up, Charles!" Jessica said, following me out of the kitchen.

"I'm trying . . ." he said, "I'm trying. . . ."

"Maybe you need to try harder," Mom told him.

"Push, push, push . . ." Charles said. "That's our family motto."

Mom ignored him and called after us, "Please be ready by eleven, girls. We're going to see Gram then."

Gram is Mom's mother. Her name is Kate Carter Babcock and she's seventy-six. She had a stroke a year ago and has lived at a nursing home ever since.

I get very depressed when we go to visit. *What's the use?* I think. *What's the use of going through a whole lifetime, then winding up like Gram?*

Gram can't talk. The stroke affected the left side of her brain. She makes sounds, not anything we can understand, though. They tried therapy for a while, but when she didn't respond they stopped. I don't know if she understands what we say, or even if she recognizes us. I like to think she does.

Today, when we got there, Gram was dressed for company. The nurse had brushed blush on her cheeks, and it stood out against her pale skin in two uneven circles. She sat in her wheelchair, facing the window that overlooks the garden. She had a soft, pastel-colored blanket across her lap. I recognized it as one of Roddy's baby blankets. When he was born, Tarren received so many she brought half a dozen to the nursing home.

I was glad Gram's chair was turned to the window, because one time we came to visit and someone had left her facing the blank wall. Mom was furious. She'd gone straight to the director to complain.

Mom opened the white florist's box we'd brought and took out a small orchid corsage. She slid it onto Gram's wrist. "Happy Mother's Day," she said, kissing Gram's cheek.

"Happy Mother's Day," Jess and I repeated in unison.

Then Charles stepped forward and kneeled beside Gram's chair. "Hey, Gram . . . remember me . . . your one and only grandson?" He paused for a moment. "So, how's it going?"

Gram turned her head toward Charles. Her eyes seemed to focus on his face. After that it was as if the rest of us didn't exist.

We took Gram for a stroll around the grounds. The tulips and daffodils were in full bloom, and the dogwoods were about to flower. I guess if you have to be in a nursing home, it's better to be in one with pretty gardens.

Mom pushed Gram's wheelchair. Dad hung back. I think visiting Gram reminds him of his own parents, especially his father. After Grandpa Robinson died, when I was in fourth grade, Dad went to bed for six weeks. I was very scared at the time, thinking he was going to die, too. That's when I started running through my *what ifs* at bedtime. My stomach was always tied up in knots. I went to the school nurse every day. Finally my teacher called Mom and asked her to come to school. The next day I was taken to Dr. Klaff for a complete medical checkup. Dr. Klaff said there was nothing physically wrong with me, except that I needed to learn to relax.

Then one day, just as I was getting used to the situation, Dad got out of bed and decided to change his life. He didn't want to be a lawyer anymore. He wanted to be a teacher. So he went back to school to get a degree in education, then got the job teaching history at the high school. We never talk about that time in our lives.

As we walked with Gram, Charles kept up a steady one-way conversation with her. "Yeah, I'm doing really well at this school, Gram. Dorrance . . . that's what it's called. I'm probably going to be class president next year and I've already made the varsity track team. That's how it is with us . . . we always have to be the best! But I guess you know that, Gram. . . . I mean, you're the one who raised Mom, right?"

"Charles . . ." Mom said, warning him.

"Yeah, right . . ." Charles answered.

Gram seemed mesmerized, as if the sound of Charles's voice were enough to make her day. I couldn't help wondering what she was thinking. Did she understand he was feeding her a pack of lies?

An hour later, as we said good-bye to Gram, Charles turned away from her wheelchair with tears in his eyes. When he caught me watching, he walked off by himself.

Gram made a few sounds. Maybe she was calling to him. Who knows? But the nurse had a different interpretation. "We're ready for our dinner, aren't we?" she asked Gram in singsong.

"Will you please not address her in that tone of

voice," Mom said to the nurse. "Will you please talk to her as if she were a healthy person!"

"But she's not, is she?" the nurse replied tartly.

Mom was about to pounce but Dad reminded her this is the best nursing home in the area. There's a waiting list to get in and if Mom makes a fuss again, the director will call, threatening to expel Gram. Wouldn't that be something . . . Charles and Gram expelled in the same week! Mom backed off and headed for the car.

The rest of us followed. Charles walked behind me, deliberately stepping on the backs of my shoes, pulling them off my feet. I thought about sticking out my foot and tripping him, but I didn't feel like making a scene. So I moved away and walked closer to Mom. She put her arm around my shoulders and said, "Don't be sad, honey. Gram's had a long life. And she's not suffering. We should all be grateful for that."

By Monday morning I was seething. And all because of Charles!

So at the bus stop, when Dana Carpenter, a ninth grader who also lives at Palfrey's Pond, said, "I hear your brother's back," I wasn't exactly thrilled.

"Is he going to the high school next year?" she asked.

"I really don't know."

"I hope he does . . . he's so cute . . . and I love his sense of humor." Dana has been going with Jeremy Dragon since Christmas. They fight a lot and sometimes break up, but they always get back together. So why this sudden interest in my brother?

The bus came along then and I got on with Stephanie and Alison.

"Now I'm *really* curious," Alison said, as we took our usual seats. "I've got to meet this brother of yours!"

"How can you be so cruel and hateful?" I spoke

louder than I'd intended and some kids turned to look at me. So I lowered my voice to a whisper. "You're supposed to be my friend."

"I am your friend," Alison said. "And I think it's cruel and hateful of you to accuse me of being cruel and hateful, because I'm not!" She looked at Stephanie, who kind of shrugged at her.

"I just don't think I can take any more of this!" I felt very weak and leaned back against my seat, closing my eyes for a minute.

"Any more of what?" Alison asked.

"I think she's depressed about her brother," Stephanie told Alison, as if I couldn't hear.

"I know that," Alison said. "I'm not stupid." She fussed with her bag for a minute. She carries this huge canvas tote stuffed with all kinds of junk. She pulled out a roll of Life Savers and offered one to Steph, then to me. I shook my head. Steph popped one into her mouth.

At the next stop Jeremy Dragon got on the bus. "Hey, Macbeth . . ." he said as he passed us. Last Halloween the three of us went to his house dressed as the witches from Shakespeare's play. When Jeremy came to the door, instead of saying *trick or treat*, we'd recited a poem.

Double, double, toil and trouble;
Fire burn and cauldron bubble.

And ever since, he's called us Macbeth. Sometimes it means all three of us—sometimes, like in math class, it's just me.

When we were moving again, Alison said, "I wonder what *my* brother's going to be like?"

"Your brother's going to be a baby," Stephanie reminded her.

For some reason that made me laugh. But my laugh came out high-pitched, not at all like my regular laugh.

"I wasn't trying to be funny," Steph told me. "I was just making a point."

"Are you saying that baby brothers aren't as depressing as older ones?" Alison asked.

"Not *all* older brothers are depressing," I said. "Just some."

Stephanie sighed. "Maybe you should see Mrs. Balaban."

"The school counselor?" I asked.

"Yeah," Steph said. "I saw her once . . . when I found out . . ." She hesitated for a moment. "When I found out my parents were separating."

"You went to Mrs. Balaban?" Alison said, as if she couldn't believe it.

Stephanie nodded.

"So did I!" Alison told her.

"You?" Steph said to Alison, as if *she* couldn't believe it. "Why did *you* go to Mrs. Balaban?"

"Because of the . . . when I found out about the . . ."

"Pregnancy?" I guessed.

"Right. . . . When I found out my mother was pregnant."

"How come you didn't *say* anything about seeing Mrs. Balaban?" Steph asked Alison.

"How come *you* didn't?" Alison asked Steph.

"I thought we were talking about *my* problem," I said, and they both looked at me.

The next morning Mrs. Balaban sent a note to my homeroom teacher, saying she wanted to see me. I was really angry. How could Alison and Stephanie betray me this way? If I want to see Mrs. Balaban, I will. But that's *my* business and nobody else's. I intended to tell them exactly that at lunch, which is our first and only period together except for gym, which we have twice a week but not today.

I stopped at Mrs. Balaban's office on my way to the cafeteria. "I'm Rachel Robinson," I said. "You wanted to see me?"

"Oh, Rachel . . . yes . . . I'm very glad to meet you," she said. "Sit down."

Mrs. Balaban is young and good-looking. The boys think it's great to be called to her office. One time she brought her baby, Hilary, to school. The girls oohed and aahed over her, while the boys oohed and aahed over Mrs. Balaban.

"I only have a minute," I said, standing in front of her desk. "I have to go to lunch."

"Well, let's see how fast I can explain this to you." She poured some sparkling water into a mug decorated with Beatrix Potter rabbits. "Want some?"

"No thanks."

She took a long drink. When she finished, she burped softly, her hand covering her mouth. "Sorry," she said. "Have you heard anything about Natural Helpers, Rachel?"

"I've heard of Natural Lime Spritzers," I answered.

She laughed. "This isn't a drink. It's a program we're going to try next fall. It's called Natural Helpers."

I felt my face turn hot. That's the kind of mistake Stephanie would make, not me. And it happened because I was worrying instead of listening.

"It's a kind of outreach program," Mrs. Balaban continued. "You know . . . kids helping other kids."

I waited to hear what this program had to do with Charles.

Mrs. Balaban took another swig from her cup. "I asked the teachers to recommend a group of mature seventh and eighth graders . . . people other kids would relate to . . . and you were one of them."

"So this doesn't have anything to do with . . ." I began.

"With . . ." Mrs. Balaban repeated, looking at me.

"Never mind. I was confused for a minute. I thought you wanted to see me because . . ."

"Because . . ."

I was so relieved this didn't have anything to do with Charles, I started to laugh.

"What?" she asked, curious.

"Nothing," I said, trying to keep a straight face.

She twirled her wedding band around on her finger. "Do you think you'd be interested in participating in this kind of program, Rachel?"

When I didn't respond right away, she said, "Of course I want you to take your time and think about it. Because the training will be fairly intense. And I know you're already involved in other school activities, not to mention your schoolwork."

"Schoolwork is no problem," I said.

She shuffled some papers on her desk. "Straight A's," she said, smiling up at me. She must have had my transcript in front of her. "Very impressive. But you know, Rachel, there's nothing wrong with a B now and then."

"I prefer A's," I said.

She laughed. "Remember, I don't want you to feel pressured to take this on, unless it's something you really want to do . . . okay?"

"Okay."

"We're having an introductory meeting next week, and Rachel . . ."

"Yes?"

"There's no rule that says Natural Helpers can't have their own problems . . . so if there's something on your mind that you'd like to talk about . . ."

"No," I said, "there's nothing."

"But if there ever is . . ."

"I have to go now," I told her. "This is my lunch period."

When I got to the cafeteria, Stephanie and Alison were already eating.

"Where were you?" Steph asked.

"Mrs. Balaban," I said.

"You actually took my advice?" she asked.

"Not exactly . . ."

Steph turned to Alison. "I knew she'd never admit she took *my* advice!"

My life at home is falling apart and Mrs. Balaban wants me to help other kids. What an incredible joke! What makes her think kids would come to me with their problems? I'm not very popular, except right before a test when everyone suddenly needs extra help. And when Steph's parents were separating, she didn't even *tell* me and I'm supposed to be her best friend! We had a huge fight when I found out she'd been lying to me. We didn't speak for seven weeks. And did Alison come to me when she found out her mother was pregnant? No. She went directly to Stephanie. So, it seems to me Mrs. Balaban doesn't know much about finding Natural Helpers!

That night I had too many *what ifs*. I knew I'd never get to sleep if I couldn't clear my head. So I went down to the kitchen to make myself a cup of herbal tea.

Charles was at the table, stuffing his face with cold mashed potatoes and leftover salmon with a big glob of mayonnaise on top. He'd refused to have dinner with us earlier. The thought of all that mayonnaise at ten o'clock at night was enough to gag me. I looked away and thought about going back upstairs. But then I changed my mind. Just because *he's* in the kitchen doesn't mean I can't have my tea. I took a few deep breaths and put the kettle on. While I was waiting for the water to boil, I opened the cupboard where we keep the teas and chose Grandma's Tummy Mint. Burt and Harry were sniffing around the table, begging for salmon.

"Come on, you guys," Charles said to them, with a mouthful of mashed potatoes. "Not while I'm eating."

"Cold mashed potatoes are disgusting," I muttered.

"To each his own," he said.

I didn't respond.

"You know . . . I'm worried about you, Rachel."

"You're worried about me?"

"Yeah . . . it's not normal for a girl your age not to have friends."

"I have plenty of friends."

"So where are they? How come they never come over?"

I chose my favorite mug, decorated with pink and lavender hearts, and poured boiling water over my tea bag. Then I set the mug down so the tea could steep. It's amazing how few people know how to make a good cup of tea. They think they can hand you a cup of hot water with a tea bag on the side and that's it.

"I asked you a question, Rachel."

"My friends are none of your business," I told him.

"I think you're trying to hide something."

I spun around. "I am *not* trying to hide anything. And I don't have to explain my friendships to you!" I knew better than to continue this conversation. So I took my tea upstairs, to the privacy of my own room.

The next day I asked Stephanie and Alison if they wanted to come over after school.

"Sure . . ." Alison said. "Will Charles be there?"

"Probably," I told her. "But don't get into a long conversation with him. Don't start telling him about your dog and how she can talk."

"Would he believe me if I did?" Alison asked.

"No, but he'd lead you on and then he'd never let you forget you said it."

"Fine . . . I won't say anything," Alison said.

"No . . . that would be even worse. Then he'll think you *can't* talk."

"Okay . . . I'll just say one or two things."

"And nothing personal," I told her. "Don't tell him your mother's pregnant."

"Got it," Alison said. "Nothing personal."

"And no questions!"

Alison repeated that. "No questions."

"You, too," I told Steph.

"All right," Steph said. "Stop worrying! I've known Charles since I was seven . . . remember?"

"I'm not worrying," I said.

The cats were sleeping outside the kitchen door when we got home. Burt woke up and stretched when he heard us. Harry didn't even move. I gave them fresh water from the outside faucet. Then I opened the door. Charles wasn't in the kitchen, so I poured three glasses of cranberry juice and set out a box of Dutch pretzels.

"The way you eat pretzels is so weird," Stephanie said to me.

"To each her own," I answered. It's true that I have a special way of eating pretzels. I like to lick off all the salt first. Then, when the pretzel is very soft, just before it's actually soggy, I chew it up. I didn't always eat pretzels that way. But a few years ago I broke a tooth on one, and ever since I eat them very carefully.

"Well . . . are we going to see him or not?" Alison finally asked.

"All right," I said. And I started down the hall to Charles's room, with Alison and Stephanie right behind me. I knocked and called, "Charles, I'm home with my friends!"

We waited but he didn't answer.

"Maybe he's not here," Steph said.

"I couldn't be so lucky," I mumbled on the way back to the kitchen. Just when I decided he probably wasn't home he appeared, fresh out of the shower, barefoot, with wet hair. He was wearing cutoffs and a T-shirt that said ELVIS IS DEAD.

"Well, well, well . . ." He smiled, surveying the scene.

I said, "Alison, this is my brother, Charles."

"You're Charles?" Alison said, like she couldn't believe it. What was she expecting . . . Dracula?

"None other," he answered, turning on the charm. "And who are you?"

"Alison Monceau." She practically drooled. "From L.A. I've heard a lot about you."

"I can imagine," Charles said. "I'm one of my sister's favorite subjects."

"Not from Rachel," Alison said quickly. "Rachel doesn't like to talk about you."

357

"What?" Charles said. "Impossible! Rachel, is this true? You don't talk about me anymore? You don't tell people how I bit you on your leg when you were two?"

"He bit you?" Alison asked me. Before I could answer, Stephanie waved her arms, trying to capture Charles's attention. "Hey," she called, "remember me?"

He looked her up and down. "No!" he said. "I don't believe it! This can't be Stephanie Hirsch!"

Stephanie suddenly grew self-conscious, touching her hair, her mouth, then crossing her arms over her chest. She tried to smile at him without showing her braces.

He was doing such a number on them! And they were just eating it up. Fools! I wanted to shout. He's just using you. He's just playing games.

"I was beginning to think the child prodigy had no friends," Charles said, making me cringe. "Why, just last night I accused her of being friendless. Right, Rachel?"

"That's it!" I said. "The party's over!"

I opened the screen door and let it slam behind me, expecting my friends to follow. But they just stood there, enthralled by my brother, until he said, " 'Parting is such sweet sorrow . . .' " and disappeared down the hall. As soon as he was gone, Stephanie and Alison burst out laughing.

"I don't see anything funny!" I told them from the other side of the screen door.

"That's your problem, Rachel," Stephanie said. She pushed the screen door open and she and Alison joined me outside. "Maybe if you treated him better, he'd treat you better."

"Why are you taking *his* side?" I asked. "You're supposed to be *my* friend."

"I am your friend," Steph argued.

"No," I said, "a friend is someone you can depend on!"

"You *can* depend on me. It's just that you always think everything's going to be a disaster!"

"Not everything," I told her. "Just *some* things!" But it was useless. They'd never understand. I turned and ran to the top of the hill. Then I lay on the grass with my arms hugging my body, and I began to roll. I rolled all the way down, like I used to when I was small, stopping myself just short of the pond.

Alison and Steph, thinking I was playing some game, followed, rolling down the hill after me, laughing hysterically. Steph stopped on her own, but I had to grab Alison or she'd have rolled right into the water. When she stood up, I steadied her. "Well . . ." I said, "are you satisfied?"

"About what?" she asked. Sometimes Alison is so dense!

"About Charles," I said.

"Oh, yeah . . . I guess." She and Steph exchanged looks. "I mean, based on what I just saw, I can see how he'd be a pain as a brother . . . but as a boy . . ."

I held up my hand. "I don't want to hear it, Alison!"

"All she's saying is—" Steph began.

But I didn't let her finish. "I am not interested in either of your opinions about my brother."

"It's getting hard to be around you, Rachel!" Steph said. "You're so . . . intense!" She turned to Alison. "Come on . . . let's go." And they walked off together.

I wanted to call after them, to tell them I needed them. But I couldn't find the words.

Instead I went home and rearranged my dresser drawers, folding and refolding each sweater, each T-shirt, each pair of socks. Then I started on my closet. When everything was in order, when everything was perfect, I sat down at my music stand, picked up my flute and began to play.

handed in my biography. I thought of taking out
the section about inventing a vaccine to prevent
hair balls in lions, but I didn't. Just because Charles
found it wildly funny or even peculiar doesn't mean
anything. Because Charles is peculiar himself.

He stays up all night watching reruns of old sitcoms
on TV—"The Munsters," "Gilligan's Island," "The
Brady Bunch." He goes to bed at sunrise and sleeps
away half the day. It's easy to avoid him on this
schedule. Maybe that's why he does it. Maybe he's
trying to avoid us. He doesn't even join us for dinner,
which is fine with Jessica and me. But it bothers
Mom and Dad. They think eating dinner together is
the single most important part of family life. They've
been seeing Dr. Sparks. They want Charles to see him
again, too, but so far he's refused.

"That quack!" Charles shouted at Mom a couple of

nights ago. "He knows *nothing*! You're blowing your money on him."

"Fine," Mom said, without raising her voice. "Then we'll find someone else. Someone you feel more comfortable with."

"Don't count on it," Charles told her.

At the dinner table we don't talk about him. Jess and I try to keep the conversation light, but you can tell Mom is stressed-out and Dad's not himself, either. He tries not to let us see he's distracted, but he can't fool me. I've seen him gobbling Pepto-Bismol tablets. And I've heard him talking quietly with Mom late at night, long after they're usually asleep. I've stopped asking them about Charles and what's going to happen, but I haven't stopped wondering if we have to live this way until he's eighteen.

On Monday my biography came back marked A+, and in the margin Ms. Lefferts wrote, *Excellent work, well thought out, delightful reading. See me.* When I went up to her after class, she said, "Rachel, I had no idea you were interested in the theater."

She was referring to my imagined career as a great actress. I'd written that Rachel died onstage at the age of ninety-seven. It was weird writing about my own death, but I suppose if I absolutely have to die — and death is a fact of life, isn't it? — then ninety-seven isn't bad, especially if I'm able to work right up to the end. Besides, since I'm just thirteen now, that gives me another eighty-four years to figure things out.

Ms. Lefferts was in one of her hyper moods, talking very fast, using her hands to punctuate every word. "I'm going to be advisor to the Drama Club next year and I certainly hope you'll join."

"Well . . ." I began.

But she didn't wait for me to finish. "I know you're busy. I recommended you for that helping program myself. . . . What's it called again?"

"Natural Helpers," I said.

"Yes, Natural Helpers . . . but the Drama Club could be a very exciting experience for you. We're going to do a fall play and a spring musical."

"I'll—"

"That's all I'm asking. That you give it your serious consideration. Because we really need people like you . . . people with a *genuine* interest in theater."

"It sounds—"

"Oh . . . and I forgot to mention we'll be going to New York to see at least two plays."

"Will we go by train or bus?" I asked.

She seemed surprised by my question. "I haven't worked that out yet. Do you have a preference?"

"Yes," I told her. "I prefer the train." I didn't add that I get motion sick in cars and buses but not on trains.

"Well . . ." she said, "I'll keep your preference in

mind. I'm hoping to get tickets to a contemporary drama and a Shakespearean comedy."

"Shakespeare is my favorite," I said.

Ms. Lefferts put her hand on my shoulder and squeezed lightly. "Mine, too, Rachel. Mine, too."

What am I going to do about all these activities? I wondered as I got into bed that night. Mom says the trick is to know your own limits. But I don't know what my limits are. I wish my teachers wouldn't expect me to do everything!

I decided to make a list. In one column I wrote down the activities I'm participating in now—Orchestral Band, All-State Orchestra, Debating Team, plus a private flute lesson each week and forty-five minutes of practice a day. In the other column I wrote down the activities I'm thinking about adding next year—Drama Club and Natural Helpers. Also, Stephanie wants me to run for eighth-grade class president. She's already volunteered to be my campaign manager and she's thought up the perfect slogan—*Rachel Robinson, the Dare to Care Candidate.*

I tried to figure out how many hours a week these activities would take, not counting president, but until tomorrow, when I go to the introductory meeting of Natural Helpers, I won't really be able to come up with an exact figure. I wonder if it's even possible to handle so many activities. I wish I could be a regular person for just one year! But then Mom would be disappointed. She'd say it's a crime to waste my potential. I wonder if she's ever wished she could be a regular person.

I turned off the light and lay down. Burt snuggled up against my hip and Harry at my feet. I closed my eyes, but my mind was on overtime. What if class president isn't allowed to participate in other activities? What if Natural Helpers turns out to be a full-time activity? What if I get a part in the school play, which means rehearsals every afternoon, when I'm supposed to be at Debating Club preparing for an interschool match and Orchestral Band is rehearsing for the spring concert and my flute teacher says I haven't been practicing enough and my grades start slipping and everybody says I'm not doing my job as class president because I'm too busy doing other things and I am impeached by the class officers? Being impeached would be even worse than being expelled. Being impeached would probably make the local papers!

Suddenly I felt my heart thumping inside my chest. I sat straight up, frightened. The cats looked at me as I leaped out of bed. But then a voice inside my head reminded me to stay calm, to breathe deeply. I began to count backward from one hundred. That's it . . . count slowly . . . very slowly . . . that's better . . .

The panicky feeling passed, leaving me drenched

with sweat. I lay back down and closed my eyes. *Psychology Today* says one good relaxation technique is to imagine yourself in a serene setting, like a beautiful tropical island with a white sand beach and palm trees swaying gently in the warm breeze. Yes. Okay. I'm on an island, swinging in a hammock, when this incredibly handsome guy comes up to me. He's carrying a book of Shakespeare's sonnets. He sits beside me and begins to read. After a while he reaches for my hand, looks deep into my eyes and, not being able to resist a moment longer, kisses me. It is a long, passionate kiss . . . without tongues. The idea of having someone's tongue in my mouth is too disgusting to contemplate.

I must have fallen asleep then, but when I awoke in the morning I had a gnawing ache in my jaw.

The next afternoon I went to the introductory meeting of Natural Helpers and nearly passed out when Mrs. Balaban presented someone named Dr. Sparks. Could he be *that* Dr. Sparks? I wondered, as I slid lower and lower in my seat. How many psychologists named Dr. Sparks can there be in one town? He must be the same one! Suppose he recognizes my name and asks if I'm related to Charles? Suppose he tells Mrs. Balaban that with my family situation I shouldn't be a Natural Helper?

I worried all through the meeting. I hardly heard a word he said.

But when the meeting ended, Mrs. Balaban thanked Dr. Sparks and he left without addressing any of us individually. I felt so relieved I let out a low sigh. Only the girl next to me seemed to notice. Then Mrs. Balaban told us we should think long and hard about becoming Natural Helpers. "I'll need your answer by the last day of school," she said. "And remember, it's a significant commitment. Helping others always is. You'll have to be aware and involved all the time."

Aware and involved all the time, I thought as I sat in the dentist's office after school. By then my jaw was killing me. I opened and closed my mouth, hoping to relieve the pain.

Unlike most of my friends, I'm not afraid to go to the dentist. I have very healthy teeth. I've had just two small cavities in my entire life. Besides, our dentist, Dr. McKay, is also a stand-up comic. He performs at the Laugh Track, a comedy club on the highway. He tries out his material on his patients, so in this case you might say, going to the dentist is a lot of laughs!

"So, Rachel . . . how do you get down from an elephant?" Dr. McKay asked as he adjusted the towel around my neck.

"I've no idea," I told him.

He tilted the chair way back. "You don't . . . you get it from a duck."

I laughed, which wasn't easy to do with my mouth

open and the dentist's hands inside. I hate the taste of his white surgical gloves.

"Hmm . . ." he said, poking around. "Are you wearing your appliance?"

I tried to explain that I'd lost it, but he couldn't understand me. I guess he got the general tone, though, because he said, "So, the answer is no?"

I nodded.

"Well, you're clenching your jaw again."

I tried to act surprised. I said, "I am?" It came out sounding like *Ah aah?*

"Uh-huh . . ." he said. "And grinding your teeth, too."

Grinding my teeth? That definitely did not sound good.

"Everything all right in your life?" he asked.

I wiggled my fingers, indicating so-so.

"Still getting all A's in school?"

I wish people would stop acting as if there's something wrong with getting all A's. I waved my hands around, our signal for letting me sit up and rinse. After I did, I said, "This doesn't have anything to do with school."

"Maybe not, but I'd still like to see you learn to relax. And so would your teeth."

People are always telling me to relax, as if it's something easy to do. When Dr. McKay finished cleaning my teeth, he moved the chair to an upright position. "I'm going to do an impression," he said.

I assumed he meant an impression of someone famous. So I was surprised when he said, "Open wide, Rachel . . ." and he slid a little tray of flavored goo into my mouth.

On the way out of Dr. McKay's office I met Steph, who had an appointment with the orthodontist in the next office. "How do you get down from an elephant?" I asked. I hardly ever tell jokes because no one laughs when I do. I don't know if this means my comic timing is off or people just don't expect me to be funny.

"How?" Steph said.

"You don't. You get it from a duck."

Steph just looked at me.

"It's a joke," I said. "Down . . . as in feathers. Get it?"

"Oh, right . . ." Steph said. "Now I do." But she didn't laugh. Then she said, "Did you hear about Marcella, the eighth-grade slut?"

"No, what?"

"She got caught in the supply closet with Jeremy Dragon."

"Is this a joke?"

"No. Why would it be a joke?"

"I don't know. The way you set it up, I thought you were going to tell a joke."

"No, this is a true story," Steph said. "It was the

supply closet in the arts center. When Dana found out she went crazy, yelling and screaming in front of everyone!"

"Really?"

"Yes . . . then Jeremy goes, 'How come it's okay for you but not for me?' And Dana shouts, 'What are you talking about?' Then Jeremy goes, 'You know what I'm talking about!' And he walks away, which makes Dana so mad she takes off his bracelet and throws it at him. It hits him in the back of his head. So he turns around and goes, 'Thanks, Dana!' Then he picks up his bracelet and puts it in his pocket."

"You were actually there?" I asked. "You actually saw this happen?"

"No," Steph said. "But everybody's talking about it. Everybody knows!"

"What was he doing in the supply closet with Marcella?"

"What do you think?" Before I had a chance to respond, Steph answered her own question. "Pure animal attraction!"

"Yes, but the difference between humans and animals is that humans are supposed to *think*," I explained, "not just react."

"But let's say you were alone in a supply closet with Jeremy Dragon . . ." Steph said. "Wouldn't you react?"

"I don't know."

"Well, I do. I'm reacting just thinking about it, like any normal person."

"Are you suggesting I'm not normal?"

"I didn't say that."

"It sounded like you did."

"Well, I didn't."

"Good, because I'm as normal as you!"

"If you say so."

"What do you mean by that?"

"Lighten up, Rachel, will you?" Stephanie said, shaking her head. "You're never going to make it to eighth grade at this rate."

I wanted to ask Steph exactly what she meant by that remark, but she went into the orthodontist's office before I had the chance. It's not as if I wouldn't want to be alone with Jeremy Dragon. But I'd choose someplace more romantic than a supply closet at school!

When Alison came over that night, I asked if she'd heard about Jeremy Dragon and Marcella. "Steph told me," she said. "I feel bad for Dana." She walked around my room touching things—the framed photos on my dresser, my collection of decorated boxes, the needlepoint pillows on my bed. "I'd do anything for a room like this." She sounded as if she were in a trance.

Since she goes through this routine every time, I decided to call her on it. "Okay," I said, "on Saturday I'm coming over and we're going to organize your room."

"Oh no," Alison said, "it wouldn't work!"

"Why not?"

"I'd never be able to keep it like . . . this," she said, opening my closet door, "with all my clothes facing the same direction, and my shoes lined up in a row."

"It's easy!" I told her. "You just have to put away your clothes when you take them off."

"But you know how I am. You know I never put anything away until my closet is empty and all my clothes are piled on the floor."

"You can do it if you want to."

"I want to . . . but I know myself. I'm too tired at night to care."

"Then you should go to bed earlier."

"That's what my mother says."

"I don't mean to sound like your mother, but you'll never know until you try."

"No, I'd just wind up feeling bad." She sighed. "Maybe someday. Maybe next year, okay?"

I shrugged. "Whenever."

"Besides," she said, looking around, "Steph says it isn't normal for a teenager to have a room as perfect as this."

"Stephanie said that . . . about me?"

"Not about you," Alison said, backing off. "About your room. We were just talking, you know, about this article in *Sassy* and . . ." I waited while she painted herself into a corner. "Steph didn't mean it personally or anything."

"I cannot believe Stephanie told you I'm not normal."

"She didn't say that!"

"You know what Stephanie's problem is?" I asked.

"Stephanie confuses *normal* with *average*. It's true that the *average* teenager doesn't keep her room as neat as I keep mine. But just because it isn't *average* doesn't mean it's not *normal*."

I absolutely detest the word *normal*. I detest the way Stephanie throws it around. And, I admit, sometimes I do wonder about myself. There's no question, I'm different from most kids my age. I don't know how to explain it. Maybe when my mother jokes to her friends that *Rachel was born thirty-five*, she knows what she's talking about. Maybe I won't find out until I actually *am* thirty-five. Maybe then I'll be more like everyone else.

Alison was running her hand over the books on my shelves. "So, can you recommend something good? I have a book report due on Friday and I forgot to go to the library."

"They're all good," I told her. "It just depends on what you're in the mood for."

"Something about a girl who lived a long time ago."

"Historical fiction," I translated. "Let me think . . ." My books are arranged alphabetically by author so I know exactly where each one is. I pulled two off my shelf—*Summer of My German Soldier* and *A Tree Grows in Brooklyn*—and handed them to Alison.

"I'll take this one," she said, thumbing through the first.

374

"Good choice," I told her. "I think you'll like it." I wrote down Alison's name, followed by the title and author, in my library notebook. Even though every one of my books has a bookplate on the inside cover, some people forget to return them. They don't mean to. It just happens. This way I know who's got what. As I was putting away my notebook, Charles opened my bedroom door. "You know you're supposed to knock!" I said.

But he paid no attention. "I was hoping for a quick game of *torture*," he said, standing in the doorway.

"We are *not* interested!" I tried to force him out by closing the door but he blocked it.

"What's *torture*?" Alison asked.

"*Torture* is having a conversation with my brother. *Torture* is enduring his witty comments."

Alison didn't get it. But Charles pushed past me and said, "An excellent definition, Rachel." He looked at Alison. "You just don't know how refreshing it is to live with a child prodigy."

Alison didn't get that, either. She sat on the edge of my bed, not knowing what to say. Charles smiled at her. She smiled back, clearly flattered by his attention.

"So, what's your ethnic heritage, California?" he asked.

"None of your business," I told him, answering for Alison.

"I don't mean to pry," Charles said to her smoothly, "but I'm very interested in ethnic heritage, given my background."

What background? I wondered.

"Well, I'm adopted," Alison said. "I don't know anything except that my birth mother was Vietnamese."

"I'm adopted, too," Charles said. "I wish our family were as open about it as yours."

"What are you saying?" I asked, totally shocked. "You're not adopted!"

"You mean you never guessed?" he asked me. "You never put two and two together?"

"You're lying!" I shouted. Then I turned to Alison. "He's lying!"

"Here are the facts," Charles said quietly to Alison, as he sat beside her on my bed. "I'm one-eighth Korean, one-eighth Native American, one-quarter Irish, one-quarter Eastern European, and one-quarter Cuban."

"How would you know all that if you were adopted?" I asked.

"I've seen the papers."

Alison was confused and so was I. "Get out of my room!" I shouted at Charles, holding the door open. "Now!"

"Goodnight, California," Charles sang as he left. "Until next time . . ." He blew her a kiss.

I slammed the door after him. "I'm sorry," I said to Alison. "He's so obnoxious."

"No . . . it's okay," she said.

"It's not okay! He's playing with your mind."

"Maybe he is adopted."

"He's not!"

"You're younger," she said. "Maybe you just don't know. Some people don't talk about it."

"It's not possible!" I said, feeling lost. "Grandpa Robinson said—" I stopped in midsentence. "I mean, he looks like my father . . . don't you think?"

"Not really," she said.

But Mom and Dad would never keep such a secret, would they? No, they believe in honesty. On the other hand, Mom is a very private person. She holds everything inside.

As soon as Alison left, I went directly to my parents' room and knocked on their door.

Dad called, "Enter. . . ." He was grading papers at his desk. I heard water running in the bathroom. Mom was probably taking a shower.

I pulled a small chair over to Dad's desk and waited for him to look up from his work. When he did, he said, "What can I do for you?"

"I have a very important question," I said.

"Okay . . . shoot."

There was no easy way to do this. I focused on Mom's collection of glass bottles. There are eleven of them sitting on top of her dresser, each with a silver top.

"Rachel . . ." Dad said.

I looked at him, then back at Mom's bottles. Finally I managed to say, "Is Charles adopted?"

Dad didn't answer right away. He reached for my hand. "I know it must feel that way to you . . ."

"It doesn't feel that way to me," I said, "but that's what he just told Alison! He told her he's one-eighth Native American, one-eighth Korean, one-quarter Irish and . . ."

Dad started laughing.

"I don't find it funny at all!"

"He's not adopted," Dad said. "He probably just feels that would explain things."

"Are you absolutely sure?" I asked.

Dad stroked my arm. "I was there at his birth, honey. I held him in my arms, same as I held Jessica and you when you were born. Not that I wouldn't love any of you just as much if you were adopted . . ."

"It's cruel to lie to someone who really is adopted, trying to make her think they have something in common."

"I'm not excusing him," Dad said, "but maybe he likes Alison and is trying to impress her."

"What do you mean by *likes*?"

Dad kind of smiled and said, "You know . . . boy meets girl . . ."

"You mean likes her *that* way!" I didn't give Dad a chance to respond. I jumped up. "That's out of the question. She's my friend. My friends are off-limits to him. You've got to do something, Dad! You've got to get him out of my life!"

"Rachel, honey . . ." Dad stood, too, and wrapped me in his arms. "It's going to be all right. I know these are difficult times . . ."

"So were the Crusades!" Mom said, coming out of the bathroom in her purple robe.

10

Charles has a tutor. His name is Paul Medeiros and he's tall, about six feet, with dark hair and dark eyes. He wears rimless glasses. He's Dad's student teacher. He's going to come to our house every afternoon for two hours. This means Charles will *not* be finishing ninth grade at my school. What a relief!

When I met Paul a few days ago, he was wearing jeans and a black pocket T-shirt. He had a pencil smudge on the side of his face. He said, "So you're Charles's older sister."

"No," Charles told him, "this is my *baby* sister." Charles was wearing a T-shirt that said ALL STRESSED UP AND NO ONE TO CHOKE. I felt like choking him!

"She doesn't look like a baby," Paul said.

"Looks can be deceiving," Charles said. "She's just thirteen." He said *thirteen* as if it were the plague.

I could see the surprise on Paul's face. But I liked

him for not making a big thing out of it. "Then you're the musician?" Paul asked.

"Well, I love music but I'm not that good," I told him.

"She's only a child prodigy," Charles said.

"Charles . . . I am not!" I wish he would stop calling me that! I've met real prodigies at music camp. Some of them are only ten or eleven and they're already studying at Juilliard. It was a shock when I realized I'll never be as good as they are, no matter how much I practice.

Paul gave me an understanding smile, then playfully shoved Charles back toward his room. "Okay, time to hit the books." He turned for a moment and said, "Nice to meet you, Rachel."

When he said my name, I felt incredibly warm inside. At first I thought I was having what Mom and her friends call a *hot flash*. But I don't think you get them till you're older. I'm not sure if what I feel for Paul is pure animal attraction or not. Either way, from now on I'll have to be very careful because if Charles ever finds out—or even *suspects*—I have an interest in Paul, he will deliberately humiliate me in front of him. Not that I think Paul would let him get away with it. Still, the damage would be done.

That night I lay on my bed reading sonnets to the cats. I imagined I was onstage and the entire audience, including Paul, was mesmerized by my voice.

Suddenly I had the feeling I wasn't alone and when I looked up, Charles was standing in my doorway. "You read Shakespeare to the cats?" he asked.

"They're very good listeners," I told him. "Now please leave!"

"You know, Rachel . . . when people start reading to their animals . . ."

"Out!" I said again. "Right now!"

I could hear him chuckling even after he'd closed my door.

I began to think of Paul every night when I went to bed. Thinking about him is very relaxing. It's better than anything I've read in *Psychology Today*. My jaw hasn't hurt at all since Paul started coming to our house. But whether that's due to my new dental appliance or to Paul himself, I really can't say.

I wonder if Tarren knows him since he's graduating from the same college where she is a junior. Next time I see her I'll have to ask.

But the next time Tarren came over, she pressed a screaming baby into my arms and said, "Where's your mother?" Her eyes were red and swollen, her hair damp and matted around her face.

Mom was at the dining room table, working on what could be her last big jury trial before she is appointed a judge. "Tarren, what is it?" Mom asked, pushing back her chair.

Tarren threw her arms around Mom and cried, "Aunt Nell . . . my life is just one big mess! I don't think I can take it anymore."

Roddy continued to scream. Mom said, "Rachel, take the baby into the kitchen and give him a bottle or something."

Tarren pulled off her shoulder bag and passed it to me. "There's a bottle inside."

I took Roddy into the kitchen, but since there's no door between the kitchen and the dining room I could still hear everything.

"All right," Mom said to Tarren. "Now calm down and tell me what's going on."

Tarren sobbed, "I got another ticket . . . for speeding. I was only doing sixty-seven, but they gave me points." She blew her nose. "If I lose my license I won't be able to get to school and if I can't get to school I'll never graduate, and if I don't graduate and get a teaching job I'll never be able to support myself and Roddy and I'll never get out of my parents' house, or have my own life, or . . ." She was crying again.

Mom sounded firm. "Listen to me, Tarren. We've been through this before. You are responsible for your own actions."

"But it was a mistake," Tarren cried. "I didn't know I was going over the speed limit."

"We all make mistakes," Mom told her. "The point

is, you can't fall apart every time something goes wrong. You've got to learn to be strong!"

"I don't know how to be strong, Aunt Nell. I want to be like you . . . you know I do . . . but I just don't know how."

"Then you're going to learn, right now," Mom said. "You're going to start by telling yourself, This is not a life-threatening situation. This is not a serious problem."

"It's not?" Tarren asked.

"No, it's not!" Mom said.

Roddy lay in my arms, sucking on his bottle, his fingers playing with my hair. I love Roddy. I love the way he smells and feels. I love his sweetness.

"And I don't want to hear you sounding like your father, Tarren," Mom continued. "Your father still hasn't learned to be strong, and he's forty . . ." Mom hesitated.

"Forty-four," Tarren said.

"Yes, forty-four," Mom repeated. Mom says Uncle Carter takes after Grandfather Babcock, who drank too much and wasted his money on get-rich-quick schemes. I never knew Grandfather Babcock. He died when Mom was just nineteen. I think she worries that Charles will turn out like him or Uncle Carter.

"Life is an obstacle course," Mom said.

I know Mom's obstacle speech by heart. *We all have to make decisions. I'm not saying it's easy. But you don't have to collapse every time you come face-to-face with an obstacle.*

"An obstacle . . ." Tarren repeated, her voice trailing off.

As Mom and Tarren were talking, Charles breezed into the kitchen. "Hey, Roddy, baby . . . how's it going?" He lifted Roddy off my lap and held him high over his head. Roddy shrieked, loving it.

"He just finished a . . ." I began to say, but by then it was too late. Roddy spit up half of what I'd just fed him, right on Charles's head.

Charles shoved Roddy back at me and ran for the sink. He turned on the faucet full blast and stuck his head under it. When he'd had enough, he turned off the water and shook his head like a dog who's been for a swim. Roddy clapped his hands and laughed. Then Charles laughed, too. "Very funny, Roddy," he said. "Ha-ha-ha."

"Aa-aa-aa," Roddy sang back.

"So what's tonight's catastrophe?" Charles asked, with a nod in Tarren's direction. He grabbed a kitchen towel and wiped his face.

"A speeding ticket," I said.

"She thinks Mom can fix it?"

"I don't know."

"Lots of luck," Charles said. Then he waved at Roddy and left.

This is what it must be like to have a regular brother, I thought. Someone you can laugh with, someone who talks to you naturally, without being sarcastic or cruel. Someone you can face every day without feeling you are walking on eggs. Why can't Charles be that kind of brother all the time?

Tarren looked less anxious when she came back into the kitchen. "I don't know what I'd do without you, Aunt Nell." She hugged Mom. "You're the most supportive person in my life. I hope someday I'll be more like you."

"You'll be fine," Mom said. "You can handle whatever life throws your way. Remember . . . obstacles, not problems."

"Right," Tarren said. "Obstacles." She reached for Roddy.

"You are about the luckiest girl alive," she told me. "You have the most wonderful mother in the entire universe!"

It's funny how people think life would be perfect if only they had different parents.

Jessica has hardly been home this week. She and her friends are looking for summer jobs. I saw them downtown this afternoon, while Steph, Alison and I were shopping for shorts and T-shirts. Jess and Kristen were inside Ed's car. They seemed to be having a heavy discussion, so I didn't wave or anything.

Later, when we sat down to dinner, Dad asked Jess how the job hunt was going. Jessica put down her fork. "I've been all over town. I've answered every help-wanted ad in the paper and I always get the same reaction. They take one look at my skin and say, 'Nothing available now.' One woman even whispered, 'Come back when your skin clears up, dear.' Can you believe it! I mean, is that discrimination or is that discrimination? I'm thinking of suing."

Jess caught the look that passed between Mom and Dad. "Well, why not?" she asked them. "You can sue for sex discrimination and race discrimination and other discriminations, so why *not* skin discrimination?"

Mom said, "It's a temporary condition, Jess. Painful, but temporary."

"Does that make it okay for people to treat me like a freak?" Jessica asked. "Maybe my skin will never clear up. Maybe no one will ever hire me for anything. Maybe I'll just wear a face mask for the rest of my life!"

"An interesting idea," Dad said, and we turned to him. "I mean," he said quickly, "the idea of discrimination based on a skin condition."

Jessica sat up, her eyes bright.

"Or could it be viewed as a disability?" Dad asked Mom.

Mom mulled that over while she chewed, then swallowed whatever was in her mouth. "The law says you can't discriminate against someone because of a disability," she said. "If we could prove that acne is a disability . . ."

"So you'll take my case?" Jessica asked Mom.

"As a judge I wouldn't be able to represent you, Jess."

We all stopped midmouthful and turned to Mom, who flushed.

"You heard?" Dad asked.

Mom nodded. "Today."

"Why didn't you say something?" I asked.

"I was waiting for the right moment," Mom said.

"Well," Dad said, "this calls for a special toast." He poured himself half a glass of wine and held it up. "To Nell Babcock Robinson, who will bring her sense of fair play and justice to the bench!"

Jess and I joined Dad in his toast, raising our water glasses to Mom. "Will you still have to finish your big case?" I asked.

"Yes, but this will be my last one as a trial lawyer." Then she said, "It'll mean a substantial cut in income."

"We'll manage," Dad said.

I love you, Mom mouthed at him.

I love you, too, Dad mouthed back.

"Does this mean we're not going to decide about my lawsuit?" Jess asked.

Mom snapped back to reality. "What I started to say, honey, is . . . as a judge I wouldn't be able to handle your case. Dad can talk to his friends at the Employment Rights Project. They might have some ideas for you."

"But not you!" Jess exploded. "Not my own mother, the greatest trial lawyer who ever lived. I'll bet you'd help Tarren, though, wouldn't you?"

Mom winced.

"Jessica . . ." Dad said, touching her hand.

"What?"

"That's not fair."

"Exactly!" Jess said.

Mom started to say, "Don't you think I know . . ."

But Jess got up from the table and marched into the kitchen with her plate.

Mom's face tightened but she continued to eat, taking very small bites.

Dad tried to reassure me. "She'll be all right," he said, knowing I was thinking about Jess. "She's just upset over not getting a job."

I nodded, trying not to show how close to tears I was, trying to eat the rest of my dinner exactly like Mom, cutting my food into tiny pieces so I barely had to chew.

On Friday night Stephanie invited Alison and me to her house for supper. Steph's mother came home from work with two pizzas—one plain and one with the works. She put them into the oven in their boxes, then went upstairs, calling, "Be down in a jiff."

Mrs. Hirsch is a lot younger than Mom. Her name is Rowena and she has permed hair and big eyes. She dresses in clothes that look like costumes. One day she'll wear a long peasant skirt—the next she's in western gear. She used to look more like your basic working woman, but since she and Mr. Hirsch split up she's become more exotic.

Steph's house is cluttered, with piles of magazines and papers waiting to be read, and odd pieces of furniture that don't make any sense, like the sink in the foyer. Mrs. Hirsch has taken off the cabinet doors in the kitchen, so everything, including cereal boxes, is right out in the open. Steph's father is the complete opposite of her mother. You wonder how they got married in the first place but not why they've split up.

Stephanie's brother, Bruce, is ten. He's a worrier, like me. He should have been *my* brother. "What's new?" I asked him, as we sat around the kitchen table.

"Only good news, Bruce!" Stephanie warned. "Nothing about the rain forest, endangered species, global warming or the homeless. We don't need any of your gloom and doom tonight."

Bruce thought that over and finally said, "The Mets beat the Cards ten–zip."

"You call that news!" Stephanie said.

"Yeah, I call that news," Bruce told her. "I call that very good news."

"I wonder if my brother's going to be a baseball fan," Alison said.

"Your brother's going to be a baby," Steph said.

"I wish you'd stop saying that!" Alison told her. "I was talking about when he's older."

Mrs. Hirsch came back into the kitchen wearing tight jeans and a lacy top. She pulled the pizza boxes out of the oven. They were beginning to smell like burned cardboard. She set them on the table and told us to help ourselves.

"Yum . . ." Alison said, taking the first bite.

As much as I enjoy pizza, I can't eat it without thinking about Jess and those obnoxious boys who call her Pizza Face.

As if Mrs. Hirsch could read my mind, she suddenly asked, "How's Jessica?"

"She's trying to get a job," I said, "but so far she hasn't had any luck."

"Tell her to give me a call," Mrs. Hirsch said. "I'm looking for someone intelligent and responsible." Mrs. Hirsch owns a travel agency in town. It's called Going Places.

"Jess is very intelligent and responsible," I told Mrs. Hirsch.

"I know that," she said. "I wouldn't expect anything less from your family, Rachel." She turned to Alison. "And how's it going with *your* mom? Is she feeling okay?"

"She says she feels fat," Alison said. "She can't see her toes in the shower."

Mrs. Hirsch laughed. "When is the baby due?"

"July eleventh."

"Tell your folks if there's anything I can do, just give me a call," Mrs. Hirsch said. "Now, who's ready for a second slice?"

We all answered at once.

When we'd polished off both pizzas, Stephanie carried a plate of brownies to the table. "Well . . ." her mother said, "as long as you're all here together, I may just run out for an hour or two."

"Where to?" Steph asked.

"To see a friend."

"What friend?"

"Really, Steph . . ." Mrs. Hirsch said, with half a laugh.

"Really, what?" Steph asked, shoving most of the brownie into her mouth at once.

"If you don't want me to go out, I won't," Mrs. Hirsch told her.

"Did I say that?" Steph looked around the table. "Did anyone hear me say that?"

None of us answered.

"I just want to know *what* friend you're going to see," Steph continued. "And I want a number where I can reach you. You *said* we should always have a number, just in case, remember?"

"Yes," her mother said, "I remember."

Alison and I exchanged glances as Mrs. Hirsch pulled the phone book out of a drawer and thumbed through it. She jotted down a number and handed it to Steph. Steph looked it over, then asked, "Who is Geoff Boseman?"

"A friend," Mrs. Hirsch said.

"I never heard of him."

Mrs. Hirsch sighed. "He's a new friend."

"You mean this is a date?"

"Not unless you call two friends having coffee together a date."

"I do if one is a man and one is a woman."

"You're overreacting, Steph," Mrs. Hirsch said. She dropped a kiss on Bruce's cheek, but when she tried to kiss Stephanie, Steph ducked and Mrs. Hirsch wound up kissing air. She gave Alison and me a kind of embarrassed smile. "I'll be back in two hours, at the latest. Keep everything locked." She grabbed her purse and headed for the kitchen door.

When she was gone, Stephanie said, "You think I was overreacting?"

"Yes," I said.

Then Steph looked at Alison, who nodded and said, "She's separated. She's allowed to have dates. But even if she was still married, she could meet a friend for coffee, or even dinner."

"A friend that Bruce and I have never heard of?"

"I've heard of him," Bruce said.

"You've heard of Geoff, with a *G*, Boseman?" Steph asked him.

"Yeah. Isn't he the guy Mom met at the gym?"

"The gym!" Steph said. "She's having coffee with some guy she met at the gym?"

"On the StairMaster," Bruce said.

"The StairMaster?"

"I think that's what she said."

"I can't believe this!" Stephanie said to the ceiling.

"Lighten up," Bruce told Steph. Exactly what Steph is always telling me.

"Yeah," Alison said, "stepfathers can be the best. Look at Leon."

"I don't *need* a stepfather!" Stephanie said.

"Isn't this conversation premature?" I asked. "I mean, one cup of coffee does not necessarily lead to marriage." As soon as I said it, I realized my mistake. Natural Helpers are supposed to listen carefully, not just to the spoken but to the unspoken. We're supposed to acknowledge feelings. But did I acknowledge Stephanie's feelings? No, I did not. And did I size up the seriousness of the situation and offer support and encouragement? *No.* If I'm going to be a Natural Helper, I'm going to have to learn to be a better friend.

At eight, Steph and I sat down to watch Gena's TV show. It's called "Franny on Her Own," and it's the only show on TV I watch regularly. Actually it's not as bad as most half hour comedies. It doesn't have a laugh track and it's not stupid. Gena plays an intelligent woman who comes to live in the city after years in the country. It's a kind of city-mouse, country-mouse story. They finished shooting for the season before she looked pregnant. Alison says Gena would rather stay home with the baby next year, but it's hard to give up that kind of salary.

"This is so embarrassing," Alison said as the show began. "I don't see why you want to watch it."

"Because your mother is the star!" Steph explained. "We know her."

"Why don't you tape it instead?" Alison said. "Then we could do something interesting."

"It's just half an hour," Steph told her. "You can read or something if you don't want to watch."

"Or play computer games with me!" Bruce said. "I couldn't care less about your mother's TV show."

"You're on!" Alison told him, and the two of them ran up to his room while Steph and I laughed over "Franny on Her Own." It felt good to laugh with Steph again. According to *Psychology Today*, laughter is the best medicine.

12

Jessica got the job at Going Places. She'll be working full-time over the summer but just three
afternoons, plus Saturdays, for now. After her first
day of work she was bubbling with excitement, not
just about the job but about Mrs. Hirsch. "*Rowena* . . .
isn't that the most romantic name?" she said on
Monday night. She was on the living room floor surrounded by travel brochures. "She's so warm."

"Who is?" Charles asked. He was passing through
with a copy of Stephen King's latest book. Stephen
King is his hero. Maybe he can go live with him in
Maine!

Jessica looked up at Charles. "I was talking about
Rowena Hirsch, my boss."

Mom came through then, with a mug of coffee.
"What about her?" she asked.

"I was just saying how *warm* she is," Jess repeated.

"How sincere. She's completely different from anyone I've ever known."

Mom raised her eyebrows but didn't comment.

"I'm thinking of becoming a travel agent," Jess said. "I mean, not right now, but later, when I finish college. I'd love to travel."

"Travel agents don't get to travel," I told Jess. "They arrange for other people to travel."

"Rowena doesn't travel much because she has kids at home," Jess said. "But there's another agent at her office who travels all the time. She writes a newsletter, reporting on hotels and stuff like that."

"You've only been working one day," Mom reminded her.

"You can tell a lot in one day," Jess said.

"A travel agent," Charles said. "That suits you, Jess."

"What do you mean by that?" Jessica asked, suddenly wary.

"I mean I can see you as a travel agent. You'd be very . . . competent."

Jessica didn't answer him. It's always hard to know when he's coming in for the kill.

"I'm glad you enjoyed your first day on the job," Mom said, "but shouldn't you be working on your English paper now?"

"It's not due until Friday."

"That doesn't give you much time."

Jess gathered up her travel brochures.

"And you've got the SAT's on Saturday morning," Mom reminded her. "I hope you've explained that to Rowena."

"I have . . . but they're just for practice."

"Still, you want to do your best, don't you?"

Jess muttered something under her breath and headed upstairs.

Charles tsk tsked. "It's not easy running your children's lives, is it, Mom?"

Mom gave him a look but didn't answer his question.

After Jessica's second day of work it was, "I love the way Rowena dresses. She has such style." The two of us were in the bathroom, brushing our teeth before bed. "And she built the business on her own. She's a real role model for today's young women."

"She's not that great," I said, annoyed at the way Jessica was gushing.

"I guess you really don't know Rowena the person, Rachel. You only know her as Stephanie's mother."

"You can tell a lot by how someone treats her children," I said. Not that I've ever seen Mrs. Hirsch treat Steph or Bruce badly, but she's not as perfect as Jessica thinks, either.

By the end of Jessica's first week of work we were all sick of hearing about Rowena and we'd pretty much tuned her out until she said, "And Rowena thinks I should be taking Accutane now." Mom and

Dad were at the kitchen table finishing their coffee and going over the household bills. Jess and I were drying the pots and pans from dinner. "She doesn't see any point in waiting and neither do I. She even gave me an article about it. Here . . ." Jess said, pulling a folded page from a magazine out of her pocket and shoving it under Mom's nose. "Her nephew's acne cleared up six weeks after he started taking it. *Six weeks!* And he hasn't had any side effects at all." She looked from Dad to Mom, then continued, "And with my salary I can pay for it on my own. Rowena even said she'd give me an advance, if I need it."

"Where did you get the idea we can't afford Accutane?" Mom asked.

"Well, it's expensive," Jess said. "And you've been making such a big thing out of your *substantial* cut in income now that you're going to be a judge."

"It's the serious side effects that concern me," Mom said, "not the cost. Our insurance would cover the cost."

Jess exploded. "The truth is, you don't want me to take it. You've never wanted me to take it!"

"Jessica, that's just not true," Mom said. "Accutane isn't a drug to take casually. Maybe Rowena doesn't know that. I'm going to call and straighten this out right now!"

"Nell . . ." Dad said.

"Don't *Nell* me," Mom told him, storming out of

the kitchen. Dad followed her into the living room.

"Welcome to another evening of fun and games with the Robinsons," Charles said, appearing out of nowhere. He opened the freezer and pulled out an ice-cream sandwich.

"Just shut up!" Jessica shouted.

Charles smiled and went out the kitchen screen door, letting it slam behind him.

"I wish I lived at Rowena's!" Jess said to me.

"You sound like Tarren," I told her. "And you know how much you love it when she gets going over Mom."

"This has nothing to do with Tarren!" Jess said.

"Why are you angry at me?" I asked. "What'd I do?"

"I'm *not* angry at you. I'm angry at *them*," she said, with a nod in the direction of the living room, "for not taking me to someone else when Dr. Lucas said I should wait before I take Accutane. And now I find out I've been suffering for more than a year just because Mom has some warped idea that bad skin makes you a stronger person."

"Mom never said that."

"She doesn't have to say it, Rachel. You've heard it often enough, haven't you? *Looking back*," Jess said, in a perfect imitation of Mom, "*I realize I am where I am today because I had very little social life during my teens due to bad skin. Bad skin has . . .*"

401

She stopped when she saw Mom standing in the doorway, listening. Then she ran from the room.

"How can she possibly believe that?" Mom asked. "Doesn't she know that I, of all people, sympathize and identify?"

I wasn't sure if Mom was talking to me or to herself.

On Monday afternoon, while I was sitting on our front steps waiting for Paul to give Charles his break, Tarren drove up. She looked very pretty in a summer dress and sandals, her dark hair pulled back, her cheeks flushed. "I have to leave Roddy for a few hours. Can you watch him? Please, Rachel, it's urgent."

"An obstacle?" I asked, looking into her car, where Roddy was napping with his pacifier in his mouth.

Tarren thought that over. "Not exactly," she said. "More of a . . ."

"A what?" I asked.

"Well, I guess you could call it an obstacle. A romantic obstacle." She looked down and fluttered her eyelashes.

"Really?" I said, hoping for more information.

"Rachel, this isn't something I can discuss with you or your mother or anyone else."

Now I was even more curious.

"He's married," Tarren whispered.

"Who is?" I asked.

"My obstacle," she said.

"Oh." Suddenly I felt very uncomfortable.

"He's my professor, at school. We're . . . involved."

Did that mean what I thought it meant?

"I know what your mother would say and I'm not prepared to take her advice," Tarren said. "Because he's wonderful. Even if he is married. Even if it doesn't make any sense. Do you see what I'm saying?"

"I think so."

"Do I have your word, Rachel . . . that you won't say anything about this?"

I nodded.

She hugged me. "Thanks." Then she opened the car door and reached in for Roddy. "Someday I'll cover for you. That's a promise."

"Do you by any chance know Paul Medeiros?" I asked, as she lifted out Roddy.

"No, should I?"

"He's Charles's tutor . . . he's graduating this month."

She handed Roddy to me. "I don't think I know him." She opened the trunk of her car and pulled out Roddy's stroller.

"What time will you be back?" I said.

"Around six, okay? If anyone asks, just say I'm at the library."

As soon as she pulled away, Roddy woke up and started screaming. "It's okay . . . it's okay . . ." I said, patting him. I tried to get his pacifier back into his mouth but he wouldn't take it. Then I offered him a bottle of apple juice, which he knocked out of my hand. Finally I strapped him into his stroller and wheeled him, at top speed, down to the pond. But he still didn't let up.

"Want to see the ducks?" I asked, lifting him out of his stroller. He thrashed around in my arms and screamed even louder.

Stephanie saw us from across the pond and waved. "Ra . . . chel," she called, "what are you doing?"

I didn't answer. It was obvious what I was doing.

In a minute Steph joined us and took Roddy from me. As soon as she did, he grew quiet and looked around. He seemed surprised to see me. Steph talked softly to him. Then she set him down on the ground and he began to crawl toward the pond, stopping along the way to pull up blades of grass that he stuffed into his mouth. We followed, also on hands and knees, making sure he didn't actually swallow anything.

Later, Steph said, "Can I stay over on Saturday night . . . because my mother has a date with the StairMaster and I'm not about to hang around the house waiting to meet him."

"Sure," I said. "Should we ask Alison, too?"

"Yeah, that'd be fun . . . like the old days."

I wanted to ask what she meant by *the old days* but I stopped myself, afraid I might spoil the moment.

Dad is a Gemini. His birthday is June 3. According to my book on horoscopes, you can't ever *really* know a Gemini. They have two sides. One you see, one you don't. I guess the side you don't see with Dad is the side that sent him to bed for six weeks after Grandpa died.

Mom left Jess and me a list of things to do for Dad's birthday dinner on Wednesday night. Jess doesn't work at Going Places on Wednesdays. The menu was honey-glazed chicken, wild rice and sugar snaps. Jess and I baked the cake—chocolate with buttercream frosting—while Paul was tutoring Charles. We decorated it with forty-seven candles plus one for good measure.

"Well . . . doesn't this look festive!" Mom said when she got home from work. She admired the table we'd set with our best linens and dishes. We'd even used Gram's silver, which was passed down from *her* mother. It's ornate and very beautiful, but we hardly ever use it because you can't put it in the dishwasher. It goes to the first daughter in the family, so Jess will inherit it someday. Maybe she'll let me borrow it on special occasions.

"What would I do without the two of you?" Mom asked, shaking two Tylenol out of a bottle, then washing them down with a glass of water.

Jessica didn't answer. She's still angry at Mom for listening to Dr. Lucas about not taking Accutane. Her skin looks angry, too—red and broken out, with swellings on her chin and forehead. Tomorrow she's got an appointment to see the dermatologist Rowena recommended.

Mom headed upstairs to get changed, and when she came down a few minutes later, she said, "Rachel . . . get Charles, would you? Dad will be home any minute."

"Charles doesn't eat with us . . . remember?"

"Tonight is a special occasion."

"We'd have a better time without him," I told her.

"Rachel, please! We have to make an effort."

"I don't see why," I muttered under my breath.

"Because that's the way I want it," Mom said, setting another place at the table.

"Okay . . . okay . . ." I said.

Charles's room is painted lipstick red, which was his favorite color when he was thirteen, the year he persuaded Mom and Dad to let him move downstairs. Last year, before he went away to school, he taped an embarrassing poster to the wall behind his bed. It shows a woman wearing only red boots. I WANT YOU! she's saying.

Mom was offended by it but Dad convinced her Charles was entitled to his privacy. So his room was declared off-limits to the rest of us, as long as he kept it reasonably clean. But keeping his room clean has never been a problem for Charles. Jessica is the one who lives in a mess. Charles likes things in order. Once, when I was in fourth grade, I made the mistake of letting Stephanie borrow one of his *Batman* comics, and he almost killed me for taking it out of its plastic wrapper.

Now I knocked on his door and when he called, "Come in . . ." I opened it slowly, not sure of what I might find. The shades were pulled, making it very dark except for a single bulb inside the slide projector. Charles lay on his bed, a black baseball hat on his head. He was munching chips dipped in salsa and swigging Coke from a can as he flipped through a tray of slides with his remote control.

"Look at this picture, Rachel . . ." he said, as if he were expecting me. "Remember when this was taken?"

I turned to look at the screen and saw a picture of the two of us at the lake in New Hampshire, where we go every summer to visit Aunt Joan. I'm about six and Charles is eight. We have a huge fish between us. We're both laughing and pointing to it. We look happy. Were we? I don't remember.

"Mom says your presence is requested at the dinner table," I told him. "We're celebrating Dad's birthday."

He cut off the projector, jumped off the bed, smoothed out his shirt and gave me a smile. "Do I look . . . acceptable?"

I nodded.

When Dad came home, he feigned surprise. "What's this?" he asked, eyeing the festive table.

"Happy birthday!" the rest of us shouted.

We go through this with each of our birthdays. Even though we're never surprised, we always pretend we are. We sit down to dinner before we open presents. Mom started that rule when we were little. Otherwise we'd get too involved in our gifts and forget about the food.

All through dinner Charles didn't make one rude remark. *Not one.* He ate heartily, complimenting us on the food, telling Dad he didn't look a day older than forty-five. He told charming stories about birthday parties he remembered. But I couldn't help noticing there were just three wrapped gifts on the table, not four. And I wondered how Charles would feel when Dad opened something from each of us, but not from him.

After the main course Charles insisted on helping

Jess and me clear the dishes. He even scraped the bread crumbs off the table like a waiter in an elegant restaurant. He asked if there was anything else he could do.

Jessica almost fainted. "I think that's about it," she said, lighting the candles on the cake.

"Wait!" Charles called, as we were about to carry it in. "This is the stuff family memories are made of." While he ran out of the room, trying to find the camera, Jess and I looked at each other. We didn't know what to think.

Charles snapped away on our Polaroid as we sang "Happy Birthday." It took three tries for Dad to get all forty-eight candles out. Then Jess moved the cake to the center of the table and we took our seats to watch Dad open his presents.

Jess gave him a book. She'd showed it to me earlier.

"What do you think?" she'd asked.

"*The Pencil*?" I said, leafing through it, amazed that anyone had written such a book. It was four hundred pages long.

"Look at the subtitle," she said. "*A History of Design and Circumstance*. You know Dad loves anything having to do with history."

And now, as Dad opened it, he seemed really pleased. "I've been meaning to check this out of the library," he told Jess. "Thank you, honey."

I gave Dad a snow globe. Inside is a tiny skier perched on a hill. Dad loves to ski. The second it snows, he straps on his cross-country skis and off he goes, around Palfrey's Pond, through the woods, even on the roads before they're plowed. One winter he got a pair of snowshoes and tried walking to school in them.

Dad turned the snow globe upside down and shook, then watched as snow fell on the little skier. "Thank you, Rachel," Dad said quietly. "I love it. It'll keep me going till next winter."

I knew he really meant it. With Mom it's a lot harder. She doesn't like most things that other people choose for her. That's why Jess and I always decide on something from the two of us. Like the Mother's Day subscription to that magazine. The sample copy is still on her bedside table. I wonder if she's ever actually looked at the pictures inside.

Then Dad opened the final box, from Mom, which held an envelope with two tickets to a concert at Carnegie Hall this coming Saturday night. Music is Dad's thing, not Mom's, but she tries for him. They smiled across the table at each other.

"Well," Mom said, "shall we cut the cake?"

"Wait!" Charles pushed back his chair. "I haven't given Dad my gift yet." He stood up and cleared his throat. "Dad . . ." he began, then paused to clear his throat again. "Dad . . . on this night, on the anniversary of your forty-seventh birthday, I give to you the gift of living history." He paused and looked at each of us. "I give you back your roots." He paused again. "From this night and forevermore . . ."

What was he up to this time?

"From this night," he continued, "I will proudly carry forth the name of our ancestors . . . from this night I will be known as Charles Stefan *Rybczynski*."

There was a deadly silence at the table. And then Jessica blurted out exactly what I was thinking. "You mean you're changing your last name from Robinson to Ryb-something?"

"I'm not changing it, Jess," Charles explained. "I'm reclaiming my true name . . . *our* true name."

Dad had a false smile on his face. "Well . . ." he began.

But Mom interrupted. "Are you contemplating a legal name change?" she asked Charles.

"Mom . . . Mom . . ." Charles shook his head. "Ever the lawyer. Does it really matter whether or not I go through the formalities of changing my name?"

"Yes," Mom said, "it does."

Charles pulled a document out of his back pocket and unfolded it carefully. He spread it out in front of Dad. "I'll need your signature," he said, "since I'm under eighteen. But I told my lawyer that wouldn't be a problem."

"Your lawyer?" Mom asked.

"Yes," Charles said. "My lawyer . . . Henry Simon."

"You went to see Henry without discussing it with us?" Henry Simon is an old family friend. He went to law school with Mom and Dad. He practices in town.

"Don't worry," Charles said. "I set up an appointment. I wore a nice shirt."

"You had no—" Mom began.

"I explained it was a surprise," Charles said. "And Henry . . . Mr. Simon, that is . . . promised he wouldn't say anything. He didn't, did he?"

"No," Mom said. "I wish he had."

"Poor Mom," Charles said. "You're feeling left out, aren't you? But you can do it, too. You can become *Judge Rybczynski*. It's easy." He looked around the table. "You can all become *Rybczynskis*."

"No thanks!" Jess said. "Can you imagine your children trying to print that name in first grade?"

I laughed. I couldn't help myself.

"Let's not get ahead of ourselves," Charles said, which made Dad laugh, too.

"Well, Charles . . ." Dad finally said, "it's a mouthful to say and a bitch to spell. . . ."

Charles handed him a pen, but before Dad could sign his name Mom said, "Victor . . . don't you think you should sleep on it?"

"What for?" Dad asked. "If Charles wants the family name, it's his." Dad signed his name to the document, then sat back in his seat. "You know . . . I remember my grandfather telling me a story about the day he got to Ellis Island. The officials couldn't say his name, let alone spell it. My grandparents didn't speak a word of English but they understood what was happening. And they were all for it. A new country. A new life. A new name. I wonder what they'd think if they were here tonight?"

"I think they'd be honored," Charles said.

"You could be right," Dad told him.

Mom picked up the cake knife. "I guess it's time for dessert," she said, cutting into the cake as if she were trying to kill it.

Later I overheard Mom and Dad in the kitchen. "We're talking about a name that's going to follow him the rest of his life," Mom said.

"Maybe . . . maybe not," Dad told her. "And either way I still think it was better to sign, without making it into a production."

"You actually *like* the idea, don't you?"

"There's a certain strength to a name like that," Dad admitted.

"Well, I hate the whole thing! It's just one more way for him to separate himself from the rest of the family."

"He's testing us . . . you know that."

"I'm tired of being tested!" Mom said. "I'm tired

of him manipulating us. And I hate what this is doing to the girls."

I stood with my back against the wall right outside the kitchen. My heart was thumping so loud I was sure they could hear it.

"Sometimes I feel . . ." Mom continued. "Sometimes I feel such anger toward him I scare myself. Then I remember what a sweet, clever baby he was." Her voice broke. "If I didn't have those memories to fall back on, I don't think I could tolerate another day of his mischief."

"Nell . . . honey . . ."

I sneaked a look into the kitchen. Dad was holding Mom in his arms. I backed away as quietly as possible, right into Charles, who jabbed me in the sides with his fingers, making me cry out.

"What?" Dad asked, rushing into the hall.

"Nothing," I said.

Charles laughed. "Rachel's very edgy," he said. "She's worried she won't be able to spell my last name."

"**H**ow do you *spell* that name?" Stephanie said. She and Alison had come over to spend Saturday night.

"R-y-b-c-z-y-n-s-k-i."

"How do you pronounce it again?" Alison asked, unrolling her sleeping bag and placing it next to Steph's.

"Rib-jin-ski," I told her.

"That's an incredible name," Alison said.

"Why would anyone *want* such a long last name?" Steph said. She pulled a stuffed coyote out of her overnight bag. She's slept with that coyote since her father won it for her at a carnival. She says she plans to take it to college with her. She says she plans to take it on her honeymoon if and when she decides to get married.

"You'd have to ask Charles," I told her.

"Where is he?"

"Stephanie!" I said. "Don't you dare ask him!"

"But you said . . ."

"She was just kidding," Alison told Steph. "Right, Rachel?"

"I was definitely not serious!" I said.

"Is Charles home?" Alison asked.

"I believe he's in his room."

Mom and Dad had left for New York on the 4:30 train. They planned to have dinner at their favorite restaurant before the birthday concert at Carnegie Hall. Mom wore her slinky black dress, the one Jessica *borrowed* for her junior prom. Jess got home from work before they left. "How come you're so dressed up?" she'd asked when she saw Mom.

"It's a benefit," Mom told her, "for the Legal Defense Fund. There's a party after the concert."

Jess seemed nervous, especially when Mom looked in the mirror and said, "I don't know. There's something about this dress. Does it look odd to you, Victor?"

"It looks great!" Dad said. Obviously no one had told him what Jess wore to the prom.

Mom sniffed herself. "It doesn't smell like my perfume," she said.

"Whose could it possibly be?" Jessica asked, sounding defensive.

"I've no idea," Mom said. "Something just doesn't feel right."

"It shouldn't feel any different than it always feels," Jessica said. I shot her a look, hoping she'd shut up about Mom's dress, but she didn't. "It shouldn't feel any different than when you wore it to that benefit for the homeless."

"Maybe I've gained weight," Mom said, adjusting the straps.

"You never gain weight," Jess told her. "It's probably that you're not wearing those dangling earrings." Jess was talking about the earrings *she* wore to the prom.

"They'd be too much for tonight," Mom said.

When Mom and Dad finally left, Jessica let out a long sigh. "Do you think she guessed?" Jess asked.

"No, but you were acting so guilty she would have in another minute."

"I couldn't help myself," she said. "I didn't mean to say anything but the words just kept pouring out. I should have taken the dress to the cleaners."

"Mom'll probably send it after tonight. Stop worrying."

Jess looked at me and laughed. "This must be a first . . . *you* telling *me* not to worry!"

Later Jess went out with Kristen and Richie. Ed and Marcy have the flu.

A few minutes before seven, the three of us took our positions at the windows in my room facing Steph's house. Even though Steph refuses to meet the StairMaster, she is very curious about him.

At five after seven, a red pickup truck pulled up to Steph's. A guy in jeans and a leather jacket got out. A guy with a ponytail. Stephanie inhaled sharply.

"It's probably just a delivery," Alison told her.

We watched him swagger up to the front door. He wasn't carrying a package. In fact, his hands were in his pockets until he rang the bell. Mrs. Hirsch answered.

"He's probably selling magazines," Alison said.

Steph didn't say anything.

Mrs. Hirsch was wearing jeans, western boots and a fringed jacket. She linked her arm through his. They laughed as they got into his truck.

"I guess he's not selling magazines," Alison said.

"I can't believe this!" Steph finally said. "How old do you think he is?"

"Over eighteen," Alison said.

"Probably thirty," I said.

"Right," Alison said, glancing at me. "And they're probably just friends. Younger men and older women make good friends for each other. I read about it in *People* magazine."

But Stephanie wasn't listening. "And with a ponytail!" she said. "This is so embarrassing!"

If I were a Natural Helper right now, what would I do? I reminded myself of the first steps we learned at the introductory meeting. *Listen, not just to the spoken but to the unspoken. Be aware of body language.* Right now Steph had her arms folded across her chest. An angry pose, a defiant one. *Be on her side. Offer encouragement and support, but not advice . . .*

But as soon as the red truck pulled out, Steph said, "Let's play Spit!" You could tell she didn't want to talk about her mother and the StairMaster.

So for the next hour we played Spit, a card game Alison had taught us. It's meant for just two players but we've invented a way it can be played with three. I used to hate it, but lately I've learned it's an excellent way to relieve tension. It's such a fast game you can't afford the time to think—you just have to react. And it's so silly we always wind up laughing our heads off and singing "Side by Side," our theme song.

Tonight, when we got to the section that goes

Through all kinds of weather
What if the sky should fall . . .

Stephanie stopped and turned to me. "That's the perfect line for you, Rachel."

"What line?" I asked.

"That line." She sang it. "What if the sky should fall?"

"I don't know what you mean," I told her.

"You always think the sky is falling."

"I do not think the sky is falling."

"You think the worst is going to happen," she said. "And that's the same thing."

"I do not think the worst is *necessarily* going to happen!"

Alison held up her hands. "Let's not get into one of these stupid arguments," she said. "Okay?"

"Who's arguing?" I asked.

"I didn't mean it was bad or anything," Steph said. "I just meant . . ."

But we were interrupted by a sudden blast of music. When I opened my bedroom door, it grew even louder. I walked to the stairway and called downstairs, "Kindly lower the volume!" My choice of words made Alison and Stephanie laugh.

But Charles either couldn't hear me or chose to ignore my request. Now the neighbors would start calling. There are rules at Palfrey's Pond and one of them is no noise loud enough to break the tranquillity of the area. I love that word, *tranquillity*. It means peacefulness, serenity.

I looked at Stephanie and Alison. "I better go tell him to turn it down." As they followed me, the phone rang. "I knew it," I said. "Neighbors."

"Aren't you going to answer?" Steph asked.

"No," I said. "Let the machine take the message."

We paused outside Charles's bedroom door. The sound of the music was deafening. "Metallica," Alison said to Steph. They know the names of all the groups. But they don't know Bach from Beethoven.

Finally I knocked. No response. So I banged on his door with two fists and shouted, "Charles . . . turn that down!"

Suddenly the music clicked off and the door opened, just enough for Charles to have a look. Stephanie and Alison giggled nervously. They find anything having to do with Charles exciting.

"The neighbors are going to call to complain!" I told him.

"It's my warden," Charles announced. As he opened his door all the way, a pungent odor hit us. It was so dark and smoky in his room, it took me a minute to realize he wasn't alone.

Marcella, the eighth-grade slut, sat on the floor with Adrienne, a ninth grader who has a major attitude. There were also two guys I'd never seen before, swigging beer from bottles. And over in the corner, looking unhappy and out of place, were Dana Carpenter and Jeremy Dragon! What were *they* doing here?

"Macbeth!" Jeremy said when he saw me. "What are *you* doing here?"

"I live here," I told him. Why would Jeremy and Dana be at a party in Charles's room, especially since everyone knows about their fight over Marcella?

"You live here?" he asked, surprised.

"This is my baby sister," Charles said. "Rachel Lowilla, the child prodigy." He grabbed my wrist.

"Come in, Rachel . . ." He beckoned to Stephanie and Alison. "Come in, girls. We're celebrating my name change. Have a beer . . . have a joint . . . loosen up!"

"No thank you!" As I tried to pull away, Dana came up behind him and rested her hand on his arm. "Charles," she said quietly.

Charles let go of me and wrapped an arm around Dana's waist. They smiled at each other. What was going on here? "You're going to read about my little sister someday," Charles told his guests. "In addition to developing a vaccine to prevent hair balls in lions, she's going to—"

"Murder her brother!" I shouted, not waiting for him to finish. Then I slammed the door and broke for the stairs, with Alison and Steph following. When we got back to my room, I slammed *my* door and woke the cats.

"I *knew* Dana liked Charles!" Steph said, flopping in my chair.

"Some people have no taste," I muttered.

"And *he* likes her!" Steph continued.

"I thought he liked me," Alison said.

Steph and I looked at her.

"Well, he acted like he did . . . didn't he?" she asked. "I mean, that night I came over to get a book, he definitely acted like he was interested. You were there, Rachel."

I shrugged.

Alison continued, "I think what happened is he realized I'm just in seventh grade and he decided I'm too young . . . for now."

"Right," Steph said. She waited for me to agree.

There was no point in hurting Alison, so I said, "It's possible."

"Anything's possible," Alison said, using one of my favorite lines.

"Right," Steph and I said at the same time.

We were quiet for a minute, until we heard a voice calling, "Macbeth . . . where are you, Macbeth?"

Jeremy Dragon?

"Open the door," Steph whispered.

I opened it.

"Hey . . ." Jeremy said.

"Hey . . ." I said back. *I could not believe this!*

"Aren't you going to invite me in?" he asked. I stepped aside. He walked into my room and looked around. "Nice," he said. "Very . . . neat."

"Yeah," Steph said, "a hot Saturday night for Rachel is folding her socks!" Then she laughed nervously.

I could have killed her!

But Jeremy thought it was a joke. He laughed and said, "So, is that what you're doing . . . folding Macbeth's socks?"

Steph said, "No . . . we're just hanging out."

"Well, if you're just hanging out," Jeremy said, "how about a game?"

"A game?" I repeated.

"Yeah, a game . . . like Monopoly."

"You want to play Monopoly?" I asked. *I definitely could not believe this!*

"Yeah," he said. "That is, I wouldn't mind."

I looked at Alison and Steph. We were having trouble keeping straight faces. I went to my closet, reached up to my top shelf and pulled down my Monopoly set, which Tarren had given to me when I was in third grade.

The four of us settled on the floor, with Jeremy seated between me and Steph, across from Alison. He chose the little race car for his token. I took the hat.

We rolled to see who would start. Alison got the high number. None of us asked Jeremy anything about Charles's party. And he didn't volunteer any information. For the next two hours we concentrated on Monopoly. Midway through the game I went down to the kitchen and brought up a bottle of apple juice, a bag of pretzels, and a tin of cookies my aunt had sent us. Jeremy ate three-quarters of the cookies and drank half the juice.

The game finally ended when Alison built hotels on Boardwalk and Park Place and the rest of us went bankrupt. By then it was close to eleven and the three of us walked Jeremy downstairs. He didn't head for Charles's room or even call goodnight to anyone at the party, which, from the sound of it, was still going strong.

I didn't want to think about Charles's party. I'm not the family warden, despite what Charles says. It's not my job to report on him to my parents. If he does something that directly affects me, that's different. If not, let them find out on their own.

"Goodnight, Macbeth," Jeremy said as he went out the door and down the path. "Good game."

The three of us went back up to my room and fell across my bed, laughing hysterically. Then we were absolutely quiet. Then we began laughing hysterically again, until our sides were splitting.

I woke up sometime later to see Stephanie sitting in the window. I crept out of bed and kneeled beside her. The StairMaster's truck was parked in front of her house. "It's been there for an hour at least," she whispered. "And don't tell me they're just talking."

"It is possible."

"Please!"

"Sorry."

"I hate this!" Steph whispered, looking over at Alison, who was totally out of it in her sleeping bag. "It's so . . . disgusting!"

I nodded.

She choked up. "If she marries someone like him, I'm moving out. I'll go live with my dad."

"You can live with us," I said.

She smiled. "Thanks."

I put my arm around her shoulder. "It must be really hard to see your mother with someone like him."

"It is . . . it's so hard." Then she cried. I held her and patted her back. "Thank you," she said after a few minutes. "I think I'll go to sleep now."

I wish I could just let go and cry like that. I wish I knew how to let my friends comfort me.

At the bus stop on Monday morning, Dana said, "Just so you know . . . it's all over between Jeremy and me."

"You don't have to explain," I told her.

"But I want to. You seemed so . . ." She paused, trying to find the right word. "You seemed so *surprised* the other night."

"I was."

"You really don't know Charles, do you?" she said. "If you'd just give him half a chance, you might be . . ." She paused again, then came up with the same word. "*Surprised.*"

"He's a very surprising person," I agreed.

She shook her head at me, obviously annoyed. "I really don't understand you, Rachel. Most of the time you seem so grown-up, and then you . . ."

I glanced over at Alison and Stephanie, who were listening to every word.

"I just hope you'll try to get to know your brother," Dana continued, "because he's a very warm and intelligent person."

"If you say so."

"And would you, please, stop acting like such a bitch!" With that, she turned and marched away from me in a huff.

Now Stephanie and Alison were really cracking up. I went over to them, took each one by the arm like a mother with two small children, and led them away.

"Is she *really* going with Charles?" Alison asked.

"It sounds like *she* thinks so," Steph said.

"What about *him*?" Alison asked. "Does *he* think he's going with *her*?"

"I wouldn't know," I said. "Charles and I haven't exchanged a word since Saturday night."

That afternoon Dana rang our doorbell. "I'm here to see Charles," she said when I came to the door.

"Charles is with his tutor," I told her. "He's busy until five-thirty."

"I know that," she said, as if she knows everything about our family. "But they take a break at four-thirty, don't they?"

"Yes," I said, "but just for ten minutes."

She checked her watch. It was quarter after four. "If you don't mind, I'll wait."

"Suit yourself," I told her. But I didn't invite her inside.

428

"And Rachel," she said, "I'd really appreciate it if you wouldn't discuss this with Jeremy again."

"Discuss what with Jeremy?" I asked, since I've never actually discussed anything with him.

"*This*," Dana said, as if I were stupid. "Charles and me."

"I've never discussed you and my brother with Jeremy."

"Oh, please!" she said. "It's not like I didn't see the two of you coming out of math class today."

But what Jeremy had said on the way out of math class today had nothing to do with Dana.

He'd said, "I can't say I like your brother, Macbeth."

"I can't say I do, either," I'd answered.

"He's too full of himself."

"He's definitely full of something."

"He's not . . . you know . . . as *real* as you," he'd said, looking directly into my eyes. The way he said it made it sound like a compliment, but I couldn't be sure.

So Dana sat on the front steps to wait for Charles. Burt rubbed against her leg and she petted him, cooing, "Good kitty . . . sweet kitty." I turned away and went back into the house.

At four-thirty, when Charles and Paul came into the kitchen for their break, Charles asked, "Is Dana here?"

"Out front," I told him.

"You could have invited her in," he said.

"You didn't mention you were expecting company," I answered.

Paul dropped an arm around Charles's shoulder and said, "No distractions during our time together. Ask her to come back at five-thirty . . . okay?"

"Okay," Charles called, on his way to the front door. He didn't sound angry or even annoyed. I don't understand how Charles can get along so well with Paul but not with any of us. If Mom or Dad had said no distractions during tutoring, Charles would have told them where to go. But with Paul, he's a totally different person. He's keeping up with his schoolwork and even moving ahead of where he would be if he were just finishing ninth grade. Of course since he's already finished ninth grade once before, that's not surprising. But still . . . As soon as Charles left the kitchen, Paul looked at me and said, "What about you, Rachel?"

"*What* about me?" I asked.

"Do you have a boyfriend?"

"No!" I answered too quickly, feeling my lower lip begin to twitch. I couldn't look at him. Instead I said, "I have to practice now. Excuse me." And I ran from the room.

"When am I going to hear you play?" Paul called after me.

"Whenever . . ." I called back.

I wish I could let Paul know how I feel about him.

I often imagine us having deep, meaningful conversations. I often imagine us kissing passionately. Sometimes I imagine *more* than kisses. If Steph knew what I was thinking, she'd be relieved. She'd say, *So you're normal after all . . . at least in* that *way!* But she can't know. No one can. Paul has to remain my secret.

Mom lost her big jury trial on the same day I won a major debate against a ninth grader at Kennedy Junior High. Toad Scrudato, the only other seventh grader on our team, said, "Rachel, you were brilliant!" Those were his exact words. So obviously I was feeling pretty good. This was before I found out about Mom. At the time I didn't even mind that Toad's father's car broke down on the Merritt Parkway on the way home from the debate and we had to be towed to a garage, then wait an hour while a new battery was installed.

I called home at quarter to six to say I'd be late. Charles answered. I asked for Dad. He said Dad was coaching at a track meet. When I asked for Mom, he said she wasn't home yet, either. "And neither is Jessica, so that leaves me, Rachel. Do you have a message for me?" I told him about Mr. Scrudato's car but nothing else.

Then Toad and I sat on the curb outside the garage and read while Mr. Scrudato made call after call on his car phone. Toad and I have known each other since kindergarten. We're sort of an odd couple. He's always been the smallest kid in our class and I've always been the tallest, until Max Wilson moved here. But we have a lot in common intellectually.

By the time Toad's father dropped me off at our house, it was after seven. As soon as I walked in, Dad took me aside and said, "Mom lost her case. She's pretty upset."

"Should I say something?"

Dad shook his head. "You know how she is. She doesn't want to talk about it."

The same way I was when I missed *sesquipedalian* and lost the state spelling championship last year.

Still, I was surprised when Mom didn't come to dinner. It's not as if this is the first case she's ever lost.

"She's just disappointed," Dad told Jess and me as he grilled hamburgers on the patio. "She wanted to go out on a high note."

"Who?" Jess asked, as if she lived on another planet.

"Mom," Dad said. "This is a blow to her pride but she'll get over it." He sounded like he was trying to convince not only us, but himself. I must have looked strange because Dad reached out to touch my arm. "Don't worry, Rachel . . ."

Until then I wasn't worried.

Charles passed by, grabbing a roll. He flipped a

hamburger onto it and smothered it with salsa. "Is it true?" he asked, taking a huge bite. "Did the perfect litigator really lose her final case?"

Dad snapped at him. "A little compassion is in order this evening, Charles!"

"Yeah, sure," he said, with a mouthful. "I've got compassion. I'm just saying, you know, we'd all be better off if we were less competitive."

"Speak for yourself," I said.

"I always speak for myself, Rachel," he said, going out through the patio gate.

After dinner I went upstairs. The door to Mom and Dad's bedroom was open a crack. I knocked lightly. "Mom . . ." No answer. I pushed the door open and tiptoed in. She was asleep with an ice pack across her forehead. I looked around and was surprised to see her suit tossed over a chair and her shoes in the middle of the floor as if she'd kicked them off on her way into bed. "I'm sorry you lost your case," I whispered as I picked them up and put them in her closet. But she didn't hear me.

I went down the hall to my room and sat at my desk, staring out the window. I wasn't in the mood for my math homework. I wondered what my teacher would do if I came in tomorrow and used that as an excuse. *Sorry, I didn't feel like doing my homework last night.* She'd probably call Mrs. Balaban, who would send me to Dr. Sparks!

While I was sitting there, Dad came in. "Tell me about the debate."

I didn't want to talk about it now. It didn't seem right to be happy about winning when Mom was so unhappy. So I just gave him the basics.

"I'm proud of you, honey," he said. "But I'd love you just the same if you'd lost today. You know that, don't you?"

"Why do you always say that?"

"Say what?"

"That you'd love me just the same if I lost."

"Because it's true."

"That's not what I mean."

"Then what?"

I wasn't sure how to explain it. "I mean," I said, trying to find the right words, "why can't you just accept good news?"

"I guess I want you to remember that winning's not the most important thing in life."

"But it's a lot better than losing," I told him. "Just ask Mom."

He ran his hands through his hair. He does that when he's thinking. So I quickly added, "Mom would be glad I won. I don't see why you can't be, too."

"I *am* glad, Rachel. I just want you to keep it in perspective." He dropped a kiss on top of my head. "I've got to run over to the library. Be back in an hour."

When he was gone, I jotted down *Keep it in per-*

spective on my math worksheet. Under that I wrote *Victor Robinson, Tuesday, June 9.*

The next afternoon, right before school ended, I was called to Mr. Herman's office. The one time in my entire life I didn't do my homework and I've been reported to the vice principal! I felt sick. I wondered if this would go down on my permanent record. When I got to his office, Toad was there, too, looking as terrified as me. Mr. Herman told us to make ourselves comfortable but neither of us moved an inch. Even though he has a friendly smile, Mr. Herman's size makes him formidable. Kids call him the sumo wrestler.

"Good news," he said. "You've both been recommended for Challenge, a new program for junior high students who excel academically. If your parents give permission, you'll be taking courses in math and science at the college next year."

As he explained it to us, I began to feel like I couldn't breathe. Another program to separate me from my friends! When he asked if we had any questions, I managed to say, "Do we *have* to?"

"Have to what, Rachel?"

"Do this?"

Toad looked at me as if I were totally insane. But I didn't care. I felt light-headed and grabbed hold of the back of a chair facing Mr. Herman's desk.

"It's entirely up to you," he said. "It's an honor just to be asked."

"A person can't do everything just because she's asked," I told him.

"A good point," he said.

I definitely could not breathe! I closed my eyes and forced myself to count backward from one hundred.

Mr. Herman never noticed. He went right on talking. "Well, I guess this has really caught both of you by surprise!" When neither of us responded, he cleared his throat. "Here's a letter to take home to your parents." He handed one to Toad and another to me. "Think of this as an opportunity not to be missed."

As the bell rang, I shoved the letter into my purse. I wish I could explain to Mr. Herman and everyone else that right now I don't *need* another opportunity.

On the bus home from school Alison said, "Are you okay, Rachel?"

"Yes . . . why?"

"You look sort of pale."

Steph squinted at me. "No, she doesn't. She's always that color."

"She's usually got *some* pink in her cheeks," Alison said. "Maybe she's coming down with that flu."

"She looks fine to me," Steph said.

While they were arguing, some guy shoved Jeremy

Dragon, who was getting off at the next stop, right into my lap.

"Sorry about that, Macbeth," he said as he pulled himself up.

I could feel my cheeks burning, especially when the driver yelled at us to quit fooling around.

As Jeremy got off the bus, Alison whispered, "You're not pale anymore, Rachel!"

"I wish he'd fall onto me!" Steph said, making all three of us laugh.

The minute I got home, I folded and refolded the letter from Mr. Herman until it was small enough to fit into the secret compartment of my favorite box. Since Mr. Herman says participating in Challenge is entirely up to me, I don't have to show it to my parents. At least not yet.

Jessica's been taking Accutane for a week. The doctor Rowena recommended told Jess about the possible side effects and gave her a booklet to read. But Jess decided to try it, anyway. I don't blame her. I'd try anything if I had her kind of cystic acne. Before the doctor gave her the prescription Jess had to sign a paper stating she would not get pregnant, because if you take Accutane while you are, it causes serious birth defects. As if Jess would be foolish enough to get pregnant even if she had a boyfriend, which she doesn't.

Jess will have to see the doctor once a month for twenty weeks. She'll need blood tests to make sure everything's going okay. She says Accutane can take up to four months to work but some patients see a difference right away. I hope she'll be one of them.

Tarren and Roddy came over for dinner on Thursday night. Tarren took one look at Jess and said, "Your skin looks . . . painful."

"Well, it's not as painful as acne," Jess told her. Her face was totally dried out and peeling. So far Jessica's only side effects are dry eyes and cracked lips. She carries a tube of medicated lip gloss with her and has to put drops in her eyes twice a day.

Before we sat down to dinner, Tarren cornered me. "Listen, Rachel . . ." she said, shifting Roddy from one hip to the other, "I wanted to thank you for that day you watched Roddy."

I nodded. "How's it going with your romantic obstacle?"

"It's going great."

I nodded again, then looked around to make sure no one was within earshot. "Have you by any chance met Paul Medeiros?" I spoke very softly. "He's a history major at the school of education."

"You've asked me about him before, haven't you?"

"I thought maybe you've met him since then."

Tarren shook her head. "Is he someone special?"

"No," I said quickly, hoping Tarren wouldn't become suspicious. "I mean, he's Charles's tutor . . . and I'm curious . . . but other than that . . ."

"Well, I don't think I know him. Do you want me to ask around?"

"No . . . forget it . . . it's nothing."

"You're sure . . . because I owe you a favor."

"I'm sure," I told her.

Charles joined us for dinner. I don't know why. He hasn't had a meal with us since Dad's birthday. He sat next to Roddy, who was in a Sassy Seat, which attached to the table.

We were having corkscrew pasta with vegetables and Mom's special lemon-and-herb sauce. The green peppers weren't cooked quite enough for me, so I moved them to the side of my plate. Tarren did the same with her mushrooms.

"Tarren," Mom said, "I'd like you to come to my swearing-in ceremony. It's the morning of June twenty-third, in Hartford. After, we'll all go out to lunch."

"Oh, Aunt Nell," Tarren gushed. "I'm honored."

I wondered how long it would take to drive to Hartford. If it's more than half an hour, maybe I can take the train. I wouldn't want to get carsick on the day Mom is sworn in as a judge.

Charles was quiet, intrigued by Roddy, who was slowly and methodically eating Cheerios. He picked up one at a time, using two fingers, brought it to his mouth, got it inside, then mashed it with his gums. He still doesn't have teeth. Tarren says he will soon.

"Was it always your goal to become a judge, Aunt Nell?" Tarren asked, as Dad served the salad.

"I really hadn't given the possibility much thought

until recently," Mom said. "But frankly, after this week, I'm beginning to think it will be a relief."

"What do you mean?" Tarren asked, wide-eyed.

"I lost a case," Mom told her. "I lost my final jury trial." She sounded wistful, almost emotional. This was the first time she'd mentioned the verdict.

"I can't imagine you losing a case!" Tarren said.

"Well, I did," Mom told her, "and I took it personally, even though I know better." She kind of sighed as she speared a tomato. "But I did my best and that's what counts."

Tarren had tears in her eyes. "That is just so moving, Aunt Nell. To know you've done your best even when you've failed."

Charles looked up, suddenly interested. Then Mom said, "I didn't exactly fail, Tarren. I lost a case that I'd rather have won, that's all. It happens." She sounded sure of herself again, like Mom.

"It's all about goals, isn't it?" Tarren asked. "In our Life Studies class we had to write down where we hope to be five years from today, then ten, then twenty. It really got me thinking."

Charles looked over at Tarren. Before he had the chance to pounce, Dad said, "What *are* your goals, Tarren?"

"Well, some of them are personal," Tarren said, with a glance in my direction, "and I'd rather not discuss them. But my professional goal is to become the best fourth-grade teacher I possibly can. To make a difference in a few children's lives."

Charles let out a snort.

Tarren leaned forward in her seat so she could look directly at Charles. "It would be a good course for you to take," she told him. "Talk about someone who needs to clarify his goals!"

Didn't she know better than to start in with him?

"My goals in life are very simple," Charles told her. We all waited for more but first Charles reached for his water glass and took a long drink. Then he wiped his mouth with his napkin. With Charles, timing is everything. Finally he said, "My main goal in life is to be Batman!"

"Really, Charles!" Mom said, as Charles lifted Roddy out of his Sassy Seat and bounced him on his lap to the theme from the Batman movie.

Roddy laughed and said, "Da da . . ."

"I'm not your da da," Charles said, "but speaking of your da da, is he still soaring?"

Tarren sucked in her breath. "As far as I know Bill is still hang gliding, if that's what you mean. We have almost no contact."

"Poor little guy!" Charles patted Roddy's head.

"He doesn't need your pity!" Tarren told Charles. "He's going to be just fine."

"That's the spirit!" Mom said, squeezing Tarren's shoulder.

"Having a runaway father is just one obstacle in his life," Tarren said. "And we all have our obstacles."

"Yeah, look at me," Charles said. "I'm surrounded by mine. My father, the *wimp* . . . my mother, the *ice queen* . . . my big sister, the *potato head* . . . and my little sis—"

Before he had the chance to finish, Jessica pushed back her chair. "I hate you!" she hissed.

"I know that, Jess . . . but you'll get over it."

Mom jumped up, her face purple with rage. "You want to hurt us, Charles? Okay, we're hurt! You want to cause pain? Fine, you have! You want to disrupt the family? Congratulations, you've succeeded!" She banged her fist on the table so hard the dishes rattled.

Roddy began to cry. Tarren snatched him from Charles's lap and whisked him into the kitchen, where his screams grew louder. By then Dad was out of his seat, grabbing hold of Mom, who had lunged at Charles, shouting, "Enough is enough!" A glass she'd knocked over rolled to the edge of the table, tumbled to the floor and smashed.

Charles folded his napkin. "Well," he said, "this pleasant evening seems to be drawing to a close."

As he began to get up from the table, Dad pushed him down again. "Stay right where you are!"

Charles looked surprised for a minute. The color drained from his face. He didn't move.

"We're not going to tolerate any more nights like this!" Dad shouted. "It's time for you to get your act together. Do you understand what I'm saying?"

Mom stood next to Dad, waiting for an answer.

Charles gave them a long look, then asked, "Is that it? Are you finished?"

"Oh, for God's sake!" Mom said, and I could feel her frustration.

"No, I'm not finished," Dad told him. "I'm waiting for you to answer the question!"

"I believe I get your point," Charles said quietly. "Now, may I please be excused?"

Dad didn't answer right away. When he did, his voice was flat. "You're excused to help clean up."

"Thank you." Charles stood, stacked the dinner dishes and carried them into the kitchen.

I ducked under the table to pick up the broken glass.

"I've had it," Mom said to Dad. "This time I have *really* had it."

"We can't give up on him, Nell."

"I'm not saying we should give up on him. I'm saying he's pushed me to the limit!"

Before I'd collected all the glass, the phone rang. "It's Stephanie, Rachel," Tarren called from the kitchen.

"Tell her I can't talk now," I said quietly, from the floor. "Tell her I'll call back."

445

But I didn't call Stephanie that night. And later, as I lay in bed watching the clock, I played the dinner table scene over and over in my mind, angry at myself for just swallowing everything I was thinking and feeling—for just sitting there, totally paralyzed, waiting to hear what Charles would say about me, almost disappointed that Jess stopped him before he'd had the chance to finish.

I got out of bed and crept down the hall to Jessica's room. But she was sound asleep, breathing evenly. How could she sleep after tonight? How could anyone?

My stomach was killing me. I needed something to soothe it. I moved silently downstairs with Harry right behind me. When I got to the kitchen, I flicked on the light switch and almost keeled over when I saw Charles perched on the counter, gnawing a chicken leg.

"Want a bite?" he asked, holding it out.

"You just about scared me to death!" I told him, keeping my voice low. The last thing I wanted was to wake Mom and Dad. "Why are you in here in the dark?"

"Is there a family rule against conserving energy?"

I didn't answer. Instead I filled the kettle and turned on the burner.

Charles jumped down from the counter. He opened the refrigerator, pulled out the grape juice and held it up, as if to toast me. "Here's to you, Rachel Robinson!" He swigged some juice right out of the bottle, then slammed the door. "Here's to my whole fucking family!"

"You better not let Mom and Dad hear you say that."

"Yeah, right. They'd call the language police. And the language police will drag me to the dictionary to find a more acceptable word for my family, like noble . . . like self-sacrificing . . . like—"

"You were despicable tonight!"

"Thanks, Rachel."

"Why'd you have to hurt everyone? What was the point?"

"The point was to get at the truth."

"Well, you didn't!" I told him. "You didn't even come close."

"Really."

"Yes, really! Mom's not an ice queen."

"Maybe not to you. After all, you're her clone."

"I'm not anybody's clone! And Dad's not a wimp, either."

"Then how come he went to bed for six weeks when Grandpa died? How come he couldn't make it in the real world? How come he gives the Ice Queen all the power?"

"He went to bed when Grandpa died because he was sad."

"Oh, that's sweet, Rachel. But plenty of people get

sad and they don't climb into bed and pull the covers over their heads for six weeks!"

"He wasn't happy being a lawyer, so he quit. What's wrong with that?" I paused for a moment. "And Mom doesn't have all the power. He's the one who's always stopping her."

"Right . . . because he's a wimp! He'll do anything to avoid confrontation!"

"He didn't avoid it tonight, did he? He told you off and so did Mom!"

"You call that telling me off?" He smirked. "I call that pathetic."

"Mom and Dad are *not* pathetic!"

"Are we talking about the same Mom and Dad? The Nell and Victor with the bedroom upstairs at the end of the hall?"

"I'm talking about *my* parents. I don't know about yours!"

"When are you going to face the facts, Rachel? This is a very screwed-up family!"

"You're the part that's screwed up."

"I don't deny it. But the rest of you . . ." He stopped and shook his head.

"All families have problems," I said, thinking of Steph and how angry she is at her mother for dating the StairMaster.

He laughed. " 'Happy families are all alike; every unhappy family is unhappy in its own way.' "

That sounded familiar but I couldn't remember where I'd heard it.

Charles laughed again. "Tolstoy, Rachel. Don't tell me you haven't read him yet?"

"I plan to . . . this summer."

"I certainly hope so. I wouldn't want you to fall behind. After all, you've got to be the best."

"I like being the best!"

"What happens when you find out it's not always possible?"

"I've already found out and I'm surviving!"

He paused, as if I'd caught him by surprise. "You know something, Rachel, you've got possibilities. With a little coaching . . ."

"I don't need any coaching from you!" I told him. "I'm figuring out life by myself, thank you."

"Whatever you say, little sister." He started to walk away.

I called, "What do you want from us, Charles?"

He spun around. "What do I want?" He looked up, as if he'd find the answer on the ceiling. Then he repeated the question, quietly, to himself. "What do I want . . . ?"

I waited, but for once Charles seemed at a loss for words.

The next night Charles didn't come to dinner. I wasn't surprised. But even without him at the table, it's become so tense it's hard to eat. The rest of us didn't have much to say until Dad announced we're going to see a family counselor, someone named Dr. Michael Embers.

"I don't see why *we* have to go to a counselor!" Jessica cried, with a nod in my direction. "There's nothing *wrong* with Rachel and me!"

"Because it's *family* therapy," Dad told her, sounding weary.

"But *Charles* is the one with the problem!" Jess argued, which is exactly what I was thinking.

Dad shoved his plate out of the way. "Please don't make this more difficult than it already is." He reached into his pocket and pulled out a packet of Pepto-Bismol tablets. He popped two into his mouth and chewed them up slowly. He looked very tired. So did Mom. I really and truly resent Charles for making them so unhappy.

"Well," Jessica said, "if we *have* to go, I don't see why we can't see a woman!"

"According to *some* people," Mom said, "there are already too many authoritarian women in Charles's life."

Does that mean us? I wondered, looking at Jessica. What a joke! Charles walks all over us. We have no authority over him!

On Monday night at six, we went to Dr. Embers's office. He shook hands with each of us, but only Charles introduced himself using two names. "Charles Rybczynski," he said. If Dr. Embers noticed Charles had a different last name, he didn't show it.

He said, "Please, sit down . . . make yourselves comfortable."

His office was arranged like a living room, with a small sofa, two armchairs, a wooden rocker and a couple of other chairs. I sat stiffly in one of the armchairs, next to Jessica, who sat in the other. Mom and Dad shared the sofa, and Charles settled in the rocker.

Dr. Embers was younger than I'd expected, with wiry light hair, washed-out blue eyes and a runner's slender body. He sat in a plain wooden chair and crossed his legs. "So . . ." he said, "you're having some problems. And you're here to find a way to resolve them."

Mom and Dad nodded.

Dr. Embers continued, "The good news is you're all healthy, intelligent people. My job is to help you understand the patterns that cause the difficulties so you can make the changes that will enable you to live together in harmony." I waited for him to give us the bad news, but he didn't.

"Okay, just to break the ice," he said, "I'd like each of you to describe in one word or phrase how you feel about being here today." He looked directly at me. "Rachel . . . why don't you begin."

"Me?" I said. "Why start with me?"

"Because you're the child prodigy," Charles said.

"You see!" I told Dr. Embers. "There's the problem!"

"You seem angry, Rachel," Dr. Embers said.

"I am angry!"

I expected him to say, *Can you tell me about that?* But he didn't. He just nodded and said, "Go on . . ."

But I couldn't. I mean, I didn't really know anything about Dr. Embers. I didn't know whose side he was on or how much Mom and Dad had told him. And I certainly didn't know if I could trust him. "I'm angry . . ." I hesitated for a second. "I'm angry because I don't want to be here."

He nodded again.

"But I've been told I have no choice," I continued. "I have to be here even though there's nothing wrong with me or my family . . . except for . . ."

"Except for?" Dr. Embers said, leaning slightly forward. His jacket fell open and I noticed he was wearing a silver belt buckle with an Indian design etched into it. Dad has one almost exactly like it.

"Except . . ." Dr. Embers said again, expectantly.

When I couldn't get the words out, Jessica did it for me. "Except for Charles!"

"Except for Charles," Dr. Embers repeated matter-of-factly.

"Yes," Jess continued. "He gets all the attention. He takes up all our time and energy. I'm exhausted just from living in the same house with him. It's like . . ." Jessica choked up. "It's like being slowly poisoned!"

Dr. Embers turned to Charles, who was rocking back and forth in his chair, a frozen expression on his face. "What are you feeling right now, Charles?"

"Nothing," Charles said. "Absolutely nothing."

But I didn't believe him.

We came home from our session with Dr. Embers with what he called a contract for family living. It runs for two weeks. By then I'll be on my way to music camp. I can't wait! In the contract we each agreed to try to respect one another's feelings, needs and concerns. We agreed to think before speaking. We agreed to exercise each day, if only for twenty minutes, because Dr. Embers says exercise is a good way to get rid of hostility. And we're not supposed to go to bed at night feeling angry. Even Charles signed the contract without any snide comments. Even he was too worn down to argue. When we got home, Dad taped it to the refrigerator.

The next day I signed up for Natural Helpers. I don't think I'd be a good Natural Helper if I came from a family with no problems. But I know what problems are. I know how they feel. So maybe I can help someone else feel better.

Charles has new wraparound sunglasses. Dana
gave them to him. I remember when she gave
Jeremy Dragon a gold dove. He wore it pinned to
his underwear. At least that was the rumor. I wonder if he gave it back to her when they broke up. I
wonder if Charles will give back the wraparounds if
he splits with Dana.

"So how about it?" Dad said to Charles. He was
trying to convince him to go to Ellis Island tomorrow
with his sophomore history classes. Ellis Island is the
place where our family name was changed from
Rybczynski to Robinson.

"I'm thinking about it," Charles said. He was wearing his sunglasses even though it was almost dark.

We were outside on our patio. It was very still,
more like August than June. Dad lit a citronella candle to keep the mosquitoes away. Mom was work-

ing late at the office again. Now that her big trial is over, she says she has so much to finish up before she's sworn in as a judge she doesn't know how she'll ever get it done. I'm worried about her. A woman like Mom needs kids like Jess and me, who don't give her any trouble!

"I can't make you go," Dad said to Charles. "But it would mean a lot to me if you did."

I really felt for Dad, so I said, "I'll go."

"Me, too," Jessica added.

"There!" Charles said to Dad. "Why don't you take your devoted daughters instead of me?"

"This isn't an *instead*," Dad said. He looked at Jess and me. "For the two of you it would mean missing a day of school."

"Nothing ever happens the last week," Jess told him. "You know that."

"This isn't the last week," Dad said.

"It's the last *full* week," I reminded him. "Next week is all half days."

"And you're going to miss one of those to go to Mom's swearing-in ceremony," Dad reminded us.

"But, Dad . . ." Jessica argued, "Ellis Island is an example of *living* history. It's not something you can learn in a classroom."

Dad laughed. He knew Jess had him, and we knew he'd let us come. Then he looked over at Charles, who was picking up pebbles and letting them run through his fingers. "Charles?" he asked hope-fully.

"I *told* you, I'm thinking about it!" Charles said.

I was thinking about Paul Medeiros, wondering if he'd be going with us. I hope so! After all, he's Dad's student teacher. Then I remembered this is a school trip and almost all school trips use buses for transportation. So I asked, "How will we get there?" I tried to sound casual, as if I didn't care one way or the other.

"There's a ferry from Battery Park," Dad said. "It's just a ten-minute trip, past the Statue of Liberty."

"No, I mean from *here* to New York," I said.

"Oh . . ." Dad said. "We've got a bus."

I knew it! I chose my next words carefully. "I could take the train and meet you in the city."

Charles pulled off his sunglasses and looked at me. "Don't tell me you still get carsick!"

"I don't want to discuss it with you!" I told him.

"Is she ever going to outgrow that?" Charles asked Dad.

"Of course," Dad told him. "When she gets her driver's license . . . if not before."

When I get my driver's license! That's three years from now. Mom used to tell me I'd outgrow it by ten, but I didn't. And for some reason the medicines that work for other people give me excruciating headaches. I *hate* getting carsick! It's so embarrassing, especially at my age. A few months ago Alison's mother invited us to visit her on the set of her TV series and I got sick on the drive into the city. We had to stop so I could throw up.

But Gena was very nice about it. She opened her purse, pulled out a pair of these things that looked like sweatbands and offered them to me. "I don't think I'd have survived the first few months of my pregnancy without my Sea-Bands."

When I hesitated, she said, "They're perfectly safe. You wear them above your wrists, with the little button pressing on your Nei-Kuan point. That's three fingers up from your wrist."

I thanked Gena and tucked the Sea-Bands into my purse. But I never wore them. Instead I slept all the way home and didn't get sick until I was in my own house.

Now I looked at Dad, hoping he'd say it would be fine for me to take the train. But before he had the chance, Charles started. "She wouldn't act like such a baby if you didn't treat her like one."

"Who are you to judge?" Jess asked him. She turned to me and said, "I'll take the train with you, Rachel."

I was so grateful I grabbed her hand.

Charles said, "What are you two . . . Siamese twins or something?"

"Yeah," Jess said. "You have a problem with that?"

"You see," Charles said to Dad. "It's always them against me. That's how it's been my whole life!"

"Oh, please . . ." Jess said. "You're not in second grade anymore, so why don't you stop acting like it!"

"You know, Jessica . . ." Charles began, "it could be a lot worse. I could be into drugs. I could be in trouble with the law. I could be a rapist or a serial killer . . ."

"Am I supposed to be grateful?" Jess asked.

"You're supposed to count your blessings."

"I do . . . every day . . . and you're not one of them!"

I waited for Dad to remind us of our contract for family living but Dana came along at that very moment, calling, "Helloooo . . . anybody home?"

Charles stood up and brushed off his hands. He opened the patio gate.

Dad called, "Be back by ten."

"Yeah . . . yeah . . ." Charles muttered.

After he was gone, Dad said, "I think she's good for him, don't you?" Jessica and I looked at each other but neither of us answered his question. Then Dad blew out the citronella candle, and Jess and I followed him into the house.

The weather broke overnight and the next morning was perfect, sunny and breezy. Jess and I were up and dressed at six. By the time Charles came into the kitchen Mom was gone, and it was just as well, because Charles looked like he'd slept in his clothes. "I have a sore throat," he said. "I think I should stay home."

Dad felt his forehead. "No fever."

"It could be Lyme disease," Charles told him. "My neck feels stiff."

I looked at him. There was an article about Lyme disease in yesterday's paper.

"Just get dressed, Charles," Dad said.

"I *am* dressed," Charles said. He was wearing his ELVIS IS DEAD T-shirt.

"Well then, have something to eat," Dad suggested.

"You're starting to sound just like Mom!" Charles said.

Dad pointed to the contract taped to the refrigerator and Charles shut up.

Dad dropped Jess and me at the train station in time to catch the 7:10 to New York, which was packed with commuters. When the train came along, we took seats across the aisle from a man carrying a canvas gym bag. As soon as the conductor collected our tickets and moved to the next car, the man, who was wearing a business suit, unzipped his bag and a small dog stuck out his head and looked around. Then the man pulled out a Dixie cup and fed ice cream to the dog from a spoon. Jess and I looked at each other and started laughing.

When we calmed down, I said, "Thanks for coming with me."

"I prefer the train," Jess said. "I always get queasy on the bus."

"I never knew that."

"Well, I don't get as sick as you, but with Charles on board . . ." She didn't have to finish her sentence. I knew what she meant.

When Jess pulled out her *Elle* magazine, I opened the book Dad had given me about Ellis Island. We read quietly for a while. Then I asked, "Do you think it's going to work with Dr. Embers?"

"It all depends on Charles," Jess said, holding her place in the magazine with her thumb. "On whether or not he wants to make the effort."

"What do you think?"

"I have no idea," Jess said. "But either way I'm not going to let him ruin my senior year!" She flipped through a few pages.

I wanted to tell her about the other night in the kitchen, when I asked Charles what he wanted from us and he couldn't answer. But I didn't.

"I'll tell you something, Rachel," Jess continued. "If he can't get along with us, that's his problem! I've got too much to look forward to, to let him get in my way." She flipped a few more pages, then tapped an ad for shampoo. "Just once I'd like to see a model in here with acne. Maybe someday they'll get real!"

When we got to the city, we followed Dad's directions and took the subway from Grand Central Station to Battery Park, which is at the southern tip of Manhattan. We were proud of ourselves for not getting lost.

Once we were there, we waited in line for tickets. Dad was lucky we went by train because by the time his bus pulled in, the lines for ferry tickets were so long we would have waited till noon.

When Charles got off the bus, I worried he'd make some rude remark about me in front of Dad's students but he didn't even glance my way. He was talking and laughing with a group of kids. I guess he'd recovered from his Lyme disease.

Paul was the last to get off the bus. I'd held my breath until then, afraid he wasn't coming after all. But when I saw him, I turned away quickly, so he wouldn't get any ideas. As Dad rounded up his students and led the way through the park down to the ferry dock, I hung back, feeling slightly out of place until Paul called, "Rachel . . . wait . . ."

I love to hear him say my name!

"Have you been to Ellis Island before?" he asked when he caught up with me.

"No, have you?"

"Once," he said, as we walked toward the ferry. "I took my grandparents for their fiftieth anniversary. They came here from Portugal right after they were married. Not exactly a romantic journey since they were both seasick the whole time."

Romantic journey! He said *romantic journey* to me!

"Victor tells me his father came over from Poland." Paul spoke as if we were actually having a conversation. It was weird to hear him call my father by his first name. I wonder what else he and Dad talk about. Do they talk about Charles? Do they talk about *me*? I tried to say something but felt like I had a mouthful of marbles.

We boarded the ferry with a large crowd—tourists from different countries speaking their own languages, other school classes, groups on outings, and families. We climbed to the upper deck and watched as two helicopters circled overhead. A group of Dad's students surrounded Paul, separating us. I looked around for Jessica but she was busy with friends.

I wandered around the deck, stopping when I heard a teacher scolding a boy, about ten. "Never mind Eric . . ." she told her class, "he's just looking for attention." When the ferry began to move, the other kids cheered but Eric sat down, clutching his stomach. Was he seasick already or just scared?

I sat next to him. He looked up at me. "I forgot my lunch," he said.

"Maybe one of your friends will share with you."

"I don't have any friends," he said. "Everyone hates me."

"That's really sad."

"Yeah, I know."

"You want my lunch?" I asked. Not that I wanted to give it to him, because I'd fixed things I really like. But I could always buy lunch if I had to, and he seemed so alone.

"What do you have?" he asked, perking up.

"Tuna with tomatoes and sprouts on rye."

"What else?"

"Oatmeal cookies, cranberry juice and a peach."

"I don't like any of that stuff," he said.

"Well then, I guess I can't help you."

"You're a geek!" he told me. "You're an ugly, stupid geek!"

"No wonder you don't have any friends!" I said, surprised at how angry I felt. Natural Helpers aren't supposed to get angry just because someone they're trying to help isn't grateful.

We stopped at the Statue of Liberty first. Eric and his class got off there. I watched from the deck as they marched off the ferry, two by two. When Eric turned and looked up at me, I waved. He stuck out his tongue. Well, at least I'd tried!

Our ferry waited at the statue while another group of school kids boarded. They were all wearing green foam Statue of Liberty crowns. As the ferry pulled out again, Dad began to recite the poem engraved at the base of the statue.

"Give me your tired, your poor,
Your huddled masses yearning to breathe free . . ."

A few kids in his class joined in, then a few more, until they were all reciting the poem together. When they finished, it was so quiet on deck I could hear the wind as it whipped my hair away from my face.

Next stop was Ellis Island. Dad reminded us to imagine ourselves as immigrants arriving by ship after a long, difficult journey. "You're tired, hungry, scared, but you've made it to the new country," Dad said. "You are about to start over in the land of opportunity!"

We entered the main building through a long portico and came into the Great Hall, which feels enormous. Probably thousands of people could fit in this room at once. The floor is made of white tile and the ceiling is so high it makes you feel tiny, even if you are the second tallest person in seventh grade.

If I were a thirteen-year-old immigrant girl coming into this vast hall, I know I'd have been scared, especially if I didn't understand a word of English, which most immigrants didn't.

Dad said we were free to look around on our own for an hour, then meet in front of the computers. Most kids went off in groups but I wandered by myself. I stopped at the first exhibit to look at the types of baggage the immigrants brought with them. There were trunks in all sizes. Some of them were made of wood, others of leather or what looked like cardboard. Some immigrants brought baskets as big as trunks. Some came with woven sacks in bright colors.

I closed my eyes and tried to imagine my grandfather as a little boy, clutching his mother's hand while his father carried their baggage into this Great Hall.

I climbed up the stairs to the Registry Room, where each immigrant was inspected for diseases and where some guard who couldn't pronounce or spell our family name, *Rybczynski*, assigned Grandpa and his parents the name *Robinson*.

On the third floor were display cases filled with

the immigrants' most important possessions—hand-embroidered clothes, candlesticks, bibles, photos, musical instruments. What would I take if I had to leave the country quickly, with just one small bag? My flute, definitely. Photos of my family and friends and of Burt and Harry. And my favorite books, the ones I read over and over again.

I checked my watch and discovered I'd been browsing for over an hour. I raced down the stairs and found Dad and his students gathered around Charles, who was seated at one of the computers. I pushed my way through the group until I was standing next to Dad.

Then I watched as Charles typed RYBCZYNSKI into the computer. In two seconds RYBCZYNSKI, STEFAN AND LEILAH popped up on the screen. I got goosebumps down my arms. These were my great-grandparents! Under their names was JOSEF, AGE FOUR. This was my grandfather! Charles moved the cursor down the screen to COUNTRY OF ORIGIN — POLAND.

Dad swallowed hard. He nodded several times, blinking back tears, and rested his hand on Charles's shoulder as Charles moved the cursor again, this time to DONOR — VICTOR (RYBCZYNSKI) ROBINSON.

Charles sat absolutely still, studying the screen. Then suddenly he jumped up and turned to face Dad. They looked at each other for a minute, but when Dad moved toward him, Charles took off, pushing

467

everybody out of his way. He ran back into the Great Hall. Dad followed, calling, "Charles . . ." I followed Dad. Charles ran outside, under the portico and around to the left. He climbed up onto the seawall, where the immigrants' names are inscribed in bronze. For a minute I thought he was going to jump into the water. So did the tourists who were sitting nearby. You could hear a gasp go through the crowd. But instead of jumping, he spun around, arms outstretched, and began to recite.

"Give me your tired, your poor,
Your huddled masses yearning to breathe free . . ."

A guard spotted him and called, "You!"
But Charles didn't stop. His voice grew stronger.

"The wretched refuse of your teeming shore,
Send these, the homeless, tempest-tossed to me:"

The guard headed for him.
"Charles!" Dad called.
Charles looked right at him. His voice broke as he finished the poem.

"I lift my lamp beside the golden door."

Dad stood in front of the wall. "Come down now."
Charles hesitated. Then he jumped. Dad caught

him, wrapped an arm around his shoulders and shielded him from the crowd. Charles hid his face against Dad. I think he was crying.

I felt myself choking up and looked away, confused, because I was also angry! Angry at Charles for making himself the center of attention again. Angry at Dad for loving him so completely. Angry at myself for . . . I don't know what. I tried to find Jessica. I needed to share this with her. But Jess was nowhere in sight.

"**W**here were you when we were at the computers?" I asked her later.

"Upstairs, with my friends," Jess said. "Don't tell Dad, okay?"

"You missed . . ."

"What?"

"Seeing our family name."

"Really?" Jess said. "Well, maybe I'll go back in and have a look."

"It won't be the same."

"Of course it'll be the same. It's a computer."

"No," I said. "It wasn't just the computer."

"Then what?"

I couldn't find the words to tell her what I sensed—that something between Charles and Dad had changed forever, something I could feel but couldn't explain. So I just shook my head and said, "Never mind."

"Rachel . . ." Jess said, "you're acting very weird!"

At the end of the day, as we got off the ferry at Battery Park, I told Jessica, "I'm thinking of taking the bus home. That is, if you don't mind."

Jessica looked surprised. "Really?"

I took the Sea-Bands out of my purse, where they've been since Gena gave them to me. "I've been meaning to try these," I explained. I slipped the bands onto my wrists, then moved them three fingers up exactly the way Gena had showed me. I hoped the buttons were pressing on my Nei-Kuan points.

"Do you want me to sit next to you," Jess asked, "or can I sit with my friends?"

"You can sit with your friends."

When we boarded the bus, I took the first seat. Mom says you're less likely to get sick if you sit up front and look straight ahead, out the driver's window.

Charles seemed like his old self as he got on, talking and laughing with a group of kids. He was surprised when he saw me but he didn't say anything. He just walked by, toward the back of the bus.

When Dad saw me, he looked concerned. "Rachel, are you okay?"

"Yes," I said. "I just want to try these." And I held up my wrists, showing him the Sea-Bands.

"Good for you!" he said.

After all of Dad's students were accounted for and seated, Paul got on the bus. "Is this seat taken?" he asked, tapping the one next to mine.

I shook my head. "I don't know about you, Rachel," he said, sinking low, "but I'm zonked." Then he closed his eyes and slept most of the way home, waking only when we made a sharp turn or a sudden stop.

I can't say whether it was the Sea-Bands or the distraction of having Paul Medeiros sleeping next to me, but I made it back without getting sick!

When we got off the bus at the school parking lot, Paul yawned, stretched, adjusted his glasses and said, "There's a concert at the college tomorrow night. Would you like to go?"

Would I like to go?

"Does that look mean *yes*?" he asked.

I think I nodded.

"It's at six-thirty," he said, "so I'll have you home by nine . . . in case you were worrying."

This time I found my voice. "I wasn't worrying," I told him.

I was bursting! As soon as we got home, I ran over to Alison's to tell Gena the good news about the Sea-Bands. But when I got there, Leon said she was resting. "Her blood pressure's up and she's supposed to stay off her feet. Only a month to go . . ."

I told him I hope Gena feels better soon, then ran up to Alison's room. She was sprawled across her bed, her head hanging over the edge. Stephanie was there, too, sitting cross-legged on the floor, jotting something down in a notebook. As soon as they saw me, Steph closed the notebook and she and Alison looked at each other as if they knew something I didn't. But for once I didn't care. I sat on the edge of the bed and gave Maizie a few pats.

Steph could tell something was up because she said, "What?"

"Oh, nothing . . . except I'm going to a concert at the college tomorrow night . . . with Paul."

"Who's Paul?" Steph asked.

I had to be careful since I'd never even hinted how I feel about him. "You know . . . Charles's tutor."

"Wait!" Steph said, holding up her hand. "If you're going to a concert, that means you can't come to the carnival with us." The Jaycees sponsor a weekend carnival every year. Steph and I always go.

"We could go Saturday, instead," I suggested.

"Dad's taking Bruce and me to the city on Saturday," Steph said.

"I'm sorry, but I can't miss this concert."

"Are you telling us this is a date?" Alison asked.

"No, it's not a date," I said, although in my mind it definitely is. "My parents would never let me go on a date with someone nine years older."

"Why not?" Steph asked. "My mother's dating someone fifteen years *younger*."

"That's different," I said.

"Maybe to you . . . not to me."

"I don't know, Rachel," Alison said. "It sure sounds like a date."

I just smiled and kind of shrugged.

"Are you saying he already has a girlfriend?" Steph asked.

A girlfriend? I thought. For the first time I realized I know almost nothing about Paul's personal life, except that his grandparents came from Portugal. But what if he does have a girlfriend? What if she meets us at the concert? Worse yet, what if . . .

473

"So does he . . . or what?" Steph said.

"I don't know."

"Who cares if he does or he doesn't?" Alison told Steph. "Rachel is the one he's taking to the concert." She turned to me and asked, "What are you going to wear?"

"Wear?" I said.

She jumped off the bed and scooped up an armload of *Sassy* magazines. "You have to think about these things, Rachel," she said, dumping them in my lap.

After dinner I cornered Mom and asked if I could borrow her black dress to wear to the concert. She and Dad have no idea this is anything more than a friendly invitation. Mom said, "That dress wouldn't be appropriate, Rachel."

"But you wore it to a concert in New York . . . when you took Dad out for his birthday."

"That was different," Mom said. "That was a dress-up event."

"But, Mom . . . this is at the college!"

"I know, honey . . . but college students wear jeans, not gowns. Call Tarren . . . she'll tell you."

So I called Tarren and she said Mom was right. She also told me she'll be at the concert, with her Romantic Obstacle. "I'll look for you," she said.

I don't know how I got through the next day, our last full day of school. On the way out of math class

Jeremy Dragon said, "Hey, Macbeth . . . you going to the carnival tonight?"

"Not tonight," I told him. "Tonight . . ." I hesitated. "Maybe tomorrow night," I called. But I don't think he heard me because by then he was halfway down the hall with his friends.

I spent most of the afternoon in the tub, daydreaming about the *romantic journey* I was about to take with Paul. When I finally got dressed, I chose a long summer skirt and my favorite tank top. It's pale green and has a matching cardigan sweater. I thought about borrowing Jessica's parrot earrings but I didn't want anyone in my family, including Jess, to grow suspicious. Anyway, Jess was at work. So I wore my silver earrings, instead. My only real dilemma was whether or not to use strawberry-flavored lip gloss. I decided to go for it.

At five-thirty, when I heard the front door slam, I looked out my window and watched as Charles and Dana took off hand in hand. Only then did I come downstairs.

"Oh, there you are," Paul said, collecting his books. "I thought you'd forgotten."

Forgotten? Was he serious? "No," I said. "I just had a lot to do this afternoon." I tossed my cardigan over one shoulder the way models do in magazines.

Paul was wearing a blue denim work shirt with the sleeves rolled up. Mom and Tarren were right. The slinky black dress wouldn't have been right. I followed him out of the house, locking the door behind me. His car was parked out front. It's an old two-door Toyota, either gray or brown—it's hard to tell since I've never seen it clean. On the inside it was even worse. The upholstery was ragged. His seat was covered with an old blanket and mine was held together with duct tape.

"Slightly messy, huh?" Paul asked as we headed for the highway.

Until then I hadn't realized I'd been cleaning things up, folding papers and collecting gum wrappers and tucking them all into the side pocket of my door.

"No, it's fine. I'm just . . ." I almost said *compulsively neat* but caught myself in time and changed it to, "a natural helper."

When we stopped at a red light, Paul glanced my way and said, "I like that color on you, Rachel."

Which color? My tank top . . . my lip gloss? I didn't ask. I just said, "Thank you." Could he tell how fast my heart was beating? Did he know the palms of my hands were sweaty and I felt like either laughing or crying? I only hoped I could control myself. I stared straight ahead, grateful the drive to the college takes just fifteen minutes. "Do you by any chance know my cousin, Tarren Babcock?" I asked, trying to make small talk. "She's an education major."

"I don't think so," he said.

"She'll probably be at the concert."

"Is she a music lover like you?"

Lover! He said the word *lover* to me! I felt myself blush. "No," I said. "She's more into obstacles." I began to fan my face with my hand.

"Obstacles?" He laughed, as if I'd meant to be funny.

"Yes." I tried to laugh, too, but it came out more like a squeak.

"What kind of obstacles?"

"All kinds," I said. He seemed to think this was funnier yet. I wish I had never mentioned Tarren's name. How was I supposed to get out of this? Tell a joke, I thought. One of those jokes the dentist told me. But I couldn't remember any of the punch lines. I was totally hopeless!

"She sounds like someone I'd like to know," Paul said.

"Who?" I asked.

"Your cousin."

"Oh, I doubt it," I told him. I didn't add that he and Tarren would have absolutely nothing in common.

When we got to the college, we parked in a big field, then walked up a hill to a yellow-and-white-striped tent. There were rows of folding chairs set up inside and people were already taking seats. A girl handed us programs as we entered, and I followed Paul down the aisle to a pair of seats in the middle.

I knew I could easily be mistaken for a college student and for once I was glad. It's not just my height that makes me look older. It's my body. Mom says she was an early bloomer, too. She says in a few years my emotional maturity will catch up with my physical maturity. But I think it already has.

Outside the tent groups of students were settling on blankets on the lawn. I wished we could sit out there, too. It seemed much more romantic, even though the sun was still shining. If only the concert began at nine instead of six-thirty!

I read my program carefully. This was the last in a series performed by visiting musicians. Tonight it was the Connecticut Valley Chamber Players, with an all-Mozart program.

When the concert began, Paul closed his eyes. A lot of people close their eyes when they're listening to music. It helps them concentrate on what they are hearing. But I couldn't tell if Paul was concentrating or sleeping. Maybe he isn't getting enough sleep at night. Maybe he needs vitamins. I looked over at his hands, which were relaxed in his lap. They looked strong, manly. I imagined them touching my face, my hair. But then I began to feel very warm and had to use my program to fan myself.

The group of fifteen musicians played in different combinations for thirty-five minutes, took a short break, played for another half hour, then performed two encores. Paul applauded enthusiastically. He said, "Fantastic, aren't they?"

"Outstanding!" I agreed, even though they weren't.

Just as we were about to head back to Paul's car, I heard someone calling my name. "Ra . . . chel!" I knew it was Tarren even before I turned and saw her. She was already weaving her way through the tent to us.

"Hi . . ." she said, joining us.

"Hi," I answered. She looked very pretty. Her hair hung to her shoulders and she was wearing a low-cut sundress, showing off more than necessary.

"Well . . ." she said, giving me a nudge in the side. "Aren't you going to introduce us?"

I really didn't want to introduce Tarren to Paul. I didn't want anyone reminding him that I am just thirteen. But there was no way to get out of it, so I said, "Paul Medeiros, this is my cousin, Tarren Babcock." I spoke very fast and hoped Tarren wouldn't ask any questions.

A tall man with thinning hair came up to Tarren then, put his hand on her naked back and handed her a paper cup. "They didn't have lime spritzers," he told her. "Just plain seltzer."

"Thanks," she said, smiling up at him. That's when it hit me! This man, who looked as old as Dad, who wasn't even good-looking, at least not to me, was Tarren's Romantic Obstacle! She took a sip of seltzer, then introduced us. "Rachel, Paul . . . I'd like you to meet Professor Benjamin Byram." She said his name proudly, then gave me a meaningful smile. I'm not sure if I smiled back or not. I felt weird, knowing this man and Tarren were involved in *that* way.

Paul shook hands with Tarren's Obstacle. "I was in your class two years ago," he said. "Paul Medeiros."

"Of course," Professor Byram said. "I remember . . ." But I could tell he didn't. And so could Paul.

A small, pretty woman with lots of pale curly hair came up to the Romantic Obstacle then and linked her arm through his. "Sweetie . . ." he said, clearly surprised. "I thought you said you couldn't make it tonight."

"Well," she told him, "the meeting didn't last as long as I thought, and it was such a beautiful evening I asked the sitter to stay."

Tarren looked stricken—the way my father had the night Charles called him a wimp. "This is my wife, Francesca Hammond," the Obstacle said to all of us.

Francesca beamed at Paul. "Paul Medeiros! How good to see you. Where've you been hiding?"

"You two know each other?" the Obstacle asked his wife.

"Well, of course," Francesca said. "Paul is one of my prize students."

Tarren looked like she was about to be sick. She'd

turned a kind of grayish color, and one hand went to her throat. I don't think anyone noticed but me.

Francesca and Paul went right on talking. "I hear you've accepted a job teaching in Westport," she said.

"Yes," Paul said.

"That's wonderful! Come in next week and we'll have lunch. I want to hear all about it." Then she turned to her husband and said, "Darling, the baby-sitter . . ."

The Obstacle checked his watch and said, "Got to run. Nice to see you again, Paul. Glad to meet you, Rachel." He turned to Tarren and held out his hand to shake hers. "If I don't see you again, have a wonderful summer. It's been a pleasure having you in my class."

He had to pull back his hand because Tarren wouldn't let go. Then he and his wife walked away, arm in arm.

Tarren watched them for a minute, then burst into tears.

"What?" Paul asked.

Tarren just shook her head and tried to stifle her sobs by covering her mouth with her hand.

I patted her back.

"Don't tell me . . ." Paul said. "Another of Professor Byram's conquests."

Tarren looked at him. "Conquests?" she managed to ask.

Paul put his arm around her waist. "Come on," he said to me. "Your cousin needs some cheering up."

Tarren leaned against Paul as he led her to his car. I got in back, by myself. *She* sat up front, next to him.

We went to a diner and took a booth, where Tarren cried and Paul passed her napkins from the dispenser so she could blow her nose. When she shivered in her sundress in the air-conditioning, I handed her my sweater. She pulled it around her shoulders. Paul dropped a couple of coins into the jukebox on the wall and selected four songs, all hard rock, which totally shocked me. Slowly Tarren began to recover. She felt hungry, she said, and she and Paul smiled at each other, then ordered hamburgers and fries while I sipped a peppermint tea.

"He was never right for me," Tarren cooed to Paul over the apple pie and ice cream they shared for dessert. "I know that now."

"You were wasted on him!" Paul told her.

"It was like . . . I couldn't help myself," Tarren said to him. They spoke as if I weren't there, as if I were invisible. I hate being treated that way!

On the drive home I think they were holding hands. But I didn't care anymore. I just wanted it to be over. I just wanted to be alone in my room.

Finally we pulled up in front of my house. I leaned

forward and thanked Paul for taking me to the concert.

"My pleasure," he said.

"See you, Rachel," Tarren said as I got out of the car.

At the last minute I leaned back in through her window and said, "Give Roddy a kiss for me."

I knew she hadn't had the chance to tell Paul she was divorced, with a baby. Well, too bad!

I will never forgive Tarren for ruining what should
have been the most romantic night of my life!
She's such a fool, jumping from one Romantic
Obstacle to another. I raced up to my room and
closed the door, praying that Mom and Dad wouldn't
ask any questions. I was halfway undressed when
Mom knocked on my door. "Rachel . . ."

I didn't feel like explaining anything to her now.

When I didn't respond, she knocked again.
"Rachel . . . there's someone here to see you."

Paul! He realizes he's made a major mistake. He
wants me, not Tarren!

"It's a boy," Mom continued. "Jeremy something.
Should I tell him you're already in bed?"

Jeremy . . . here? I began to get back into my
clothes. "No!" I told Mom. "Tell him I'll be right
down."

"Okay," Mom said. "But it's getting late."

Why would Jeremy Dragon come to my house on a Friday night at nine-thirty? It didn't make sense. Nothing made sense!

I had to shoo Harry out of the bathroom sink so I could splash my face with cold water. Then I fluffed out my hair, put on more strawberry lip gloss and flew down the stairs. I opened the front door but didn't see him.

"Pssst, Macbeth . . . over here."

I followed the sound of his voice to the maple tree.

"Hey," he said. He was wearing his dragon jacket. "How come you're all dressed up?"

"I just got back from a concert."

"Who was playing?"

"The Connecticut Valley Chamber Players."

He didn't act like that was unusual. He said, "You're really into music, huh?"

I nodded.

He smiled at me. "How about a walk?"

"Sure," I answered.

"Don't want to run into . . . you know . . . them."

Charles and Dana were about the last people I wanted to run into, too.

"So," he said, fishing something out of his jacket pocket. It was his token race car from Monopoly. "I meant to give this back to you right away . . . then I forgot . . . sorry."

"That's okay. Nobody's played since that night."
Our hands touched as he gave me the car.

We walked around the pond. I was glad it was dark
so none of the neighbors, including Stephanie and
Alison, could see us. When we got to the tree where
the raccoons live, Jeremy stopped walking and faced
me. "Macbeth . . ." His voice was hoarse.

"What?" I think I sounded alarmed.

He leaned toward me and before I even knew what
was happening, his lips were on mine.

"I've wanted to do that for a long time," he said.

"Really?"

"Yeah . . . ever since Halloween when you came to
my house reciting that stupid poem. I liked the way
your mouth twitched."

"It does that when I'm nervous."

"Like now?"

I touched my mouth. Was it twitching and I didn't
even know? He took my hand away. "It's very kiss-
able . . . you know?" He put his arms around me,
pulled me close and kissed me again. My legs felt so
weak, I thought I might fall over.

On our third try, I kissed him back. I felt a surge go
through my whole body. My mind went blank for a
minute. Never mind animal attraction, this was *elec-
trical* attraction! When I came back to earth, I asked,
"What does this mean?"

"Mean?" he said. He held my hand and we

started walking again. "It doesn't mean anything. It was . . . you know . . . just a couple of kisses."

No, I wanted to tell him! I don't know. This is all new to me. This is nothing like kissing Max Wilson at the seventh-grade dance. But I didn't say anything.

He walked me home. We kissed one more time in the shadows. Then he smiled and said, "See ya . . ."

Just when you think life is over, you find out it's not. Just when you think you'll never be foolish enough to fall for somebody else, it happens without any warning! I hope this doesn't mean I'm going to be like Tarren, jumping from one Obstacle to the next. I don't think it does. I don't think it means anything except life is full of surprises and they're not necessarily all bad.

The next morning Stephanie called. "How was the concert?"

"Boring."

"What do you mean by *boring*?"

"You know . . . the music wasn't that good and everyone there was ancient . . . over twenty, at least. I couldn't wait to get home!"

"So I guess you're glad it wasn't a date."

"Very!" I paused, lowering my voice. "I have important news but I can't tell you over the phone."

"Well, what are you waiting for? Come right over!"

"I kissed Jeremy Dragon!" I threw myself backward onto Steph's bed, falling on top of about thirty stuffed animals. "Not once," I told her, "not twice, but four times!"

Steph's mouth fell open. "Rachel . . . I'm so jealous!" I love the way Steph says exactly what she's

488

feeling without worrying about it. "How did this happen?" she asked.

, "I don't know. It was so bizarre. He came over to give me back a Monopoly piece and it just . . . well . . . happened."

"Does this mean you're going together?"

"No. It doesn't mean anything. It was just a . . . couple of kisses."

"Did you react?"

"You *must* be joking!"

"Rachel!" she squealed. "I can't believe this!"

"You think *you* can't!"

Mom was sworn in as a judge on Tuesday morning. I think Charles was disappointed when he introduced himself to the governor as Charles *Rybczynski* and the governor didn't say anything. I wonder if he's going to get tired of his new name.

Tarren wore a white suit and three-inch heels. She looked very . . . adult. She thanked me over and over for introducing her to Paul. They've been seeing each other every night. She says he's wonderful with Roddy. I don't want to hear about it. I made sure I wouldn't be sitting next to her at lunch.

Mom seems relieved now that she's the Honorable Nell Babcock Robinson, though she still doesn't know which court she'll be assigned to. I think she's also relieved Charles has a summer job working at the bakery in town. No one has said for sure what school he'll be going to next fall, but Jessica and I think there's a good chance it will be the high school, which means he'll be living at home. I'm trying to learn from Jess, who says we should stop thinking about him and just let Mom and Dad work it out with Dr. Embers. *I wish!*

Charles seems less angry since Ellis Island but I can't say he's changed. He's probably never going to change. He'll probably take pleasure in annoying me my whole life.

With Jessica it's completely different. We're always going to be close, no matter what. Still, I was upset when she said, "I heard about that program at the college."

"What program?"

"Challenge. Toad's brother told me."

"Oh." Until now I'd managed to put Challenge out of my mind. "You're not mad, are you?" I asked.

"Why would I be mad?" Jess said. "I learned long ago not to compete with you, Rachel. If I did, I'd just wind up resenting you and that wouldn't be good for either of us. Besides, no matter what happens at school you're still my *little* sister." She laughed and gave me an elbow in the ribs.

"Don't mention anything about Challenge to Mom or Dad, okay?"

"How come?"

"Because I haven't decided if I'm going to do it."

"Why wouldn't you do it?"

"I have my reasons," I told her. "So promise you won't say anything."

"You know I won't."

On the last day of school we got out at ten because the ninth graders were graduating at noon. When I passed Jeremy in the hall, he was carrying his red cap and gown.

"So, Macbeth . . . you hanging around this summer or what?"

"I'm going to music camp," I told him.

"Play a song for me, okay?"

"Sure."

"See you in September."

"I'll be back the end of August."

Some of his friends came along then, slamming into him. As they dragged him away, he looked back at me and waved. I waved, too. I can't believe I actually kissed him! And that come September, I might kiss him again.

"Nice that you and Jeremy get along so well." I spun around. It was Dana, dressed in her cap and gown. But her cap wasn't fastened yet and she had to hold it on with one hand.

"Nice that you and my brother do," I said.

I didn't want to go to the bakery after school but Alison insisted. She still has a *thing* for Charles. He was working behind the counter, wearing a white apron over his

T-shirt and jeans. "Well, well, well . . ." he said, "if it isn't the triumvirate! What brings you here?"

"Hunger," I told him.

He plucked a dog biscuit out of a jar and held it up. "These are quite savory. They appeal to all sizes and breeds."

"Woof, woof . . ." I said.

Steph and Alison tried not to laugh. They each bought a giant-size chocolate chip cookie. When Charles handed Alison her change, he said, "I'm still waiting for you, California."

"What about Dana?" I asked.

"Dana is my date *du jour*," he said, using the French expression. "But California is something else."

Alison had this ridiculous look on her face. I hope that's not how I looked when I was with Jeremy. "Come on . . ." I grabbed her by the hand and led her away. Steph followed.

"Good-bye, my lovelies," Charles called after us, giving Stephanie and Alison both a profound case of the giggles.

When we were outside, Steph bit into her cookie and said, "He just likes to tease you, Rachel!"

"Because you take everything so seriously," Alison added, breaking her cookie in half and sharing with me.

"I don't take *everything* seriously!" I told them. "Just *some* things."

On the way home I invited them to my house for

lunch. I felt safe knowing Charles was at work. Before we went inside, Alison said, "Guess what? As soon as Matthew's born, we're going to L.A."

"But you'll be back in time for school, right?" Steph asked.

"I think so," Alison said. "I hope so."

"But Alison . . . you have to be!" Steph said. "You're running for class president." As soon as she said it, she clapped her hand to her mouth. She and Alison exchanged a look. "We were going to tell you before you left for camp," Steph said.

"We were just waiting for the right time," Alison added.

"I mean, you acted like you didn't want to run," Steph said, making excuses. "You acted like you were only doing me a favor." She paused for a minute. "And Alison's so popular. She has a real chance of winning."

"We just thought the Dare to Care Candidate was too good to waste," Alison said.

I didn't know what to say! It's true I was going to tell Steph I can't run because of all my other activities. But I hadn't told her yet. And I certainly never imagined she'd find herself another candidate and give away the slogan she thought up for *me*.

"You're not mad, are you?" Alison asked.

"Let's just say I'm surprised," I told her.

"I want you to work on my campaign," Alison said. "You will, won't you?"

"If I can fit it into my schedule," I said, sounding

as snide as Charles. "I'm going to be really busy between Natural Helpers and Challenge."

"What's Challenge?" she asked.

"It's this program at the college for—"

But Steph didn't let me finish. "You're going to college?"

"No, it's for eighth and ninth graders. It's like . . ." I tried to find a way to describe it. "It's like enriched math . . . except . . ."

"It's for geniuses!" Steph said.

"We're not geniuses."

"It's for prodigies!" Alison said, trying out Charles's favorite word.

"We are *not* prodigies!"

"Even so," Alison said, sliding her arm around my waist, "I love having such a smart friend!"

A born politician! I thought.

"And you'll still work on my campaign, right?" When I didn't answer, she said, "Steph . . . tell Rachel you *want* her to work on my campaign."

"Dah!" Steph said. "Who'd want Rachel!" Then she tackled me to the ground and Alison jumped on top of us.

On Sunday morning I carefully packed my flute in its case and tossed my last-minute stuff, like my hairbrush and Walkman, into my backpack, along with *Anna Karenina*, the novel Charles quoted the night we had our private talk in the kitchen—the one that begins, "Happy families are all alike . . ."

This is the first time I'm going to camp by bus with everyone else. I've always gone by train before. I put on the Sea-Bands and adjusted them. I hope they work! But what if they don't? What if I get sick and the driver won't pull over and . . . I stopped myself. I'm not going to get sick! Mom and Dad promised we'd be at the bus early enough for me to get a seat in the first row.

I walked around my room one last time, stopping to touch the box with the secret compartment. It's always hard for me to leave, even when I really want to. I'd said good-bye to Jess last night. Now that she's working at Going Places six days a week, Sunday is her only chance to sleep late. She says she expects her skin to be clear the next time she sees me. I hope she's right.

I went down to the kitchen to get a box of crackers for the road, just in case. Charles was standing at the counter, wolfing down a bowl of cold leftover pasta.

"What am I going to do without you for six weeks, Rachel?"

"Yeah . . . who'll you torture?" I asked.

"I don't know . . . it won't be easy." He swallowed a mouthful, then puckered up. "Kiss your big brother good-bye?"

"I sincerely hope you're kidding."

"Would I kid you, little sister?"

"You would if you could."

"I'll be counting the days till we're together again."

"Me, too," I said. "I hope they go really slowly."

"Rachel, is this possible . . . you're developing a sense of humor?"

"Anything's possible!" I told him. Then I walked out the door, laughing to myself.

About the Author

Judy Blume spent her childhood in Elizabeth, New Jersey, making up stories inside her head. She has spent her adult years in many places, doing the same thing, only now she writes her stories down on paper. Her twenty-three books have won more than ninety awards, none more important than those coming from her young readers.

Judy lives on islands up and down the East Coast with her husband, George Cooper. They have three grown children and one grandson. You can visit her at www.judyblume.com.